SHOCKING SOJOURNS

ANTHOLOGY OF SPLATTERPUNK & EXTREME
HORROR

EDITED AND ILLUSTRATED BY
SIDNEY SHIV

CONTENTS

TROTTERS

HARRISON PHILLIPS

PRESENT DAY

What in the name of God was that thing?

Leah ran through the trees, the thick bramble tearing at her shins, the ragged points of fallen branches digging into the soles of her bare feet. But she ignored the pain—she *had* to —and continued to run, her lungs rattling with every racked breath. She could still taste Stan's blood on her tongue, bitter as it tainted her saliva. The image of his head imploding—his eyeballs bursting in their sockets, his tongue severed as he involuntarily bit through it—still haunted her. She could still see his scalp tearing open, broken shards of skull, and mangled grey matter leaking out of his cracked cranium.

It had hit him with a sledgehammer…

It had hit him with a fucking *sledgehammer!*

What was supposed to be a peaceful, romantic getaway had turned into a nightmare.

It had been Stan's idea. He'd insisted they should take a weekend away together, just the two of them. Leah had assumed he meant a city break or a few days at a spa, perhaps. When she realised he actually meant camping out in the sticks, she'd been less than enthusiastic.

Camping was hardly her idea of a good time.

Still, she had to admit it'd be good to escape the city for a few days, get away from the pollution, and get some fresh air into their lungs. It'd be nice just to spend a few days in each other's company, too.

It was a four-hour drive to the place where Stan said they should camp, somewhere deep in the Brecon Beacons, Wales. It was the middle of nowhere, but that's exactly what Stan had wanted for them, to get away from everything; no phones… no internet… nothing.

As they drove along the winding streak of tarmac that snaked through the countryside, Leah couldn't help but admire their surroundings. On one side, vast open expanses stretched out endlessly over rolling green hills, while on the other side, dense woodland obscured all from view. It truly was beautiful.

Leah hadn't realised they'd be wild camping; she'd assumed they'd be staying at a campsite, at the very least. Technically, wild camping was illegal, but Stan had assured her that everything would be fine, that people did it all the time. *But where was she supposed to shower? Where was she supposed to shit?*

She should've refused at that point. She should've told him to turn around and drive them home. Had she done so, he'd probably still be alive.

But it was too late, she supposed. They were already there, so she'd at least give it a go.

Stan found a place off the beaten track to park the car. From there, they hiked into the woods. It was the middle of summer, and though the canopy of the trees offered some respite from the sun's heat, the air was still thick with humidity. Sweating, Leah had soon stripped down to her bikini top and denim short-shorts. She and Stan paddled in the first stream they found, the icy cold water a blessing against her bare feet.

They hiked for another hour or so before finding a clearing in which to pitch their tent.

Stan built a fire and cooked sausages over it. They drank beers, sitting on opposite sides of the fire in their camp chairs. As the sun began to set and a chill perforated the air, Leah changed out of her clothes and into the oversized hoodie she often slept in, the hood pulled up over her head.

She sat on Stan's lap, complaining that it was cold, telling him that he needed to warm her up. He was more than happy to oblige. He wrapped his arms around her and pulled her in close. She rested her head on his shoulder. Then, they were kissing. Stan's hand slid up under her hoodie, his fingertips gliding gently along the side of her stomach until they found their way to her pert breasts, her nipples standing to attention.

God, how she loved him. She wanted him so badly. She *needed* him inside her.

But then, that *thing* attacked them…

Neither of them had heard its approach. It must've moved through the forest as silent as a ghost. It was just *there*.

It was huge and vaguely human-shaped, like a large man —it must've been at least seven feet tall–with broad shoulders and a round belly. Its arms and legs seemed disproportionately short; they were stumpy and thick with muscle. Its neck was as thick as a tree trunk. But it was the tumescent head that was the most ghastly. It was wide and flat, entirely misshapen, nothing like that of a human. Scrappy tufts of wiry hair sprouted sporadically from the flaking scalp. It didn't appear to have any ears. A pair of small, pinprick eyes, like tiny black marbles, were set deep into its skull. They looked *too* small, like maybe they were loose in their respective sockets. The front of its face was squat, like the edge of a cliff. And instead of a nose... it had... there was nothing there!

Leah screamed.

The events following her scream seemed to happen in less than half a second. Stan had barely gotten a chance to look over his shoulder when the monstrosity standing behind him had swung the sledgehammer high over its head and brought it down full force in the centre of his skull.

Stan's head popped like a plump zit. His blood splattered Leah, cutting her scream off dead and sending her sprawling to the ground.

Stan's headless corpse remained upright momentarily, sitting in the camp chair, ragged ribbons of torn meat hanging loose from his neck stump, blood squirting from his savaged arteries. Seconds later, he fell limp, slumping to one side, falling to the ground. It was only then that Leah noticed the creature was naked. It had a small, round nub where its dick should've been and a colossal scrotum the size of a grapefruit, with skin just as thick.

4

Wheezing and snorting as if it were suffering from a severe case of asthma, the beast lifted the sledgehammer once again and began to hit Stan's body over and over again. The sickening crunch of breaking bones and the wet tearing sounds of ravaged flesh filled the forest.

As devastated as she was, her brain feeling like a mulch of overcooked scrambled eggs, she knew she needed to get the fuck out of there. She pushed herself backwards, away from the monster, away from Stan's corpse. She scrambled to her knees, forced herself to her feet, and then took off into the trees.

It was pitch black in the forest; not a single sliver of moonlight seemed to make it through the thick canopy overhead. Thankfully, her eyes soon adjusted to the darkness, allowing her to just about navigate between the trees. When she finally broke from the treeline, she saw nothing but endless fields and steep hills.

Still, she continued to run.

Something was out there, far away in the distance, little more than a pinprick of light in the blanket of darkness that seemed to smother the Earth.

Salvation, perhaps?

As Leah approached, she saw it was a farm.

There were a few small barns and a small house. The lights were on inside, and smoke billowed from the chimney.

Leah felt on the verge of collapse, her muscles burning as lactic acid built up in the fibres. But she ignored the pain and pushed on, driving herself forward towards the safety of this house. She scrambled over the waist-high fence, splinters from the rough-sawn timbers digging into the soles of her bare feet and nipping at her thighs.

She almost fell as she slammed into the solid wooden door. In an instant, her energy drained out of her, and her entire body went numb. But she managed to prop herself up and hammered on the door with the heel of her palm.

She heard the locks opening.

And then the door swung open.

A woman stood in the doorway, little more than a silhouette against the warm glow emanating from inside. "Eh," she said, her accent thick and heavy. "Wha's goin' on 'ere?"

"P-p-please," Leah mumbled, hunched over, breathing heavily. " You h-have to help me. Th-there's a monster…"

The woman looked puzzled, the soft features of her face seeming to bunch up into a frown, her thin lips pursed. She was a plump lady with wide hips and an ample round bosom. Her arms were thick, as were her legs. She wore a blue floral summer dress with a yellow apron cinched around her waist, the knot at the side on the verge of breaking. "A monsteh, you say? Now, that don't sound right t'me. Best you come in."

The woman waved a hand, the rolls of fat hanging from the underside of her arm jiggling as she ushered Leah inside.

Leah crossed the threshold into the farmhouse.

It was like stepping back a hundred years. The single room was illuminated by a number of candles mounted on the whitewashed walls. A large fire burned in a stone hearth. On one side of the room was a table with two chairs placed beside it. A bundle of wool lay on the table, two thick knitting needles embedded into the ball, standing upright. On the other side of the room, a staircase led to the floor above. A large ceramic sink and an ancient-looking stove were at the back of the room. And in the middle of the room was a threadbare sofa, the arms practically worn through to the wooden framework beneath. A sizeable wool blanket was draped over the back, no doubt knitted by the woman now escorting Leah into the house.

"Now," said the woman, directing Leah to the sofa. "You just take a seat right here, while we try an' figure out wha't'do with you."

Leah didn't have enough willpower left in her to refuse. She allowed the woman to direct her to the sofa. "P-please…" she said, taking a seat, sinking into the soft cushioning. "You have to phone the police. My b-boyfriend… this… this… *thing*… it came out of nowhere. It k-killed him!"

The woman didn't seem to hear her. "A pretty lil' girl you are," she said, smiling. "Very pretty indeed."

"Please… listen to me… there's a monster out there! You have to phone the police!"

The woman smiled kindly. "We don't got no phone, I'm 'fraid. Can't be callin' nobody."

Leah frowned. She didn't understand. No phone? Confused, she looked around the farmhouse once again. Only then did she consider the fact that there weren't any electric lights in this place, nor was there a television. No lights, no TV, and no phone, apparently.

"I tells you wha'. Let me make you a nice cup of tea, an' you can tell me all about wha' you think you seen out there, all right?"

Leah didn't want a cup of tea. What she wanted was some fucking help! She needed to get out of there. She needed somebody to find the godforsaken thing that killed Stan! But then, the more she thought about it, perhaps she was thirsty. Her throat was sore, and her tongue felt bone dry. "Sorry," she said, "but could I maybe just have a glass of water?"

The woman shook her head. "No can do, I'm 'fraid. The water's all used up."

Leah didn't understand. "What do you mean, *'used up?'*"

The woman headed to the back of the room, where a teapot simmered on the stove. She reached into the sink and

1

picked up an empty plastic bottle. Leah could see by the label it was once the container for spring water. "We got'a use bot'led water 'round here." She lifted the teapot from the stove and poured the contents into a mug she took from the sideboard. "The pipes are no good, you see? You'll catch somethin' nah'sty if you drink from the faucet, you will."

Leah thought she was just as likely to catch a disease from the filthy mug the woman held out before her. Feeling obliged, she took the mug. The liquid inside was as thick as gravy. A foul odour emanated from it, like the woman had boiled the contents of their septic tank—if they even had such a thing; it seemed just as likely they might be doing their business in a hole outside. The thought of having to drink this vile substance turned Leah's stomach.

Thankfully, it was the woman herself who saved her from this fate worse than death. "Now, you be careful," she said, using her foot to push a small side table over towards her. "That there's real hot. We don't want you burnin' yourself, now, do we?"

Leah offered a weak smile and nodded. She placed the mug on the table. There was no coaster, but something told her the woman wouldn't mind too much. "Please," she said. "If you don't have a phone, do you have a car? Maybe somebody could drive me into town?"

"Sorry, missy," said the woman. "But I don't drive, you see? Ain't got a license."

"D-do you have a… a husband?"

"I do. But he's asleep upstairs."

Leah felt herself frowning. Was this woman stupid or something? Didn't she understand she needed somebody to help her? Stan was dead, for fuck's sake! "Well… can't you wake him?"

The woman snorted a laugh. "Wake 'im? Not much

chance of that I'm 'fraid. Once he's out, he's out. Dead to the world!"

"Please! He has to drive me into town right now! I told you somebody is dead!"

"An' I told you he's sleepin'."

"No, he ain't," a gruff voice came from the stairs.

Both Leah and the woman looked. A man was standing halfway down the stairs, peering over the banister. He wore a white shirt, stained with sweat and grime, and dirty corduroy trousers held up with braces. Like the woman, he was a large man, his round belly straining against his shirt, the buttons just about ready to pop off. He had thin grey hair on his head and a wiry beard. He smiled, exposing yellow teeth, his gums stained brown. "Now, 'oo d'we have 'ere, then?"

The woman smiled. "Well now, this pretty young thing came poundin' on't door. She says her boyfriend got killed out in the woods."

"Th-there was a m-monster," Leah confirmed.

"A monsteh?" said the man, making his way to the bottom of the stairs. "Ain't no such thing as monsters, lil' miss."

"I'm telling you what I saw! It was huge, like some kind of… of… deformed man! His head was all messed up. He killed Stan, my boyfriend. He hit him with a fuckin' sledgehammer!"

The man and woman shared a knowing look. A palpable silence befell the room.

After a brief moment, the man cleared his throat. "Well," he said, "that don't sound like no monster to me. I know exactly what it is that you be talkin' 'bout, you see?"

"Y-you do?"

"Oh, aye. But, trust me, it ain't no monster."

"So, what *is* it?"

"Well… there's a bit of a story to it," he said, "but I'll tells you if you want. But you gotta understand this whole thing's gonna sound crazy, like the ramblin' of a madman."

"Tell me."

"All right then." The man sighed wearily as he took a seat on the sofa beside Leah. "The story goes like this…"

———

1974

Out in the valleys, folks like to keep themselves to themselves. That's as true now as it was way back when. These were hard-working people. They worked their fingers to the bone, toiling the land on the farms they'd inherited over numerous generations. They grew their crops and raised their livestock. Then, they sold their produce at the local farmer's market once a fortnight. It was a simple life they led, but it was all they'd ever known.

Being so remote, these people hardly ever saw anybody else. Other than at the markets, they might go for months on end without laying eyes on another soul. These were isolated communities, way off the beaten track. Nobody ever went there… other than those who lived there, of course. These people had no gas and no electricity. Most didn't even have running water. There were no shops, no hospitals, no police. But they took care of themselves. They got by.

Carys was the daughter of one such farmer. A pretty young thing she was, only fifteen years of age. She had blue eyes and blonde hair cut into a simple bob. Her skin was pale, as white as snow, her face littered with freckles.

There was this boy she used to knock about with named Owain. He was a good lad. His father owned the neighbouring farm. Owain worked there most days, but in the afternoon, after most of the work was done, his father would always allow him to go and see Carys.

To many an outsider, they might have thought Owain was infatuated with Carys, but that *wasn't* the case. In actual fact, Owain was homosexual. But, of course, that wasn't acceptable back then, so he kept it a secret. Carys was the only person he'd ever confided in.

Anyway, one of those afternoons, after all the farmwork was done, Carys and Owain had decided to go for a dip in the swimming hole at the base of the waterfall, deep in the woods. It was summertime, you see, and the sun was blazing overhead. The water was cool and refreshing. Kids often climbed to the top of the waterfall and jumped in, but neither Carys *nor* Owain had ever been brave enough to try it.

Still, it was nice just to paddle there.

That was until the Awbrey kids showed up.

There were four of them—quadruplets, they were. Although they'd shared their mother's womb, none of the four children was identical. In fact, one of them was a girl. The boys were named Elis, Emyr, and Gethin, and the girl was named Rhian. Carys couldn't be sure of their age, but they were most certainly older than she was, sixteen or seventeen, perhaps.

There were stories about these kids. Their ma had died during childbirth. That much was true. But rumour had it that she'd only birthed Rhian before she bled to death, so their daddy had had to cut her belly open and drag those boys out one by one, kicking and screaming. As bad as that may be, there were other rumours, too, which most ordinary folk might've had a hard time believing. You see, it was alleged that the Awbrey's mother and father were actually brother and sister. They said their whole family had been inbreeding for generations. Supposedly, these kids' great-great-great-grandfather kept his own daughter captive, tied up in the cow shed, and that he used to rape her on a daily basis. Any girls she gave birth to, well, once their flower blossomed, then he'd impregnate them too. Eventually, after he died, the men and women of the family started breeding with each other; fathers had sex with their daughters, while mothers were impregnated by their sons.

It was an abhorrent tale, scarcely believable. But if you ever saw the Awbrey kids, you'd know straight away that it was true. Those kids were the ugliest sons-of-bitches you could ever lay eyes on. Their heads were all misshapen, with overbites and buck teeth and eyes that protruded out of their sockets. None of the boys had a single hair on their head. Rhian did, however; it was jet-black but thin, fragile, and prone to falling out, leaving her with patches where her scalp was visible. She, too, would be bald by the time she reached her twenties.

Anyway, these kids weren't exactly the most pleasant. They were the type who liked to cause trouble. They were always fussing and fighting, inflicting their misery on others.

"Aye, aye," said Elis as the four Awbrey kids emerged from the treeline. "Wha' do we 'ave 'ere then?"

Carys's heart sank the moment she laid eyes on them. She'd heard all the stories about them and knew they were always up to no good. She'd seen them around on a handful of occasions but had always done her best to avoid them. She didn't like the way they spoke or behaved; it was almost feral. But what unsettled her most of all was the way they *looked*. Their abnormal, nearly inhuman features terrified her.

"We ain't doin' nothin'," said Owain, "just dippin' our toes is all."

"S'that right?" said Gethin. "You ain't causin' no bother out here?"

"Naw… nothin' like that."

The four Awbrey kids made their way to the edge of the creek. Rhian looked Carys over. Carys was wearing a yellow two-piece bathing suit that showed off her midriff. Rhian rolled her eyes and then looked back to Owain. "She got a nice body on 'er, don't she?" she said. You fuckin' 'er?"

Owain frowned. Carys could see he didn't like the question as it implied she was some sort of whore. But Carys was still pure. She'd never even kissed a boy, except for Owain, and that was only because she wanted to know what it felt like; she knew he didn't like girls in *that* way. "Not that it's any of *your* business," Owain said, "but, no, I'm not."

Rhian scoffed, a sly smile on her face. "Why not? She looks like the sort'a girl who'd know how to suck a dick real good." She looked at Carys. "*Do you* know how to suck a dick, lassie? How'd you like the taste o' cum?"

Carys felt her cheeks reddening. She felt as if the world might open up and swallow her whole. Part of her wished it would. Why was this girl talking to her like that? She didn't even know her…

"She's way better lookin' than you!" said Owain before Carys could offer a response. He puffed out his chest, like it might somehow make him look more intimidating. "Your he'ed looks like a fuckin' potato! It's like you fell from the top o' the ugly tree an' hit every branch on the way down!"

Rhian's smile melted away. In its place was a fearsome scowl.

"Think you's funny, do you?" said Elis. "You don't wanna be talkin' to my sister like that!"

"Fuck you, you dumb retard! Look at the state o' you! Inbred fucks, the lot o' you!"

Carys grabbed Owain's arm, hoping that she might stop him from provoking them. It was never wise to poke the bear, so the saying went...

"Wha'chu just call me?" growled Elis.

"I called you a fuckin' retarded inbred! Now, why don't you go home an' suck your daddy's dick?"

"Fuck you!" yelled Elis.

"Fuck you!" yelled Owain.

Then, a heavy rock slammed into the side of Owain's head. Carys hadn't seen, but one of the Awbrey boys must've thrown it. There was a cracking sound as it bounced off his skull. It sounded like branches snapping, or... or... bone breaking. Blood immediately cascaded down the side of his face. A brief moment then seemed to pass before his eyes rolled back in his head, and he slumped down, face-first, into the water.

Carys screamed.

The Awbrey kids... well... they just laughed.

"Please!" Carys howled, her heart pounding, threatening to tear itself out of her throat. "You have to help him!" She did her best to drag Owain towards the shoreline.

"Oh, sho-ore," said Emyr. "We'll help him. We'll help both o' yous!"

They were on her then, dragging her out of the water, leaving Owain behind, face down in the water, leaving him to drown... if he wasn't already dead.

"No! Please! Leave me be!" Carys begged. She was frantic, trying to pull herself free from the boys' grasp. But they held her tight. "He's goin'a die! You can't leave him there!"

"How much you wan'a bet?" asked Rhian, a twisted smirk on her face.

Carys knew then that even if they hadn't intentionally

killed Owain, the fact he was going to die didn't concern them at all.

"C'mon," said Rhian, "let's take 'er back t'farm."

The Awbrey's lived on a decrepit farm in the middle of the woods. Carys was too out of it to pay much attention, but she saw the old stone house was on the verge of collapse. Two of the boys were holding her, one on each side. They dragged her towards the house.

It was Rhian who stopped them. "Don't be daft!" she said. "You're sure to cop it off Da' if he finds you bringin' this girl home… take 'er inta the barn."

The barn was constructed from rotting, worm-ridden wood, with corrugated tin sheets nailed to the roof. It looked as though it might not survive the next storm.

It was here the boys took Carys.

Inside the barn, a cacophony of noise rang through her ears. It was the pigs. They were squealing and snorting, sniffing at the intruders through the galvanised bars of their pen.

They dumped Carys unceremoniously onto the ground. Immediately, she tried to stand, but, immediately, she was knocked back down, a swift kick to the gut sending her sprawling. It was Rihan who'd kicked her. "P-please," she cried, "don't do this! Please! L-let me go! I won't say nothin' 'bout what you did to Owain, I promise."

Rhian shrugged. "But, we di'n't do nothin' to nobody."

Carys stared up into her cold, callous eyes. She knew then they meant to kill her.

Rhian continued: "And these boys, they ain't gon' do nothin' to *you* neither… except for fuck you and kill you!" She was laughing then.

Carys screamed as the boys circled her like a pack of wild

dogs closing in on their prey. They were on her then, tearing off the two-piece swimsuit she'd been wearing, stripping her down until she was as naked as the day she was born. She tried to cover her breasts and her … *privates*… but Rhian grabbed her wrists and yanked them back behind her, allowing the three boys to grope her, to touch her wherever they wanted. They pinched at her nipples. They put their fingers inside her.

Somebody grabbed her by the hair and forced her down onto the ground. Before she even knew what was happening, one of those boys was on top of her, pushing his rock-hard *thing* into her. An agonising pain shot through her body, setting her nerves ablaze. The others were there, holding her down, tormenting her while their brother raped her.

They all took their turn.

They used every hole.

Rhian watched the whole thing, laughing the entire time. Once they'd had their fun, she stepped forward, towering over Carys' crumpled remains. "You know what happens now?" she asked, her voice low and gravelly. Now, we need to feed the pigs!"

Gethin bellowed a laugh. "Aw, yeah! Pigs'll eat anythin', you know? They'll strip the meat right off your bones, and they don't care if you're still alive and kickin'!"

"That's right," chuckled Elis. "We's gonna send you back to yer daddy as a sack full of pig shit." He snorted a laugh then, sounding almost like a pig himself.

"Pick 'er up," Rhian told the boys, "an' chuck 'er in!"

Elis, Emyr, and Gethin lifted Carys from the ground and carried her to the pig pen. There, they dumped her over the railing. "Dinneh time, piggies!" Emyr laughed. "Come an' get it!"

Exhausted, broken, every joint aching, Carys could do nothing as she lay there, face down in the muck, as the pigs circled her, snuffling at the ground, nipping at her skin, drawing blood. She squeezed her eyelids tight shut as a tear ran down her cheek. She knew she was about to die.

But then the pigs started squealing and backing away. They stopped biting her.

When Carys opened her eyes, she saw why.

The biggest boar she'd ever seen was standing over her. It must've been five feet tall at the shoulder. It could've stood eye to eye with any regular man. Judging by the size of it— and not that Carys was much good with estimating weights— this thing must've weighed at least five hundred pounds. *It's as big as a goddamned house*, Carys thought to herself.

"Aw, damn," chuckled Emyr. "Looks like Hector wants you all to himself!"

Hector? Was that the name of the pig?

Whatever its name was, it began to snort and sniff at Carys' body. It pushed its warm, wet snout between her legs, forcing them apart. She could feel its warm breath on her cooch. Then its tongue, as rough as sandpaper, probed her.

Carys screamed again.

There was nothing she could do to stop Hector from mounting her, his massive weight forcing her down into the sodden mud. His trotters scratched and scraped along her back, pinching her flesh as he moved to position himself. Then, he forced himself inside her.

Most people aren't aware of this fact, but male pigs have a corkscrew-shaped penis. It's a natural adaptation to aid in the mating process. You see, male pigs are too heavy, so the corkscrew shape of their penis allows them to stay *tied* with the female long enough for insemination to take place.

Of course, Carys wasn't a sow. Her genitalia wasn't designed for this. As such, it felt to her as if she was being raped with a bale of barbed wire.

The Awbrey kids just laughed as the boar fucked her.

Carys sobbed and screamed as she felt Hector ejaculate inside her. He pulled out, then lapped at her vagina once more, tasting the sweet mixture of blood and semen leaking from her, before sauntering away.

Rhian was still laughing. "Get her out'a there."

"Whut?" asked Elis. "We gon' let the pigs go hungry?"

"They gots their slop, ain't they? Just get her out'a there!"

The boys did as they were told.

Carys could hardly stand. She was filthy, a burning agony shredding through every inch of her body. She was barely conscious as the Awbrey kids re-dressed her.

"Now you go on home," said Rhian, "and you tell your da' how you done had sex with a pig!"

They were all laughing again.

Carys wasn't sure how she managed to make it home. She must've wandered through the woods in a daze, her subconscious mind somehow guiding her home. When she got there, she told nobody about what had happened, not Owain being killed, not the Awbrey boys raping her, and most certainly not what had happened with... that... *pig*.

Nobody knew.

Until...

Nine months later, Carys gave birth to a baby of her very own.

Her father had chastised her once he realised she was pregnant. He'd accused her of sleeping with every boy in the valley. She tried to tell him what happened to her, but he never believed it. Who would? It was a crazy story. It was much easier to think that she'd been impregnated by one of the many boys she'd quite obviously fucked.

Not until he saw the baby with his own eyes did he believe her.

This wasn't a normal baby. Its genes were all messed up on account of the fact that those three boys had all put their seed in her belly, as well as Hector. It was huge, for one thing, with a round belly, wide shoulders, and a massive head attached to the torso by a thick neck. Its arms and legs were short and stumpy, and its fingers and toes were somewhat fused, making them look almost like trotters. It looked only semi-human—almost like a pig.

It looked like its daddy.

Somewhat thankfully, Carys never got to see the baby; she died of blood loss during childbirth.

Carys' father knew he should've put a bullet in that baby's brain before it even got the chance to take its first breath. But he couldn't do it. He couldn't kill his offspring, no matter how inhuman it might appear to be.

Still, Carys' father vowed revenge. He'd find the Awbreys and make them pay for what they had done to his daughter.

But not yet. Not until her son—his *grand*son—was old enough to seek vengeance himself.

He named him Carwyn.

The time for vengeance came much sooner than expected. Carwyn grew at an abnormal rate, reaching adult size by the time he was only six years of age. Pigs don't live as long as people do, so six years was about the equivalent of a human boy being around eighteen. That made sense; Carwyn was half-man, half-pig. As he'd grown, his body had changed. He walked upright like a man, but his face was very much that of a hog. Most important, though, was the fact that he was intelligent. He was as clever as any ordinary man. He couldn't speak, only communicating in grunts and squeals, but he understood everything he was told.

Carwyn understood what those Awbrey kids had done to his mother. He understood that he needed to take revenge.

One night, shortly after midnight, his granddaddy took him through the woods to the Awbrey farm and handed him a sledgehammer.

Carwyn entered the house, and by the time he came out, all those boys were dead.

———

Present Day

Leah's mind was racing. The story this man had told her was entirely fantastical. It didn't make any sense. It wasn't possible. But then… that thing in the woods… the monster… it had looked only vaguely human. "So," she said, "are you saying the thing that killed my boyfriend was this… this… pig-man? This… Carwyn?"

The man scoffed a laugh. "Aw, no," he said. "Carwyn is long dead. He aged rapidly, died at probably around twelve years old."

"How can you be sure?" said Leah, growing almost frantic once again. "And if that wasn't… erm… Carwyn out there in the woods, then who—or *what*—was it? Are you saying there's more of those things out there?"

"Oh, sho-ore there is," said the man. "There's a whole fam-lee of 'em out there!"

Leah's heart raced. Just the idea of some half-human creatures stalking through the woods terrified her. "What? How?"

"I told you Carwyn killed all the Awbrey *boys*. I di'n't tell you what he did to Rhian."

"What *did* he do?"

"He fucked 'er, o'course! He an' his granddaddy took 'er

back to their place and used 'er as their own personal sex toy! She herself gave birth to many a pig-baby!"

Leah was speechless. The cogs of her mind turned at a furious pace, a migraine building behind her eyes. So, it was the offspring of this man-pig-monster that had killed Stan? None of it made any sense. And the way this man told his story, it sounded like he was somehow impressed. She needed help. "P-please," she stuttered. "Can you t-take me into town now? I need to speak to the p-police."

The man nodded his head. "Aye, o' course I can take yer. Follow me."

He stood from the sofa and headed for the front door. Leah stood and followed. She looked over her shoulder at the woman, who offered a reassuring smile. "It's okay, dear," she said. "Nothin' to worry 'bout. We'll get you all sorted out."

The man led Leah out of the house and across to one of the barns. "I got mah truck parked up in 'ere," he said, ushering her forward.

Something felt odd to Leah, out of place, like she was caught in some sort of trap. She wanted to turn and run back into the trees, into the darkness. But she needed these people to help her. What else could she do?

She stepped forward, and the man opened the barn door.

Leah stepped inside.

Immediately, a foul smell filled her nostrils. It was bitter, like the scent of rancid meat and rotten eggs. And then her eyes fell on the corpse of the woman, strapped to the wooden table in the middle of the space. She looked to have been at least sixty years old when she'd passed. She was completely naked, her withered body streaked with dirt, sweat, and maybe a little blood, too. A rag had been stuffed into her mouth and tied in place with a length of rope. Her glassy, dead eyes stared right at Leah.

"Oh my God!" Leah whimpered, almost under her breath. She turned, hoping to flee the barn. But the man and the woman were standing there, blocking her path. Both had deranged looks on their faces. "Wh-what is this?" she asked. "What's going on?"

"This 'ere is the girlie I told you 'bout," said the man. "This is Rhian Awbrey."

"Wh-what?"

"Carys—the girl who gave birth to Carwyn—she were my second cousin, she were. I have been lookin' after Rhian here for the past twenty years now after Carys' daddy died. She done helped us expand our family. Only problem is, those babies she's been pushin' out her cunt mostly got the same deformities that Carwyn had."

Leah's legs felt as if they'd turned to jelly. It was all she could do to keep herself from collapsing into a heap on the ground.

"I'm guessin' it were Gruffudd who killed yer boyfriend. An' I am sorry 'bout that, but he's been lookin' for a new sow to breed from for a while now. As you can see, Rhian 'ere went an' died, so she ain't been givin' us no new babies for a lit'le while now. And besides, fuckin' a dead body ain't anywhere near as fun a fuckin' a live one. I can tell you that!"

Every ounce of energy leaked from Leah's body. The air emptied from her lungs. She tried to speak or to scream, but little more than a whimper passed her lips.

A sudden cacophony of noise came from behind her. She spun just in time to see the same monster who had killed Stan bursting into the barn through the second set of doors behind her. She tried to raise her hands in defence but found they were as heavy as lead. The monster... the pig-man... *Gruffudd*, Leah remembered... lifted his sledgehammer, and slammed the butt of the handle into the side of her head. She dropped, semi-conscious, to the floor.

"She a poo'er dab, ain't she," said the woman. "She do look all out of sorts, she do."

"Not to worry; Gruffudd will get her all straightened out, won't you, son?"

The pig-man snorted and nodded his head.

Leah, still dazed, looked up at the hideous beast towering over her. The nub that was its penis seemed to have split in two. Worming its way out of it was a long, thin appendage. It was pinkish-red and curled tightly like a… a… a corkscrew.

Leah's eyes widened.

"Sorry, lass," said the man, "but this is how things is around 'ere. People call us sheep shaggers, but they don't know the truth; we don't fuck the livestock… the livestock fucks us!"

The pig-man squealed gleefully as he tore the clothes from Leah's body, his trotters ripping painfully at her flesh. He then thrust his corkscrew cock into her cunt, sending a wave of torturous agony sweeping over her. It felt as if something was shredding her insides like she was being raped with a broken bottle. She could feel the blood splattering her inner thigh, pooling around her buttocks.

The man and woman linked hands and watched with pride as their son dutifully inseminated the new breeding stock.

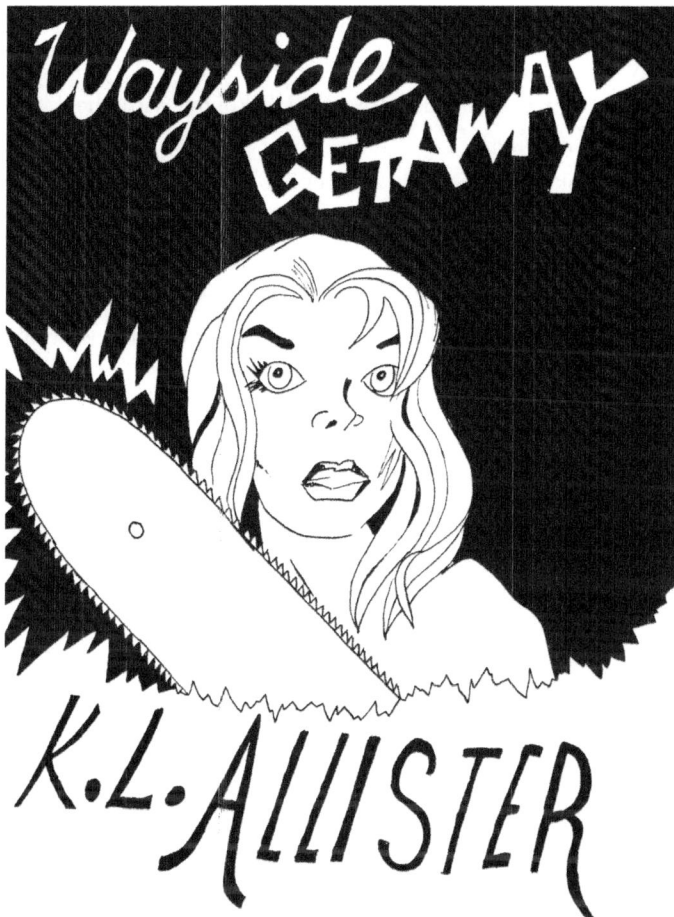

Wayside Getaway

K.L. Allister

I LOOKED over at my husband longingly as we drove. The brisk autumn air flooded over the barely cracked windows, providing a much-needed breeze. We gradually transitioned from suburban to rural, with more trees showing up on either side of the road in their amber and bronze flavors. It was quiet in the car for once.

The wooded area surrounding us gave me a sense of solace. The suburban din had become a continuous whining, similar to tinnitus, in my ears. These trees had quite the opposite effect.

"Do you think your mom will be okay with the kids, Ethan?" I inquired.

He looked at me with a sheepish grin. "Tabby, I'm sure they'll be fine. Well…" he paused for a moment. "I know Jackson will be, but Denise… She's a certified rabble-rouser."

We laughed at the thought of our little girl giving my mother-in-law hell. But really, she was in for it while we took some time away to recharge our batteries.

I researched quaint, rural getaways within a three-hour radius and found a cozy B&B near the borderline. We talked to Ethan's mom, Lorraine, about it, and although she was reluctant, she realized we'd been burning the candle at both ends. We needed a break.

"How much further until we're there?" I asked.

"Almost there. The GPS says we're only ten minutes away." He let out a deep sigh. "I cannot wait to relax, just me and you."

"Me too, babe, me too."

———

We pulled up to the building, and it oozed curb appeal. The Groupon description hit the nail on the head. Over two thousand five hundred square feet, two stories, massive wraparound porch, and the building's facade was painted a fresh baby blue balanced perfectly by firetruck red shutters. Bushes and trees were abundant around the home, but it was listed as "rural," so I couldn't fault them for that.

As soon as we closed the car doors, we were met by an elderly lady shuffling out of the front door. Her stature didn't exceed five-foot-two, and she had a slight curvature to her spine. Gray curls cascaded over her thick-rimmed glasses and down to the middle of her earlobes. She was wearing a green knitted cardigan draped over her shoulders. Despite her petite frame, her voice carried with resounding excitement.

"Oh! You must be Ethan and Tabitha Taylor! Welcome, welcome, welcome!"

She pulled me in for a tight hug. For an older woman, she was damn strong!

"Gertrude Weathers, proud proprietor of the Wayside Bed & Breakfast, pleased to meet you both! I trust you had no trouble getting here?"

"No, not at all," my husband replied. "And we packed light, so just lead the way, and we'll make sure all our stuff gets inside. Thank you!"

She nodded and smiled politely while we gathered our things from the trunk.

"Nice pick, babe! This place looks great! I wouldn't mind staying here longer than the weekend."

I gave Ethan a wide smirk, happy I'd picked a good spot for us to relax.

Gertrude led us to our room, a spacious area consisting of an Alaskan King bed with a deep brown frame and a matching dresser with more than enough space for our belongings. There was one window with a great view of nature's domain. No TV, though, which was probably a good thing. That damn thing sucks the life out of you anyway.

Gertrude stood in the doorway as we dropped our suitcases on the bed.

"So, staying for the weekend, right?"

We nodded.

"This is the Couple's Suite," she nudged Ethan and winked a few times. Breakfast will be served promptly at seven a.m., lunch at noon, and dinner at 5 p.m. There are many trails leading in and out of the woods. The lake's a quarter mile down the road, and not another soul for five miles! Just us and good ol' Mother Nature."

God, that sounded great—definitely the detox we need.

"I do have a few other people staying here. They arrived just ahead of you. Feel free to say hello and share a kind word with them. Two are exploring the trails, and two are still upstairs." She squinted at her watch and smiled. "Oh, goodness! It's almost time for dinner! I'll let you get settled. Wash up and meet us in the dining room in a couple hours, yes?"

As she turned to scuttle away, Ethan lightly grabbed her arm, slightly startling the elderly lady.

"Mrs. Weathers, thank you so much for your hospitality," he beamed.

"Oh, dear, *Miss* Weathers. My Winston is two years gone now." She smiled pensively. "Anywho, call me Gerty! Everyone's family under my roof."

"You got it, Gerty. Thank you again!"

We finished unpacking and took time to stretch from the long car ride. We waited until about five, then meandered to the dining room. Our 'suite,' as Gerty put it, was situated on the same floor as the dining room and the master bedroom, where I assumed our hostess slept. There were three other bedrooms on the upper floor and, from what Groupon said, a fully finished basement. All of its amenities catered to the overall rustic motif.

Gerty locked eyes with us as she set the table. There were seven place settings. I saw two men coming down the steps, and they immediately introduced themselves once their soles met the bottom floor.

"Well, hello!" one man said. He was dressed in a floral print shirt unbuttoned at his sternum. A gold chain adorned his neck while black dockers completed his ensemble. "I'm Thomas. It's nice to meet you both!"

His companion wore a lilac-colored Stefano Ricci dress shirt, navy tie, and beige slacks. "And my name is Raul," he said with a thick Hispanic accent.

"It's a pleasure to meet you," Ethan said, shaking their hands. "Are you both here for the weekend, too?"

"We sure are!" Thomas said. "Celebrating our three-year anniversary by getting away from that suburban life. *Ugh!*"

"I love your shirt, Raul," I started. "Stefano Ricci, you wear it very well."

Raul's eyes lit up. "Ooooh, *mamacita*, you have a good eye for fashion! *Digame,* tell me, do you work with clothes?"

I modestly brushed my hair behind my ears. My humble five-five, one hundred and fifty-five-pound frame with cookie-cutter brunette hair was as simple as they come, so it was probably shocking that a 'plain Jane' like me worked with fashion. "Yeah, I work in the fashion industry. We work with his line all the time, among others, of course."

"That is stunning, queen," Thomas added before looking at Ethan. "And what do you do for a living, stud?"

Raul shot Thomas a telling glare.

Ethan chuckled, brushing off the flirtation. "I work in construction. I manage teams of builders and delegate work projects around the burbs and in the city."

"Ooooh, intriguing, wouldn't you say, Raul?"

Another piercing glare.

Just as we were getting acquainted, Gerty made her way out of the kitchen. "Dinnertime!" she bellowed. "Ethan, be a dear and help me bring the food out, would you?"

My chivalrous husband bolted to help the old lady carry a smorgasbord of food to the dining room table. The table was littered with ham, smothered chicken, shepherd's pie, mashed potatoes, garlic bread, and French onion soup, among other things. It was more than a death row inmate would get, that's for sure. The aromas were exquisite and coalesced in my nostrils, nearly making my mouth water. I was starving from the trip.

Gerty looked around the table. "We're missing a couple, huh?" She folded her arms in a 'disappointed grandmother' sort of way and tapped her foot on the hardwood floor.

Suddenly, the front door swung open with an overexertion of force and booming voices.

"—and that's what I fucking told you," A man's voice said. "Don't worry about it. I'll handle it when we drive back."

A woman followed him in. They both had dreadlocks and wore baggy clothing. The man was easily six-foot-one, and the girl came in at five-eight. They looked like a couple of dirty hippies.

"Mister, I told you when you got here," Gerty cut in. "I will not tolerate that language in my home."

He rolled his eyes at her, disregarding her instructions. He and his female companion sat at the table and joined the conversation.

————

We were all deep in the throes of eating and stuffing our gullets like it was our last meal on Earth. I learned the names of our hippie friends—Marigold and Bodhi. They were originally from Los Angeles but backpacked across the United States, somehow ending up here in rural Michigan.

"So, *mira*," Raul said. "You just get in anyone's car and go? You don't care where they take you? *No les importa?*"

"Yeah, man," Bodhi replied. "We don't give a shit where we end up."

Gerty shot him a look, to which he pantomimed zipping his lips shut.

Ethan looked at me lovingly. Despite the diverse company, he seemed to be having a great time. I could tell Bodhi made him nervous, and honestly, he made me nervous, too. As for Thomas and Raul, I was hitting it off with them famously. We were sharing our love for fashion, having girl talk, and just having a great time. Everyone had cleared out most of the food, leaving scraps here and there on their plates. The table was like a barren wasteland, picked clean by vultures and other birds of prey.

I looked over at Gerty, and she stood to address us.

"I'm so glad you all are enjoying the dinner I prepared! I'm a quarter Italian, and my mother always said her calling in life was filling tummies!" She held her hand over her mouth as she giggled softly. "But, if you'll excuse me, I have dessert in the oven for everyone! It will take another thirty to forty minutes to finish baking, though. So, if you want to relax in your rooms, I'll get this cleaned up and have my special dessert out for you in a jiffy!" She pushed her glasses up the bridge of her nose and retreated to the kitchen.

———

Ethan and I returned to our room to recover from the buffet-style dinner Gerty prepared for us. Thankfully, I didn't eat too much, and Ethan didn't either. I was interested to see what she made for dessert, though.

"This has been incredible so far, Tabby," he said, putting his hand on mine as we lay on the bed. "This woman is gonna put ten pounds on us by the time we head back!"

I laughed. "Yeah, maybe." Then, a mischievous idea came to mind. "Unless…"

"Unless, what?"

"Unless we engage in some *extracurriculars* to combat all the food."

I moved my hand out from under his and put it on his crotch, rhythmically stroking him. He looked at the door's vintage gold doorknob like we were teenagers about to get caught by our parents.

"Tabby, what are you—"

"Shhh," I put my finger over his mouth. I unzipped his blue jeans while kissing his neck, reaching through the folds of fabric until my hand gripped his length. His hard cock was eagerly waiting to be set free.

I pulled his jeans down to his knees and took him in my mouth. I saw his eyes close and his head fling back—my absolute favorite reaction. It got me so goddamn wet. After a few repetitions, I pulled up my yellow sundress, straddled him, and put my hands on his toned, barreled chest. My eyes rolled back as he entered me.

I started grinding on his dick, his shaft playing a game of ping-pong inside my pussy. The bed creaked loudly as my intensity picked up. He cupped my tits in his hands as I rode him like Seabiscuit. His lips grazed my nipple, and the tip of his tongue resembled Picasso as he swiveled and masterfully worked each of my areolas in turn, provoking my pleasured groans.

"Oh my god, Tabby," he moaned with his eyes closed. "I'm gonna come."

My fingers ran themselves through my hair. "Almost there, cowboy. Just hang in a little longer."

I gyrated my pelvis against him faster and faster. Before this, we hadn't had sex in five months, and I wasn't about to squander the opportunity. I was so close. I kept up my pace, and our moans crescendoed into a thunderous forte.

"I'm gonna—Oh God, Ethan, I'm gonna—"

THUD! THUMP!

I was startled out of my orgasm.

Someone was at the door. I instinctively pulled a blanket over my nude body. Ethan followed suit and covered his throbbing member. We froze as we stared doe-eyed in the direction of the sound. It was shortly followed by a hurried scuffling of feet against the floorboards.

We both looked at each other and mouthed: "Gerty?"

———

Putting Gerty's apparent snooping out of our minds, we joined everyone else at the dining room table for dessert. She had made two decadent cobblers—one strawberry and one peach. They looked like something from one of those baking competitions. They were *flawlessly* executed.

"I hope you all enjoy! An old gal like me isn't too good at much anymore, but I know my way around the kitchen!"

She smiled at everyone sitting around the rectangular wooden table. All the guests grabbed their utensils and started digging into the delectable dessert. A devious smirk formed on her face when she came to me and Ethan. That was the first time Gerty unnerved me in the handful of hours we'd been there. And it surely wouldn't be the last.

"Oh my god, girl," Thomas began, "Gert, you *have* to give me this recipe. It is *delish!*"

"I agree," Raul said. "*Muy delicioso, doña.*" He raised a chef's kiss to his lips.

"The peach one is awesome," Marigold piped up, saying

her first words since we'd arrived. "You certainly know your food."

"Oh, why, thank you!" Gerty blushed and put her hands to her chest. "Too sweet, the lot of you, I swear!"

I looked at Ethan, who had already started devouring his strawberry cobbler, and joined him. I dug my fork into my peach cobbler, and it was one of the greatest things I'd ever tasted. It had the perfect balance of acidity and savory, setting my taste buds ablaze. Before I knew it, I was glancing down at my empty plate.

The room filled with conversation, just like it had at dinner. Laughter was abundant, and friendships were quickly being made.

I looked at Marigold, wondering why she hadn't spoken much. I waved at her and offered her a friendly smile. She returned the gesture as she nursed a cup of decaffeinated coffee, being one of the first guests to finish dessert.

She blinked rapidly and shook her head as if she had a migraine or was in a daze. Suddenly, her head THWACKED loudly against her plate, rendering her unconscious. Panicked looks spread around the table, and the laughter ceased.

"Babe? Mari, what's the—" Bodhi didn't get to air his concern fully. His eyes grew heavy, and his head slumped toward his breastbone.

Thomas and Raul passed out next. Raul fell out of his chair as he was getting up to check on the hippies. Thomas's head lolled back against the chair's headrest.

Ethan's hand was on my shoulder.

"Tabby, what the fuck is—"

His head landed on the table's edge, his fork still clutched between his fingers.

"Gerty? Wh—what's going on?" I managed to utter. My vision was fading in and out. "Did—what did you—why?"

The petite old lady looked at me, smiled, and sipped her coffee.

"Oh, sweet child. Didn't anyone ever tell you? Not everything is as it seems."

The last thing I heard, as my vision failed, was her squeaky giggle and the CREAK of the basement door.

———

I woke up to a humid and muggy atmosphere lit by a lone, smoky light bulb. My hands and arms were shackled, hanging over my head. As I lifted my chin upward, I saw Bodhi in front of me. His hands were manacled, and the chain was looped onto a thick metal ring protruding from the ceiling. It occurred to me that I was in the same situation, and we were in the basement. The dilapidated space was littered with thick dust and household tools, some more common than others. It was like Home Depot and Lowe's fucked and had a baby down here.

My eyes wandered down the line, and I saw all of Gerty's guests. We were lined up like cattle in a slaughterhouse. The air was palpable and so thick you could taste it. Unlike our dessert, it was bitter, and the tang of mildew coated my throat.

I tried to retain my composure, attempting to piece together any shred of reasoning behind this. My eyes darted left and right, and a blur shot out from my peripherals. What I was confronted with couldn't, in good conscience, be categorized as human.

He was massive, at least six-foot-eight and three hundred pounds. His age must have been somewhere around fifty to fifty-five. His face was mangled, a bulbous growth spanning from his hairline to his left eye socket. The ashen hair on his head was patchy and barely covered his many bumps and cysts. His nose was missing entirely, and the exposed bone was visible as mucus dripped from his open nasal cavity and down to his denim overalls.

His haunting visage was congested with pustules and boils. Some were throbbing and yielding white and yellow, cheesy pus, emanating a vile stench that assaulted my nostrils as he stood less than two feet from me. His breath made me retch and dry heave. He was undoubtedly the victim of a severe lack of hygiene.

His upper lip sported a thin, graying mustache, split in half by a cleft lip. The right side of his mouth was a gaping hole. He liked to push his tongue through the opening and lick the outside of his cheek. I could see very few teeth through the hole, a combination of gray and yellow, crooked in their placement.

One abscess exploded, and its contents landed on my top lip. I moved my head left and right, trying to shake off the rancid discharge. He flashed a morbid smile at me as his hand inched closer. His index finger scooped up the secretion, and he ogled it for a brief second. Then, without warning, he shoved his disgusting digit into my mouth. My body couldn't take it, and puke spewed from the corners of my mouth and around his big paw.

"Hey man, what the fuck are you doing?!" Bodhi woke up. "Leave her the fuck alone!"

The large mystery man jolted at the sudden noise and pivoted toward the source. He cocked back his monstrous hand and smashed the back of it into Bodhi's face. Bodhi's head slacked and slumped to the side. I saw him spit up blood and a couple of fragmented teeth.

I heard more grumblings from some of the other guests as they came out of unconsciousness. The man paid them no mind and stomped off into the dark. The basement door creaked open, and someone slowly made their way down to us.

"Well," a familiar voice rang out. "I see you've met my son, Atticus. He's the one who brought you all down here, being that I am less capable in my old age." She chuckled as if any of this was normal, then sat in a chair adjacent to the steps.

"Gerty?" Bodhi managed to slur out amongst broken chompers. "What the fuck is all this, you crusty old cunt?!"

"Mr. Bodhi, I've told you many times. I do not tolerate that language in my home."

"No, fuck this!" He looked straight at me across the way, then to the others. "Let us the fuck out of here, man! Tell your retarded, mongoloid son to unhook us and let us go! You're making a big fucking mistake!"

Gerty folded her arms and nodded her head toward the dark. I saw the shadows move and shift behind Bodhi.

"This is fucked up," Bodhi started crying. "Man, this is all some fucking joke, right? This shit isn't real. I bet it's like one of those shows where—"

A sudden, resounding staccato rocked my foundation as I was showered with viscera, gore, and bone fragments. Bodhi's head burst open from Atticus's shotgun pellets, the blast resounding in my ears, and I was staring at a bloody chasm where his face used to be. His neck gave way, and his head, or what was left of it, crumpled against his sternum.

My face was cut up in various places from the accosting of his displaced osteology. A river of scarlet poured from what used to be Bodhi and congregated below his dangling feet.

"Now," Gerty resumed. I understand the circumstances are...unsavory, so I would expect a little bit of 'self-expression.' Still, if any of you thinks of slandering my perfect boy, you will join Bodhi most expeditiously."

Gerty's chagrin quickly morphed into a devious and demented smile, stretching from one temple to the other.

I looked at Ethan, my eyes willing him to be freed. Thomas and Raul were in a state of shock, and Marigold was inconsolable. She had just lost her partner. I couldn't even begin to fathom how hard that would be for me.

"I'm going to choose two of you for...let's call it a little game. If, for some reason, you decide you don't want to play..." she trailed off and pointed her hand at Bodhi. We got the point. "Hmmm...who should I pick first?"

Gerty perused us as she walked between the two lines of her soon-to-be victims. Raul closed his eyes and started praying in Spanish. I couldn't make out all of it, but from what I gathered, I could surmise that it was the Lord's Prayer. Something in the pit of my stomach told me the Lord wasn't listening tonight.

"My first pick is Thomas," Gerty said. "Atticus, be a dear and let the faggot down, will you?"

Raul's eyes turned to Gerty. "¿A quién se estás llamando gueco, güey? Voy a pinche matarte, puta!"

"Raul, I don't speak Spanish," Gerty cleared her throat. "But I'm assuming you're not too happy with my decision or my *colorful* language." She smirked again.

Atticus reached up and removed the chain from the hook, letting Thomas down. Tears were streaming down his face as he mouthed 'I love you' to Raul over and over again. Thomas dropped to his knees, hands still bound, and placed a kiss on Raul's feet.

Marigold was still screaming and had pissed herself, Ethan was shell-shocked and donned a thousand-yard stare, and I was having an out-of-body experience. I prayed to whoever would listen that this was just some fucked up dream. My peripherals betrayed that notion as Gerty stood in front of me.

"Congratulations, you filthy harlot. It's you and Thomas, my dear."

Harlot? For fucking my own husband? That's rich, bitch.

Atticus sauntered over to me and started getting me down. I didn't realize it immediately, but Ethan was screaming, ripped from his stupor. The players had been chosen—me and Thomas. Now we'd find out what kind of sick and depraved game Gerty had in mind.

———

The screams had subsided for now. There was some hyperventilating here and there, but all eyes were on Gerty. Everyone was hyper-focused on what she was going to say next.

"Now that we have the players, we will start the game," she said. "We're going to see just how sick you puppies really are. *Control* will shift between both players, Thomas and Tabitha, and whoever is in control must pick someone to *play with*. We want creativity, depravity, and wanton destruction of the human body. If you lack in these departments or decide you don't wish to continue, you will end up looking like poor old Bodhi over here. We will accept nothing but your best performance, won't we, my sweet boy?"

She turned to Atticus and was met with a gappy smile and a throaty groan.

"I suppose we should exercise our manners, yes? Ladies first. Tabitha, take it away, my dear."

I stood there in abject terror. Did she expect me and

Thomas to kill these people? To kill my husband? Would she let us go afterward? There was only one way to find out.

"Oh, and Tabitha?" Gerty said, catching my attention. Do act with some fervor, yes? I wouldn't want anything bad to happen to your children, Jackson or Denise."

I was blindsided. "How—how the fuck do you know our children's names? You so much as look in their direction..."

I saw Atticus make a move toward me. I thought better about what I wanted to say. Gerty lifted her chin at me and smiled. The petite, frail-looking woman was in complete control; there was no doubt about it.

I had to choose. Naturally, I wasn't about to choose Ethan, and I'd bonded too much with Raul during dinner. Unfortunately, Marigold was my pick. Atticus obliged and lowered her to my level.

I glanced around the basement to all the tools strewn about. Surely, they would approve of something here. I grabbed a pipe wrench off the work table and walked to Mari. There was hesitation in my movements, but I eventually managed a swing. The blow connected with her temple, and she let out a pained groan. A gash formed on her head where I hit her, and I gazed at Gerty.

"You're going to have to do better than that, dear," she said in sheer disappointment.

Shit. They won't let me stop until I kill her...or however many of them I could. I needed to get me and Ethan out. It's either them or my kids. And those babies need their mother and father.

I reached for pliers and started to work on Mari's teeth. Metal met enamel as I yanked and prodded, ripping bone from root. Reservoirs of blood poured from her mouth as I took four...five...six...*seven* teeth.

"Tab—Tabitha...look what they did..." Mari spit out a glob of gore. "Look what they did to Bodhi."

"I'm sorry," was all I managed to say. "Atticus, hold her still."

The oversized man looked to his mother for direction. She nodded, and he complied with my request. To appease these monsters, I needed to become a monster. And to do that, I needed Mari to be still.

I revealed a cordless Dremel tool in my other hand and secured the spherical cutting wheel onto its head. It thrummed to life as I flipped the power switch on, and a loud whirring sound reverberated through the enclosure. She didn't move, as Atticus held her head still, but she was screaming so loudly that she coughed up opaque mists of blood.

I closed the gap between me and Mari, and the tool crept closer and closer to her right eye. The tool's motor drowned out her screams as I leveled my death implement horizontally across her eyeball. I pressed the Dremel to her eye, cutting through the gelatinous outer shell, passing the sclera, and into her corneal and retinal layers. I was immediately sprayed with blood and vitreous fluid, the tool exacerbating the damage and worsening the wound.

I didn't stop there. I repeated the process for her left eye, not stopping until I hit bone. Her face represented a train-wreck of gore and bodily fluids. The eyes she once had now appeared like a goopy, grisly porridge.

Her thrashing became more intense as I cut into her. She flailed and throttled her body back and forth and ended up kicking Atticus in the balls. He grunted loudly and almost dropped her. Once he regained control, he brandished a serrated knife from his overalls and dragged it across the top of Mari's head. Once he opened the ghastly incision, he grabbed hold of her long dreadlocks and yanked with all his might.

Hair separated from her scalp, followed by an audible tearing sound. Blood spurted all over me and Thomas like a burst water main. After the hippie headpiece was dissected, Atticus threw it to the cold ground, vengeance for his gonads exacted.

It was time to finish this and put Mari out of her misery. I eyed the electric weed whacker leaning against the worktable. I squeezed the trigger on the handle, and it revved up. Mari was too stunned by her impromptu pairing to pay me any mind. I dragged the gardening tool across her neck, letting free not only her lifeblood but her very soul.

The force gave way, and my hands dropped to the floor. Consequently, the implement was still pressed to Mari's skin. The metal brush cutters ripped through her chest, performing a gruesome autopsy in a sloppy curvature spanning from her sternum to her pubis. Gore poured forth like we were at the Splash Zone at SeaWorld, and her entrails surged out of the newly made cavern. Mari was *very* dead.

The screams from Thomas and the others were deafening. I could barely hear the constant thrum of the weed whacker. Atticus jumped up and down and clapped his hands at the grotesquerie. He dragged Mari to the corner of the room, where he removed his overalls and squatted over her.

He grunted with effort until a watery deluge of orange and brown excrement rapidly filled Mari's chest cavity. The audible splatters queued up a revolting dirge through the basement. Atticus pulled his overalls back up and let out a loud guffaw aimed at Mari's decrepit face. Almost as abruptly as Bodhi's life had been snuffed out, he brought his enormous boot crashing down onto Mari's face. Her facial bones shattered and caved in on themselves, splashes of crimson gracing Atticus's gargantuan stature.

"What the actual fuck…" I heard Ethan whisper as his body convulsed from panicked shakes. "This can't be happening…"

Raul vomited all over himself, and Thomas was still screaming. Thomas then did the unthinkable and rushed Atticus. He rained blows on the mammoth's shoulder—but to no avail. Brushing off the mild hindrance, Atticus grabbed Thomas by the throat and threw him to the ground.

"Now, Thomas," Gerty chirped. "We will not do that again. If you decide to be so brave, Atticus will have his way with you. Do I make myself clear?"

Thomas rubbed his neck to abate the pain and wiped the tears and snot from his worn-out face. He nodded reluctantly and stood on his feet.

"Good! We don't want to wear out Tabitha. Thomas, your turn."

I saw Thomas's eyes shift between me, Raul, and Ethan. Given that I still had the weed whacker in my hands, I doubted he would want to come after me, so that left Raul and Ethan. I knew exactly what his decision would be.

"A—Atticus," Thomas said with barely a whisper. "Hold Tabby still."

My eyes went wide as Atticus moved with unexpected speed for someone his size. Before I knew it, he was behind me, snaking his large arms under my armpits, instantly subduing me.

Thomas was off near the worktable, rummaging through the tools of torture. He spent a couple minutes doing so until I saw him land on the nail gun.

"Let me go, you *fuck*! Thomas, no!" I started kicking.

Despite what he was wielding, he approached me with a

calm gait that was almost reassuring. Although I'd only known him for a day, we'd bonded considerably, and I knew he was kind-hearted. He wouldn't hurt a fly unless he absolutely needed to. Unfortunately for us, we'd become slaves to necessity.

He put the palm of his hand on my cheek. Thick, dark bags hung heavy under his eyes, and his gaze conveyed a look of utter ruin and despair. His apologetic demeanor would have been comforting under any other circumstances.

"I'm so sorry, Tabby," he said.

He shifted to his left, pressed the nail gun against Ethan's chest, and pulled the trigger six consecutive times. Groans and gurgles intensified as metal drivers were thrust into my husband's being, riddling his skin.

"NO! Thomas, no! Ethan, baby…" My eyes bulged with surprise. "Shit! Oh no, Ethan!"

I pleaded and cried and flailed with reckless abandon. Atticus's vice grip kept me immobile and in place, making my efforts futile. Thomas dropped the nail gun and threw his hands in the air. I glanced over at Ethan and heard sharp, airy wheezes.

"There! I did it. I can't do this anymore…" he cried.

Gerty squinted her eyes in disappointment. "Have you ever watched a game show, dear?"

"Wh—what?"

"A game show," the old woman reiterated. "Have you ever watched one on television?"

"Well, yeah…who hasn't?" Thomas replied, confused.

"Would you like to 'ask the audience'?"

Thomas gawked at her but played along. "What? Yeah, sure, whatever."

"Perfect! I love interactive games!" She clapped her liver-spotted hands vigorously. "So…Ethan works in construction, right?" Thomas nodded. "There should be a chisel around here somewhere."

Thomas's mouth was slack in disbelief. "You're joking, right?"

I heard Atticus groan aggressively right in my ear. Gerty scoffed in disapproval.

"Fuck..." Thomas muttered. He resentfully trudged back to the shop of horrors that was the worktable and its surroundings, then came back with a rusted chisel, a claw hammer, and a large crowbar. I was still struggling against Atticus's hold, and Raul was trying to talk sense into his partner.

"Baby! *Mirame,* look at me! Please, don't do this, *mi amor!*" Raul pleaded as he tried to catch his breath from the constant hyperventilating. "*Te quiero,* don't..."

Raul's words fell on deaf ears as the twisted game continued.

Thomas lined up the chisel against the bridge of Ethan's nose. Once he situated it right between my husband's eyes, he aligned the hammer against the bottom. He took a small phantom swing to make sure he hit the chisel and not Ethan's face—not like it fucking mattered either way.

Thomas lifted the hammer over his head, tears still streaming down his face, and drove the chisel deep into Ethan's nasal cavity. Metal crunched the cartilage and cut deep into his face. Blood cascaded on either side of his nose, drenching his shirt in red. A second strike met with a meaty squelching, and a third disconnected his nose from his face. It met the basement floor with a faint *slap*!

The force of the blows ripped the hook from the ceiling, and Ethan fell to the ground face-first. He coughed, kicking up dust and asbestos and spitting out a couple of bloody teeth. He reserved himself to staying still, not knowing what these sick fucks might do next.

"I can't fucking do this anymore!" Thomas said again, staring directly at Gerty. "I've had enough! I won't keep torturing Tabby's husband, or anyone for that matter, just so you sickos can get your fucking rocks off!"

Gerty ponderously perched her hand on her chin. "So, you want mercy for this man?"

"Yes! Yes! I want mercy for him. For all of us!"

Gerty pursed her lips and raised her eyebrows. "Mercy it is, then." She snapped her fingers, and Atticus immediately let me go.

I got up and started toward Ethan, but Atticus was in my way. "Get out of my fucking way, you—"

His clenched fist rocked my jaw. Not enough to knock me out, but enough to knock me on my ass and distort my vision.

The beast grabbed a large cinder block from the corner of the basement, near the crawl space, and placed it a handful of feet in front of me. He dragged Ethan over and positioned his teeth over the cinder block's cold and stoney surface. My fear doubled over itself as I realized Atticus was about to curb-stomp my fucking husband.

Just then, Raul's shouting reached ungodly levels and bothered Atticus enough to divert his attention for a split second. He strode over to the bound man and backhanded him, temporarily silencing his yells.

My body betrayed me, and I tried like hell to crawl over to Ethan. His head lightly swayed back and forth, meaning to look at me. I managed to move one foot…two…slowly inching closer to my lover, my person, my partner. Did we have our problems? Sure. But he was an above-average husband and father, and he tried his damnedest. I wanted, more than anything, for him to live.

As I crept another foot, he slowly turned his head and looked at me. I stopped to hear what he was about to say.

"Tabby," he wheezed through the coagulated wreckage of his face. "I lo—"

Atticus's foot crashed onto Ethan's head, executing the curb-stomp…but not as intended. The cinder block smashed through the top of his jawbone and cut into the side of Ethan's face, slicing from his temple, through his left eye, and to the middle of his forehead. His lifeblood drenched the gray stone and the floor beneath it.

My husband was gone. His life force had been extinguished just a few feet from me.

Atticus pulled my head up by my hair, stared at me with a devilish grin, and spoke his first word since this ordeal began: "*Merrrcccyyyyyy.*"

He cackled ferociously as he unhooked Raul. There were three of us left. My sadness and despair quickly turned into rage. I was the only parent left for Jackson and Denise. It was me or them.

Thomas looked white as a sheet. He knew what was next. He ran to Raul but was quickly intercepted by Atticus. Atticus knocked him to the ground and was on him in an instant. There was a loud snap as Atticus splintered Thomas's right leg into two pieces, his toes now readily able to touch his upper thigh.

I moved swiftly, and my eyes grew wide as I ogled the chainsaw under the table. I revved it up and sauntered to Raul. Before I could even register Thomas's screams for me to spare his soulmate, I had already dug the spinning blade into Raul's left arm, right below the elbow. Tendons and ligaments gave way as I grew sodden with his blood. His arm flopped to the floor beside his body.

I was a woman possessed—filled with rage and desperation.

If you fuckers want sick and depraved, I'll fucking show you sick and fucking depraved, I thought to myself.

I rolled Raul onto his stomach and yanked his pants down to his ankles. I then snatched up the severed arm and viciously rammed it into his anal cavity. The blood proved to be the perfect lubricant as I proceeded to assfuck him, violating him with his own dissected appendage. If he or Thomas were shrieking, I couldn't tell anymore.

I flipped him over once more and grabbed the chainsaw in earnest. It broadcast the sound of death as I ripped the cord. Grabbing the handle upside down, I drove it into Raul's groin, ruining his sex and ravaging his pelvis. More blood rained down on me as I worked.

I let the saw do its job as I stood over him, dragging it toward his head. The tool-turned-weapon cut his spinal cord down the middle. Gummy tissue and meaty organs gave way to my determination, leaving a hot pile of ichor in its wake. I stopped only once I reached the top of his vertebrae, marrying viscera, gore, and cerebrospinal fluid in a grisly medley of mortality.

Gerty nodded her approval with a shocked smile on her face. I shot the cunt a glare as deadly as a shotgun. My momentum would not be interrupted. I looked around to finish this, as Thomas was still impaired.

I investigated the space around me. Next to the crawl space was a medium-sized wooden chest that I didn't remember seeing before. I walked over to see what was in it.

Gerty quickly got up from her chair. "Wait, Tabitha, don't open that chest."

I'd played their game thus far, so I exhibited some well-earned moxie. "Oh, you mean *this* chest over *here*?"

"Yes, that one. Please."

"Fuck you, cunt."

The lid had the name Winston stencilled on it, and I assumed the contents were belongings of Gerty's late husband. When I flung open the lid, I realized I was dead wrong—sort of.

It *was* Winston. He was in an advanced state of decay, and the smell was horrid. He mostly consisted of bones teeming with maggots, cockroaches, and worms. I grabbed the deceased man's fibula—or what I believed to be his fibula—and quickened my gait back to Thomas.

"What did I say?" Gerty blurted out. "If you don't follow—"

"Shut the fuck up," I interjected as I looked down at Thomas's incapacitated state. "Do you want me to finish this or not?"

Gerty's wrinkled cheek twitched. After a few seconds of silence, she nodded with a hefty helping of reluctance.

I straddled Thomas, my ass firmly placed on his chest.

"Tabby," he coughed up a red cloud. "W—What the fuck, *chica*?"

"I'm sorry, Thomas," I said with my telling eyebrows. "But I have kids to get back to you. It's either me or you."

His yearning glare quickly turned into a grimace. He pursed his lips, reared back, and hocked a big phlegm-ladened loogie onto my face. I rolled my eyes as it descended toward my chin.

With that, I sat him up and packed his taut throat with the demised bone. He promptly started choking on both the dead man's essence and the creepy crawlies I could see distending his esophagus. I pressed down further, perfo-rating his trachea. His body instinctively tried to cough up the mass but was only successful in propelling another chunky bit of blood and plasma. My face was a primal byproduct of the irreparable death I was bestowing upon this young man.

I reached for the crowbar that Thomas previously acquired and wedged it against the roof of his mouth. I dug in and felt fleshy resistance as I pressed harder. My body weight pressed on the longer part of the crowbar, and the counter-pressure started to diminish slowly. I threw all my strength toward Thomas's feet, and the resistance ceased completely. The crowbar tore through his face, taking the upper portion of his mandible and half of his sinuses. The fibula, still firmly lodged in his throat, swayed gently back and forth like a spring. He pawed at his face in futility as he bled out on my feet.

I was the last one standing. I surveyed my environment, and it couldn't have been more of the polar opposite of the beautiful nature scene above ground: wrecked bodies, viscera, gore, and a myriad of standard household tools soused with claret.

"Well, color me impressed, young lady," I heard Gerty say as the ring of tinnitus fled my hearing.

"Fuck you, you depraved old bat," I retorted as my eyes scanned from her to Atticus and back. "I did what you wanted. Now I'm free to go. That's the deal."

"Ha! My dear, have you glanced at the wreckage you've caused? You are one to talk of depravity. That would be… what's that old adage? 'The pot calling the kettle black.' You, dear, are the pot. I am the kettle."

I rolled my eyes in annoyance. "I've had enough. I just want to get back home to my kids."

"Yes, yes, of course." She motioned her hand toward the steps leading upstairs.

I paused and waited for the other shoe to drop. I inched

my way toward the bottom step, and still nothing. Two feet away, I briefly closed my eyes and sighed heavily. It was over.

As soon as I opened my eyes again, Atticus's deformed and blister-stricken mug was two inches from my own. Another massive backhand kissed my cheek, sending me flying and a few teeth asunder.

I fell back on my ass but managed to quickly get back to my feet despite the throbbing pain coursing through my body. Atticus stood over me and rained punches into my puffed-up face with his overgrown chode chokers until my resolve gave out.

He unfastened his overalls to reveal his abhorrent and colossal uncut member. It reeked of stale piss and dried-up shit. Unsurprisingly, his cock was engorged to full mast and festooned with sores, cysts and pus-filled blemishes. Crusted smegma gathered around his foreskin, clearly begging for hygiene's sweet embrace.

He forcibly inserted himself into my bloodied maw and started fucking my mouth. I closed my eyes and tried to take myself far from the degradation of which I was an unwilling participant. The corners of my mouth nearly split under the stress of his girth's bulk. Before I knew it, a thick, acrid gravy let loose on my tongue.

Oh, thank God this motherfucker is done.

I couldn't have been more wrong. His consistent thrusting caused a batch of pustules to burst onto my tongue. The innards of his abscesses leaked forth and blended with his and my blood. I tried to repress the urge to puke, but I was wholly unsuccessful. I spewed chunky digested bits of food and bile around his cock, causing him to laugh uncontrollably.

He quickened his movements and bulldozed into the back of my throat. Tears gushed down my face. I was being used as nothing more than this mongoloid's personal fleshlight. I was debased and defiled but relieved that this nightmare was almost over.

He jettisoned an unholy amount of his revolting, sticky semen down my esophagus. I was never very good at blowjobs, so naturally, some flew out as he took his cock out of my mouth. Atticus was pointing and laughing at me like some deranged baboon.

After his overalls were pulled back up, he walked past me, leaving me on my knees. I gagged and panted as I looked up to Gerty.

"Satisfied?" I asked, wiping my mouth.

"Not even remotely, darling," she replied.

Atticus was behind me in a flash and grabbed the top of my head. He sawed and hacked away at my neck viciously. Blood drained from my neck and discolored my sundress. I felt a faint detachment as Atticus's amusement reached unprecedented levels. My vision bobbed up and down as I caught rapid glimpses of the steps leading upstairs. A door creaked open, and I heard a clomping of heavy feet.

I was tumbling through the brisk autumn air, then met soft grass. The floundering stopped. Thirty feet away, the last thing I saw was Atticus jumping up and down and laughing at my decapitated head. It was then that my last thought crossed my dying mind. I would never see my children again.

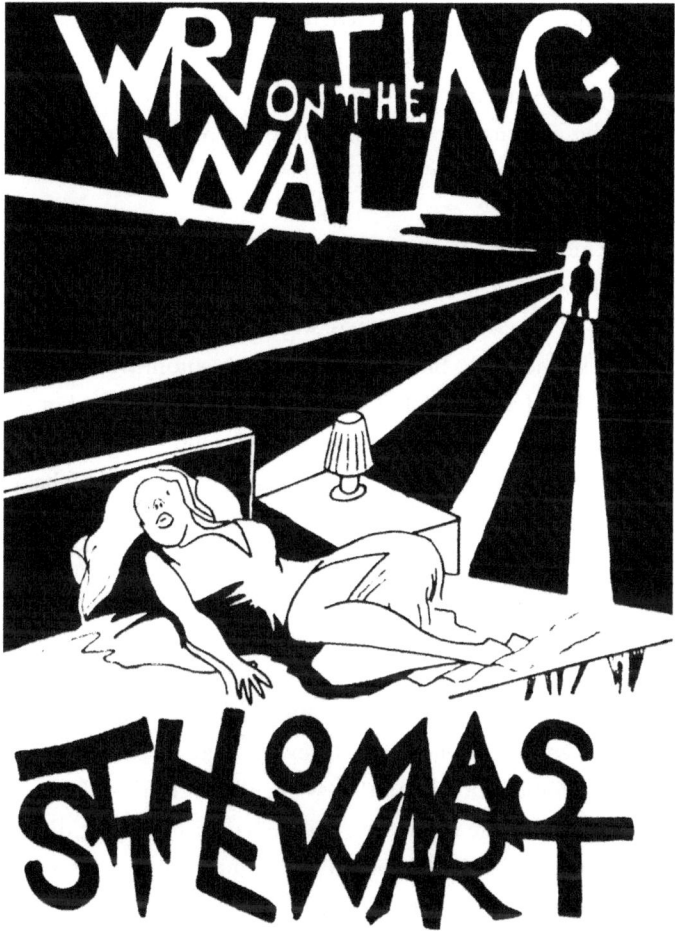

WRITING ON THE WALL

THOMAS STEWART

CELESTE WOKE to what she thought was the sound of crying coming from the hallway. She sat up in her bed and listened. The halls were silent again, so she rolled over and went back to sleep. Only about five or six minutes later, the sobs returned, and she bolted upright again. This time, she sprang to her feet. But when she went to the door, she heard nothing.

Frowning, Celeste cracked the bedroom door open and

peered out. The hallway stretched far longer than she'd ever remembered—perhaps even longer than the house was supposed to warrant. She stared for a good minute and a half down the abysmal corridor, listening intently for something —any*thing*.

Silence.

Her mouth dropped open. She felt the urge to call out into the darkness, but at the last second, she thought better of it. There was no sense in provoking what or whoever was lurking in the dark. She leaned forward, squinting to see if she could find anything, but she found only the first foot or so of the flooring ahead of her. She waited another ten seconds before finally closing the door, turning, and climbing back into bed.

No sooner had her eyes closed than she heard it all begin again. The sobs were louder this time and clearer, too. They were from a little boy, she could tell, one who couldn't be any older than about six or seven years old. Now, she couldn't help it; she had to ask. Once again springing from her bed, Celeste went over to her door, threw it open, and cupped her mouth, shouting into the darkness ahead, "Hello?"

Even before she called out, she noticed the sobbing didn't subside. After she did, she immediately had to cover her ears, thanks to the escalation in tone and pitch. What sounded before like a little boy crying now sounded like a little boy's cries of unimaginable agony. As much as this frightened and disturbed her, she couldn't keep her heart from dropping from her chest and into the pit of her stomach, wanting to ease this child's pain.

"Hello," she called out again.

"What do YOU want?" replied a small, distorted voice changer.

She froze for a moment. What *did* she want?

"I-I'm Celeste," she replied timidly, "I've been hearing your sobs for a while now, and so I wanted to ask if you were—

"You have your answer," he replied, his voice almost wholly swallowed with malice.

Her mouth went dry at this. Shivers shot down her spine, and she was less than a second away from slamming the door again when the sobbing returned.

"I'm sorry," the voice cried aloud. *"I'm sorry. I'm so sorry…"*

Anxious and hesitant, Celeste chanced asking him, "Sorry for what?"

"I wasn't talking to you!"

Once again, she couldn't help but shrink back. Shortly after, the foul and distinct miasma of rotted meat seized her senses. The smell alone was enough to make her stomach go on the fritz. The fact that there was no sight of where it came from or what could be causing it only exacerbated her nausea. And there was still no explanation for how anyone had gotten into her house, given that her doors and windows were latched and locked—something Celeste herself hadn't even thought of before speaking out. She began gagging, and in turn, the crying escalated again, drowning out Celeste's nausea.

"Why can't I be good? WHY?!"

Before she knew it, the world dropped into a gigantic cloud of fuzz, and for some reason, she felt an extreme warmth pass over her back. When she turned to look, she saw nothing again, but the pain wouldn't cease. The burning across her back only intensified when she turned around.

She could feel nerves searing themselves completely, rendering them inoperable. Her skin felt like it was peeling back—like she was being stripped from her bones. She cried out in pain, but there was no one there to hear her pleas. Eventually, her gasping slowed, and she found herself out cold.

No dreams or nightmares came to her the rest of the night —just the house…the quiet, empty house.

When she woke up again, this time, she found herself in the hallway where she'd been standing the last time before collapsing. The first thing she noticed when her vision came back to her was that the walls of her hallway were now decorated with graffiti. Symbols and other inscribed messages were all penned in dark red.

In other places, the walls had been dinged, had holes punched, or been beaten with a hammer. Celeste rose to her feet, taking in the rest of her surroundings. She was appalled and genuinely shocked at what was happening. Looking at the wall, the graffiti read: **"I'M SO SORRY! Please forgive me, Mommy?"**

She frowned. *"Mommy?" What the hell is going on? Who the hell is this little boy?*

She traveled further down the wall and saw more scribblings of the same question. Along with these were paintings —stick figures of various sizes, some holding various-sized weapons. The first few Celeste saw were pretty tame, just things she might expect to see in a child's sketchbook. But the further she went along, the more she realized some of them appeared connected, bound in a sequence of events that told a story.

Going along even further, Celeste saw multiple paintings like this, all different and telling their own stories. Not happy or savory plots, but twisted, even gruesome scenes were portrayed. All of them consisted of stick figures interacting with crudely drawn environments. One artwork showed figures running around a playground, all armed with various weapons. They appeared entangled in a violent dogpile, eviscerating each other in the most gruesome manner possible for stick figures.

In another scenario, the figures were in a mass grave or pit sort of setting—perhaps it was a blacktop. She couldn't quite tell because the paint was smudged. Only three or four figures were shown, all lying on their backs around the pit's perimeter. They all appeared to have been murdered, judging by the smeared paint running down their bodies. Celeste shuddered at how small they were, realizing the figures depicted children.

Who, how, and why someone would paint such atrocities were all questions she was asking herself but couldn't allow herself to dwell on. It wasn't long before she realized she couldn't see the end of the hallway anymore from either end. Immediately, her attention was shifted from the walls to the darkened end of the hall. All that remained was a wall of black.

Her heart was now a Mach-7 engine, sending her plunging into the unknown abyss ahead. Due to the sheer panic of the situation, her breathing became heavy. The hallway stretched for at least ten miles, about nine and a half more than it should've been able to, and continued on. In that distance, she couldn't see or feel anything—no walls, no objects on the floor, nothing.

There was nothing all around her.

The crying echoed again from the back of the hallway. She stopped and turned back around. Still, all she could see was a wall of black. But the way the crying sounded, it was getting closer. She took several shaky steps backward.

"Wh-Who are you?" she whimpered.

"I don't know!" cried the little boy's voice.

"What? What do you mean?"

"*I mean, I don't know. I'm not like you, Celeste.*"

Her eyes widened. "What are you talking about?"

"*No one knows who I am. I don't even know who I am.*"

"You're not making any sense. Look, I just want to go back to bed, please."

"*Then why did you come out?*"

"B-Because I wanted to help you."

"*'Help me?' Really?*"

"Yes."

"*And how the hell were you going to do THAT?*"

Celeste's tongue went dry. How was she supposed to know?

"*What, were you going to tell me everything would be alright again? Do like you did last time and hold me close, saying you'd never let go?*"

Her heart stopped. "Hold on a second. '*Again?*' What are you talking about? '*Like last time?*'"

"*This has all happened before, Celeste.*"

"What has?"

"*This… Look around you.*"

She moved her head about the hallway again. The walls were now visible again, exhibiting their graffiti once more.

"*All of this has happened already.*"

"I… You're not making any sense. What *is* all of this? Why is it all over my walls?" She felt a draft creeping up in front of her. Closer and closer it came. Her flesh had already begun breaking out into goosebumps while turning a pale shade to match.

"*You don't get it, do you?*"

"No, I don't. Please, tell me what's going on."

"*This is everything I've seen happen, Celeste.*"

"What? These…" She pointed to a scene on the left wall in which one figure held up a pike with another figure's head

58

skewered through it. "You're telling me you've seen people doing this?"

"Yes. I see it all the time, since the beginning of time."

"Huh?" The pounding of her head now seemed to match almost in perfect synchronicity with her heartbeat. Too much more of this, and she'd drop right there in the hallway. The darkness would have her forever.

"I can't stop seeing it. I don't want to, but I still have to." The voice sobbed loudly before asking, *"Why can't I just go already?"*

"Where?"

"What?"

"Go where?"

"You know, the beyond."

"Where? What's the be—"

"'Heaven,'" the voice replied, somewhat coldly. *"'Nirvana,' 'Valhalla,' whatever you want to call it. The afterlife. It's where we're supposed to go after we die."*

"Why can't you go?" asked Celeste.

"Because I never got to live!"

The draft was now biting her—pricking and shocking her. She wanted to step backward again, to turn around and run back to her room, but something kept her feet firmly planted.

"I didn't get to have a life, so now I'm stuck here, constantly forced to see all of this. I don't know why, but I just am."

"What am I supposed to do?"

"I already told you… You can't help me! I don't want help."

"Then what do you want?"

"For someone else to know. So someone might have a solution for me, not just a pat on my back."

"I-I… I don't know anyone."

"I know already. You didn't even back then, either."

"'Back then?'"

"I've known you for a long time, Celeste. But because time is a joke for me, it means that years, even decades, can vanish without a trace. Yet I still see it all, over and over again."

"Where? Where is any of this coming from? Why?"

As if on cue, the pathway ahead began to glow, piercing through the darkness. Like a moth to a flame, she dashed forward. Had she *really* managed to find the end of all of this?

"Come here, to the light," said the voice.

Celeste stopped in her tracks.

"Come here, Celeste, so I can show you."

"Show me *what*?!" She wasn't entirely aware of it, but she began to clutch at her chest.

"Show you what I see."

"Why can't you show me here?"

"If I could do that, I would have already. I want you to see, though, see what I see. See the truth."

Celeste's foot shook as she raised it. The glint ahead gleamed bright, almost blinding her with its contrast to the otherwise all-encompassing abyss around her. This made it inviting, in a way, when offset by the ominous circumstances and their uncertain nature. She *wanted* to go to it, yet her subconscious mind wouldn't permit her body to move a single inch forward.

Who was this little boy? Was this even an *actual* boy? Why's it so dark? What's he talking about, "*Seeing time pass*"?

Why's it so dark?

(*What does this writing mean?*)

Why can't she see him?

(*What does this writing mean?*)

Why won't he show her?

(*What is this writing here?*)

What's he going to do if she goes into the light?

(*Why's the light getting brighter?*)

60

What does he want to show her?

(WHAT IS THIS WRITING?!)

Suddenly, she noticed the light seemed to grow, becoming larger and brighter. When she looked down, she realized why; her feet were moving her closer and closer, without her consent or knowledge—an utterly unconscious act, and one that, even now, she couldn't hinder.

Her feet continued to move her forward until she was face to face with the light. From it, she could feel a blistering warmth, a scalding scorch that made her skin want to peel away. The hair on her arms began to singe.

"Come on," urged the little boy's voice, *"Just one more step."*

"If I do," she said, shaking, her foot raised to enter, "What's gonna happen?"

"I don't know."

Her foot raised itself higher, preparing to step backward again.

"I've never talked to anyone like you."

"What do you mean?"

"I told you already. I can't explain anything to you except to show you."

The light blazed momentarily, reddening the skin on Celeste's arm. Strangely, unlike she expected, it wasn't all that painful—at most, it was like a small pinch. The real damage, though, would've been to her eyes, with this blaze causing the aura to burn ten times brighter than before. She was forced to close them, and even this had only a marginal effect on preserving her retinas from being seared.

"Come on, Celeste. I promise I won't hurt you. I'm not like you. I want you to see so you can understand."

Once more, she felt the urge to stop and turn around again. All the questions returned to her, and she wanted to ask them again. Looking around at the walls, at all the different graffiti, she couldn't help but wonder if she'd see these scenes of gruesome violence when she stepped through. Would they be anyone she knew?

Would HE know any of them?

He said he'd seen them all before, been with them before, and even talked to me before…

She looked up and down at the light, wanting to voice her inquiries, before figuring she'd only get the same half-assed answer. Without thinking, her foot breached through the light. Unlike what she was expecting, her foot didn't burn or hurt in any way.

In fact, she couldn't feel her foot *at all* anymore!

She tried retracting her foot, only to find that it was caught in the light and unable to move. She pulled and pulled, tugged and jerked on her leg, which resulted in her losing her balance and falling forward into the light. As sudden as the fall was, her mind wouldn't comprehend anything for the next thirty seconds when she managed to pick herself up and open her eyes to take in the new environment…

…what little environment there appeared to be. All around was an expanse of golden light stretching for bound-less horizons. Celeste found the warm radiance of her surroundings inviting, if only because it was a welcome distraction from the eternal night.

"You came."

Celeste snapped around, jumping, to be met by a little boy whose eyes were lumps of coal in their sockets, leaking a venomous ichor. His head leaned to the side. On the boy's pale, gaunt face was an expression as malicious as it was empty—the face of a psychopath engraved on an innocent child—the face of wrath.

"Who… Who are you? What is all of this?" she asked, turning her head left and right.

"This is nowhere."

"Nowhere? What? You're not making any sense. I thought you said you were gonna answer—"

"And I am," the boy interjected. "You asked me where we are, and I've told you."

"'Nowhere'? How are we Nowhere?"

"This is where things that didn't exist, or maybe don't exist anymore, go."

"I… I… I don't…" Her hands grasped her temples. Her entire body shook violently. Her brain and heart appeared to beat at the pace of a race engine while slowing to a snail's crawl.

"Calm down, Celeste," he said in a tone as dead and hollow as the rest of him appeared. "You give out here, and you won't be able to get back."

She continued hyperventilating. She couldn't make it stop. She couldn't make *any* of this stop.

That's all she wanted… for this to finally…

Stop.

The little boy put his hand to her chest. Amazingly, her heart's pace slowed drastically. She didn't know how he did it and didn't have the patience or mental stamina to ask. Eventually, it caused her to fall unconscious. Little by little, the all-encompassing darkness devoured what little of her vision still lingered.

Deep in her mind, she could hear the little boy's voice singing: *"Go to sleep, little angel, don't say a word, 'cause momma's gonna bring you a sheep to herd. Wipe those tears from your little eyes, 'cause momma doesn't want you to cry…"*

The further into drowsiness she slipped, the more her throat clenched. Something about that rhyme, the lyrics… so somber, yet so… *familiar…*

"Go to sleep, little Cherub, don't make a sound, 'cause happiness

will be found. Don't you cry, little one, 'cause when you do, a piece of dear momma's heart dies…"

She could feel her heart, though stagnant, beating out of control. Despite the fatigue, her mind pounded with the question of what was happening and where she—and especially *he*—knew that song from. Her knees gave out beneath her.

"Go to sleep, little baby, and sleep well, so that your harmony may be found. Do not wake yet, my dear, for there is nothing left to fear…"

Her stomach twisted itself into square knots. The pounding of her mind and heart escalated, though her body couldn't move. She collapsed from the inside out with each progressive verse of the rhyme.

Where did she know this rhyme?

(What was that writing on the wall?)

The little boy's voice faded entirely, and she slipped into a calm slumber. It was peaceful despite the chaotic circumstances, which only a stoic mind could've endured. There were no dreams or nightmares, and when she awoke—God only knew how much later, and God only knew where—she was well rested.

Her eyes were met with a confusing display. Surrounding her were stars—millions upon millions of stars.

No…

Something was different about them. They seemed to follow her…

No… They were *watching* her!

She looked at the ground. Beneath her was a black abyss occupied by more of the specks. She had no idea how she was standing or what she was standing on. Her closest guess was that she was defying gravity, floating within a boundless purgatory and spied upon by these mysterious lights around her.

Where the hell am I? She wanted to shout but didn't. Her mouth wouldn't allow her to voice anything. Instead, it hung slack, gawking and gasping in every direction she turned.

"This is nothing," spoke the little boy from behind her.

She let out a sharp scream and spun around.

The little boy was standing there. He gazed at her with his head cocked to his right. His coal-black, ichorous eyes drilled into her heart. "Where everything that never got to exist is."

"This… This is… What… What is this?" She passed her arms around the expanse.

"These are the windows into reality. It's how I've been keeping watch with you."

"Windows? Jesus Christ, none of this makes any damn sense!"

"Because you won't allow your mind to expand."

"Expand? To what, exactly?"

"To the truth beyond your mortal coil. To the fact that, though you might not want to accept this now, it's what's necessary… that you don't know anything."

"You're not even explaining it to me."

"Granted, but in the end, it's entirely up to you if the tether is severed."

"Okay, look, I can't understand any of this. Who are you?"

"I told you, I don't have a name."

"What, didn't your parents name you when you were—"

"NO!" Shrieked the little boy. "Don't you get it? I couldn't have a name because I never existed, Celeste."

He pointed to an area at his right, and all the specks flocked to her. All at once, her eyes turned to slag as the first one blinded her, just as it had before. After the flash, her eyes opened, and she beheld a glimpse into the mortal plane. It was a garden. Two people. They were distantly whistling, caught in each other's embrace, laughing and giggling.

"What? Who is this?"

"It's you."

Her eyes doubled in size. Her tongue quickly dried up, nearly shriveling completely. "M-M-Me?" she asked, shaking. What're you talking about?"

"I mean what I just said." He pointed to the orb again. Celeste squinted and saw he was right. The garden was simple and tall. She and a man she'd never seen before ran through it. This only raised more questions. The only thing she knew for sure was that she *wasn't* hallucinating.

Then the next one came, and something began to click, a sense of familiarity. She'd never recognize this scenario itself, but...

But perhaps she would second-handedly.

She closed her eyes and tried to imagine the walls again. All the scenes, the gruesome and torturous artwork, made her want to curl up into a ball and quiver. Suddenly, she opened her eyes to find the most damning scene of them all—the one most prevalent in the pictorial drawings: The playground.

In the orb, all Celeste could see were hundreds of people, men, women, and children, all of whom were in the act of brutalizing and murdering one another. The violence only ended several minutes later, after the final victim had been claimed by...

By...

"Yes," said the little boy. "This is you, too."

Celeste stepped backward. Her breathing quickly turned into hyperventilations, desperate gasps, incapable of sounds.

"Now you're starting to see, aren't you?"

"WHO ARE YOU?!" Her throat was only a second away from tearing in half when she screamed this.

"I'm your son."

Even in her panic, these words made her body and

mind go numb. The dryness of her mouth, the loosening of every muscle in her body, and the blurring of her vision all went unnoticed by her. The world, whatever parts of it she could interpret as *her* world, stood still. Her mouth fluttered. Breaths were taken, but no sound was produced.

"You did those things, Mama. You hurt them all."

She stood still, saying nothing.

"I've seen it all happen. You're a monster."

"NO!"

Her body seized. Her brain reeled. "No. This isn't real!"

"If it isn't real, Celeste, then why did you wake up to see me?"

"Shut up!" She clamped her palms to her ears. "Shut up! Shut up! Shut up! SHUT UP!"

The entire void around her started to shake. The little boy stood motionless, unphased by any of this, remaining as cold and stoic as he'd been the entire time.

Celeste's body was now a supercell, shaking and convulsing at a supersonic rate. Her fingers dug into her scalp, almost breaking the skin. The world blurred from exhaustion. She grimaced, each quake of her head causing her great pain.

The little boy merely watched, unmoved. "I'm sorry, Mommy."

"SHUT UP!"

"We're all sorry." The boy's voice took on the echo of several others. Some were other childlike voices, like his own, while others were deeper in pitch. "We're sorry that you have to learn the truth, Celeste. We're sorry that you're in pain and that we couldn't help you."

She crumpled to her knees, still clutching her head. The little boy stepped closer. Each step he took was another earthquake throughout the void. The surrounding lights began to converge upon her.

"NO, NO, NO! GO AWAY!"

"We won't go away, Celeste. We're sorry, but we are a part of you now. All of us."

Celeste screamed a banshee-like wail that should've instantly damaged the boy's eardrums.

The little boy walked forward. "Most importantly," he said, reaching his hand to her shoulder. "I'm sorry, Mommy."

"GO AWAY!"

One last hellish shriek echoed, and then the world itself silenced once more for her.

***

Butch and Gary bolted down the hallway, rapidly passing every patient's room, following the echoing screams. Neither man felt a bit of hesitation, fear, and far less sympathy for their intended patient. Both knew good and damn well who this was and how they were going to have to deal with it.

Still running, Gary patted his side pocket, feeling for his needle. "Got the harness?" he asked Butch.

Without responding, Butch held up the restraints.

The shrieking escalated in pitch, more so than either man had previously dealt with this patient or any other. Not only that, but the fact that her vocal cords managed to sustain the hysterics *this* long meant it was a *particularly* bad episode.

Gary gritted his teeth, remembering what happened the last time. He took a look back at Butch, trying to picture what his predecessor looked like. He'd been a friendly younger man with a bright disposition towards the patients. He was an idealist. An optimist. "He has a damn good head on his shoulders," his friends and colleagues would say of him.

Well, *had* one, anyway… Before her.

Gary and Butch rounded the corner and found the patient's room. The patient, Celeste Warner, despite being a "mousy little cunt," as Gary often joked to himself, was in the act of smashing her bed to pieces with her bare hands. Her howls and shrieks of rage, completely animalistic and devoid of humanity, were so loud to both men that their ears rang.

Smeared on the walls in her blood and feces were the words *"I'm sorry"* and *"Shut up."* The latter was fresh, indicated by the darker, wetter coloring. Her palms were coated in the biological paint. She scowled, wielding a rod from her bedframe.

Gary and Butch lowered themselves into stances, ready to catch and detain her the moment she leaped to attack. For a moment, the room stood still, with neither side pushing to make the first move, until finally, Celeste took the opportunity to lunge at them.

She raised the steel rod to bludgeon them. They immediately threw out their hands, catching the rod as it came down and jerked it from her grasp. From there, it was more or less a cakewalk for them to restrain her, fit the harness over her, and dope her up with the 11 CCs of tranquilizer Gary kept in his pocket.

It was at least a full minute before Celeste's body finally relaxed. When she did, she was spread-eagle in the middle of her room floor, surrounded by excrement and the dismantled bedframe. Her gown was stretched and worn, barely holding to her body enough to cover her privates.

The two men stood, assessing whether the threat had been neutralized before Gary finally turned to leave.

Butch called out for him, "Hey, wait. Aren't we supposed to get her back in bed? We can't just leave her on the floor, can we?"

Gary stopped and looked sideways at his partner. "Why not? She wants to beat her fuckin' chest and scream like an animal. I say let her lay there like a fuckin' animal."

Butch glanced at him and the unconscious patient.

"Besides," continued Gary, "*What* bed?"

Butch took one last look into the room, nodded, and followed his partner's lead. Back out in the hallway, Butch asked Gary, "Is it true? I mean, she didn't *actually* do all that shit, kill all those people, I mean, right?"

Gary chuckled. "Butchy, my friend, you really are a naive son of a bitch, ain't ya?"

"What're you talking about?"

"For Christ's sake, were you *not* just in there? Did you not see what I just did back there? That woman is an animal, through and through. Yes, she massacred those poor bastards in the park, just like the papers said, and yeah, she was pregnant when she did it, too."

"Pregnant," exclaimed Butch.

"Yeah. About eight and a half months in, I believe."

"But… But why?"

"There you go again, naivete."

"I just don't get it. Why would she have done that?"

"Butch, you've been here, what, three months? You need to open your eyes and realize that these motherfuckers aren't getting dumped here because they're just a little quirk. These people are dangerous. That's why we're here—to make sure no one else can end up like those people in the park. You hear me?"

Butch nodded.

"Besides," he continued, chuckling once again dryly. "If you want insight into what's going on in her batshit-assed brain, go back and read what's on the walls."

NO GRACIOUS DEMISE

CHUCK NASTY

THE WHISKEY WAS GOING DOWN QUITE NICELY, and the jukebox was blasting some good tunes. Not to mention, the women in the bar were barely wearing anything due to the aggressive heatwave of the past week. Nope, not a goddamn thing was going to ruin my mood. That was until everyone's favorite bartender, Jimmy Holmes, walked over to my side of the counter.

"Ya got a phone call, Eddie!" he announced loudly,

making sure he was heard over the volume of the music. Only one person had ever contacted me at my favorite bar, and it was usually never a good thing.

"Hello?" I answered, already knowing whose voice was about to speak up.

"I figured I'd find you there. Thought you quit drinkin'?"

I sighed. "Four months ago. Guess you could say I leaped off the wagon," I responded before taking a double shot of whiskey.

"Well, no one expected it to last long, anyway," he replied.

The little laugh hidden behind his words made my nostrils flair. It never mattered to that son of bitch that we'd worked together for many years before he decided to turn his back on me when he became my boss. I guess I can't be too shocked. He always had a way of revealing he was a closeted asshole when we shared an office.

"Well, it's good to know that no one has hope for me. What the hell can I do for you, Jack?" I growled, motioning to Jimmy that I needed another shot of whiskey.

Jack snickered. "Eddie, don't get your feelings hurt. But, as much as I wish I had the time to bust your balls about how pathetic a human you are, there are other matters at hand."

He wasn't always such a prick, but when he got his hands on a little bit of power, it shot right to that big fucking head of his. "Get to the point, Jackass. I am over here trying to enjoy my vacation time!" I snapped back.

"Ummm…it's a suspension, asshole. Not the same thing!"

"Whatever." Jimmy, the bartender, placed a shot in front of me, and I pulled a cigarette from the soft pack on the bar top.

"Look, somehow, I am still trying to figure out how. But you are good at what you do, which is why you still have a fuckin' job." I could tell by the pauses and the sound of ice sliding into the glass he was also having a drink.

"What's the pay?"

"Goddammit! Is that all you care about?" he shouted.

I laughed, hearing the frustration in his voice. "Why the hell do you give me so much shit, Jack? You know, at one time we were friends? In case you forgot!" The heated exchange brought the attention of the patrons sitting to my right. Jimmy hadn't moved from his spot, awkwardly staring at me. Not wanting to be rude to the old guy, I spun my bar stool around, stretching the chord of the phone.

He didn't reply right away like he had been. He paused, but it wasn't to take a drink. I could hear his breathing; it was heavy. "Eddie, Mayor Thompson called me a few hours ago. Chief Sutherland is dead, and his wife and kids are missing."

"Bert's dead?" Although I was licensed as a journalist, I was a private investigator first. The mayor and the chief had been on my side for a long time, and frankly, the chief had become a father figure to me. The news that Chief Sutherland was dead was disturbing enough. His wife and children being taken made it so much worse. "How?"

Jack's tone calmed. He sighed before speaking. "You don't want to know."

"The hell I do?" I shouted into the phone. This time, it wasn't just the people at the bar who turned to glare at me. The tables in front of me did as well.

Even though the man proclaimed he hated my guts, he knew the news would mess me up. "From what I was told, he had been tortured and," he paused and sniffled, "and his head was removed."

I went silent, staring out at nothing, dazed at the memory of my now-fallen friend. A tear welled up in my eye. I blinked, and it traveled down my cheek. Then the other news hit me. "Any idea who did this? Any idea who took Wendy and the kids?" I asked with quivering lips. I could hear Jack gulp down the last of his beverage.

"Well, it's sensitive."

"Sensitive?"

"We have an idea of who might have done this. Look, can you stumble your way to the office so we can talk in person?" He asked.

Any other time, I would tell Jack to piss off. However, this situation was personal. "Yeah, see you in thirty."

After hanging up the phone, I hollered to Jimmy for another drink. He had moved to the other end of the bar to help a couple of big-breasted women who'd just arrived. Since he didn't hear me, I reached over the bar and snatched the bottle Jimmy'd been pouring my drinks from, which he'd left sitting a few inches away. Fuck just pouring a shot. I placed the bottle to my lips and turned it up, getting a few gulps down before Jimmy noticed and came running down the bar at me.

"Hey now! You gotta pay for that whole bottle, puttin' your lips on it and all!" he yelled, shaking his fists at me.

"Calm down, Jim, I got the cash." I threw him a wad of cash before getting up off the barstool and strolling to the door.

I could hear Jimmy behind me as the door closed. "Thanks, Eddie! See you tomorrow!" He was right. He probably would.

———

When I finally got to the office, Jack was waiting for me, tears pouring from his eyes and himself pouring a glass of scotch. He sat the bottle on his desk and looked up, not saying a word. I could tell the scotch was taking effect on him as he lumbered toward me.

"About five minutes before you walked through the door, my phone rang again. This time, it was from Cody down at the morgue. There is no easy way to say this, so I am just going to say it." He took a few seconds to compose himself. I'd never seen him so torn up. "Pat Sutherland's body is down there. His gut had been sliced open, and something was stitched up inside of him. It was a Polaroid of Wendy and the kids." I feared the next words from his mouth. "It's a picture of all three of them bound and gagged."

"Jesus Christ!" I sat on the couch in his office and put my head in my hands. Jack wandered back over to his desk and sunk into his chair. "What do you need from me? We have to get whoever did this," I mumbled.

"There's something else, and this hasn't been made public yet. In the past three months, there have been four other murders. The cops didn't want us to say anything. Chief Sutherland told me to keep things hush for the time being, so I never announced anything." He sipped from his glass.

"So, do we have any idea why this happened?" I asked, pulling a cigarette from the pack in my jacket pocket and putting it to my lips.

"Our guess is the Chief was too close to something, and someone wanted him quiet."

His expression told me he knew something he wasn't saying. "There's something you aren't telling me, Jack. I can see it all over your fucking face! I'm a big boy. I can take whatever you are afraid to tell me!" I took a long draw off my cigarette, exhaling in his direction.

"There was something else Mayor Thompson told me." He leaned back in his brown leather chair and stretched his arms, bringing them down on each armrest. Jack let out a sigh. "Apparently, the only thing close to a lead on these recent murders—they seem to think the one possible suspect may be a few hours away from here." He picked up his glass and sipped. "There isn't enough evidence for law enforcement to travel and harass people over what seems to be a hunch."

I walked over to his desk and put my cigarette out in the metal ashtray. "Let me guess, Mayor Thompson thinks I'm the man for the job?"

"Well, yeah. I told him you were on suspension, and I wasn't sure how you would feel about traveling. He insisted you be hired to go where they need, snoop around, and report back what you find." Before I could reply, Jack started up again. "So yeah, you'll get paid. Nicely." I could tell by his words that he was disgusted at me for asking about payment earlier. But to be fair, I asked before I knew about Chief Sutherland and his family.

"I realize my reputation isn't the greatest, but give me a break. My friend was just brutally murdered, and his family is about to be next. Don't give me shit about getting paid when you know for a damn fact I have been struggling lately." If I hadn't closed my eyes and taken a deep breath before I kept speaking, I may have reached over that desk and strangled my boss.

Realizing he had offended me, Jack raised his hands and grinned at me. "Just because tragedy has struck doesn't mean you get a pass from me giving you shit." He reached into the drawer to his left and pulled out a pad of paper, immediately tossing it to the front of the desk.

"What's that?" I asked, looking down at the words and numbers scribbled on the paper.

"That's all the information you wanted to know," Jack

replied, staring at me with his eyebrows raised, waiting to see my reaction.

I read it out loud. "Find Eddie." One part was scribbled. "Springer County." This would be the name of the fucked-up place I was about to journey to. "Payment: twenty-thousand dollars!" That part threw me off. "Am I reading this correctly?"

Sighing, Jack stood up from his chair and walked over to his jacket hanging from a hook on the wall. "Yeah." He tossed an envelope at me, which I caught before it flew past. "Thompson had his secretary, Lacey, drop that off. I was also told to tell you you'll get the rest once you return with good enough intel."

Figuratively speaking, my jaw was on the floor. I wasn't complaining. I was bewildered at why they would pay me that much right upfront to go to some town and bombard people with assuming questions. I opened the large envelope. The contents inside were indeed cash, very tightly packed at that. "How much is in here?"

"Not sure. I know it's a nice chunk. Be enough for your trip and whatever else you need money for. Just think of all the booze you can guzzle down when this is over." He laughed— that snide bastard. "There's more than just money in that envelope. There should be a piece of paper with the name of the hotel you will be staying at and a key to the room."

Reopening the envelope, I noticed the well-compacted bills were all hundreds. There was also a folded piece of paper along with a silver key. "Yeah, they're here."

"Eddie, look, I know you and I don't see eye to eye on things these days, but I mean it when I say that I wish you the best, and I know you will find something to bring back worth a shit. You're a slob of a human, but you're a damn good journalist and an even better private dick." Jack snickered, knowing what he said.

I rolled my eyes, not remarking on his comment. "Well, I appreciate that, Jack. And coming from a backstabbing megalomaniac like yourself, It must mean I'm doing something right."

Jack glared at me. "Don't you have somewhere to be?"

"About that. When do I need to leave?"

"As soon as possible. Why?" he asked, bringing an eyebrow up.

I stretched my arms over my head and yawned. "To be honest, I am not going to be worth much of a shit if I don't get a few hours of sleep before I get on the road."

Jack darted over to me, poking me in the chest as he spoke, "You go home, and you get a good little nap. Hope you can sleep knowing there's a woman and her two children scared to death somewhere, and every second counts."

"I'm aware, but I need to sleep this drunk off so I can make it to my destination without being arrested or killed. I am beyond exhausted. I swear. It will only be an hour or so." I know I must've sounded like a prick. It was true, though. Without some time with my eyes closed, I wouldn't be able to get much done.

"Get the hell out of my office," he muttered with frustration. I took heed and did just that, knowing damn well that I was going to buy a half-pint of whiskey to really knock myself out good.

———

After swallowing the brown contents of the small bottle in a matter of minutes, I smoked a cigarette and lay down face-first on my bed. In a matter of minutes, I was in dreamland.

Did I dream? I don't think I did. However, the rest didn't seem to last long enough. My alarm clock's obnoxious beeping opened my eyes. Barely awake, I lifted myself from the bed, stumbling into the bathroom. I stripped naked, kicking my clothes to the corner, then proceeded to get into the shower. Turning the nozzle over to get a colder water temperature, the quick blast of freezing liquid to my face opened my eyes.

I was on the road almost an hour after waking up. Jack called me when I was almost ready to get the fuck out of dodge. He was pretty pissed that I hadn't left yet. I explained to him that I had to take a major shit, shower, and wake up more. He scoffed at me before he hung up. But I left shortly after the call.

About halfway to Springer County, I remembered I'd left most of a joint in my car ashtray. Without taking my eyes off the road, I used my fingers to find it resting nicely against the corner of the tray amongst a pile of ash. I put it to my lips, about to take a flame to it when something caught my eye up ahead. Because it was still dark and I hadn't slept much, I had to wipe my eyes and blink to see someone walking on the side of the road. The closer I got, the more I could tell it was a woman.

She looked to be in her late twenties. Her dirty blonde hair, up in a ponytail, swayed behind her head as she approached the car. "Hey there, I hate to ask, but do you think you could give me a lift?" she asked with a smile, leaning in my open window.

"Well, that depends. Where ya headed?"

"Springer County, I think it's called."

What were the odds?

"No shit? That's actually where I'm headed. You got family there?" I asked, watching her open the passenger side door, placing a leg in first and then the rest of her body. Her shorts were cut off a little below her crotch, and her white tank top was soaked in sweat, leaving nothing to the imagination. She had clearly forgotten her bra before she left. I wasn't complaining.

"Not exactly." She giggled.

Her vague answer was strange, but I didn't pry. "Well, what has you all the way out here at this time of the morning?" I asked, then put my lighter's flame to the tip of the unfinished joint. "Ya' mind?"

"It's a long story, but I guess I owe you some kind of reason since you're giving me a lift." She sighed. "Honestly, I was dropped off by a biker ex of mine. We had a fight. I guess I should be grateful he just let me hop off the bike this time." She looked at the joint and answered my other question. "Hell no, I don't mind!"

"This time? What happened last time?" I asked before taking a long drag from the cannabis stick. Then I handed it to the young woman.

She took the joint and replied, "Last time, he pulled the bike over, got off, then picked me up by my neck. Bastard flung me into the bushes and rode off."

"That's pretty heartless. Whatcha' do to piss him off?" I asked as I grabbed the joint back and took another long drag from it.

Before answering, the woman leaned her seat back and stretched her smooth legs. "I have been dying to stretch out. I've been walking for about an hour now," she continued, throwing her arms up and resting them behind her head. "Oh, my name is Alecia, by the way." She sighed. "The reason he was pissed…well, I wouldn't get fucked up and have fun with him and his friends."

"Fun?" I ignorantly asked, not thinking.

"Yeah, they throw these biker orgies all the time. I was even told they would pay me." In the corner of my eye, I could see she had turned her attention off the road and was staring right at me.

"Oh."

"Yeah, last time I was sore for a month, and my pussy got all swollen and purple. I guess it was to be expected, taking multiple cocks at once." She laughed.

I had no response.

We passed a sign saying WELCOME TO SPRINGER.

"Look at that!" I hollered. "Looks like we are now in Springer County." As intrigued as I was by the information Alecia had shared, I needed to keep my head out of the gutter. "Where ya' need me to drop you off?" I asked, taking the envelope from my jacket pocket and fishing out the folded piece of paper with all the information needed. I glanced down at the part that read: Marks Street Motel.

"Yeah, there's an adult bookstore not far from here. You can drop me off there. Could use the quick buck." She turned down the mirror above her and checked her make-up.

It was all making sense after she spoke her last sentence. She was a lady of the night. It wasn't that I was really that shocked. It had more to do with how almost innocent Alecia's demeanor was, as well as how goddamn gorgeous she was. She didn't give off tweaker vibes, and minus a few purple bruises on random spots, the color of her skin looked fine, not pale and sickly. If anything, I was impressed. Most of the whores I'd met were usually so far gone on smack and methamphetamines that their minds were blown.

When we arrived at the adult bookstore, I eased my car into the parking lot. Alecia seemed pleased at the number of vehicles parked in front of the store. Before swinging the door open on her side and quickly running out, she leaned in and kissed my cheek, laying a twenty-dollar bill between my legs.

I grinned. "What's that for?"

"It's not often I get to pay someone for taking some stress off of me." She winked, then off she went to take shelter beyond the blackened double doors and relieve every penis in the building with her mouth.

———

When I finally found the damn motel, my eyes were getting heavy. After only sleeping five hours in the past three days, it wasn't unexpected. The only thing I desired was a pillow to slam my head onto. Of course, it wasn't that simple. Marks Street Motel had three deaths and a violent rape, all within a couple of hours before I came pulling into the parking lot.

Two ambulances and three cop cars lined the driveway from the motel entrance to the parking lot, blocking access to the lobby. I shook my head, mumbled, "Goddammit," and put the car in park. Not giving a shit that the ass end of the car was in the road, I stepped out and headed to the entrance.

One ambulance had the rape victim sitting on the back. Chunks of her hair had been ripped from her scalp. Her face was smeared in blood, and her eyes were busted, circled with purple and green bruises. She couldn't have been any older than twenty-three. When her eyes met mine, I quickly lowered my gaze to the ground as I walked.

EMTs were loading a gurney onto the second ambulance when one of the EMTs lost his balance, resulting in the mangled corpse spilling out from under the white sheet and splatting onto the concrete. I heard the EMT shout, "Sonofabitch!" Glancing down at the body, I was horrified to see that the man's throat had been sliced from ear to ear, and his gut had been ripped open. Innards slid from the giant gash onto the blacktop.

A big fucking cop stood at the door, blocking me from getting into the building. The giant asshole just stared at me. When I tried to pass by him, he wouldn't budge. "Mind moving your ass so that I can go check in, please?" I asked, gnashing my teeth.

"Sir, in case you can't tell, this motel is an official crime scene," he responded.

"What's your point?" I unkindly inquired, making a fist in my pants pocket.

He crossed his arms. "Look, buddy, I can't let you in until I get clearance." He spit at the ground below my feet. It took every ounce of energy I had not to introduce that ape to my knuckles.

A woman dressed in official motel garb walked out from behind the large swine on two legs. She wasn't what I would refer to as "hot," but she was an attractive woman nonetheless. Her hair was in a ponytail, and her glasses had red rims with rubber tips. "Officer, this man has a reservation with us. Mayor Thompson paid for his room."

"You heard the lady! Move the fuck out of my way. Wouldn't want to have to call the mayor and let him know he needs to talk to your people about how big of an asshole you are." I said with a shit-eating grin stretched across my face. The cop moved to the side, mumbling something under his breath. I walked past him and followed the young woman into the motel lobby.

"Sorry about that, Mister…?" The woman said, ending with an inquiry.

"Just call me Eddie, and it's all good," I replied. "If you don't mind me asking, how did you know I was me?"

The brunette motel worker pulled a printed-out picture from her pocket and handed it to me. It was a picture of me.

"Interesting," I said, handing the printout back to her.

"Mayor Thompson's office sent it over when they paid for your room. They just said here's who we are sending, and here is a wad of money, and if it weren't enough by the time you leave, they would send more." She spoke with a semi-professional tone.

"Damn. The mayor is spoiling me on this one, isn't he?" I joked.

She smiled. "Follow me. I will show you to your room and brief you on some things."

I did as I was told, following her butt cheeks as they wiggled in front of me. *Not bad at all,* I thought.

————

Typically, motels have outside-facing doors to the individual rooms. However, some motels also have rooms along interior hallways. I had never been to one like it, but the Marks Street Motel was designed this way. The halls were painted dark tan, while cheap thrift store paintings hung in the gaps between rooms.

"Here we are," she said as she slid the key in and twisted the knob.

I followed her into the room. She stopped while I wandered to the well-made bed in the middle of the room. I fell backward onto the mattress. The sponge-like texture felt like clouds. I just wanted to sleep. Well, after thinking naughty thoughts about the motel worker, I wanted to jack off and then go to sleep.

"Don't mind me. I am going to just lay here with my eyes closed. Feel free to start the briefing anytime." I stretched my arms and legs. To the woman standing before the bed, crossing her arms and smirking, I probably looked like a child waking from a nap.

"Okay, then." She went to the table in the corner and sat in one of the two chairs. "Mayor Thompson said you know the gist of things. However, he also wanted me to let you know that he lied to you."

Quickly, I raised my head with concern draped across my face. "Lied about what?"

The once adorable smile on her face went straight.

"He said he regrets informing you that Chief Sutherland's family is not being held hostage. They are, in fact, already dead."

"What the hell? Why would he lie to me about that?" No longer lying down, I found myself pacing the room.

"That, I don't know. That isn't all…" She lifted her head and stared me in the eyes.

I stopped pacing to anticipate whatever was coming next. "Do tell."

"The objective was to get you here. Now that you are here. You have one main task." She pulled out a key to the room and a folded piece of paper. "These are directions and a key to a cabin not far from here. That is where they believe the killer has been staying."

My feet carried me to the table. I picked up the directions and looked them over. "A cabin? What the hell is this? Something smells fucked up!" I threw the paper back on the table, then turned to the sitting woman, grabbing her by the top of her arms and pulling her up. "What kind of fucking joke is Thompson trying to play?" I could tell by her eyes bugging out that she wasn't expecting my outburst.

"I-I don't know what he's doing. I am just doing what I was told," she pleaded.

I let go of her arms, and her butt fell back into the chair.

"Who are you? You sure as shit aren't a motel employee. The mayor wouldn't give that kind of information to just anyone." I pointed my finger inches from her trembling lips.

"My name is Amanda Peters. Mayor Thompson used to pay me for my services."

"Of course he did," I groaned. "So, did he say anything else about this cabin?"

"He did. But, seeing as you have seen the events that have taken place here tonight, I didn't feel it was necessary to tell you."

"What was that?" I asked.

"That you need to be careful. The killer may be back in town. With two dead bodies, a woman raped and beaten so badly her eyeballs almost popped out, with her vagina bleeding and anus prolapsed, I'd say it's a good sign he was right. Dontcha' think?" she said as she walked to the door." Before leaving, she told me she would come when I needed something.

———

After getting the sleep I hadn't gotten in weeks, it was nice not to wake up in a pissed-off mood. I looked at the clock on the wall. It was Three in the afternoon. I whistled while undressing and walking to the bathroom to shower, whistling in there as well. When done, I pulled the shower curtain to the left side. The mirror was foggy at the top but not as much on the bottom. I stared down at my dick, admiring the girth, then reached over to grab a towel. My mind started to imagine that Amanda chick walking in and dropping to her knees and slipping my cock in her pie-hole over and over until baby batter filled her mouth. There was no fighting it, and since I hadn't before I'd fallen asleep, I aggressively masturbated until ropes of jizz fell into the bathroom floor.

A coffee maker was sitting on the dresser next to the TV. I made myself a pot and began planning my next move. I knew there was no point in going to the cabin during the day—too much of a chance the killer would be there. The nighttime was the best. That's when killers kill—more time to snoop with less chance of getting caught.

There wasn't much to do beforehand, so I figured riding into town to get lunch would be a good idea. People would surely be talking about the incidents at the motel the night before. I sat at the edge of the bed, studying the directions while looking at a map from one of the dresser drawers. From what I gathered, Amanda wasn't kidding. The cabin was in the woods, not far behind the motel.

————

I was proven right as soon as I entered a little sandwich shop and heard a group at a table gossiping about the gruesome killings. I ordered a meatball sub and waited for it to be done while leaning against the wall. Waiting for my food was perfect! I was just a guy ordering food instead of a dude trying to eavesdrop.

"They said all three victims were sexually violated," a woman added to a conversation among three older ladies. "Apparently, the only reason the one survived was because the killer heard someone parking their truck directly in front of the room he was in—that poor girl. My daughter is a nurse at the hospital. She told me the victim's privates had been stretched so wide they were torn to ribbons like a large wild animal had sex with her."

Hearing this, I became even more intrigued with this

weird investigation I'd been assigned. I was glad I kept my mini notepad in the pocket of my shirts. I pulled it out with a pen and started to write what I had just heard, mouthing the words as I wrote them.

A woman came from behind the counter with my food on a tray, smiling as she handed it to me.

As I devoured my sub, scenarios ran through my head of how the evening would go. The possibility of everything going belly-up and me finding myself in a fucked situation was high. This son of a bitch could come back earlier than planned. What if there were dogs trained to kill anyone trespassing? These were plausible risks. It wasn't the first time I'd landed in the middle of a dangerous case. But the nature of this one was worse than the others.

On the flip side, what if things went better than planned? I thought about that as well. I thought about how it would be if the guy just said fuck it and turned himself in, or he couldn't take the guilt of his crimes and ended his life with a shotgun or something before I showed up. Something told me these scenarios weren't likely.

————

My lunch had been so delicious that I felt I should celebrate by returning to my motel room, ordering an adult feature, and seeing how much of a mess I could produce this time. Making excuses to viciously stroke my stiff member to completion was something I'd always done to ignore the fact that I did so much that some would call it an addiction.

Glancing out the window, I saw it was almost dark, but I had enough time to tend to myself beforehand. Like most things in my life, things didn't go as planned. I ordered a porn titled: *Pussy Eaters and Cum Guzzlers*. I wasn't ten seconds into the feature before I whipped my dick out, stroking slowly at first. The more faces I watched get glazed, and the more pussies I watched get licked, the harder I got. My stroking became more intense. I could feel the cum about to shoot from the head of my dick—like a blowhole on a whale when it fires water into the air…

There was a loud scream.

As I was about to climax, a woman's cry for help could be heard by anyone within a mile of the woods. It may sound like a douchebag move, but I wanted to orgasm before sneaking off to the cabin. My anxiety told me it might be the last time I would be able to. I took major advantage. The moment I came, the woman screamed again.

I cleaned up and got dressed in my all-black "spy" clothes. Then, I poured a cup of cold coffee and chugged it down. I knew I needed to be on guard, and the caffeine kick would help.

―――――

The wind was starting to blow more aggressively. A storm was on the way, and it couldn't be at a worse time. I stood in the woods, armed with a flashlight and a revolver. The trees swayed back and forth; their shadows looked like black wraiths dancing in circles around me. To be honest, I was pretty fucking scared. The darkness seemed to swallow the beam of my flashlight.

"That damn Mayor, I'm gonna' kick his fucking teeth down his throat!" I muttered to myself as I walked, feet pausing every few steps. "Yep. I'm gonna kill him!" All I could hear was the wind blowing through the trees and branches cracking. Without thinking, my feet started to move faster than ever. I ran in fright, losing direction as I veered from the path. The sounds of nocturnal nature surrounded my every move; the chirping of birds and howling from four-legged animals sounded like screaming. Those woods held fear.

Stopping to catch my breath, everything went completely silent. I gripped the revolver, hoping not to have to use it because in my other hand was my dick. Being as afraid as I was, the urge to piss hit hard. As the last few drops fell, something snarled behind me—then *BAM!* Something struck my cranium, knocking me to the ground and causing me to black out.

———

"Shit!" I hollered, waking up with a sack over my head, stretched out on a wood floor. My hands were tied behind my back, but my legs weren't shackled. Someone was walking around me; their footsteps were heavy. A few loud steps made me think my head was about to be crushed. "Who the hell are you?"

The person let out a distorted laugh. "Don't act so damn tough with me, Eddie."

The voice was familiar. It couldn't be...

A hand pulled the sack from my head. Mayor Thompson stood before me. To my left was that back-stabbing prick, Jack. There was something off about both of them.

"Wait, it's both of you? Why?" I wiggled my hands around, hoping to get them loose. No luck.

Jack looked down at me with a scowl. "It wasn't supposed to be like this, Eddie. It really wasn't." He looked away.

"No, but this is where we are in life." Thompson laughed, pulling a syringe from his khakis. "This powerful little substance is the reason for everything."

"Explain!" I demanded, gritting my teeth.

Thompson lifted his sleeve. Track marks ran the length of his arm.

"What…are you a couple of dope fiends or something?"

They both laughed.

"No, don't be silly. This is way more than just a means to get fucked up." Thompson plunged the needle into a vein in his forearm. "Being Mayor has weird perks. I get to meet some interesting people. It just so happens…" His words trailed off as he fell to his knees, dropping the syringe and gripping his stomach. "…a gathering of very important people, coming together to ingest the finer things in life." He snarled and gripped his stomach more tightly. "We have some chemists in the group. It was supposed to be a cure for erectile dysfunction for us old fucks." The snarling became more bronchial. He stood up. His eyes were glowing green, while his face looked more rigid.

"We were the lucky ones to test this shit out." Jack raised the syringe to his face, appraising the amount of solution left within. His sleeves were already rolled up, and, like Thompson, his arms were heavily pocked. Immediately after shooting the remaining drug into his veins, he tensed up and fell to the ground. "Instead of just helping with our hard-ons, it changes us into fucking monsters!"

"Literally!" Thompson shouted, still in pain.

Even through their howls of pain, both men laughed at the comment. Then, they fell to their sides and started twitching.

I knew it was time to find a way to break free. The rope holding my hands together behind my back was starting to slip off when Jack jumped up and grabbed me by the back of the neck. He tossed me to the other side of the cabin. My head hit the wall, gashing my forehead.

"No, you don't get to leave, Eddie!" Thompson stood and walked over to a closet.

"So, you two are the ones who have been killing everyone around here? The Chief? His family? Why?" The rope around my hands snapped, but Jack, whose body was bulking up before my eyes, blocked my exit.

Thompson's voice was nearly unrecognizable. "Originally, the plan was to frame you. But things went amok. Now, you get to witness what we do!" He reached into the closet. I was horrified as he pulled a body out by the hair and tossed it on the floor. It was Alecia, the hitchhiker from earlier. Her eyes were covered with a rag, and it looked like she was still breathing.

"You bastards! You followed me!"

"Of course we did! Jack was on your tail from the start." Thompson chuckled. He reached down and patted Alecia's face to wake her up.

"Yeah, why do you think I was so pissed you took forever to get going. I was down the road waiting for fucking hours for you to leave. Asshole." Jack added.

"What's going on?" a dazed Alecia inquired.

Jack and Mayor Thompson had grown in size. They walked with hunched-over gaits, their spines bent below their shoulders. Their teeth had grown long and sharp.

"I am so hungry!" Jack said before removing his pants and dropping them to the floor.

Thompson followed his lead. I had to blink and shake my head. What the hell was I looking at? Their bodies had become hairy, and dangling between their legs were the most ungodly-sized cocks I had ever seen! Those dicks were the size of an adult forearm.

"I'm scared. This isn't funny. Please let me go!" Alecia shouted, trying to get up.

Jack put his wolf-like foot down on her chest, knocking her painfully back to the floor.

She started to weep. "What are you going to do to me?"

I'd never felt so goddamn horrible as I watched this poor, beautiful woman shake with fear. Her clothes were barely together, hanging off of her. Her tank top had been sliced while her shorts were gone. All she had covering her goods was a pair of piss-soaked panties. She looked so helpless lying there with those creatures looming over her. "Stop! Don't!" the words finally shot from my mouth.

"Eddie?" Alecia asked. But before I could respond, Thompson slammed his deformed hand down on her throat. His strength immediately cut off her airway. She flopped around like a fish out of water.

"Goddammit! Leave her alone!" I screamed, looking around for something to fight them off with.

It was too late.

Thompson had already sunk his fangs into her throat. He ripped out a chunk of flesh and gobbled it into his snout, chewing with elation.

Jack got on all fours, joining in on the massacre by ripping open Alecia's shirt with his claw-like hands and sinking his fangs into her breast, promptly tearing away the meaty flesh. Blood ran like a sacrilegious offering from the young woman's throat and breast; A pool formed like a crimson baptism around her mangled body.

"She tastes so good!" Jack announced, looking back at me with a glare and a smirk. He reached down, taking one of his overgrown fingernails and poking a hole in the middle of Alecia's panties, ripping them off with ease.

Thompson growled, knocking Jack's hand away from the corpse's thighs. "I'm first!" He snarled, taking his monster cock in his hand, using his free hand to spread Alecia's legs, then violently shoving himself into her. With each thrust, the grisly sound of her flesh splitting became more wet and sloppy.

Jack paced the room, impatient for his turn. He crawled to Alecia's face and removed the rag from her blank, open eyes. Leftover tears dribbled down her face as he forced her mouth open, carelessly breaking her jaw. Laughing, he raised her head to his crotch and stretched her dead throat with his sweaty member. Her esophagus sheathed his mammoth tool all the way to his hanging balls. His fist-sized glans tore through the remaining sinews of her neck and poked through the gash in her throat.

Then it hit me. The revolver... Where was it? There was a good chance they had it in the cabin. I moved my eyes around the room. There it was, sitting on a chair in the corner. My first thought was to dash past the necrophiliac depravity that was occurring and grab the gun. However, seeing how fast those assholes were moving, I knew I would need to be sneakier about how I went about things.

Jack and Thompson were having so much fun fucking and feasting upon the flesh of Alecia's carcass that they had taken their sights off of me. Sighing, I crept toward the wall, keeping to the shadows as much as possible. Inches away from the chair, I was startled by the sound of both man-creatures about to orgasm. "For fuck's sake!" I shouted, falling but managing to grip the handle of the revolver in the process.

They growled like the savage beasts they'd become, and at the same time, they pulled their disgusting, engorged beast-cocks from the corpse's body. Jack pulled from the gash in Alecia's throat, and Thompson removed himself from her atrociously gaped anus. The flood of lime-green liquid that sloshed out of the young woman's abused openings was like nothing I had ever seen before.

The sound of me cocking the gun got their attention.

Jack howled as he ran at me to rip my head off. My response was to turn and aim the gun at the middle of his forehead. I fired, sending a bullet through the center of his head, blasting from the back. Blood sprayed into Thompson's rigid face. Jack fell to the floor.

"I'm going to dig out your insides and fuck the wound!" Thompson shouted.

My reflexes weren't quick enough to point the gun at his face. He grabbed me by the top of my head, slamming me over and over into the brick of the fireplace. The way the blood was leaking from my head, I knew the gash had widened. "Fuck!" I was struggling to see. So much blood blinded my vision while being attacked by that damned mutant, Thompson. My concentration was skewed. I felt razor-like teeth chomp down on my shoulder. "You son of a bitch!" The pain was beyond severe.

"Don't fight it, Eddie! Just let me end your pathetic existence!" Thompson proposed, taking another bite out of me, this time almost severing my right arm.

"You motherfucker!" I cried out, looking down at my mangled limb. Still being on my back, my leg was directly under Thompson's mutated fuck-stick and saggy nut-sack. My leg first smashed into his testicles, then kicked into the fat head of its monster cock. They both flopped up. Thompson's eyes rolled back in his head, and he doubled over, groaning.

The revolver was in arm's reach. I turned my body over, snatching the gun and shooting in Thompson's direction. He moved quickly enough to avoid taking the shot dead center of his face; it only blew a small part of his head off.

I crawled out from under him, scooting backward. His

face was blank as he crawled slowly over to me. I scooted back until I couldn't anymore. Thompson raised his arms and started to lift himself off the floor. His raging erection almost smacked me in the face. I placed the barrel of the gun to the side of his dickhead and fired. The explosion was fierce.

He fell back on top of Jack's body, shaking and crying. "I'm going to kill you," he mumbled, hacking wads of blood from his throat. Before he could say anything else, I stood up and stomped repeatedly on his melon-fucking-head. The noises he made sounded like a dog being beaten. Then he went silent as his head split open.

———

I walked away from the cabin, broken, bloody, and eaten, making my way to a local hospital, They amputated my mangled arm; It didn't surprise me. The damn thing was hanging on by a chunk of bone and some skin.

After I had a few days to heal, it was revealed to me by a couple of detectives that Chief Sutherland and his family had been brutally tortured and violated before being devoured by Jack and Thompson.

When I finally healed up enough, I decided to get the fuck out of the PI business and move. Which is exactly what I did.

I think about Alecia every now and then. What happened to her taught me a valuable lesson. Whether you're a whore or a drunk PI, if you play too long with wolves, you're bound to get the fangs.

COUNTDOWN TO FUR-DER

SHAUN AVERY

FRIDAY 8:00 P.M. – *The Argument*

Grant told her he wouldn't be judgmental when he found her furry cat outfit at the back of the walk-in cupboard. He even took her in his arms, could tell she was upset, and led her to the bed, where they snuggled. Grant told her not to worry, that everything would be all right.

Amy let herself believe him.

But then, the very next night…

It was her own fault, really. She said she'd meet him for drinks with some of his office friends after work. As lovely as Grant could be when it was just them—and there were enough surprise meals, back rubs, and tender sessions of lovemaking to show just how nice he sometimes was—something changed in him when he got with his colleagues, especially this one called Cath, who, naturally enough, was there that night.

She frowned when she saw this.

It was the two of them there. *Just* the two of them there. No other colleagues.

Amy almost backed out. Standing in the bar's doorway, she wondered if she could turn and leave before her boyfriend saw her. But she hesitated, something she did often when not in the suit, and so he noticed her, stood and smiled, and waved her over.

She headed to the corner table where they were sitting. Still letting herself believe things would be fine, that all the guys she'd been with in the past were bad. But Grant was different, Grant was good, Grant was—

Looking at her.

With a slimy sort of grin on his face, one she'd never seen before. Amy's stomach dropped. *He's going to tell. I know he is…*

In her despair, she looked away and glanced towards the bar. She briefly caught the eye of a man standing there, and perhaps it was just her imagination, but she was sure she'd seen the same person watching her as she'd approached the table she now sat at. She only half-registered him then, thinking no one had any reason to look at her. But now she was sure of it, and Amy wondered why.

She turned back to Grant and opened her mouth to mention the strange man. But he was already embroiled deep in a conversation with Cath. Was it her imagination again, or had they moved their chairs closer together when her attention was elsewhere?

"I hate Old Man Carruthers," Cath was saying.

"Yeah," Grant agreed, nodding. "That old bastard. And his breath!"

"Yeah, but that's not the worst." Now it was Cath's turn to cast a sneaky glance at Amy, which she did when Grant reached for his pint of lager, attention diverted. "The worst thing is, he's always touching." She laid a hand, the fingertips so finely manicured and painted a deep shade of red, on Grant's leg for a beat. "Like this."

Amy wanted to scream at her to stop. And, oh, if the suit had been there...

All she could say, though, voice small and quiet, was, "Who's Old Man Carruthers?"

"This new boss we've got at work, babe," Grant explained, "when Crusty Collins is on the sick. He's the reason it's just me and Cath here. He's got everyone else working late."

"That's right." Now, Cath turned her gaze to Amy. Cath's heavily made-up face was so pretty and hard to look at. "But that gives us girls a chance to talk." She smiled with thick red lips. "Right, Amy?"

Amy managed a weak smile of her own.

"So, tell me about yourself," Cath went on. "What do you do?"

Amy always hated this question—rather, she hated that it was one of the first things people asked when trying to get to know her—as if a job was the most important detail about somebody. Still, she tried to be polite and replied, "I'm a secretary." But a very modern one. One whose notes to type up and meetings to plan were mainly sent via e-mail—not much human contact was needed.

"How interesting," Cath replied. But she didn't *sound* very interested. She looked down at her phone as she spoke the words.

Seeing this, Amy could not help but notice an air of disappointment from Grant—like the answer she'd given, though truthful, had been the wrong one and had brought a reaction from his colleague that he had not wished to see.

But then that slimy grin from earlier returned, and suddenly Amy knew—just knew—what he was about to say and do.

"Hey," he said. Cath was still looking at her phone, but he went on regardless. "It's not her *job* you should be asking Amy about."

"No?" she asked disinterestedly, still looking at the phone.

Now Amy felt a sudden urge to ram the thing right up her fucking nose. Force it up into one of her nostrils and deep into her brain until blood and *stuff* pumped out, and then—

"That's right," Grant said, cutting into her thoughts and bringing her out of them, much to her regret. He looked at her, and she stared back, searching deep inside his eyes, trying to find the man who gave her back rubs and ran her baths but seeing nothing of that person. "Amy's got an interesting hobby. Haven't you, babe?"

"Grant," Amy said. Trying to make the word sound like a warning, but it came out more like she was pleading, all thoughts of anger and violence gone from her now. "Don't. Please."

Cath finally looked up from her phone. "Yeah?"

Grant's grin grew wider when he heard this. Excitement shone on his face as if he knew what he was about to do and how it would impact Amy, but he did not seem to care.

Amy looked away from this scene for a second and glanced into the bar. Her eyes locked onto the strange man again. And it was odd… For a second, it seemed like he would move towards her and take a step away from the bar. She didn't know why, but this thought excited her—made her sit up in her seat. The man did not follow through, though. He merely returned to his drink and removed his eyes from her.

Dejected, she looked back to Grant and Cath. The pair was *definitely* closer now, arms almost touching on the table.

"Tell Cath what I found in your cupboard, babe," he went on.

Babe, babe, she thought, hands tensing into fists upon her lap. *Always fucking "babe" to you. My name is Amy!*

"This gonna be kinky?" Cath asked, eyebrows raised, sounding excited by the idea.

"It's okay, babe," Grant said, and as he reached a hand towards her, Amy caught a trace of the *other* Grant in his voice, the *nice* Grant. It suddenly struck her that she was seeing the *real* him now, that he could turn on the charm whenever he needed to, whenever he wanted something from her—money, sex, a place to stay. *An act*, she realized. All one big fucking *act*.

"Don't worry," he continued. "We're just having a little fun here. A little furry fun, that's all." He winked as he said this, but at Cath, not at her. And his hand was coming closer, moving across the table towards her. But in Amy's mind, it was suddenly not a hand anymore. It was something disgusting—some fat, slimy alien slug—and she did not want that thing anywhere *near* her. She was almost sick when she thought of it touching her naked body in the heat of the night. So she swept it away, disgusted… but then crashed back into the reality of the moment when her action knocked his hand into his pint of lager, tipping it over, cascading thick brown liquid onto his lap.

"Shit!" Grant jumped out of his chair, and the mask was gone for a second, revealing the true Grant, the slimy alien creature beneath. "What did you do that for, you crazy bitch?"

Amy leapt up, too, tears in her eyes, finally seeing him for what he was. Then she turned and walked away.

But he wasn't done yet.

"Yeah," he said. "Go back to your cat suit, you fucking weirdo."

She shook her head. Tears flooded down her face now—tears of rage and sadness. But she would not look back at him. Would not give him that.

Instead, she ran from the bar and into the night. Thinking of home. And safety. And—of course—the suit.

———

Friday 5:30 p.m. – The Calling

He entered the Club, so packed with many different animals tonight, both fulls and halves, all of them having great fun—dancing, drinking, even a couple of orgies going on in various corners of the place. Usually, he'd join them—suit up and get involved. But it was business rather than pleasure that called him here tonight, so Simon headed straight for the Sanctum instead.

The Host was waiting for him. Though he saw it as a bear, he knew others saw it differently and viewed it as whatever their furry identity happened to be. Whatever its visage, though, one fact always remained: it was their mentor. Too, it was always looking out for others of their kind. Hence, Simon and the other agents like him.

"Welcome," it said. "How fares you today, Simon?"

"Tired," he replied, which was the truth. He'd been busy of late, seemingly more furries around than ever before, going on trip after trip to find them, to bring them in. But it wasn't tiredness that was worrying him. Not really.

The Host must have caught this in his voice and asked, "What troubles you?"

Simon wasn't sure he had an answer. It was just a vague sense of discontent troubling him lately. He'd just come from his latest furry, the most recent in a long line of hundreds. It had been great to see their face when he explained things to them, to realise how happy they would now be. Yet somehow, that no longer seemed enough. He realized he didn't get the same thrill when he helped one of their kind get through a Blooding. No, he wanted something more. He just wasn't sure what.

"Nothing," Simon said. He sat on the floor in front of the floating Host and crossed his legs. "You got another one for me?"

"Are you ready?" it asked. "Don't you need some rest time?"

Simon didn't. He could do without the time to think, to brood about what was bugging him. But the Host surely already knew the answer and would not have called on him if he hadn't been prepared. So he said nothing. Instead, he waited the spirit out.

"Very well," it eventually said. "Yes, I have discovered a new one."

"Where?"

It named a town nearby. It added, "There's an entry house in the area. You can go through that."

"No thanks," he said. "I'll drive."

The Host chuckled. "Still indulging your humanity, Simon?"

He shrugged. The truth was, the Host was right. He did indeed like to treat his human side from time to time. And really, what was more human than driving, than going on another little journey in his car? Nothing. At least not so far as he could see.

"Who am I supposed to be looking for?" Simon asked.

It brought up the image of a woman before him, and suddenly, there was a flash inside Simon that made him forget his worries. There was something different about this one, and he was instantly attracted to what he saw.

"Like her?" the Host asked. "This one is close to your age."

Simon reluctantly dragged his eyes away from the image to look at the Host. "Where can I find her?"

"There's a bar she sometimes goes to," came the reply. "That is where it starts."

Simon nodded, looked at the image once more, and licked his lips, thinking there was something to feel excited about again. He was suddenly very eager to meet this new woman about to go through her Blooding.

This pretty woman called Amy…

————

Friday 11:00 p.m. – The Deal

It was most uncommon for him to have thoughts of any sort this close to orgasm… except a couple of times with Amy, when he'd got bored of looking at her lying there like a soggy sack of potatoes and decided to look at himself in the mirror and strike a few poses to keep himself interested. Yet, as he now shot his hot load into Cath's wet mouth, it struck him that his girlfriend had done him a favour by soaking his trousers.

At first, Grant felt bad about going off at her like that. It wasn't as if he disliked Amy or anything. It was just that he'd always preferred Cath from the office, especially now.

As if sensing this thought, she pulled away from him, looked up, and winked. Then, she made a big show out of swallowing every drop.

He leant back against the alley wall, wet trousers round his ankles, content.

Apart from all that stuff with Amy, the evening had been like something from a dream. It had started normally enough that morning, with him and his colleagues making the usual Friday night arrangement to go out for drinks, something they had to do more and more often in the deranged reign of Old Man Carruthers, the cranky jobs-worth in charge of the place when their usual boss, crusty old Collins, was recovering from a heart attack, the selfish fucker. Only one by one, people started dropping out, citing family occasions or plans with non-work friends until only a few of them remained. That was when Grant started hoping, *praying,* for the one thing he'd wanted to happen all along—the chance to be alone with Cath, the dark-haired beauty who was always there but part of too big a crowd for him to make an impact with.

Finally, there was just him, her, and Brian left still in, and Grant had sighed internally, seeing his style cramped once again. But then Brian put down the phone with a dejected look, saying, "Sorry, guys. Deanna's got to work late. I've got the kids."

Grant had looked to Cath, fearing the worst. But she'd shrugged and told him, "I'm still game."

Hallelujah! Grant thought.

But it was common practice for people to invite their partners along, and he couldn't quite bring himself to cancel on Amy. Instead, he'd hoped his girlfriend, like his colleagues, would drop out. Or, if she *did* come, that she would go home early. That was why he'd made up the lie about everyone else at the office working late, doing so on the spur of the moment, not wanting Amy to suspect anything untoward was going on with his intentions for Cath, and God bless his hot colleague for going along with it without even missing a beat. Yeah, he had known just what—*who*—he wanted all along. But the way it happened was better than anything he could have imagined.

Now, staring down at Cath, he was almost ready to go again, and he reached for her shoulders, meaning to pull her up, wanting, *needing* to kiss her, dick lips and all. But she smiled, stood, and stepped away from him. "No," she said. "Not yet."

He looked at her, eyes wide.

"I like you, Grant," she said. "Have for a while. But I want our first time to be special, you know?"

This was news to him. It should have been music to his ears. Yet he suddenly found himself struggling to believe her. She had not met his eyes when she spoke, and there was something slightly *off* in her tone—like the words were not spontaneous—like they'd been prepared—rehearsed in her head when she was doing her thing on him.

"So," she went on. "I think we should—pull your pants up, will you, darling? That's kind of distracting when we're talking."

He glanced down at his exposed cock, the organ starting

to wilt once more, the second wind diminishing. Aware he sounded like a sulky, needy teenager as he pulled his trousers back up, he said, "But I thought we were going to…"

"Oh, we are, we are," Cath assured him. She motioned around the grimy back alley, the one she'd pulled him into when they were supposed to be on their way to the next bar. "Just not here."

"Then where?" Hoping she didn't say his house. Place was a shit-tip, hadn't been hoovered in God knew how long. That was why he'd spent most of his time at Amy's.

"Know what I want to see?" she replied, ignoring his question. "What would really get me hot?" Her fingers trailed down her body, lingering at her breasts, fondling, caressing, making her nipples rise against the thin white material of her blouse, jutting, huge and proud. "Want me to tell you, babe?"

His cock started stiffening again. "Yes," he replied. "I do."

She smiled. "That furry suit your little girlfriend has at home."

He blinked, surprised. He'd gone into further detail about the suit after Amy had left—how he'd found it, what it looked like—and noticed Cath growing steadily more interested as he did so. He had assumed this was an increasing attraction to him and continued to think this when she later dragged him into the alley and started kissing him, then slid to her knees and pulled down his still-damp trousers. Now, seeing the glint in her eyes when she mentioned the suit, he thought maybe he'd been wrong all along.

She turned her back to him, pulling down that thin blouse to show him a shoulder. Grant gasped, hoping she was about to put out after all… But then he took a closer look at the shoulder—at all the things he now saw *on* that shoulder.

"Whips," she told him. "And burns. I like the way they

107

make me feel. I've got them all over my body." She looked back over her bare shoulder at him. "Wanna see?"

Looking at those burns and bruises, he wasn't so sure he did.

But in his silence, she continued, saying, "Then get me inside. Let me see that suit for myself. And I'll let you see everything." She pulled up the blouse, turned back to face him, and licked her lips. "That a deal?"

In the end, it was the lip-licking that did it.

He had to see her *other* lips.

"Yes," he told her, a little breathlessly.

"Good." She held out her hand. "Let's go."

He took her hand and did so, loving the way her fingers felt somehow soft and rough at the same time. With his other hand, he hunted deep inside his damp trouser pocket, finding the key he'd had cut for Amy's place.

The one she didn't know about.

————

Friday 11:30 p.m. – The Surprise

She'd thought of the man as she walked home, the strange man she'd seen at the bar, and the more she remembered, the more she was sure she knew him from someplace, though she couldn't think where. *But why,* Amy asked herself, now sitting in her living room, *are you even thinking about him? When you should be thinking about—*

Grant.

Well, it was over with him. That much was for sure. He could come crawling back to her all she liked, even pretending to be the nice back-rubbing, bath-running Grant, and still, she wouldn't be convinced. No, all she would remember, now and forever, was the guy she'd last seen, the guy standing up and insulting her—and the suit.

Still, though, she wondered… *where was he now? And was he still with Cath?*

The suit would know. Or rather, she'd know when she was *in* the suit. It was difficult to tell the difference sometimes.

She bought it online about five years ago and had always felt something was missing in her life until it arrived. She'd been going out with Paul then but had known even before ordering the suit that she would not tell him about it. Instead, she'd put it in a locked cupboard drawer, and she had worn it only when he wasn't due to come around. And should he have arrived unexpectedly and turned up at her door unannounced, she'd have just pretended she was not in. That was why she hadn't let him have a key to her place—had not done that with *any* of her boyfriends.

Grant, though…

She'd thought—hoped—Grant was different. That was probably why she'd become lax about locking the suit away and left it out in her cupboard. Of course, maybe it was desperation behind her hope. Amy was thirty-five and wanted to settle down and have kids with someone—which some people on the furry websites she frequented found strange. *We're different,* they'd say. *Why do you want the same thing* everyone else *wants—that all the* normal people *want?* Well, she didn't know, but it *was* what she wanted. And she didn't see why her love of wearing a furry suit should get in the way. Why couldn't she have both? Why couldn't she *be* both?

She smiled at the thought—the fantasy—then headed upstairs to grab the suit.

She stripped naked before she wore it and, like always, took a chance to admire herself in the big mirror she had in her bedroom. *Not a bad little body,* she thought. It was the stuff inside she had the problem with.

But not in the suit, no, never in the suit.

She pulled it on, looked herself over in the mirror, and liked what she saw even more—liked the bulging cat breasts and the swishy cat tail. Put one paw on the former, the other on the latter. Stroked and pulled. Stroked and pulled. Started feeling pretty hot—wished someone else was here to join in this fun.

That was when—like something from a nightmare that made no sense—she heard the impossible sound of a key turning in the front door lock.

———

Friday 11:30 p.m. – The Wait

What the *fuck* had he been thinking?

He'd been a furry agent for a long time, for more years than he cared to remember—ever since that day when he was twenty, when he was scared to go to work at the office where that arsehole, Portland, was bullying him. His only release came from the secondhand bear suit he'd bought online. Until a beautiful woman called Kim knocked on his door and told him what he was and what he had to do. And then…

Man, how Portland had bled. His body had come apart bit by bit, strip by strip, in Simon's claws as he had fun with the guy—as he made it last, Kim watching. And then…

So, yes, he was experienced. That was the point; that was what he was thinking about, what he should be thinking about, pleasant though the memories of that little bit of revenge and all that followed were. So what the hell had he been playing at earlier, almost approaching this woman, this Amy, before the Blooding even started?

Strange. Tonight felt so strange. It had ever since he parked and headed to the bar. Part of him even wondered if he should pull out of the mission. But he didn't want to. And so Simon remained, standing in the shadows across the street, watching the house.

Amy's house.

He hadn't followed her from the bar—he hadn't needed to, as now that he had her scent, he could pick it up wherever he wanted and follow her from there. He'd wanted to, though... yeah, how he had *wanted* to. He didn't know why, but it wasn't lost on him that since beginning this mission, he hadn't once thought of his earlier discontent. That alone was reason enough to speak to the woman, to see what she was all about. But there was also that whole thing when she'd had the row with a man Simon guessed was her boyfriend. It seemed that Amy had some balls on her. Which made him kind of want to put *his* balls *in* her.

Maybe, anyway.

It depended on how she felt about that prospect.

Simon wanted to find out.

But not yet.

So, instead of following her, he'd waited—sat up at the bar and ordered another drink. He'd kept a sly eye on the woman's two companions, watched them leave, then stood and followed them. Left the pair to it when they disappeared into the back alley, guessing what they'd get up to in there. Proven right when they came out smelling of sex and semen. Wondered where they would be going next.

But he knew.

They were heading towards the woman's scent.

They had to be a part of the Blooding.

From the shadows, Simon now watched as they approached the house—felt the bear pulse inside him, eager to be fed. But he felt something else as well—something he'd never felt before.

Wait, he told them both. *Be patient.*

Almost time.

———

Friday 11:25 p.m. – The Destination

They'd walked hand in hand at first, but she'd taken it away. He'd felt disappointed, only for her to reach down and give his cock a squeeze, then come closer and lick his ear. Her breath and lips were so warm and promising. Grant didn't know how he'd managed not to come again. The way she made him feel and that glint she got in her eyes whenever she mentioned the suit made him think it wouldn't take much to tip *her* over the edge, either. So he would have his way with her, just like he'd always dreamt of. Oh yes. Whether Amy liked being a party to it or not, it was a shame that it had to end this way. He'd kind of liked the girl. But she'd brought it all on herself, had she not? Yes indeed. Bitch shouldn't have made that scene with him earlier in the bar.

Grant nodded to himself. He looked to Cath, now a few steps in front of him, let his eyes take in her perfect ass cheeks, and wondered how they'd taste beneath his tongue and his fingers. Knowing he'd soon find out, he felt his cock twinge once more.

Then, finally, they were there—at Amy's place.

"Wonder if she's wearing it right now," Cath said, that lust in her voice again.

Grant almost felt a sense of guilt for whatever was about to happen with Amy, for all that had come before, back at the bar. But then he remembered the blow job, Cath's hot lips around him, and he knew he needed more, much more from her. He thought to himself, *yeah, you know, all things considered —fuck Amy*.

Smiling, he pulled the key from his pocket.

"Let's find out," he said.

————

Friday 11:35 p.m. – The Blooding

Amy froze, eyes wide behind the cat mask. Shock coursed through her as she heard the door swing open, followed by footsteps heading up the stairs.

Grant, she thought. Who else could it be? But not *just* Grant, she realized. No, two sets of footsteps were coming closer, one of them the clacking of high heels.

High heels?

Cath.

She found herself snarling.

Then suddenly, there they were.

They stood in the doorway of her bedroom, staring at her. She liked the look of awe on Grant's face and remembered he had not yet seen her in the suit. *Look at what you're missing out on, Buster,* she thought, with a grin... But her sudden glee faded when she glanced across at Cath. The woman was clutching at her breasts, nipples standing out through her blouse.

"Oh my God, that's so fucking hot," Cath said. She briefly looked at Grant before returning her gaze to the suit, to Amy standing there in it. "Go and take it off her, babe. I want to touch it."

No, Amy said to herself. *You won't touch it, touch me. I'll kill you first.* It was the sort of thought she always had while in the suit if thinking about someone she hated. But all those other times, it was just a figure of speech, just fantasy talk. Not tonight, though. Tonight, she felt lethal—would not let either of these fuckers touch her.

Touch the suit, a voice inside her mind told her. *You mean you won't let them touch the suit.*

But *no,* she realised. She did *not* mean that. Did not *just* mean that, anyway. She wasn't sure what the distinction was, but she knew that it was there, was suddenly—or not so suddenly—there.

Grant, meanwhile, seemed doubtful. "Um," he said, "I don't think that's what we…"

Cath's breath was coming in sharp bursts now, her fingers trailing down to play between her legs. "N . . . now, babe. It'll be worth your while."

Grant shrugged and gave Amy a mournful look that seemed to say *I'm sorry.* Then he went for her.

"Stay back," she warned him, standing beside the bed, a bed she could not believe she once shared with him. "I mean it, Grant."

He ignored her and kept coming. His face was no longer mournful but something else instead. And those hands moving towards her, like back at the bar before, this time reached for her mask, meaning to pull it off.

She screeched.

Lashed out with her cat claws. Raked open his cheek.

"Bitch!" he called, and he raised his hand to strike her.

"Uh-uh," came a voice. "I wouldn't."

They all turned towards the sound.

The man was standing just behind Cath.

She leapt away from him and said, "Who the fuck are you?"

But Amy knew. This was the man she'd seen earlier, the man from the bar.

"You butt-heads left the front door open," he said, looking between Cath and Grant. "That's dangerous. But I guess you wanted to make a quick escape afterward, am I right?"

Grant didn't reply. Instead, he looked at Amy and asked, "Hey, who's this?" sounding aggrieved and betrayed.

"Simon," the man replied. I'd shake your hand, but." He let his eyes roam over Cath, his face wrinkling in disgust as he did so, apparently not liking what he saw. "I don't know where it's been."

"Hey, fuck you," Cath shot back, placing her hands on her hips, not sounding quite so aroused now. "What the hell are you doing here anyway?"

"I came for her," the man said, waving a hand at Amy. As he did, his eyes locked on those of her cat mask... But somehow, it was still like he saw her, the real her. And she saw something in him, too. She wasn't quite sure what that was. But it made her groin tingle.

Cath sneered. "You another freak, then?" Then motioned to Grant. "Sort him out, darling."

Amy saw Grant's expression when Cath said this and did not think he wanted to obey. But then, she'd thought a lot of things about Grant before tonight, and not a single one of them had turned out to be true. Still, she hoped he would tell Cath, "No," and the two of them would get out of there, leaving her alone with this man, this Simon. And what might happen then?

Her groin tingled again.

But she felt different down there somehow. Wetter. Wider. Like there was more of her waiting to be filled than there had ever been before. But that made no sense. Did it?

Shaking the thought away, as she had with the last one she could not answer, she returned her attention to Grant. Amy sighed inside, feeling she'd not known him at all.

An angry look fell across Grant's face, and he told Cath, "Fucking right, babes."

Simon shook his head. "if you insist," he said, then lashed out with an arm.

Amy had to blink at what she saw, unable to believe her eyes. His arm had suddenly changed, becoming something else: a giant and hairy bear paw topped with razor-sharp claws, claws that sliced clean through Cath's throat, taking her head off.

Grant screamed, and as blood gushed from the stump of Cath's neck and her head sailed up to smack the ceiling before falling to hit the bedroom floor, Amy felt like she should be doing the same. But she was not. Instead, she felt that tingling more than ever. Her hand went to her tail and pulled.

Simon watched her as she did and winked. Then he stepped further into the room, closing the door behind him as Cath's dead body slumped to the floor, stump still spurting blood.

Grant stopped screaming and slid to the ground, his back against the bed, blood still streaming down his cheek from where Amy had cut him. He looked up at her, panic on his face, and asked, "Amy, who the fuck is this guy? You see what he just did?"

She heard the terror in his voice and was disgusted by it. She wondered what she had once seen in this... this *man?*

This man who now grabbed at her legs, not with aggression but out of sheer desperation, and hung onto her, begging, "Please, please, don't let him hurt me!"

Amy shrugged him off. She didn't think about the action; she just did it, almost as if her body had a mind of its own. But then she wondered: Was it her body… or the suit?

There were those distinctions again.

Simon stopped before her. Grant was a quivering, pathetic mess between them. Amy imagined her old self trying to comfort him, but then her face hardened behind the mask, and she told herself, *fuck him.* Instead, she turned her attention to the other man. She looked him over long and hard and finally asked him the question she'd been wondering all night.

"Why do I feel like I know you from somewhere?"

"You recognize your own kind," he replied. "We all do."

"Own kind?"

He nodded. "You're confused, I know. But that's okay. It'll all make sense after the Blooding."

The Blooding. The words made something click in her.

"Yes," he went on. "There are two types of us—Fulls and Halves. Halves just wear their suits. The Fulls… our bond with the suit is so great that it becomes a part of us." He flexed his bear paw once more, illustrating his point. "But for that to happen, first you've got to go through the Blooding."

Amy raised her paws to look at them and flexed her flesh fingers beneath them. She imagined the two being as one. But how could that be?

Amy wanted to know. *Had* to know. "How?"

Simon looked down at the shaking, moaning Grant, grinning as he told her, "Sacrifice."

Grant whimpered at the word, looking at Cath's headless body and seemingly seeing his own future there.

Simon laid a hand on the other man's shoulder.

"Normally, you have to hunt one down," he said. "Not often does one come to you."

"Yeah," Amy said, not looking at Simon as he spoke, instead staring down at Grant. She tried to remember the good times but only saw the actions of this evening.

"Please," Grant begged. "Please, Amy. I love—"

She sliced her fingers across his throat, cutting off what she knew would be another lie.

He fell backwards, clutching the gushing wound, and crawled for the door.

Simon stood back and looked at her. "Well," he said. "That's a start."

"Don't worry," she replied. "I'm not done yet."

She leapt onto Grant, using her claws, and when they weren't enough, she pulled off the suit and used her teeth, ripping into him, tearing him open, starting at his already damaged throat and sinking in deep and *pulling* before moving on and down. When it was done, when he'd finally stopped thrashing, when the room was littered with his body parts, she felt the urge in her groin again. It was maddening now, a hunger that had to be fed. But it was no longer just *her* groin, she realized, but the groin of the suit, too. It was no longer on the floor where she had left it but was now within her, joined to her by some kind of bonding magic. Looking in the mirror, she saw she was naked. But all she had to do was think—and *poof—t*here it was. There *she* was, no longer just a woman wearing a suit, but now the suit was a part of her, as vital as her hands and heart.

Thinking this, she looked at Simon and said, "*Come here,*" growling the words, unsure if she was Amy or the cat, but comprehending she was now *both*. Cat-Amy. There *were* no distinctions anymore. Seeming to sense this, Simon shed his clothes. Then he changed, too, becoming Bear-Simon. He growled back and leapt at her, and then—

It lasted hours, time almost coming to a stop. Surrounded by the body parts of the enemies she'd killed and coated in their shed blood as she and her equally animal partner rolled around the bedroom, she came like she had never come before. She realised that she probably hadn't, for she was Cat-Amy tonight… Tonight and forever more. Yes, she had been Blooded. Reborn.

But in what should have been the afterglow, what should have been the comedown period of the best night of her life…

Doubts hit her—the habits of a lifetime too hard to break. She turned to Simon as they lay amidst the blood and asked him:

"What… what are we going to do with the bodies?"

———

Saturday 2:30 a.m. – The Future

Simon began to explain it all to her. He told her that since she had gone through the Blooding, she could make any place an Entry and Exit point to the Club, and any Full furry could do the same, no matter where they were in the world. She didn't believe and who could blame her? He'd been just as skeptical back when Kim first came to him. It wasn't until they'd made hot, sticky love in the forest, Portland's severed head next to them, that he saw the truth.

That had been a one-time thing. Kim was married in the real world but had an understanding husband who let her make love to the men she brought through their Blooding, who understood it was Gorilla-Kim, not human Kim, letting herself go with all those guys. As one-off experiences go, though… it had been pretty good.

He smiled at the memory and told Amy, "Watch."

Simon waved a hand. A door appeared in the room. He laughed as her eyes grew wide and offered his hand to her. "Come on," he said.

"But I'm naked!" By this point, they were both in human form, suits now back inside of them.

"There are a lot of people naked where we're going," he replied.

And he was right.

Heading back into the Club, he saw a bunch of the same people from earlier, still fucking where they'd been hours ago. Like before, he wanted to join in… wanted them *both* to join in, for tonight, at least. But also, like before, he was there for business—Blooding business.

"You did it," he told her.

She blinked, surprised. "What?"

"You went through with it," he explained. "The Blooding. Not everybody does. Some fail at the last minute. That was why I had to wait, see if you fought back."

"You mean… When I hit Grant with my claws?"

He nodded.

"It felt good," she said.

"I know," he said. It struck him that he'd been very glad when she did so. He always was, of course, when someone embraced their true self. But it seemed different with her— seemed *more* somehow. He was getting soft, he guessed. He was getting on, too. In his early thirties, he wondered what came next, which is maybe where his earlier feeling of discontent came from.

She looked around the Club. "Where is this place?"

"Downtown," he told her. "Halves can only enter through

its actual location. But us Fulls can come here anywhere we make an Entrance."

"Wow," she said. "But what happens to me in my old life now?"

"That's up to you," he replied. "We can get rid of the bodies, of course. But people might remember you were the last to be seen with... those two sacrifices. There might be questions asked. You can stick around to answer them. Or we can take you somewhere else and start you up a new life." He remembered he'd have to go back for his clothes either way—his car, too. Human side or not, he was fond of travelling in that thing.

"Where?"

"We have places," he said. "The Host can introduce you to some powerful people."

As if confirming this, a police chief waddled past dressed up as a duck.

"Is that what you do?" she asked.

"Yeah." He lived from place to place, sleeping at the Club when necessary. But that suddenly seemed to be getting old like everything else.

She shook her head. But he knew the place was working its magic on her, with all its dancing and fucking. Before his eyes, she became the cat again, pulling at that tail. Then she looked back at him and said, "I still don't get how all this works. Like how before, your suit came on above your clothes. How can that be?"

"There's a lot to get used to," Simon admitted. "Don't worry. The Host will explain everything."

"You said that before," she replies. "What's the Host?"

He pointed to the open door of the Sanctum.

"Oh." She sounded disappointed, hand freezing on the tail. "Now?"

He got her meaning. As he looked at her cat breasts and her furry vagina, he suddenly wasn't very interested in talking either.

"No," he said, reaching for her. "Later."

But she became human again and stepped away from him, a sudden sad look on her face. "I have to tell you something," she said.

Simon hoped she wasn't about to ruin this. He'd begun to think there really was something different this time... But what? The fact they were almost the same age? He wasn't sure. But suddenly, he believed it was no coincidence that the Host had picked him for this one.

"What?" he asked her.

"I want..." She paused, met his eyes, and started again. "I want children. At some point. Will any of this change that?"

He laughed. "Is that all?"

Amy's eyes hardened, and it hit him that he couldn't just be his usual smart-mouth self with her. No, he had to think about what he was saying. This was not something he was used to or had ever felt was necessary. But looking at those eyes, seeing the way she tensed her body and stood her ground, made Simon think she would be worth it.

"Sorry," he replied. "I just meant to say it will be fine. Our kind have children all the time."

"How? I mean, are they human, or are they..."

"Human," he replied. "*Just* human. That's how *we* start out, so that's how our kids are born."

"Oh," she said again. Then her eyes softened as she looked away from him, and she continued with an almost shy air. "But do you... Do you want that, too?"

Simon didn't know. But he *did* know that he felt no discontentment around Amy, which might not mean much in the long run. Maybe it would be just a one-night thing like it had been with Kim. But he didn't think so. Suddenly—or not so suddenly—he didn't think so.

"I'm not sure," he said. "I never really thought about it before."

But as he pulled her towards him and kissed her, he realised…

He'd like to figure it out with her.

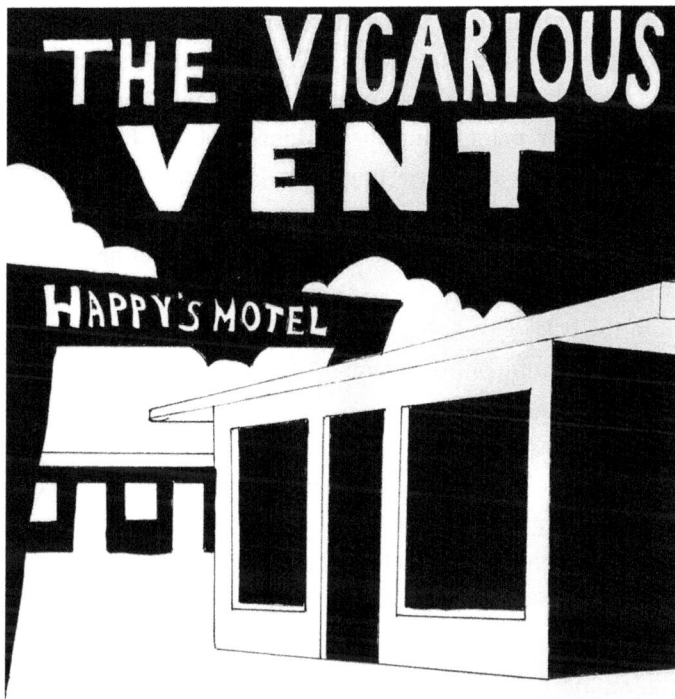

THE VICARIOUS VENT

HAPPY'S MOTEL

SARAH DeROSA

LANCE'S KEYS dangled from the belt loop of his creased khakis. They jingled harmoniously, bouncing off the top of his leg with each step forward. He pushed his heavy Coke bottle glasses up the bridge of his crooked nose. Ohio's summer humidity made his pores excrete an oily coating that could rival the slickness of a slip n' slide.

As he cleared the cigarette-studded parking lot, he coughed into his clammy palm. After examining the mixture of sweat and saliva, he smeared it onto his belted waist. Stubborn grass popped through the gaping cracks of the broken concrete. The greenery peppered the lot, complimenting the faded yellow paint lining the parking spots on the cement. Lance hocked a loogie, ejecting a stringy concoction of mucus and spit with rapid fire.

"Here we are." He announced to himself under his breath, struggling to unhook the scratched metallic carabiner clip from the belt loop. A stray beige thread entangled itself with the nose, snaring onto his pants.

"Gad bless it."

Once again, his glasses slid to the tip of his nose as he tucked his chin to his chest. His underbite jutted out, uncovering his bottom row of rotten teeth. The exposed bones resembled popcorn kernels embedded in his gums. Lance yanked the clinking keys free of the thread with a snap.

Even in the early morning sun, he could feel beads of perspiration welling up beneath the thickness of his mustache. The weatherman had warned of record temperatures today. He hated the polarizing weather of the Midwest, but he couldn't deny that the extreme changes were good for business. Everyone wanted to be in his air-conditioned rooms this time of year, even if they could only afford an hour's worth of relief.

From an early age, the little things always annoyed him the most. Although his property remained in disarray, his mind demanded order when it came to minor inconveniences. The upset of that daunting task sent his mild agitation over the edge. Heat only heightened his sensitive temper.

Lance sighed as he approached the sprawling beast, already exasperated with the day ahead. The building was twenty years overdue for a new coat of paint. In its prime, the mint green radiated off the glowing vintage sign that stoically hovered, beckoning the weary traveler. The humming neon lights flashed the word Vacancy in highlighter pink lettering.

Due to its convenient position near a highway exit, he was able to keep the neglected structure in business regardless of the thick overlay of grime. However, it wasn't exactly considered a treasured piece of history. The old girl was rarely revisited by anyone other than the town's most unwanted misfits.

He vowed to work on sprucing the place up in honor of the lovely couple who once owned it. Maybe it would appeal to a classier clientele, and then he would really be in business. As soon as the thought was there, it passed as he calculated how much elbow grease and money that would take.

"Another day in paradise," he muttered to himself, kicking a condom wrapper into the heap of dried leaves and trash collecting in the corner next to the office's door. With a subtle, disapproving shake of his head, he rotated the key into the lock.

The regulars at Happy's Motel usually paid for rooms hourly or for weeks at a time. However, the local landmark didn't discriminate against desperate road trippers, usually families—the Americana types with, at minimum, one terrible child motivated to listen solely by the threat of being deprived of technology—an unhappy wife in tow with a permanent scowl and pinched nose, dressed in bunched capris and a visor like that of a casino dealer.

If the women were pretty enough, he usually knocked ten bucks off the nightly rate to convince them to stay. Typically, that was all it took for the dads to reach into their cargos and pluck their credit cards from the frayed corners of their bulky trifolds. It could be said that the motel wasn't wife-approved, as the women usually complained to their husbands. The soccer mom types were the worst to interact with but the best to spy on.

Once those capris slipped off for the night, it was long legs with healthily dabbled cellulite and stretch marks. Usually, those women wore flower-speckled cotton hipsters with no hint of ass cheek in sight. These women reminded him of his Patty, making them favored by default.

Seldomly, a zesty twenty-something and her boyfriend would unknowingly put on a show for him. They generally sported thongs with the deep crescents of lace fabric framing their accentuated rounds of flesh. He loved viewing woman at their most vulnerable, young and old alike. After some time, he'd refined his skill of guessing what kind of undergarments he might see.

The original owner left the motel to Lance in her will, saying it was what her late husband would have wanted. His devotion as their literal whipping boy had paid off, and now, he could reap the benefits of their triad for the remainder of his golden years. Still, he ached for their company and would have gladly exchanged Happy's for just one more day with the two of them.

The two-bedroom bungalow he'd called home for decades gifted him with reminders of the couple's presence everywhere. Ben's oil paintings were proudly displayed on the vivid robin's egg walls. Patty's cookbooks were nestled on the shelf in the kitchen with heart-shaped cutouts scaling the sides. Her cherry curio cabinet crowded the living room. Crystalware and flashy collectibles were frozen in time behind the glass.

Relief couldn't be found in his outside world either. Their own personal oasis shared a parking lot with the business. When they'd bought the property, Patty insisted she wanted to be as close as possible to keep an eye on her precious venture.

Patty's eye for design made it easy to see what the hotel's

profit had gotten wrapped up in. Lance always admired her fondness for the gaudy and frivolous junk. She was perfect, from her costume rings with bulging rhinestones to the signature silk cheetah print robe she often garnished to set the mood.

Her tastes were bold and advanced for their time. Throughout their relationship, he often felt inferior to such a fearless woman. Living in her unchanged quarters made him feel less lonely—like maybe she was just off frying eggs in the kitchen for her two men.

He slept in the old heart-shaped bed they'd rescued when they remodeled the honeymoon suite ten years back. It was the original bed the young, ambitious couple had purchased in the late seventies. They excitedly calculated the return of upcharging married couples willing to pay for a romantic experience. Sure, it had some stains, but the custom satin sheets covered them with class.

Patty also demanded the glossy red jacuzzi from the suite be salvaged and reinstalled in their bungalow. It held many stories of the throuple as well as other guests. Lance recalled one of his earlier experiences when he sat on his haunches in the heart-shaped tub and sucked Ben's girthy penis. Meanwhile, Patty poured champagne over his unsuspecting mop of hair.

Ben had held Lance in place by his ears, suffocating him with the flabby skin overhanging the base of his member. A stomach-churning yeastiness wafted into his nasal cavity, encompassing him. Pre-ejaculation oozed down his windpipe to the symphony of his nostrils rapidly flaring for air. He struggled against Ben's firm grip, fighting to breathe in the fizzy stream of the luxury water torture.

The couple had instructed him to drown in the waterfall of carbonation if it meant keeping Ben's swollen member in the recesses of his mouth. The force of it got Ben off in minutes, blasting salty loads to the back of Lance's esophagus. Ben's semen tasted of curdled milk as if the man himself had expired. It wasn't Lance's favorite escapade, but he loved being the third to the kinky couple.

In a Freudian way, he'd treasured their maternal and paternal bonds to him just as much as the sexual ones. Especially Patty. She'd initiated the whole thing.

At the time, he'd left his parent's house after a big fight and was couch-surfing around town with his stoner friends. A sense of urgency pulled him onward, knowing he was beginning to overstay his welcome at most places he cycled. Lance needed a job to afford his own place, so he started looking around town.

It quickly became a challenging endeavor since he lacked many skills and had zero experience. Despite the lonely, unwanted feeling taking root, he tried to remain optimistic. He persevered with a "fake-it-til-you-make-it" philosophy. When he saw an ad in the paper for a maintenance job at the local Happy's Motel, he jumped in without the slightest bit of expertise.

Patty interviewed him first. The ringlets from her blonde perm bounced along with the jiggling tops of her exposed cleavage as she discussed the position. As she asked him questions, she nonchalantly maneuvered the tip of her pen to her freckled collarbone and traced downward, not breaking eye contact once. His mind had to race to remember what she just asked. The mature woman didn't seem to care, studying him with amusement.

Shortly after being hired, she started coming onto him. He was boyishly dumbstruck by his luck. She and her husband were in their prime in their 40s, but Patty, especially, was stunning. With similarities to the models in pop commercials, she was the tanned, toned, and tight blonde of his dreams.

Back then, he'd often see her stroll past him, announcing she was leaving for jazzercize, in neon unitards that held the slightest pocket to cover up the outline of her vulva. He would have to make a mad dash for the laundry closet and frantically jerk off. The image of her bulging pussy lips sandwiching the hot pink spandex as it rubbed against her clit was too much for him to bear.

With the help of his racing right hand, he'd blown an unthinkable load onto a stack of folded guest towels, neatly waiting in a laundry basket to be delivered. It became a biweekly ritual the two of them shared. There was no doubt in his mind the teasing was intentional. She gave him a knowing look, understanding how much he lusted over her and making him feel naked under her gaze.

Lance found it odd at first that an older married woman would have any interest in a teenage boy. When he'd left his parents in search of a better life, he couldn't even drive. Against all odds, he was grateful to discover his place in the world in the gap of Patty's motherly breasts.

Patty sold him the extra perks of the job with her manicured fingertips squeezing his shoulders from behind. The smoothness of her juicy tits hovered at the back of his neck. Rich perfume overwhelmed his senses. He was intoxicated by her. He couldn't believe his ears as she explained that she *and* Ben were an adventurous couple looking for new experiences.

She confided that the maintenance job wasn't a necessity, but they'd created the ad to find a lover who could appeal to both of their tastes. They both had heightened sex drives and required daily intimacy but wanted to remain discreet about their lifestyle. Initially, Lance hesitated.

He had never been with a man but often fantasized about

it. Ben fulfilled the role of a sleazy business mogul in a bowling shirt with a wifebeater poking out and a garb of silver wiry chest hair surrounding a gold chain. The sides of his dome sprouted thinning grey strands while the top remained black. His significant age gap with his companions also added to his appeal.

He was baritone, manly, and broad. As soon as Lance agreed to test the compatibility as their third, Ben became his *daddy* as much as his father figure. Ben's flourishing desires yielded cravings for the same sex that were every bit as strong as his lust for his wife.

Their configurations as a threesome were just as enticing as the individual intimacy he shared with them separately. Lance's favorite was the position where Patty rode one of them while the other penetrated her taut asshole. It stretched her out wide like the forming O of her mouth. Her eyes would roll back in her head as she screamed, violently gyrating and smacking the top of her pussy with wet thwacking sounds.

Ben and Patty's experimental appetite had adopted darker undertones upon learning about the BDSM movement sending shockwaves from New York to the Midwest. They played catch-up with the trendy swingers in their previous network and were influenced to delve into a more shocking side of sexual culture. Together, they used Lance to explore their depraved fantasies.

At first, it had been innocent enough with the champagne shower. Shortly after, chintzy leather whips and purple fur-lined handcuffs became part of the repertoire. Soon, their range as a threesome expanded with the introduction of Ben's thick leather belt instead of the gag-gift quality whip. They bought chastity belts, a hogtie kit, a few different dildos, a D-ring, and a special strap-on for Patty to fuck them with when they were being bratty little boys.

Lance learned explicitly how to ride the line of pain and pleasure as they took turns plugging his holes and testing his boundaries. Moons caused by the extinguishing of rotating cigarettes were burned into the skin spanning his chest. While the range of experiences had been mostly pleasurable, he still felt more satisfied when they would spend nights entertaining his fantasy.

Lance's kinks centered around voyeurism. Patty and Ben didn't have to interact with him at all. In fact, all he required was a chair to sit in as he stroked his throbbing dick at the sight of Patty being rammed from behind by her husband so hard she was yelping. Her eyes often held his gaze until he sprayed jizz all over his stomach and dropped his head in exhaustion. She would always hold back her own orgasm to watch his.

He truly loved their compatibility and planned on happily spending the rest of his life with them. They shared general companionship and deep-seated interests buried inside their taboo psyches. They reciprocated, allowing him to blend in with the striped wallpaper interrupted by large peonies. In exchange, he dove into their catalog of body torture kinks, blood, pissing, and incestual scenarios.

The void left in his chest by their unexpected deaths made him lonelier than ever. Happy's Motel struggled to maintain the same luster in their absence. Everything appeared dull without Patty's flamboyant personality and Ben's toothy smile to light up the place. The anniversary of Patty's suicide was approaching.

Initially, he began inflicting his tendencies on the unsuspecting customers as a distraction—a way of coping with the loss of the only people he ever felt understood him. The wounds left by Ben's fatal heart attack and Patty's subsequent overdose were still fresh after only three years. His coping mechanism shifted into an obsession with the secret lives of strangers behind closed doors.

After the couple's deaths, he refused to change anything about the rundown motel to preserve Patty's unique vision of utopia. However, he did make one exception to his rule by installing a new duct in the office closet. It served as a door to eavesdropping on the world that cast him as an outsider for the entirety of his life. Silently, he would hover over his desired room, peering through the slits in the overhead vent.

Lance's petite stature enhanced his ability to roam without making too much noise. Instead, he wormed through the maze of ductwork by crawling on his stomach. His pockets were deep enough to hold his supply of tools, allowing him to explore with a miniature notebook securely tucked in his armpit.

Sighing, he plopped into his ratty office chair behind the front desk. Strips of duct tape hung limply from patching years of neglect. Ben had bought it new and fought to keep it in its aged state against his wife's protests. Variations of the fight stretched over the ages, echoing in Lance's thoughts.

"Just take it to the dump, Ben. For chrissakes! It's old and worn. We can get you a new one."

"You're old and worn, but I'm not replacing you, am I? Plus, I already broke it in. Look, it's got my ass carved into it!"

"That's because you don't do anything around here but sit in that damned chair all day!"

Lance smiled in amusement at the memory of their bickering. Most of the time, it was lighthearted and playful. From a spectator's perspective, he could see their immense love for each other, and it warmed his heart to call them his people.

As the owner, Lance got away with working a morning

shift and made a habit of disappearing into his office once his star employee, Veronica, arrived at three. She worked most days until about midnight. He loved her for her fierce respect for privacy and lack of curiosity about his endeavors. Her only request was that it be reciprocated. The two had an unspoken understanding, only once interrupted when Lance ventured to ask her if she was in college shortly after meeting her.

Their town was quiet enough to have an unsupervised front desk, and most of the time, he slept in the cot in his office anyway. It kept him from the sad reminder of the empty heart mattress awaiting him and was convenient after a long night of remarking on strangers' behavior in his notebook.

Veronica texted him that she was running late, extending the last hour of his shift. Lance silently cursed her and her entire useless generation. No one had respect for their employers anymore, let alone a work ethic. Forget about taking initiative, judging by the impressive mountain of trash huddled in the corner of the building's exterior.

In his own bout of hypocrisy, he avoided tending to the property, thinking it was beneath him. As far as his minimum wage employee was concerned, there was paperwork to do. Instead, he sat at his mahogany office desk, scratching his balls and thumbing through old Hustlers from Ben's original stash.

The hulking dark wood beast had been Patty's choice, and she would not budge on the matter. She insisted they had to look like professionals. He kept the office door open, trusting the old-fashioned bell attached to the lobby's front door to warn him of guests.

He peered through the blinds at the sound of a car screeching to a halt outside the office window. Heavy metal rattled from the car's interior all the way through his window. Scowling, he watched as Veronica, clad in black, exited the golden Taurus she'd named Pearl as if it were a human. Kids…

Even running late, she walked up to her favorite wall, leaned on it with her leg propped up, and lit a cigarette. Lance glanced at the clock. It was nearly five in the afternoon. Moments later, a black SUV pulled into the spot next to Pearl at an equally alarming speed. The windows were tinted to a point of unnerving secrecy. Veronica delivered an unflinching stare toward the vehicle between deep drags of her cancer stick. She tilted her skull back, blowing smoke at the cobwebs infesting the wobbly soffit of the low roof.

"Don't worry, Veronica, I'll get this one," Lance muttered. He glowered, hoisting himself from the desk chair and burying his shirttail into his khakis.

The bell rang just as he buckled his belt. A couple approached the desk with an immediate sense of impatience. The man reminded him of Ben when he first started at Happy's. If he had to guess, the man was in his mid-sixties yet had a taut body and straight posture. He was immaculately dressed in a designer suit and twinkling leather dress shoes. His pinky finger was studded with a man's ring containing a glittering ruby. Lance's insecurities swelled with self-conscious awareness that he was at least twenty years younger and much more doughy.

A gaunt young woman, well under half his age, quietly stood behind him with her arms crossed in front of her chest. Her eyes darted around the lobby as if afraid to look at him or anyone. While most women had a knack for protesting, unafraid to insult Lance's motel, she stayed silent. Something about the pair was bizarre.

The girl's damaged hair was off-putting. Lance could tell

she was a dark brunette underneath the botched bleach job. Her chocolatey brown irises and olive skin tone also deceived her brassy top coat. The girl was probably as tall as he was, maybe 5'4. A truck stop sundress with large tropical flowers and a tie-dye print did nothing to conceal nor accentuate her frail frame. The brightness and loose form only enhanced her sickliness.

"We need a room," the man in the suit demanded.

"Of course! Mr.?"

"John Smith," the suited man stated with a smirk.

Lance stared, reeling for words to accompany his customer's brashness in giving him the obviously false name. "Of course, *Mr. Smith*. I have one available with two queens or just a single."

His eyes flitted to the girl, who looked more and more underage by the minute. Perhaps the mysterious female was his daughter. He could only hope.

"One bed will do us."

Then again, perhaps not. Lance's moral compass was a little off-kilter, as were the two people who trained him on all parts of life. He was aware that the sex worker scene was filled with young runaways.

"Okay, I just need an ID and credit card."

Nervously, he watched the man dig into the silk-lined pocket of his pants and pull out a designer wallet. He plucked two crisp one-hundred dollar bills and set them on the raised ledge of the counter. "I was hoping to pay cash."

A beat skipped before Lance nodded and slid the money off the counter, clutching it in his grip. He ran his thumbnail along the raised ridges of the payment. Upon confirmation that the hundreds were real, he placed the key in his customer's tense, outstretched hand.

As long as they're not little kids, look the other way, darlin'.

We're here to make money, and so are they, Patty's words echoed in his head.

Veronica walked through the door, ringing the bell overhead with raised eyebrows. She entered behind the desk, smelling fragrantly of Djarms. Previously, when Lance first spotted the black filtered sticks, he shook his head at her, joking that even her smokes were gothic. In return, she told him he was cringey in a flat voice.

The duo had a complicated relationship. He'd hired her after the loss of Patty to help him balance his business and grieving. She wasn't a star employee as far as going above and beyond, and sure, she scared the everloving shit out of him, but she was also the only one who'd responded to the "NOW HIRING" sign in the window.

Beggars can't be choosers. Besides, he loved that she kept to herself. Was she the most inviting person to be the face of Happy's Motel as a front desk worker? Not in the slightest. Did she care or ask questions when he stayed in his office all day and night? Also no.

They had a silent agreement to look the other way for each other. If she heard a noise in the ducts, which she often did, it was that pesky raccoon again. No questions asked. If Lance caught her going out to smoke a clove every half hour, it was her break time.

She took her spot on her equally destroyed desk chair and propped her feet up with a heavy thud, one combat boot crossing the other. Without acknowledging her boss, she reached into her floppy bag and plucked her newest macabre novella, clenching it between her black nails. Where other girls her age strutted around with designer purses, she was proud to show off her cotton tote, which brandished the tarot card for death printed on it.

She turned to him once the guests were out of earshot. "Were they hourly?"

He chuckled nervously, uncomfortable under her burning gaze. Then he feigned a *can-you-believe-it* tone and said, "No, they wanted to stay the whole night."

"Well, look at that."

His cheeks burned underneath her judgmental scrutiny. She rolled her eyes, refocusing on finding her page in her book. He detested the sick content she was capable of reading and couldn't keep up with how fast she zipped through them. There was a new title every couple of days. This one's cover revealed an unnerving drawing of a girl with no teeth and some sort of BDSM mask that covered the upper part of her face.

The last time he asked about her book, he regretted it wholeheartedly. He'd squirmed as she went into vivid detail about a man torturing people in the most unimaginably heinous ways. However, he needed a diversion from the topic of the guests.

"*Run Red*, huh? What's that one about?" He questioned with nonchalance.

"Do you *really* want to know the answer to that, Lance?" She tilted her head.

"I- uh… Yes, I do."

She sighed. "I don't believe that. You know that girl is young as fuck, right?"

He shifted uncomfortably.

"Did you even ask to see her ID?"

"No. That's not our business. Dammit, Veronica! We didn't card the ten-year-old from Farmington Hills, did we?"

"No. He was with his family," she stated firmly.

"And how do we know she's not that man's daughter?"

"How many beds?"

Lance stayed silent.

"How many beds, Lance? One or two?"

"V, I'm your boss. You shouldn't talk to me like that," he said weakly.

"You shouldn't be letting trafficking or underage sex fly under your fucking radar."

She had a point. Morally, the situation wasn't great, but she knew how skeezy he was. She revealed that much to him when she accused him of putting cameras in the rooms during a spat. However, business was business, and this was the cost of paying the bills. Still, it weighed on Lance's conscience that she acted angrier than usual.

"Did they pay with cash?" she badgered him.

"Of course they did. Who doesn't at this place? You can't judge people by that."

"You are so lucky I need a job right now because this immoral shit is fucked." With that, she flipped *Run Red* open, and her eyes dropped to the page.

"You're lucky I need an employee. Otherwise, *you'd* be fucked," he muttered, storming into his office. How did someone who read the most twisted books for leisure have a stronger moral compass than he did? He hated how inferior the girl made him feel, even if she was being the voice of reason.

Lance looked at his watch. It was too early to start spying on his guests, but Lance didn't care. He made the rash decision to kill two birds with one stone: blow off steam by starting his nightly quest early and prove his overly suspicious employee wrong about the occupants of room twelve.

The bottom drawer of his desk jerked open under his frustrated force, and he retrieved the pocket-sized notebook from the back corner. He licked his finger to flip it open and turn to a blank page. The less movement in the ducts, the better.

The front side had been used with a cryptic list scrawled in his sloppy penmanship.

Becca

Est. 5'2

130 lbs?

D cup

Med. Blonde hair.

Missionary

Lance stepped inside the closet and closed the door behind him. This had been his nightly ritual for years now. He yanked the cord, illuminating the closet with the bare light bulb hanging overhead. After unfolding the six-foot ladder, he climbed up and removed the plate from the vent.

His first stop would not only ensure that Veronica was wrong but also allow him to delve into a tight wet pussy. Lance reminded himself to take detailed notes on this one. He was already sweating by the time he hoisted himself into the vent.

Like a giant rat, he scurried toward room twelve. It was his favorite room to put guests whom he'd taken a particular interest in. A sickening concoction of stenches wafted through the vents, combining with the humid moisture on the metal. He'd become used to the heady scents of body odor, sex, shit, and cigarettes that his guests provided.

His arrival placed him directly at the foot of their single queen bed. To his disappointment, the couple was not engaging in foreplay. Fear ran through him, and he worried he was too late or early.

Instead, he was met with the disturbing truth—Veronica could very well be right. Suddenly, he faced the conundrum of someone who cared. Beneath him, the girl was a tiny ball leaning against the stained cloth headboard with both knees to her chest. Her tear-streaked face was barely visible beneath her unnatural mane of hair.

John Smith was setting up a tripod at the foot of the bed. A bead of sweat rolled down Lance's nose, plopping onto the metal grate of the vent with a ping. The man paused, looking around.

"Did you hear that?" he asked the girl.

Between hiccups and sniffling, she struggled to provide a verbal answer and instead shook her head. A knock at the door made her jump.

"What the fuck is going on?" John Smith said, strolling to the door.

Lance exhaled, not realizing he'd been holding his breath.

John cracked the door open enough to expose half of his face. "Yeah?"

The girl on the bed was shaking profusely. Lance couldn't peel his gaze away from the strange scene. That was until he heard Veronica's bitchy tone fall flat on the room's vile carpet from the other side of the door.

"Hi, I'm the manager here at Happy's. I just wanted to make sure you had everything you needed for your stay with us."

"Yeah," the man replied with pure annoyance before trying to close the door in her face.

This didn't deter Veronica, who managed to jam her Dr. Marten between the door and its frame.

"Are you and your daughter only here for one night?" she asked pleasantly.

"Jesus, Veronica," Lance whispered to himself.

"What gives lady? We're trying to relax in here. We're tired," the man said.

"Oh, are you traveling? Have you guys ever been to Canada? It's just north of here. You should go... if you and your, uh, daughter, have passports," she said, blatantly ignoring his irritation.

"Yeah, I'll make a note of that," he replied, seething.

"Well, my name's Veronica. If you should need anything, call the front desk. I'll be here watching and waiting. Oh, and I know we're in a sketchy part of town, so I just wanted to assure you that we have an advanced security system equipped with camera surveillance all over the property." She started withdrawing her foot from the door. "Given how bad crime is…you know, with the border and all. Lots of human trafficking in these parts from what I hear."

The man tensed, reaching in the back of his waistband for what Lance could tell was a concealed gun. He silently willed Veronica to shut the hell up and leave before she got herself killed meddling in other people's business. He couldn't help but think that he had told her so, and this was her own fault for being nosey.

"Great. Listen, we don't want to be disturbed anymore. Can you pass that on to housekeeping, too?"

"Of course. Just a reminder that checkout is at eleven AM. You and your wife have a great stay." She removed her foot from the door jamb as she dropped the sneaky remark, trying to trip him up.

He closed the door in her face and turned back to the girl who was visibly shaking on the stained duvet.

"Christ, I think she knows something somehow," John said more to himself than to the girl. "Eh, I'll deal with her later if I have to." He waved his hand dismissively at his thought.

John turned to the frightened ball of flesh huddled against the headboard. "This is your fault, you stupid bitch. You acted like a fuckin' nut job when we checked in and tipped them off." Angrily, he raced toward her and punched her jaw with a closed fist.

Lance winced at the crack her bone made. She whimpered, withdrawing even more inward. He was appalled at the senseless act of violence. Clearly, she was terrified of the man, so what more did he have to gain by hurting her?

"If Don hadn't paid for you already, I'd have killed you by now. Your age and body are the only things keeping you from being a pile of human trash in a shallow grave. You got that?"

The girl nodded with a quivering lower lip. Pinching her chin between his thumb and index finger, he raised her head to meet his scornful glare. Momentarily, her eyes matched those of her abuser before their familiar flightiness ensued.

Without warning, John drew his hand back and slapped her. "You look at me when I'm talking to you!" he shouted.

Lance audibly gasped from the vent. John stopped his tirade of terror and stared around the room with acute curiosity. Lance covered his mouth with his sweaty palm. He felt the ongoing perspiration trickle through his eyebrows and blinked rapidly to rid himself of it. He was a self-admitted pervert, yes, but watching the abuse on a meek and helpless woman was a whole other ballgame.

"I swear, if that fuckin' nosey bitch is spying on us, I'm going to blow her brains out and then yours," John said cold-heartedly, lifting his gun out of his waistband and aiming it at the girl's head. Her face wrinkled in despair, and a sob escaped her.

As much as Lance wanted to, he couldn't bear to look away. It took him back to watching crime shows with Patty in their free time. He knew he should call the police but refused to move back down the vent. Aside from that, he understood the man in the suit did not make empty threats. One sudden move, and he risked Veronica's life as well as the young girl's.

An idea bloomed, and Lance silently whipped out his notebook from the deep pocket of his khakis. He jotted down descriptions of the two below him. Although he hated to admit it, Veronica was right about this one. Not only was her intuition spot on, but she also exemplified unrivaled bravery for knocking on the door of a man she was suspicious of, especially with a girl just a few years younger than she was.

John Smith attached a professional-grade camera to the tripod, tweaking the height and angle as he rambled on to her. "Now, are you going to do anything stupid if I go take a shit? Because if so, it's better to let me know now so I can tie you up. Otherwise, when I catch you, you'll wish you were dead. Understand?"

She nodded rapidly, hugging her bruised knees.

With that, the man abandoned her, making his way to the small bathroom. At first, Lance couldn't believe he trusted his captive, but to his surprise, the girl didn't budge. Her unknown previous traumas seemed to paralyze her with fear. Aside from that, she had to be half of his weight and severely malnourished. She would be far too weak to overcome him even in full health.

Not without a weapon.

Lance's heart stopped as an idea sprang to life. Serpent-like, he slid his arm down his body with a wiggle in the claustrophobic space and fished for his screwdriver. The handy tool was used to remove the screws from his main vent in his office. He always had the diligence to be cautious about making sure everything was in its proper place, with paranoia about one day being raided by the police.

With all his strength, he bent and twisted the chintzy pocket-sized tool he'd acquired at the town's dollar store. To his surprise, the handle separated with ease. The flathead tapered to a thicker, narrowed cylinder.

The odor of his own body suffocated him in the compact area, but he shimmied his arms above him, overcoming his own stench, which had the potency of an onion. He quickly scribbled a note to the girl on a fresh page in the notebook.

"Psst."

The noise was almost inaudible but enough to grab the girl's attention. Then he slid the note through the vent and watched it flutter to the floor. Her swollen eyes transformed from puffy slits to half dollars. She tilted her head toward the ceiling and stared at the metallic square.

Timidly, she scooted off the edge of the bed in silence and crawled on the filthy carpet to where the note from her heavens had landed. With cautious curiosity, she picked it up and read it.

Use this. Kill him. His inky scribbles loosely hung on the parchment. Her thick eyebrows knit together in confusion.

A rustling from the toilet paper holder echoed through the connecting vent. Lance was running out of time to get the weapon to the girl. Carefully, he slid the narrow part of the flathead through the slits of the vent. As the end of the metal thickened slightly, it came to a halt, jammed between the vent's slats. He worked as quietly as possible to rotate the metal back and forth to widen the opening. To his relief, it worked just enough to prevent the scraping of colliding metal. The detached head of the screwdriver dropped to the ground with a thud off the carpet.

Hastily, she crawled to the landing spot, never moving her stare from the vent. Lance was sure she couldn't see him from his perch, but he matched her large brown eyes filled with gratitude. He could tell by her expression that she was aware the mysterious metal piece had given her a second chance at surviving.

The toilet flushing made them both jump, snapping them

out of their human connection. She wadded the paper and tossed it under the bed before scurrying to the mattress. Lance smiled when she tucked the weapon into the pillowcase just as the door to the bathroom swung open.

Atta girl! He thought to himself.

"Ahhhh, that's better." John rubbed his stomach with relief beneath his now untucked shirt. "Now, where were we?"

The camera's screen sprung to life with the jab of his finger on a button. His other hand dangled at his side, casually holding the gun. The heavy metal thudded against the veneer as he dropped it on the table next to the door and unbuttoned his shirt.

"Now, here's how we're going to do this. You are going to wipe your eyes and stop crying. The people I sell this shit to want you to look happy—like you want this."

Scumbag, Lance thought, twisting his upper lip into a grimace.

The girl used her palms to wipe her eyes, rubbing her lashes free of the welled-up droplets. John continued his instructions. "Now, I want you to slowly take off your dress while looking at the camera. After that, I'm going to come into the shot and fuck you like you've never been fucked before."

With that, she stifled a sob before a new flood of tears cascaded down her reddened cheeks. "Please, no," she whimpered.

Impatiently, John picked the gun back up from the table and stared at her, waiting for her to protest again. She cupped her hand over her mouth until she was under control. Using the bottom fabric of her dress, she wiped the ongoing trail of snot dribbling from her nose and collected herself.

A red light popped on as he pressed record. Lance felt

himself biting his lip hard enough to draw blood. He clenched his notebook, leaving it damp in his palms.

The girl reluctantly did as she was instructed and stared directly into the camera as she began to strip. She grabbed the hem of her skirt, stained with mucus, and lifted it to expose her upper legs. Lance cringed at the sight of the bruising that was mirrored on her inner thighs. Her limbs looked like they could snap in half with the slightest pressure. Hesitating, she paused uncomfortably.

"C'mon. Keep going," John's irritated voice boomed.

Her panties were decorated with several splotches of blood. Lance had never seen the aftermath of a girl's period before but guessed the scarlet staining the length of the polyester was from something far more sinister. Her trembling hands moved upward, revealing a sunken lower belly adorned with bloody slashes and cuts. Some looked fresh, dawning congealed blood. Others oozed yellow pus from caked-on hardened skin bursting at her slight movements.

Flinching as the scabs brushed the thin fabric, she raised the dress the rest of the way over her head. A rigid ribcage came into view, matching her gaunt facial features. Her collarbones were sharpened blades hiding under a thin sheet of flesh. Nonexistent breasts heaved with the rising and falling of her chest. Scratches cloaked her pert nipples from their resting spots on her soft mounds.

"Good. Good," The shirtless man strode toward her, carrying himself like a predator stalking his prey. "Now, let's get this party started."

Lance watched, hypnotized, as John undid his belt buckle. He slid the leather effortlessly through the loops with a snap, folding it tight in his clutches. The girl flinched involuntarily and awaited the inevitable.

Lance's thoughts blazed, warning him to look away before

he saw something that would be permanently stamped on his mind. Yet, his voyeuristic tendencies made the task impossible. He had to know if she would be okay, regardless of what he was about to witness.

He watched as John fought to pull down his expensive dress pants and boxers. His bulging erection snapped against his happy trail upon release. He stepped out of them and climbed onto the filthy mattress, wearing only his socks.

Even as the situation unfolded before him, Lance was repulsed by John leaving his socks on. Something about the image was intensely disturbing to him. Truth be told, he silently judged everyone he watched who neglected to take them off before sex and sometimes marked it down in his notes.

The girl scooted back against the headboard as if she could distance herself enough to delay the inevitable. He closed the gap in seconds.

"C'mon, baby girl. Let's have some fun." He reached her fried hair with a sweet caress but got his ruby pinky ring stuck. His tone changed from charming to aggressive, as if it were her fault. "God dammit."

He yanked it away from her scalp, and she cried out in pain. A plethora of strands still stuck in the ring, now detached from her head. He plucked them out and examined his jewel while she sobbed, holding the sore patch where her hair had been.

He positioned himself in between her thighs, aligning her tense body with his. "There we go. Show Daddy how good you can be."

Without warning, John crammed his engorged cock inside her hard, causing her to yelp out in pain. Lance realized he'd been clenching his teeth the entire time and worked to relax his jaw. He could tell John enjoyed her suffering while she lay there helplessly. His moans quickly grew louder.

"Fuck, you're still so tight." John groaned. "Even after that last video." He pumped harder and faster as she squealed and gripped the duvet for relief. "Remember that one, little girl? Being fucked by all Daddy's friends at once." His eyes squeezed shut, and he tilted his head back.

Lance had a perfect birdseye view from directly above the foot of the bed. He studied the man's concentrated face. Then he shifted to the girl, who startled him with her intense gaze. She locked eyes with the vent as she reached her right arm above her. His heartbeat pounded in his ears as her limb disappeared into the pillowcase.

"Ah, fuck. I'm gonna come." He snarled with pure euphoria.

The silver of the flathead glinted in her tiny grasp. John's eyes opened wide as he started shuddering, gyrating into her with choppy motions. She jolted up and jammed the screwdriver into his neck in one swift movement. As the object dug in, piercing the skin, she twisted before yanking it back out to stab him once more. Blood squirted out, raining onto the corded telephone on the nightstand.

He fell to his side on the bed, cupping his throat in panicked shock. His mouth moved like a fish gasping for air, and his eyes were wide. A stream of crimson flowed onto the duvet. Lance watched in awe as the girl hopped off of the bed and bolted for the gun. She snatched it from its resting place on the table across the room and aimed at the bastard.

Her trembling hands steadied slightly as she took a deep breath and focused on her helpless target. John's body had begun to tremor in shock, and he reached toward her as if to signal for her to wait. She squeezed the trigger without a second thought.

Lance's ears ached from the overwhelming sound the moment the bullet was expelled. A ringing faded in and out of his ear drums. The girl stood in shock with shaking shoulders and dropped the gun. She looked up at the vent through tearful eyes and mouthed, "Thank you," before dressing and running out of the room.

His phone vibrated from his pocket. He pulled it out to see an alarming message from Veronica: *Gunshots. I think from 12. Calling 911.*

Lance smiled to himself and started the trek of shuffling backward through the ventilation system. That girl needed a raise.

THE GETAWAY

R.J. DALY

"SHUT THAT FUCKIN' kid up, for Christ's sake!" Garrett growled.

"Please… Do what you want to me. Just leave my wife and granddaughter alone!"

"I'm calling the fuckin' shots, Grandad!" Garrett spat, before slamming the butt of his pistol into the old man's cheek.

"Yeah! He's calling the fuckin' shots!" Margo parroted,

pushing the phone into the bloodied face of the slumped senior. "What are we gonna do with her!?" Margo asked excitedly as she spun around, the image of a white-haired woman on the phone's screen.

"Oh, I'm gonna *do* somethin' alright!" Garrett said in a hushed, sinister tone as he undid his zipper and freed his dick. It was already stiff from the violence he'd just dished out. He quickly grabbed the grandma and pushed her rickety frame onto the dining table.

"Please... Don't!" The old lady begged.

Garrett sniggered as he swatted away the elderly woman's feeble attempts at retaining her modesty and tore open her nightgown.

He stared at her sagging breasts and the bone-white pubic hair covering her mound. "Well, Gramps, I'll bet you've had your fun over the years with that, but I think I'm gonna cut me a new tight one. I'm not too psyched about wadin' through all that fuzz!"

The old woman's eyes doubled at the sight of the blade. They widened even further, and she opened her mouth to scream before the tip of the knife separated her wrinkly skin and penetrated the fatty flesh beneath. Her groans of anguish shot up an octave as Garrett slipped himself inside the gash and thrust his hips forward.

As he found his rhythm, the young child picked up on her Grandmother's distress and joined her wails of despair.

"I'm not going to ask you again! Shut that fuckin' thing up, Margo!"

Margo lowered the phone, nodded, and headed for the crib.

The commotion caused the old man to stir from the seat where he was slumped and turn towards the screaming infant.

Margo reached inside the cradle and grabbed the squirming baby with her free hand. Her face was red and blotchy from crying. The redness doubled in colour as Margo held the screeching child upside down—but only momentarily. She released her grasp and let the baby girl fall headfirst towards the floor, her little arms and legs rotating wildly before she hit the deck.

Upon impact, the room went silent—all eyes on the lifeless form. Even Garrett stopped and watched.

Then, the crying started up again.

The pitch and intensity were becoming unbearable to someone as strung out as Margo.

With a shrug, she raised her foot and fiercely drove it down. The child's soft, developing shell crumpled beneath the sole of her boot, and a rain of liquified biology evacuated the girl's orifices in all directions, painting the walls and furniture in ghastly streaks.

Garrett smirked and resumed pumping at the old woman.

"You…You, Monsters!" The old man roared. He made the sign of the cross before trying to pull himself up out of the chair.

"Now, that's an accurate description!" Garrett cackled and raised the gun. Before the elderly gent got to standing, the weapon roared to life. The bullet struck the same place Garrett had pistol-whipped him earlier. The impact of the round caved in his weathered features, and his body promptly returned to a slumped position in the chair.

"Oh, boooy! I'm just about done here, Granny! Do you wanna wave at the camera before I send you off to be with your loved ones!?"

The old lady didn't reply. Tears leaked from her closed lids as she clutched a gold crucifix hanging from her neck. Her lips moved, but she made no sound.

"I'll have that!" Garrett's grubby fingers reached down and ripped the religious jewellery from her grip.

As it left her hand, she opened her eyes, turned towards him, and spat in his face.

"Fuck yeah! Now, that's what I call spunk!" Garrett shouted. He shot his load, then shot two rounds into the old lady's face at point-blank range as her saliva dribbled down his. "What a fuckin' hoot!"

Margo stood and watched as he withdrew from the wound in the woman's side, his body peppered with sweat. Still hard, he wagged her closer. When she was on the opposite side of the table, he looked directly into the phone's camera and tapped it twice with the gun barrel. "That's all for tonight's wild adventures, folks. But I'm sure we'll catch up again *real* soon!"

———

"This will do us good, Cassandra. More importantly, it'll do *you* good after everything you've been through."

Cassandra hesitated, contemplating her husband's words. She'd barely left the house since the accident, which was close to a year ago. Although she had the time to heal physically, the scars of recovering mentally ran much deeper. She turned towards Michael and said, "Maybe you're right. It might be nice to go someplace outside of these four walls."

"It will! Trust me. A getaway like this is just what you need," he said, smiling enthusiastically. "I took a run out there last week and checked it out. This place is perfect. The cabins look comfortable, and it's only about two hours north of here. So, should I call them back and make a reservation?"

"Erm…" Cassandra hesitated, then said, "Yeah, that would be nice."

"Great, I'll do it now." Michael smiled, pulled the phone from his pocket, and headed for the door.

"Michael?"

He stopped and looked back over his shoulder. "Yeah."

"Thank you."

"You're welcome," he replied, then returned his attention to making the booking. Michael selected the number, and with the phone held to his ear, he left the bedroom and walked out into the hallway.

The last year had been hard on them both, particularly Cassandra. The shock of the accident. The subsequent miscarriage. The exhausting rounds of treatments and the harsh finality of the end result. Not to mention the endless explanations and excuses they had to invent about the scars littering Cassandra's body.

"Hello, I called you earlier this week about booking a cabin… Yes, that's right. Is it still available? … It is? … Excellent… Yes, that's my name… No. That will be fine… Perfect. Thank you."

When Michael returned to the bedroom, Cassandra was still perched in the same spot at the foot of the bed. He sat down and gently put his arms around her. With her head resting against his chest, he tenderly stroked back her hair, tucking it behind her ear. Leaning forward, he kissed her brow and held her close.

Today was a major advancement—one that Michael had been waiting patiently for. She didn't speak, nor did he; their silence was comfortable. Cassandra's body relaxed in his embrace. From the outside looking in, it might not have looked like much, but for Michael, this was progress.

———

The following day, Michael awoke to his wife humming as she went about packing a case. He folded his arms behind his head and watched. The glow of the aura she once possessed had partially returned. He could see it in her, hear it in her. As he looked on smiling, she eventually stopped—sensing his gaze.

"How long have you been awake?"

"Long enough," Michael replied, a smug grin on his face.

"I know that look! It's your '*told you so*' look!"

"I'm just happy to see you happy!" He sprung from the bed and wrapped his arms around Cassandra. He felt a rigidness constrict through her body and relaxed his embrace.

"Let me finish up here. I've packed for the both of us," she said. An uneasy smile crossed her face when she looked up as Michael's morning wood brushed her thigh.

"Sure. Why didn't you wake me? I could've gotten the cases for you."

"I'm not a total invalid, Mike. This one was already in the closet from my last stay at the…" Cassandra stopped midsentence and forcefully poked a hoody into the remaining space using the stump of her left arm.

"I'm sorry."

"Don't be! There's no need." She zipped the luggage and upended it so the wheels sat on the carpet. "Listen, you grab a shower, and I'll load up the car. Let's get out of here before I change my mind. Okay?"

"We need this, Cassandra. We need to get back out in the world and start living our lives again. Just like we used to. Being cooped up in here hasn't done either of us any good. What we've been doing isn't natural for us."

"I know. Let's just take things slowly. Okay?"

"Whatever you need."

She smiled and said, "What I need is for you to shower so

we can get out of here! We can stop for breakfast and pick up some supplies on the way. I haven't had a drink in, I don't know how long!"

"Now you're talking!"

"I'll take this down while I'm waiting."

Michael paused and looked at the case.

"Go shower!"

"Alright. Alright," he said and headed for the bathroom. When he turned around, she was already hauling the luggage out of the bedroom with her good arm.

———

Standing in line to pay, Michael looked back at his wife as she sat in the booth and sipped her coffee. The plate in front of her was empty, a good sign her appetite had returned. Her eyes were on the many vehicles entering and exiting the busy lot of the roadside diner they'd chosen for breakfast. As she watched the bustling traffic, gentle sunlight spilt through the window, illuminating her skin with a healthy glow.

"That'll be twenty-six dollars, please. Was everything alright for you today?"

The cashier's question broke Michael's stare. "Eh, yeah, thanks. It was great. Here's thirty, keep the change."

"Thank you. Have a nice day."

"Thanks, you too," Michael said and smiled politely, tucking his wallet into the back pocket of his jeans. As he made his way towards Cassandra, he noticed a young couple sniggering amongst themselves several booths up from where she was seated. Their attention was trained on a smartphone the man held at arm's length in front of them. They laughed loudly and pointed at the screen.

"You ready to hit the road?" Michael asked.

His wife was already standing when Michael directed his attention away from the back of the blonde woman's head.

"Sure, let's get going."

―――――

Outside, Michael checked the map on his phone. "There's a place to refuel and pick up some supplies a little further up the road."

He opened the car door, and Cassandra got in. After closing it, he glanced back towards the diner. The morning rush was ending, and the seats lining the windows were now empty, including the booth where the young couple had sat. As he scanned the lot full of vacating patrons, he caught sight of them as they walked across the lot towards a black SUV.

"Are you going to stand there all day?" Cassandra asked through the crack she'd opened in the car's window.

"Yeah, sorry," Michael replied absentmindedly and made his way around the front of the vehicle. Keeping his eyes trained on the SUV, he tugged open the door and climbed into the car as the young couple pulled out onto the road.

"What's the matter?" Cassandra asked.

"Oh, it's nothing," Michael replied and started the engine. He looked at his wife and gently squeezed her thigh before pulling out of the parking lot. "I'm just looking forward to our trip!

―――――

The further they drove, the more Cassandra fiddled with the radio, searching for a station that wasn't filled with endless news bulletins or shitty country music. Eventually, she gave up, turned it off, and stared at dense woodland that sprawled for as far the eye could see in every direction. "It sure is desolate out here."

"Not that desolate. Look!" Michael said and pointed. "There's the gas station up ahead." He looked down at the fuel gauge. The tank was half-full, but he decided it would be a good opportunity to top it off. He activated the turn signal and pulled in, stopping by the pumps. He rolled down the window, half expecting to see an attendant. But even this far out in the sticks, technology reigned supreme, and refuelling was self-service. "I'll fill up. Why don't you go grab some food and drinks."

"Sure," Cassandra replied.

They both exited the car at the same time.

Michael stretched before sliding his bank card into the slot on the machine and watched his wife walk towards the store. He opened the fuel cap and then pulled the pump free. With the nozzle inserted, he squeezed the handle, and the digital numerical readout sprang to life, catching his attention. As the numbers clocked up, a logging truck barrelled down the road at speed. Its wheels kicked up a plume of dust in its wake. *Probably trying to beat the rain forecast for later*, Michael thought and looked at the darkening sky. When he turned back around, the pump clicked off, indicating the tank was full. He pulled out the nozzle, rehoused it, and retrieved his card, opting not to bother with a receipt.

After clicking the fuel cap into place, he closed the flap and turned to see Cassandra exiting the store. Michael wiped his palms against the seat of his jeans. "We're only staying for a couple of nights, you know?"

"Never mind your teasing, and come help me!"

"Sure. Sorry," Michael replied and briskly walked over to her, relieving her of the heavy load.

"Thanks. The cashier said the place we're staying is just another thirty or forty minutes up ahead."

"That's good to hear," he said, placing the bags in the trunk. Now jump in, and let's get going. I want to get there before the weather breaks. I don't fancy driving around these parts in the middle of a downpour."

Before pulling out of the service station, he clocked a black SUV parked at the side of the store. Michael glanced towards Cassandra, who was busy checking the receipt for the snacks and alcohol she'd purchased, then back towards the SUV, then towards the store. He spotted the greasy, blonde hair of the young woman moseying around inside, her male acquaintance a short distance behind her. Michael started the car as he continued watching. "What's with those two?"

"Hmm?" Cassandra asked. She looked up and followed Michael's stare towards the service station. "Oh, them! They were in there goofing around on their phone."

The cabin was at the end of a road winding up the hillside. On the way up, Michael didn't notice any cars outside the other properties. Heavy raindrops began pelting against the windshield as he pulled up outside their accommodation. "Just in time! You go open up, and I'll grab our stuff from the trunk."

"Open up how?" Cassandra asked, a confused look on her face. "We don't have a key!"

"The key is in the little black box by the door. The code is 1911."

Cassandra shoved open the car door. Once outside, and in the rain, she raced towards the cabin's porch. After bounding up a couple of steps, she pushed in the four-digit code, and the flap on the black box opened, revealing a key inside. She plucked it out, inserted it into the lock, and pushed open the door.

The sound of the trunk closing caused her to turn. She laughed as Michael sprang towards her through the downpour, his arms full. Once he'd closed the distance, she stood aside and let him enter first.

Michael stumbled into the cabin's main room and tossed the cases and bags onto the couch.

"What in the hell are all those?" Cassandra asked.

"Just the essentials we need for a trip like this," Michael said, smiling.

"What do you mean?"

"You know I always like to be prepared. We're gonna have some fun. Cut loose like we haven't done in a long while."

"Really!" Cassandra exclaimed—a quiver of excitement in her voice.

"Really. Now, why don't you start a fire? I'm just going to grab the last of our stuff. It doesn't sound like it's going to let up, so I may as well get it over with."

"Sure. But don't be too long. I'm starving!"

————

"Stop the car!"

Garrett looked towards his girlfriend, who was hunched over in the passenger seat. "What'd you mean stop the car! We only left the fuckin' gas station half an hour ago."

"I don't feel so good."

"For fucks sake, Margo! This weather is already gonna slow us down—hang on!" Garrett scanned the road through the downpour, looking for somewhere suitable to pull over. When he spotted a lay-by, he pulled hard to the right and screeched to a halt. "What the hell is wrong with you anyway?" When Garrett looked at his girlfriend, it became apparent what she needed. He reached for his phone and went live on the platform they'd been active on all week. "Hey, everybody! Garrett here with a pasty-lookin' Margo! Guess who the fuck's dope sick again? That's right—this junk-hungry cunt!" Garrett pointed the phone towards Margo as she opened the car door and puked. "That's it! Classy as ever, baby!"

"Fu—fuck you!" Margo retorted and wiped away the strings of saliva clinging to her chin. "I need a fix! And get that fuckin' phone out of my face!" She yelled, slamming the door shut.

"Not here, you don't. No way I'm cookin' you a fix on the side of the fuckin' road."

"Fuck you!"

"I love you too. Here!" Garrett extended his hand. "This is the best I can offer."

He zoomed in as Margo leaned over and snorted the small mound of powder from the back of his grimy hand. "Feelin' better?" He continued to watch as she slumped back in the seat and pinched her nose, sniffing loudly. And just like she's fixed! Well, for now anyway. Over and out, folks!" Garrett flipped the camera and pointed at the screen before ending the stream.

"Why did you do that?" Margo asked softly.

"Why the hell not! They see us at our *highest*. Might as well see us at our *lowest*!" Garrett stopped and thought about what he'd just said. The profound statement struck something inside of him, although after a couple of seconds, he wasn't sure just what. "Well, it's time we got on the road again. I don't like sitting stationary for too long."

"We've been on the road for days!" Margo protested. "Can't we just take it easy for once?"

Garrett looked towards his girlfriend. Even in her jittery, whiny state, the girl had a point. Despite her pleas, he remembered exactly what they were running from. He reached for the key in the ignition.

Click.

"What the fuck!"

Click.

"What's wrong?"

This piece of crap won't start! Shit!" Garrett slammed the heel of his hand into the dash in frustration.

"What are we goin' to do now!?" Margo's inky pupils were large with panic in the overhead light.

"Shit! I don't fuckin' know…" Garrett paused, then wiped the condensation on the windshield with the sleeve of his jacket. "There!" He pointed through the smeared glass.

"Where?"

"Up there on the hill, the lights. Are you blind!?"

Margo ducked down a touch and peered through the foggy glass. "Oh, I see it!"

"This is probably as good as we're gonna get out here. Just grab what you need, and let's head on up there. Looks like you're gettin' a night off the road after all!"

Margo turned towards Garrett and grinned as he pulled the handgun from the waistband of his jeans. After he opened the door, she slipped on her flip-flops and climbed out of the car.

———

From high on the hillside, Michael looked down at the serpentine road that wound through the trees below. It was free from traffic. Any vehicle driving in the unsettled weather would have its lights on, making it easy to spot.

He pulled up the zipper on his jacket and stepped into the downpour. The sodden foliage squelched beneath his boots as he covered the short distance to the car. A sharp gust of wind peppered his back with raindrops. He quickened his pace towards their vehicle and popped open the trunk. Inside was the remaining item of luggage he'd packed. He'd purposefully left the metallic case till last. He reached for the handle, pulled it out, and slammed the trunk shut. When Michael turned around, he paused, the inclement deluge stinging his face. Through narrowed eyes, he surveyed the surrounding terrain.

It was deserted. The only sound was that of the weather.

After a couple of minutes, he gave up. A combination of the fading light and rain had won as cold droplets of water trickled down the back of his neck.

Michael climbed the steps to the cabin and slid the key into the latch. He'd no sooner entered and closed the door when a set of headlights stopped at the bottom of the hill.

———

Cassandra turned around as Michael stepped inside and shut the door behind him. He was soaked, his boots muddy.

"What took you so long?"

The roaring, amber glow of the fire cast Cassandra as a shape. The light of the leaping flames arched and curled around behind her. Michael tossed the keys onto the dresser. They clattered noisily against the timber surface before the keyring eventually came to rest. "Nothing. I just brought in the last of the luggage. What's all this?" He set the case close to the wall and nodded towards the table. Its surface was covered with an array of plates.

"Oh, just a bit of this and that and some of the treats *you* decided to bring! Now, get out of those wet clothes and wash up, then join me."

Michael's eyes darted from his wife to the spread she'd laid out and back again. "Give me five minutes. Tops!"

"Keep movin' Margo! And quit whinin'. You're giving me a fuckin' headache!"

"Sorry. This hill is a *bitch*!"

"I know it is, and this rain ain't helpin'. But we're nearly there. Then we can get inside and have some fun, just like we always do!" Garrett said.

"You sure we don't need to scope the place out a little first? See who we're dealin' with?"

"Quit fussin'! I told you already, whoever's rented a place like this is probably just some middle-aged couple from the city, and certainly nothing to worry about. Come on! We've taken on much more than the likes of that over the past couple of months, haven't we?"

"Sure have," Margo said and laughed.

"That's my girl. Just a little farther. Look, I can see their car now. When we get closer, we'll stop and catch our breath. Then we'll mosey on up to the front door and announce our arrival!"

"If you say so."

"I do!" Garrett scowled at Margo, losing patience with her negative attitude. "Listen, this is all we've got out here, and I need you onboard. Understood!?"

Margo said nothing and nodded.

"Good. Now, our car has broken down, and we need some assistance. I'll do the talking. You just stand there and shiver like you're doin' now. It'll be a cinch. Trust me. After all, we're kind of tellin' the truth anyway."

Margo mustered a smile and tucked the wet strands of hair that plastered her gaunt face behind her ears. Despite her boyfriend's optimism, something nagged at her guts. This time, it wasn't a lack of drugs. This feeling was different. She hadn't felt it in years—a sense of unease.

———

When they reached the top of the hill, they paused at the edge of the treeline and watched. After a couple of minutes, Garrett started towards the cabin and motioned for Margo to follow with a wag of the pistol.

Both of them closed the distance quickly. The weather masked the sounds of their feet as they dashed across the wet ground towards the property's entrance.

With the gun held behind his back, Garrett raised his grubby hand and stalled when his knuckles were mere inches from the door. *Best to try the easy route first, knucklehead,* he thought to himself. His eyes darted towards Margo, who stood beside him as he lowered his hand towards the door's handle. He wrapped his fingers around the cold metal and pushed down.

Click.

The door was locked. Then he saw the metal box on the wall. *Shit!* Having dealt with similar properties before, Garrett knew the only way in from outside was with a key.

"Gonna have to do this the hard way," he muttered, raising his hand again. His fingers tightened around the grip of the pistol, and he clenched his jaw as he knocked three times in quick succession.

He glanced at Margo and elbowed her in the ribs. She flinched and rubbed where he'd hit her. "Don't look so fuckin' guilty. We ain't done nothin' yet! Straighten the fuck up, would you!?" Garrett hissed.

She nodded and, as usual, did what she was told.

———

"Time to dig in!" Michael said excitedly as he hurried towards the lounge. Cassandra had slipped into something more comfortable and was seated on the couch before the roaring fire, the spread laid out in front of her, untouched.

"This way! I waited for you before I started. Can you grab more wine from the counter on your way past?"

"You've drank a whole bottle already!?"

"No!" Cassandra laughed. "I just don't want to get up again once we're comfortable."

Michael grabbed another bottle by its neck and made his way towards his wife. He set it on the table and selected a slice of the meat. He lifted it to his mouth to take a bite and stalled.

"Quit teasing me! Hurry up and eat it!" The anticipation dripped from Cassandra's words.

"What was that?" Micheal asked, his head cocked to one side.

"What was what? It was probably just the wood crackling in the fire."

"I'm sure I heard something." His voice hushed.

"Stop messing around and…" Cassandra was interrupted by three loud raps at the cabin's door.

"Told you I heard something."

Cassandra said nothing. The intrusive sound shattered their intimacy. She looked towards Michael for guidance. His brow creased as he stared at the door. After a few seconds, he carefully placed the meat back onto the plate.

"I want you to get it, Cassandra."

"Me!?"

"Yes," Michael replied, his tone serious. "This might be the chance we've been waiting for!"

"I said I wanted to take things slowly!"

"I know you did, but things might move a little quicker than I anticipated. There's no need to worry. I'll be right here." Michael quickly went to the metallic case he'd brought in from the car. First, he extracted his handgun, and next, a small bag of white powder.

"What do you need that for?" Cassandra asked.

"The drugs or the gun?" Michael asked and smirked

"The drugs, of course!?"

"Keep your voice down!

"What exactly are you going to do?"

"When you open the door, you'll find out!" Michael said as he quickly refilled their two glasses before spiking the fresh bottle of red. He recapped the bottle and shook it gently. Content that the powder was sufficiently mixed, he set it down and unscrewed the lid. Moving towards the fire, he stashed his firearm between the cushions of the armchair.

Someone knocked again—harder this time.

Michael looked at Cassandra and motioned towards the door with a nod.

"Michael! I don't like this! It's all happening too quickly!"

"Listen, if they're genuine, there won't be a problem. If they're not…" He shrugged and winked. "It's not like you haven't done this before… And you're an excellent judge of character."

Before stowing himself behind the long drapes in the lounge, he kissed his wife.

Cassandra shook her head and muttered as she tightened the sash on her gown. Whatever it was, their impatience was growing, and her casual saunter ensured they'd wait just that little, aggravating bit longer.

———

Garrett raised his hand again and brought his calloused knuckles down on the timber. This time, the force and speed were a sign of his frustration. For a moment, he regretted his impatience—until the door opened.

He cracked a smile as he looked at the pretty face and the sliver of a petite female frame illuminated in the slight gap.

"Can I help you?"

"Eh… Yeah, sorry for troublin' you. My girlfriend and I had some trouble with our car," Garrett said, pointing over his shoulder towards the road below with his thumb. As he waited for a response, he shifted about from foot to foot, a boyish look of hope on his face. "Listen, I know it's late. But we couldn't get any signal on our phones, and we saw the lights and thought…"

"And what was it you thought?" the woman interrupted in a matter-of-fact tone.

"You know…" Garrett stopped mid-sentence, then roughly ploughed into the door with his shoulder. The speed and aggression of his actions caught the woman off guard and sent her tumbling backwards into the room—eventually coming to a stop on her ass.

With the gun raised, Garrett barged inside and towards the woman who was sprawled on the floor, Margo on his heels. They approached her cautiously as she began shuffling backwards on her elbows. "Don't try anything stupid!" Garrett said, sweeping the gun around the empty room. When he closed the gap, he leaned over and dragged the woman to her feet by her hair. Once upright, he pushed the barrel of the gun into her face. "You all alone?"

The woman didn't answer and stared at him with a sideways glance.

Garrett shook her roughly by the hair, "I asked you a question! Are you alone, bitch!?" His tone was gruff as he leaned into her face. When he yanked her head back, she moaned.

"Pull a little harder. She fucking loves it!"

Both intruders spun around to face the voice. They were met by a man sitting in the armchair closest to the fire, nursing a glass of wine.

"Motherfucker! Where in the hell did you come from!?"

"Oh, from about two hours south of here. How about you?"

Garrett sucked his teeth noisily, then said, "Looks like we got ourselves a wiseass, Margo!"

"Yep, and they don't tend to fare very well!" Margo replied.

"That's right," Garret said and sucked his teeth some more. "Particularly when they're a half-breed!"

Tightening his grip on the woman's hair, he asked, "How about you, honey? You got a smart mouth, too?"

The woman said nothing.

"Nah! I'll bet that mouth of yours is *real* sweet," he said, encircling her lips with the pistol. He stopped, mashed the barrel against her teeth, and looked at the man. "Any more of your smart remarks, and I'll blow this fuckin' bitch's head off!"

"Won't it be hard for you to enjoy her mouth if you do that?"

"What's that?" Margo interrupted when she spied the bottle.

"Just some wine and foo…"

"Wine!" Margo exclaimed, cutting the man off again. Always the addict, she hurried towards it like her life depended on it. She snatched the bottle from the edge of the coffee table and began gulping it down.

"Hey! Hold up, Margo!"

"Don't worry, we have plenty."

"That's not my concern, motherfucker!" Garrett grumbled, his gun now trained on the man. He forcefully shoved the woman towards her husband. After several stumbling steps, she regained her composure and came to a stop. With the gun pointed in the couple's general direction, he marched towards Margo and yanked the bottle from her grasp. He lifted it towards the light. It was half gone. After a sniff of the contents, he raised it to his mouth and took a tentative sip. He licked his lips several times, raised the bottle again, and slurped down a healthy dose of the claret fluid.

"You're quite the connoisseur, I see," Michael said, the corner of his mouth upturned. "Oh, I'm a connoisseur, alright." Garrett wiped his mouth with the back of his hand and looked towards the spread of meat on the table.

"Go ahead and help yourself."

After studying the selection, he stopped and looked towards the woman. "I'm thinkin' I might help myself to a piece of *that* instead! Me being a connoisseur and all," Garrett said wryly as he looked her up and down. It was only then he spotted the stump. "What happened?" He asked, motioning in the direction of her missing appendage with the weapon.

"A car wreck. It's pretty much all healed up now." The

fingers of her remaining hand moved to cover the pink scar tissue.

"No need to be ashamed or nothing. I'm gonna be *seein'* and *feelin'* every inch of you very soon. Now, lose the fuckin' robe!"

"Better do what he says!" Margo said in a childish voice. "Before he goes and loses his temper."

Michael nodded, and Cassandra moved to loosen the garment.

"That's it! Get it off!" Garrett shouted excitedly. He raised the bottle to his lips and polished it off. Empty, he slammed it down onto the table and grabbed a piece of the meat, stuffing it into his mouth. He chewed loudly as he watched the woman undress. "That's some damn fine jerky!"

"Yes, she pairs well with the wine."

Garrett shot the man a look and furrowed his brow.

"I don't feel so good!" Margo shouted, clutching her belly.

"Shut up, Margo! I'll fix you a fuckin' hit when I'm done over here," Garrett spat, his mouth full. "Come on, turn your ass around already!"

"She's chemically dependent!" the man exclaimed.

"Hey! Fuck you! We all have our demons, mister," Margo groaned as she started to double over.

"That we do! That we do!" The man replied. "Cassandra, why don't you spin around and give these fine folks an eyeful!"

Garrett watched bug-eyed when she turned to provide a full-frontal display. It wasn't what was there that shocked him. It was what was missing that rattled his reasoning. A nipple-less tit sat adjacent to a mass of misshapen scar tissue where her left breast should have been. Random sections and chunks had been carefully carved from her stomach and midriff. Most had sufficiently healed over, but some still looked tender.

"What the… What the fuck happened to her!? That didn't happen in no car wreck. Where are all those missin'… bits?"

The man laughed. "There's some of it on the table and some of it in your belly. Oh, and a little bit is stuck in your teeth, too," Michael said, pointing at the perplexed expression plastered across Garrett's face. "She really is something else, isn't she!?" A blend of pride and lust beamed in his eyes. He picked up a piece of the dried meat from one of the plates and held the strip against his wife's torso. Albeit it had shrunk a little, the piece fitted perfectly into the fleshy puzzle adorning her abdomen. "Get the idea?" The man asked before taking a bite.

Garrett's guts suddenly felt like a washing machine on a spin cycle. His head shook along with his hand. His face flushed with sweat as he tried to control his aim. But it was like a giant magnet in the floor was pulling on the gun. No matter how hard he resisted, the pull of the ground seemed to grow stronger.

"Garrett! Garrett! S—some… Some—thing—thing's not right h—here," Margo slurred and looked up from the incapacitating turmoil enveloping her. The swirling motion of her stomach no longer existed in that location alone. It had spread to each of her extremities like a fire. After knocking out the rigid support system her limbs once provided, she tumbled to the timber floor.

Garrett wavered on the spot. The pistol pulled him downwards as ropes of saliva spilled from the corner of his crooked, open mouth. He could feel the last strength of his legs being sucked away as if it were being vacuumed from his body. When his knees finally folded inwards—he hit the deck.

Looking up, through blurred vision, he tried watching as

his hosts looked down and laughed. Their smiles morphed into warped grimaces as his battle to stay conscious was lost.

———

Michael emptied the duo's pockets. Apart from a few crumpled twenty-dollar bills and additional rounds of ammo, all he found were some drugs, Margo's rig, and a smartphone. As he sat looking through the phone's contents, he sensed someone's eyes upon him. When he looked up, he saw that his captive was awake. "Nice videos! You've got quite the collection on here."

"Fuck you," Garrett slurred, his voice still groggy from the drugs. "How'd you get that open?"

"Such charming behaviour from a guest!" Michael said and held up Garrett's severed thumb.

Garrett couldn't see his bound hands, but the instant he saw his detached opposable digit, a surge of pain registered in his right hand instantly. "You dirty motherfucking monkey!"

"Listen, I'm gonna be straight with you."

"Oh yeah!" Garrett hissed.

"Yeah. There's something you should know about us. Cassandra and I..." Michael paused and raked the stubble on his chin with the nail of Garrett's grubby thumb, then sat it down without taking his eyes off the phone's screen. "Well, let's just say we're not like any of the other people you've encountered on the hellbent path of destruction you two have been carving out." Michael stopped and looked at Margo as she moaned on the floor, still out for the count. He stood before he continued, loosening the sash that held his robe closed. When it finally parted, it framed his broad, distorted physique, revealing a landscape of misshapen tissue where flesh had been dissected and removed. The scarification started at the centre of his chest and worked outwards like a 3D roadmap of a sprawling metropolis.

Garrett sucked back a shriek and began to buck wildly in the chair he was fastened to. "What the fuck is wrong with you people!?" He tried to recoil as Michael approached but couldn't. Each step the man took in his direction allowed for the tangled mesh of pink and brown tissue on his torso to become slightly clearer. The crisscross pattern of a blade was evident.

"I see you've regained your full faculties. That's good. You're going to need them. Now, as I was saying… Cassandra and I aren't your typical run-of-the-mill married couple. On the surface, yes. But beneath our front of normalcy, we're anything but!"

"Definitely not!" Margo chimed in as she tossed another log onto the fire.

"You see, Garrett, to put it plainly for you, we consume flesh. Human flesh."

Garrett whimpered and wriggled some more.

"Now, to do so meant collecting meat from those willing to donate, and you'd be surprised at how many people are into that. And from gutter scum like yourself? We always harvested forcefully." Michael paused and watched Garrett's throat bob up and down as his words sunk in. "That said, we haven't been actively hunting in the past several years because we decided to settle down and start a family. To try and ween ourselves off eating people... To try and live as 'normal' a life as possible… hence our scars. We haven't collected, harvested, or eaten any part of another human—except for each other—in over two years. And everything was going swimmingly until Cassandra's accident."

"Not only did I lose part of my arm…" Casandra paused,

composing herself before she continued. "We also lost our child. A child I carried for seven months... A child who would have changed everything for us..."

"A child who was taken by reckless people—people just like *you two*!" Michael roared. Seething with anger, he paced around the room and then abruptly stopped. "And now, here we are, in this cabin." Michael outstretched his arms before continuing. "I decided to book this trip as a way for us to enjoy a final foray of sampling each other before I introduced the idea of hunting again. And look *who* decided to barge into *our* fucking world! You and your strung-out whore, *Garrett*!" Michael doubled over in hysterics, slapping his thighs.

"Please, we didn't..."

Michael stopped laughing and straightened up, his face hard. "You didn't what!?"

Tears started coursing down Garrett's cheeks. "P —please."

"After all this—that's all you've fucking got!" He reached forward and grabbed a fistful of oily hair, twisting Garrett's neck to an unnatural angle. "You bust in here, all full of piss and vinegar, and now you're screeching worse than that toddler she stomped on! A big man when things are going your way, and you've got a gun, huh?" Michael laughed, relinquished his grip, and tossed Garrett's head back with enough force to cause whiplash. He stepped away and eyed the sorry mess before him, "Oh, I forgot! Do you still want to fuck my wife? She's right over there."

Cassandra smirked, took a sip of her wine, and opened her legs. "It's all yours, big boy! You man enough, though?"

Garrett gawked in disbelief at Cassandra's wet hole and shook his head frantically. The distorted, mangled entrance to her canal sent a shiver through him.

Michael stepped forward and placed his hand on Garrett's

shoulder. "Not too long ago, you were strutting around, willing to use two weapons—one made of metal and the other flesh. What's the matter, son? Lost your sexual dominance? I'd love me a nice slice of pussy right about now."

"Her! Take hers! It's still nice and neat," Garrett pleaded, looking at Margo sprawled out on the floor.

"Ahh, young love." Michael sneered. "I was wondering how long it'd take you to offer her up. I bet you've rented out her cunt more times than you can remember. Anything to save your sorry ass. Am I right?" Without waiting for a reply, he continued. "Leeches like you disgust me. Disgust us! And I wouldn't touch that skank even if she was the last piece of skirt on earth. Cassandra, come on over here. Let's wake up Sleeping Beauty. It's time she joined the party, don't you think!?"

"Absolutely!"

———

Garrett tried weighing his options. There weren't many, and with a mind racing at light speed, his thought process was muddled. But, as usual, he eventually arrived at the same conclusion he always did when caught in a sticky situation—self-preservation.

"This! This has to be some… of the worst I've seen!" Cassandra announced, her voice hitched in aggravation. Some may consider us depraved, but we're fulfilling a need! This is no different than those small-dicked trophy hunters—just killing for the fun of it. It's just… Wasteful!" Her grip tightened around the sadistic imagery playing on the phone's screen, and her jaw matched the pressure exuded by her hand.

"Well said. So, what do you propose we *do* about it?"

Garrett watched as stern expressions quickly settled upon his captor's faces. When their eyes locked on Margo, he instantly knew what video they'd just viewed. Knowing what they'd both just watched, he realised he was safe—for the moment, at least. He took a deep, shaky breath as the couple bypassed his sweat-laden, squirming body and focussed their attention on a non-responsive Margo, her body still passed out on the floor.

————

A flip-flop tumbled to the ground when Michael lifted Margo's left foot and wedged her ankle in the crook of his muscular arm. Once he'd locked her limb in place, he snaked his hand around the slender appendage. Happy with the position, he smiled at Garrett, then folded Margo's foot backwards.

The sickening snapping sound filled the room, quickly followed by Margo's screams as pieces of fractured bone jutted through her skin. Before the girl realised what was happening, Michael swiftly dropped the destroyed limb and focussed on the other leg—repeating the same vicious routine.

"Ah! There's nothing like that popping sound to get you all revved up!" he announced loudly after demolishing her other ankle.

Garrett stared, his face filled with confused despair, as he dry heaved at the destruction he'd just witnessed and heard.

The girl was now wailing like a banshee, and with her feet pointing in unnatural directions, Cassandra added to the crippling discomfort and kicked her legs apart. Just as she suspected, the track-marked skin of Margo's thighs kept on going to reveal her bare crotch. Her modesty was scarcely concealed beneath the short skirt she wore.

"You were right," Michael said as he peeked at her pussy beneath the hem of denim, then looked at Garrett. "It is nice and neat."

"Not for long!" Cassandra announced and reached for the empty bottle. Clenching her teeth, she took aim and roughly rammed it into the girl's well-tended slit.

Upon entry, Margo's screams instantly turned to guttural bellows as her body attempted to accommodate the foreign object; the sound she emitted was like that of a wounded animal. Cassandra looked down at the cylindrical base still protruding from the girl's bulging cunt. Crimson rivulets trickled across the wine-stained label, somehow making their way out from the snug gap where her tissue involuntarily hugged the glass. A ring of red quickly encircled the bottle's circumference.

With her hole now lubricated in a less-than-orthodox manner, Cassandra pushed the remainder of the exposed glass deeper inside using her foot. The last quarter-inch's resistance caused an ache in her calf as Margo writhed in agony against the savage insertion. Once the bottle was housed inside the stretched opening, Cassandra wasted little time raising her leg. With her foot cocked high, she stomped down ferociously on the girl's pelvis.

Beneath each frantic, frustrated stomp, she felt the cylindrical shape roll away from the force of her blows as bones broke and tissue gave way internally. The thought of the child she'd lost to the drunken degenerates who'd T-boned her car fed Cassandra's fury. The images from the recording she'd watched on the phone added further fuel to her fire.

She raised her leg again and gave it all she had.

The fourth shot finally shattered it.

The three that followed reduced the hunks of glass to even smaller fragments. Each blow caused the girl's stomach to flex wildly in protest against the savage barrage as garbled wheezing sounds rushed past her lips.

Finally content with the level of destruction, Cassandra took a step back and watched as a slurry of blood and shards replaced the rivulets. She crouched down for a better look, then turned towards Garrett. "Not so neat now, huh?"

Garrett didn't respond to the question. He just sat and stared, his mouth open—his breathing sharp and shallow. He continued watching the glass-ridden wetness pour from between Margo's legs as her body convulsed.

Cassandra turned away from the girl, marched towards the counter, and lifted a small container. "So, Michael, you want in on this one? Or are you going to sit and play with this shitbag's phone all evening?"

"I thought you'd never ask!"

"Here. I'm sure you can use your imagination!" Cassandra said as she handed over the small package.

Michael took it, then gave her Garrett's phone. Cassandra held the phone beside her as Michael reached behind him and pulled out two masks. "So, you wanna be the pig or the cow?"

"I'd rather be neither!"

"Well, we are in the countryside, and you'll have to choose one for when we go *live*! I've made my choice. I hope you don't mind." Michael slipped the pig mask over his head and grabbed a pair of scissors.

"Smile, Piggy!" Cassandra shouted.

With the porcine disguise in place, Michael spun around and snapped the blades of the scissors open and closed menacingly.

Garrett sobbed as he looked towards the pool of blood that was steadily spreading around Margo. Although, his tears weren't for her. They were a salty mix of fear, frustration, and embarrassment as Michael cut away his pants and under-wear. After the third tug, the bare skin of his ass connected with the seat to which he was zip-tied.

"W—what are you doin'?" Garrett asked, his voice trembling.

"I'm going to have a little fun! Not so sure about you, though. Now, say hi to your *fans*!"

Garrett couldn't muster the courage to look. He hung his head in shame and continued to sob.

Michael sniggered as he took hold of Garrett's shrivelled cock. "Remember how you wanted to instil fear with *this*?" he asked as he squeezed it. "Well, here we go!"

Despite the dread and disgust that boiled in the pit of his gut, Garrett started to harden in Michael's hand. Confusion fractured his mind at the fact that another man's touch aroused him, let alone a man of colour. He squeezed his eyes shut and shook his head, trying to will the erection away. His attempt failed miserably, and he bloomed fully after a few more strokes. Once his manhood stood to attention, he watched as Michael slid his hand to the bottom of his shaft, pulling his foreskin back and squeezing the base of his cock. The applied pressure opened his urinary duct.

Michael stared at the moist slit intently before plucking several pieces of pointed wood from the packet. He let the toothpicks linger at the centre of Garrett's helmet for a couple of seconds, stabbing down playfully a couple of times.

Growing bored, he casually pushed them into Garrett's urethra.

As soon as the miniature sticks entered his plumbing, Garrett began roaring and thrashing wildly. It felt like his dick was on fire. He clenched his jaw and twisted his head from side to side as the wood slid deeper inside of him. The next assault on his senses came when he felt the first tug. The man looked Garrett directly in the eye from behind the mask as he molested his member.

The breath hitched in Garrett's chest as a blob of blood gathered at the tip of his manhood, eventually dribbling down to the fist clamped around his cock, relentlessly sliding up and down its length.

"Having fun yet?"

Garrett squeezed his eyes shut and growled through gritted teeth as excruciating pain pulsed through his penis.

Then, there was a pause. He panted for breath, opened his eyes, and looked down to see the man admiring his handiwork.

When Garrett saw him lift the disguise and spit, then felt his firm grip return, it was all too much. He leaned to the side and emptied his guts.

———

Cassandra zoomed in as Michael increased the speed of his fist pumps. She could tell from the way Garrett was starting to twitch he was close to orgasm despite having just had several three-inch skewers shoved into his dick. His groans of pain had morphed into grunts as he pushed his ass up off the chair to meet the downward strokes.

"Ughhh!" The sound of satisfaction rolled from Garrett's throat as he threw his head back. The plastic restraints bit into the skin of his wrists and ankles as his body quivered. When he climaxed, no ordinary rope of cum shot from his cock.

Instead, his pink-tinged seed leaked lazily around the pointed wooden stems poking out just proud of his piss slit. His brief moment of ecstasy was soon replaced with agony as Michael pushed them back inside with his thumb and resumed pulling on his engorged member.

Cassandra continued recording and watched on the phone's screen as Garrett looked down at what was happening. The veins in his neck and temples bulged, and his face flushed red like he was about to explode before he unleashed a slew of expletives. The outburst caused strings of saliva to shoot from his mouth in the way that his prick should've shot its load.

Michael stopped and looked up. "What's wrong? You want me to stop?" His voice had an air of sarcastic sincerity.

"Please! T—the pressure! The fuckin' pressure inside…" Garrett trailed off. Laced with bullets of sweat, his head hung forward, snot bubbling from his nose and tears coursing down his cheeks.

A sickly mixture of semen and blood continued dribbling from his clogged penis as Michael scratched his head in thought. "Got it!" he said excitedly and pushed one of the sticks through the side of Garrett's throbbing pecker.

Then another…

And another…

And another.

Despite the desperate wails and empty pleas, Michael continued until the box was empty and Garrett's penis resembled a cactus. "Any better?"

There was no response. When Michael looked up, Garrett was unconscious.

Michael shrugged his broad shoulders and sunk back onto his hunkers, still staring at the prickly dick he'd created. "What now?" He asked, looking towards Cassandra.

Casandra ended the recording, sat the phone to one side, and looked at Margo's glass-filled gape.

The shock was wearing off. Rolling around, the girl clutched her belly and moaned continually. The hitched-up faded denim skirt she wore was now scarlet around her waist.

"I think I have an idea."

———

Garrett came round to the sound of breaking glass. The smashes rang out like they were somewhere in the distance, each becoming louder. His senses were sharpening, and eventually, his ears could distinguish the individual shards skittering across the floor. He realised he was lying on something soft, and whenever that something moved, pain bolted through his groin. At that moment, he remembered what had happened, and his eyes shot open.

He lifted his head and saw the woman walking backwards, away from him. Glasses tumbled from the armful she held against her chest and shattered against the floor, leaving a trail of translucent splinters in her wake. When Garrett looked down, the softness he felt beneath him was Margo. Along with the hellish discomfort that radiated from his groin and up through his stomach, he also felt a warm wetness.

Margo stirred to life beneath him, slapping her hand down into the razor-sharp shards as she tried to pull herself forward. The instant she inched ahead, the pain in his privates elevated to a new height. The wriggling momentum beneath felt like his cock was being cut to pieces—shredded.

Blind panic consumed Garrett, and he desperately tried to separate himself from Margo. But the more he bucked, and the more she pulled herself forward, the more excruciating the sensation became. The pain allowed for clarity in his mind, and Garrett looked up to see Margo's motivation standing on the opposite side of the kitchen.

Michael stood with a fully loaded syringe. The liquid inside was brown. The shiny hypodermic glinted like a beacon at its tip—calling to her. Garrett tried to pull away from her again, knowing she wouldn't stop until she got the drugs. Then it began to dawn on him why he couldn't and what the additional agony his genitals were being subjected to actually was. His face dropped, and he began to shake his head desperately and whimper. "No! NO!"

"Well, you were the one who didn't appreciate my hand-job! So, Cassandra thought it'd be nice for you two to be together one last time. Intimately, of course." Michael smiled down at Garrett's bewildered expression. "Now, we both know she won't stop wriggling over here until she gets this prize," he said, wiggling the drugs around enticingly. "And I'm sure you figured out that there's no way for you to dismount as we've taped you both together. She's going to be some fucking mess by the time she gets here! And so will you! The more she cuts herself, the more she'll slip and slide in the blood. And the more she moves around, the more the glass inside of her snatch will cut you to ribbons. This is going to please a lot of the sick fucks you've been streaming your shit to, Garrett. I bet you feel on top of the world! Talk about being the star of the fucking show!"

———

The sight of the drugs spurred Margo on despite the additional weight on her back. She clawed and slapped franti-cally at the floor, inching herself closer bit by bit towards the one thing that had always allowed her to escape the pain of everyday life—and now the pain that was burrowing into her insides needed to be numbed at any cost. She steadily pressed on even as she ripped her hands and forearms to ribbons. In her mind, the damage was considered collateral as she battled onward. Even the barrage of desperate bites Garrett delivered to her neck and the back of her head did little to deter her.

Like a zombie, Margo kept moving forward, focussed on the one thing that mattered most to her: heroine.

———

"Stop! For fucks sake—stop, Margo!" Garrett roared. With his hands bound, he resorted to plunging his teeth into the top of her scalp and shaking his head like a rabid dog. The savage assault did nothing to quell her advances. Realising this, he pulled away with a mouthful of her greasy mane and a missing incisor. "You stupid bitch! It's cuttin' my fuckin' dick off!" Garrett bellowed. Strands of Margo's hair fluttered from his mouth, and blood trickled from his chin, a slight whistle in his protest due to the newly formed gap in his enamel. He hung his head in defeat as Margo somehow managed to close the distance on her prize.

"And that, folks, is what desperation looks like, even when there's a devil on your back!" Micheal's eyes burned with contempt for the animal that rode across the sea of glass on the girl. "Trust me when I say addiction is a power that can supersede everything else. Very sad indeed. I think it's time I put you out of your misery."

Once she reached his feet, Margo looked up longingly. Like a dog looking for a treat, her tongue hung out of her mouth.

Michael leant down and plunged the hypodermic into the bulging blue vein on her forehead.

It didn't take long for the opioids to flood her ravaged

frame, and her head hit the deck with a slap, after which a series of violent tremors erupted throughout her body. White foam poured from between her lips in her final moments.

Garrett began to howl as Margo's expiring body spasmed beneath him. The glass inside the cavity into which he was inserted tore and shredded what was left of him even further. "You good for nothin' junkie cunt!" Garrett howled.

"Is your little outburst finished?" Michael asked in a calm voice as he knelt beside the man.

Defeated, Garrett raised his head and looked at him.

Michael patted him on the shoulder reassuringly, then said, "You know what, Garrett?

"W—what?"

"Your pain is only about to begin!"

Michael stood and walked away from the snivelling excuse of a human being who lay slumped on the dead body of his girlfriend. He raised his mask, pinched the bridge of his nose, and sighed.

"Your turn."

———

Cassandra had captured everything. The live feed was still running. She handed the phone to Michael and slipped the cow mask over her face. After a deep breath, she carefully swiped her foot from side to side, clearing the bloodied glass from the floor where she would work.

"We're all about equal opportunities in our relationship," Michael said as he panned the phone over the bloody chaos before him. He didn't realise the scale of the mess until he viewed it from a different angle. "Isn't that right, my love?"

"Most definitely!" Cassandra replied. "We both give *and* receive!"

Garrett tried looking over his shoulder, a dumbfounded look on his face as he tried to process their words.

"Relax." Cassandra cooed. "And..."

"And... And what?" Garrett groaned, his quaking body pressed against Margo's cooling corpse.

"And... remember to breathe," Cassandra whispered into his ear just before she thrust the stump of her amputated arm into his puckered anus.

"Garrett's screams erupted instantaneously. His shrieks ricocheted around the cabin as Cassandra roughly plundered him from behind. Once she was elbow-deep, she paused and watched the rapid expansion and contraction of Garrett's ribcage as he hyperventilated. She gave him a couple of seconds... Then quickly pulled out.

The effect of her rapid withdrawal resulted in a cocktail of clotted faeces pouring from his dilated sphincter. The lumpy river of brown and red coated Garrett's thighs before splashing onto Margo's legs and the surrounding floor. The repugnant discharge quickly filled the small space with its offensive odour.

The sudden evacuation of his bowels did little to discourage Cassandra. She just spread her feet a little wider to accommodate the mess as best she could before ramming her arm back inside him. The addition of some fluids allowed her movements to be swift and powerful. After the fourth insertion, he became so slack that it allowed Cassandra to probe a little deeper. As she leaned her weight forward, something gave way internally, and she suddenly found herself buried up to her bicep. Garrett's howls abruptly concluded, and he briefly coughed and sputtered before falling silent. In the absence of his protests, the wet, sticky sounds accompanying the rapid penetration of his limp form filled the air.

Michael walked around the bodies. Garrett's head was

laid on top of Margo's. Her eyes were shut. His were blood-shot and bulged from their sockets. A white froth leaked from her mouth. A steady stream of bloody vomit seeped from his. Both excretions dripped down steadily, intermingling on the floor beneath the deceased bodies they'd originated from.

Like a doctor delivering bad news, Michael shook his head solemnly, and Cassandra ceased assaulting Garrett's ruined rectum.

She straightened up and went about removing herself from Garrett. When she slid her arm free, it sounded like a boot being pulled from boggy ground. She looked down at the mixture that coated her limb and shook the excess onto the floor before walking towards her husband.

Once she was standing at Michael's side, he raised his arm and reversed the phone's camera. The masked couple appeared on the screen, and the impressive backdrop of carnage they'd created lay behind them.

"And that concludes this evening's entertainment," Cassandra said. "I trust you found it… *satisfying*! I know I did. And I suppose you could say it was rather fitting in the end—what goes around, comes around."

"Very true!" Michael said and pointed his finger directly at the camera. You see, karma is a wonderful thing. And remember, you never know when it might pay a visit to a home just like yours!" With that, Michael pressed his thumb against the button, ending the connection.

He slid the mask off his face and turned to Cassandra. "Well, that escalated quickly. I thought you said to take things *slowly!*"

"That prick deserved every minute of it! I just wished he'd lasted a little longer," Cassandra said as she singlehandedly wrestled the mask off her head.

"It's great to see that fire back in your belly! Didn't I tell you this would do us good?" Michael said, that smug 'told you so' grin on his face.

"Yeah, yeah… Since you're so great at making plans, why don't you look up who we plan to visit next?" Cassandra asked and looked towards the phone. I'm sure there are plenty to choose from. You can pick. I'm going for a shower."

"What do you mean, *visiting*?"

Cassandra flicked some shit from her forearm and pointed towards the bound corpses on the floor. "Well, I sure as hell ain't eating either of those two! And…"

"And what?" Michael interrupted.

"And I've worked up quite an appetite."

fulfillment

Sid Shiv

MARK GOODFELLOW'S vision became fuzzy as he lay in his hospice bed. In his waning cognizance, he understood these were the last minutes of his life.

A tall, white figure stood at the foot of Mark's bed. Its brightness stood out like an aura against the dimness of the room. Mark knew this figure wasn't a nurse or orderly. Its presence filled him with warmth and peace. He even thought he could hear soft music, like a choir of angels, over the din of the room's air conditioner and the erratic beeping of his heart monitor. He knew this glowing personage must be his guardian angel.

Mark looked back on his life as he marveled at the other-worldly being. From the time he was young, he lived to serve others. Raising money for the poor and starting nonprofit organizations that provided aid to less developed countries was his work, as well as his passion. Rolling up his sleeves and living in the trenches—building schools, bridges, and homes all over South America and Africa—was more important and rewarding than simply offering his financial prowess. Living from one project to the next, never hoarding his earnings, was his way of life. He always put everything he had into the mission.

Mark's one regret was that he'd never had a family. He was always too busy with his work to think about it. Now that he was on his deathbed, the idea of sharing his legacy with progeny seemed nice—sons and daughters to carry on the work of making the world more livable for everyone. But alas, it was not meant to be. He supposed family life wasn't in the cards for everyone. His legacy would have to live on in the hearts of those he'd helped—God willing.

As Mark's vision darkened and his breathing slowed, the idea of heavenly rewards for a well-spent life never entered his thoughts. He regarded the angelic figure at the foot of his bed. With his last breath, Mark asked, "How could I have helped more?"

The heart monitor's staccato beep was replaced with a high-pitched hum. As the last light faded from Mark's vision, a dark, hooded figure stood beside the angel. The last thing Mark saw before his earthly life ended were eyes as red as hot coals staring at him from the blackness beneath the hood.

———

A black delivery van trundled down an interdimensional highway. The company name, Star-Infinitude, was displayed in sleek grey lettering on the van's side. Accompanying it was a gaudy logo of an infinity symbol with a shooting star protruding from it. Two dark, hooded figures with glowing red eyes occupied the front of the van.

"You nervous?" Stuart, the driver, asked.

"No. Should I be?" the passenger, Dan, replied.

Stuart snorted. "Nah. This job's a fuckin' cakewalk. How long have you been with SI?"

"Two tours," Dan replied.

Stuart nodded his approval. "Very nice! Only two tours, and you've already made it to the big show. What did you do before?"

"My first tour was in Receiving, and my second was Sales."

"Damn. The usual career path starts in Receiving, followed by tours in Sorting and Loading—and then Sales. At least, that's what I had to do before they even considered bumping me up to Reaper Fleet. They skipped you right up to Sales?"

"Uh-huh."

"Better not piss you off. You'll probably be my boss one day." Stuart laughed and clapped Dan on the shoulder. "Well, welcome to the fleet. First things first. Let's get you through this probationary period and make a full-fledged fleet reaper out of you. What do you say?"

"Sounds good."

"Great! Let's get the boring shit out of the way. I know you've heard it all before, but I have to give you a quick overview of our mission to check that box off as your trainer."

"I'm all ears," Dan said.

"Good. As you know, Star-Infinitude is a fulfillment company responsible for reaping, sorting, storing, selling, and delivering the souls of recently depleted *terrestrial bodies*. Our boss—the Big G, or the Big D, depending on your station—cultivates these souls on earth. They are activated in earthly bodies, grow, and make moral choices. How they live their lives within the confines of their *t-bodies* determines whether their aptitude leans light or dark. A Guardian Angel, or *GA*, watches over and evaluates them. When their mortal bodies die, their souls are ready to return to the fulfillment center where they will be sorted—SI Dark or SI Light. Then, they are marketed and sold. SI Light is the marketplace for angels, cherubs, and whatnot who reside in Heaven. SI Dark caters to demons, fallen angels, and dark overlords in Hell. The souls marketed through SI Dark go to buyers in Hell, where they are punished and tortured. The souls sold through SI Light go to buyers in Heaven, where they typically sing in choirs, play harps, or sound trumpets. So, they get sold, go to either Heaven or Hell, and their buyers outfit them with their *celestial bodies*. Finally, the energy outputted by these souls within their new *c-bodies*—either being tortured in Hell or singing in Heaven—is collected by the Big G-or-D and used to produce more souls. It comes full circle. Any questions so far?"

"Nope," Dan answered. He'd heard this spiel several times before but understood it was incumbent on Stuart, his trainer, to tell him again.

"Awesome! Aside from the good and evil souls, some fall smack dab in the middle of the spectrum on their GA evaluation. Do you know what becomes of the elite few souls who land between the forty-eight and fifty-two percent mark?"

"They become reapers," Dan replied in a lackluster tone.

"And why is that?"

"Because we have the ability to travel within both Heaven and Hell."

"Correct. Since our aptitude lands right in the middle of the spectrum, we can withstand the extremes of both environments. If your ordinary angel were to set foot in Hell, they would ignite fairly quickly. Their wings would burst into smoldering flames, and their flesh would melt off their bones —mind, body, and soul flash-fried instantly. Likewise, if a demon were to venture into Heaven, the choirs and heavenly trumpets would rattle them. The reverberations of the music would shake their bodies and souls apart, and their heads would quickly explode like that guy in the movie Scanners. You ever see Scanners?"

"Yeah. Scanners is awesome."

"Damn right, it is!"

"What happens if a Heaven-bound orb finds its way into a c-body designed for Hell?" Dan asked.

Stuart grimaced. "From my understanding, the c-body would provide just enough protection to keep the soul from being destroyed. But the psychological damage it would sustain is the type of shit you wouldn't wish on your worst enemy. And the same goes if a Hell-bound orb gets placed in a heavenly c-body."

"What about misdelivered souls still in orb form—before they get placed in their c-bodies? Without the protection of their c-bodies, how do they survive?"

Stuart nodded with approval. "That's a very insightful question. You see, a soul is protected as long as it's in orb form. They aren't susceptible to harm until they are paired with their c-body and activated. Otherwise, we'd have souls popping like popcorn in the back of the van as we made our deliveries between Heaven and Hell."

"Damn. That's some crazy shit!" Dan exclaimed.

"You ain't just whistling Dixie. So, our unique ability to travel between Heaven and Hell qualifies us as reapers. As reapers, we're responsible for reaping—gathering or harvesting, if you will—the cultivated souls ready to come to the fulfillment center. This would be our inbound stock. When a human is about to die, their GA enters a reap order. We must be timely with our reap orders because a soul can't leave its body until we arrive on the scene to receive it. In other words, the poor sap can't die until we get there. When we get the order, we go to the GA's location, where they sign the soul over to us. Then, the soul is transmuted as an orb, and we add it to the inbound stock in the back of the van. We also deliver outbound stock as we make our way along our route. At the end of a run, when we get back to the fulfillment center, all the inbound stock is unloaded by warehouse staff, who also load the van with new outbound stock. Did they issue you a Scythe?"

"Yep. Got it right here." Dan patted the pocket of his black cargo shorts. "Brand new Scythe 9."

"They're issuing the nine now? Shit! I'm going to have a word with IT about getting upgraded. I'm still using the Scythe 7." Stuart tapped the screen of a smartphone secured in a phone holder on the dashboard. "Anyhow, the Scythe is the hub through which we conduct all our business. It maps our routes, stores invoices, and collects the digital signatures of all our customers. Your contact list should be preprogrammed with your whole chain of command. I'm in there. Don't hesitate to contact me when you get out on your own if you ever find yourself in a bind or have any questions."

"I appreciate that."

"Okay then. We're ready to get started. I'll drive for the first few shifts, and you can make the pickups and deliveries.

Then, once you're comfortable with that, we'll switch. Sound good?"

"Sounds good."

"Punch up our route map. Let's find out who our first customer is."

Dan fingered the Scythe on the dashboard. His red eyes squinted as he deciphered the information on the screen. "It looks like our first stop is a reap order for Hallowed Hearts Hospice."

"Good work. We'll be there in five minutes."

One exit and two turns later, the Star-Infinitude van pulled into the hospice's parking lot. Stuart pulled the Scythe off the phone holder and handed it to Dan. Dan took it and looked at Stuart for further instructions.

"Click the order. It should tell you where to go and who your point of contact is. At the bottom of the screen is a button for Chain of Custody. That's where they sign the soul over to you—technically over to me since it's my Scythe. Don't forget to get their signature."

"Will do," Dan replied.

"You don't mince words, do you? I admire that. Go get 'em."

Dan nodded and got out of the van. He clicked the reap order on the phone. He was supposed to meet his point of contact, a Guardian Angel named Michael, in room 217 to collect the soul of Mr. Mark Goodfellow. Straightening his black hoodie with the SI logo on the left breast, he headed into the hospice.

It wasn't hard finding room 217. Dan discovered the GA, Michael, standing over an old man's bed. Michael had earbuds in and was listening to music. The volume was so loud that Dan had no trouble hearing The Mormon Tabernacle Choir's version of the Halleluiah Chorus. He had to tap Michael on the wing to get his attention.

Michael turned with an expression of brief surprise on his face. He pulled his earbuds out and shoved them into his robe. "Oh. Sorry, dude. I was just rockin' out with my cock out. Not literally, though. Angels don't have cocks. You heard the new MoTab?"

"Can't say I have. I'm here for a reap order. Mr. Mark…" Dan scanned the order on the Scythe. "Mr. Mark Goodfellow."

"Yep. That's this geezer right here. Been evaluating this dude for eighty-seven years. I'll tell you what. I've been doing this job a long time and have never seen an evaluation like it. This mother fucker makes Mother Theresa look like one of the Real Housewives of New Jersey."

"You don't say." Dan hoped Michael would dispense with the small talk.

"He'll fetch a good price over at SI-Light—become the envy of some rich angel's choir."

Dan clicked the Chain of Custody button on the reap order and scrolled to the signature block. He held the Scythe out to Michael. "I need your signature. Then I can take him off your hands."

"Far out! Not a moment too soon, either. I could use a taco." Michael used his finger to scrawl his signature on the screen. "He's all yours."

"How could I have helped more?" the dying man in the bed asked.

Dan turned to the old man—Mark Goodfellow—and watched as a glowing orb of light rose from his chest. The slow, intermittent beat of the heart monitor became a high-pitched hum. The sphere drifted slowly through the air, down the length of its used body, and came to a floating rest in front of Dan's face. Dan gently grabbed it out of the air before heading back to the parking lot.

After securing the orb in a bin for inbound stock in the back of the van, Dan returned to the passenger seat and joined Stuart, who was finishing a Twinkie.

Stuart brushed some crumbs off his hoodie. "How'd your first reaping go?"

"It went fine." Dan looked quizzically at Stuart. "You know, I have a question, come to think of it."

"That's what I'm here for. Go ahead with it."

"Okay. We're reapers, so I understand why we pick up the newly departed souls. That part of the job makes perfect sense. But why do we make deliveries to customers? That end of it seems a bit undignified to me. The ancient reapers didn't make deliveries to asshole customers like fucking mail carriers. They were the feared and respected harvesters of souls." Dan shook his head and sighed.

"I see what you're saying. Nowadays, it's hard not to see it that way. Let me explain it in a way that might answer your question and restore your pride in our honored profession." Stuart said in a reassuring tone.

"Please do," Dan said, gazing down at his bony, black hands.

"Back in the olden days, when reapers wore long robes and carried actual scythes, the earth's population was way smaller than it is now. The Big G wasn't cranking out a fraction of the souls he does today. There wasn't the need for a fulfillment center or a fleet. The reapers delivered the souls to the boss, and he would harvest their energy himself. Now, there are so many souls that he has to outsource the energy production to angels and demons. In that way, the old reapers did make deliveries. They were just going directly to the Big G or D. So, you see, we're doing the same job on a much larger scale. Our godlike ability to travel between Heaven and Hell saddles us with making the deliveries. It allows production to increase and secures our positions as essential."

Dan turned to Stuart. "But what about the fear and respect the old-school reapers got? They inspired awe and terror in their black robes. Humans quaked in their boots at the mere mention of the Grim Reaper. I feel like a douche in this uniform. These work boots with the black cargo shorts and hoodie are lame as fuck. And the company logo, the infinity symbol with the shooting star... It looks like a cock and balls."

Stuart Laughed. "I can't argue with that. The logo could use some work."

"I don't mean to bitch," Dan said. "The job just isn't what I thought it would be."

"I felt the same way back when I started. But the job is what you make of it. Besides, it's much easier now than it used to be."

"How so?" Dan asked.

"For one thing, we don't have to report directly to the Big G or D. I wouldn't wish that stress on any reaper. I heard tales from old timers about reapers getting kicked down to Hell for misplacing souls or being seen by humans too many times. It's easy for us to navigate the cosmos now with our new Scythe phones, but it was a different ballgame back then. They had to map their own routes. They used their old-school scythes to cut tears in the cosmic veil to travel from point A to point B. Now, we have the interdimensional highway system, which adds infrastructure to the existing cosmic tears that the old timers made. It was easy for them to end up in a not-quite-right time or place and get spotted by humans. That's how they ended up with all that folklore about us being these fearsome, banshee-like creatures. The way I see it, we are supposed to carry out our jobs like ninjas—in and out without a trace."

Dan nodded. "That's an interesting way to look at it. But what happens if we mess up and lose a soul? We don't get sent to Hell, do we?"

"That's my second point," Stuart answered. "The beauty of how it works now is that the process is so convoluted that no one gets blamed if a soul gets lost or delivered to the wrong place. As long as the Big G or D is happy with the numbers, he doesn't give a shit. He keeps his beak out of the business end of the fulfillment center. He's happy he doesn't have to deal with anything except harvesting the energy and making new souls."

"What happens when a soul gets misplaced?" Dan asked.

"The customer just has to log into their account and report it or call the help desk. Then it all gets sorted. The new technology is a miracle."

"Do souls get misplaced a lot?"

Stuart shrugged. "I can't say it doesn't happen from time to time. There's bound to be a margin of error for the numbers we're dealing with. But that's the cost of doing business when you sacrifice quality for quantity."

———

"Well, fuck my angel ass! Goddammit! You've gotta be fucking shitting me!" Cassiel angrily sifted through an open Star-Infinitude box.

Raphael peeked up from his morning paper. "What is it, Cass?"

"See for yourself." Cassiel dumped the box's contents onto the table, where Raphael enjoyed a bagel and read the morning's Shangri-la Sun Gazette. Seven glowing orbs rolled onto the table's surface.

Raphael stared down at the orbs, not understanding what his partner was getting at. He accepted Cass could be temperamental sometimes and understood that strong emotions went hand in hand with artistic genius. As one of the top-tier choir directors in Heaven, Cass was a savant. Raphael looked up inquisitively. "Uh, yeah? Aren't these the souls you ordered?"

Cassiel huffed in exasperation. "Most of them. But this is only seven. I ordered eight. And, wouldn't you know it, the dipshit reapers at Star-In-shit-itude fucked up and left out the most important one. They could have fucking lost all seven of these other orbs for all I care. I'm so mad I could spit!"

"Calm down. I'm sure it can be resolved. What was so important about this particular soul anyway?"

"I've had my eye on this soul for a long time, just waiting for it to come on the market, so don't tell me to calm down," Cassiel huffed as he paced back and forth in the kitchen.

Raphael rolled his eyes and raised his hands in acquiescence. "Sorry."

Cassiel turned toward Raphael and sighed. "No, I'm sorry. I didn't mean to snap at you. I'm just really frustrated. This soul belonged to a man named Mark Goodfellow. This guy's GA evaluation was off the chart. He makes Fred Rogers look like Fred Krueger. He would add the bass to my choir that would have all the angels on this side of the Pearly Gates shitting their britches."

"Sweety, your choir is fine. Your bass and tenor sections are too legit to quit."

Cassiel folded his arms across his chest and cocked an eyebrow. "Don't think I haven't heard what that cow Muriel has been saying around the water cooler—that my choir is all screechy treble and has no ass."

Raphael shook his head and smiled. "She's just jealous. Her piddly little choir doesn't output a tenth of the divine energy that yours does. She's just trying to troll you. She wants to get under your skin and poke you until you retaliate, hoping you'll make an ass out of yourself. She'd love for you to slip up because she's a nobody. *You're* the one cranking out the big numbers. *You're* the angel Big G is taking notice of, not her."

"I appreciate that. I feel a little better now."

"Good."

"I'm still going to call these assholes at SI and see if I can get this sorted out." Cassiel picked up his phone from the counter and dialed. He placed it to his ear and paced around the kitchen. After a few moments, he sighed, took the phone away from his ear, and turned on the speakerphone.

A recorded voice cut into the elevator music melody of "Feels So Good" by Chuck Mangione. "Thank you for calling Star-Infinitude Light. We are experiencing a heavy call volume right now. If you remain on the line, a representative will be with you shortly. Thank you for your patience. You are caller number one-million-eight-hundred-forty-six-thousand-five-hundred-thirty-two." The Mangione tune came back on.

"Fuck my life," Cassiel sighed as he set the phone on the counter.

Some period of celestial time incomprehensible to humans later, a voice cut into the droning cycle of the elevator music and recorded message. "Hello. Thank you for calling Star-Infinitude Light. Sorry for the wait. This is Reba. How can I help you?"

Raphael watched as Cassiel picked the phone up and spoke into it, holding it close to his mouth. "Thank God. Yes. I did not receive an item I ordered. I think it must have been misplaced or delivered to the wrong address or something."

"Can I have your order number, please?" Reba asked.

"Sure. One second." He grabbed the open SI box off the table and studied the label. When he found what he was searching for, he recited the order number to Reba.

The sound of Reba typing could be heard over the speakerphone.

"Sir, the package in question was delivered to Mr. Cassiel at 32 Charity House Way earlier today."

"Yes, that's me."

"And your item wasn't delivered?"

"That's correct."

"So, it wasn't you who signed for the package?"

"No, I signed for the package—"

"Then you received the package?"

"No—yes. Just listen—"

"Calm down, sir. I'm just having trouble understanding."

"Jesus tapdancing Christ," Cassiel mumbled under his breath. I received a package. The package had several orders in it, but one of the orders was missing. DO YOU UNDER-STAND NOW?"

"Sir, I'll ask you to refrain from using an abusive tone with me on this call," Reba said in an icy voice.

"Fine. I apologize. I would just like to get this sorted out."

"Good. That's what I'm here for. What was the item that's supposedly missing?"

"It's not *supposedly* missing. It *is* missing. Plain and simple," Cassiel said.

Raphael recognized the tone of Cassiel's voice and knew that his temper was escalating. He got up from the table, went over to Cass, and began to massage his shoulders, hoping to calm him down before the conversation became heated.

"Okay. What was the item?" Reba asked.

"The orb of Mark Goodfellow. I paid out the ass for this soul, and I would appreciate it if we could get to the bottom of this," Cassiel replied as he huffily shook off Raphael's attempt to pacify him.

Raphael got the message and rolled his eyes as he sat back down. *I tried*, he thought. *If it has to happen, it's better to let poor Reba take the brunt of it than to have him turn his ire on me.*

"Sir, I don't appreciate your hostile language. I will ask you again to refrain from using an abusive tone with me on this call."

"I'm sorry. I don't feel like I'm being heard."

"I'm doing everything in my power to help you. What was the name of the soul?"

"Mark Goodfellow," Cassiel said.

"Uh-huh. It shows that you signed for the soul of Mark Goodfellow this morning," Reba said.

"I signed for a package. The package contained several orders. But Mark Goodfellow was missing. And he was the only one in the order that I actually cared about. Do you understand? Can you see why I'm aggravated?"

"Did you check inside the package?"

Raphael watched as Cassiel gritted his teeth, scrunched his shoulders, closed his eyes, and slowly exhaled.

"Of course, I checked the package," Cassiel said.

"And it wasn't in there?" Reba asked.

"That's correct. It wasn't in there. All of the other items I ordered were in there. But not Mark Goodfellow," Cassiel said.

"Did you check with your neighbors to see if it was delivered to them by mistake?"

"No, I did not. I'm sure the item would have been packaged in this box along with the others. But it wasn't. I can say for certain that it did not get delivered to my neighbors by mistake. It was supposed to be in this box, but it was NOT IN THIS BOX."

"If the order wasn't delivered, then why did you sign for it?"

"I didn't know it was missing! I just signed for the fucking box and let the shithead delivery boy go on his way! Forgive me for assuming I was dealing with a company that wasn't composed entirely of inept fuckwits!"

There she blows, Raphael thought, squinting sheepishly down at the table.

A long pause ensued on Reba's end of the conversation. The sound of typing and clicking came clearly over the speakerphone.

"Sir?" Reba asked, breaking the silence, a slight sneer in her voice. "I've gone ahead and set your account to limbo status pending an investigation into your missing item."

"No—"

"I hope this call has been helpful."

"No, wait! I'm sorry!"

"Thank you for calling Star-Infinitude. Have a lovely day."

The call went dead.

"Shit fucking cunt!" Cassiel threw the phone with all his might and anger.

Raphael ducked as the phone sailed over his head and shattered against the wall.

———

"Wakey, wakey. Suck my snakey."

Al heard these words as he labored to wake up from his

afternoon nap on the couch. In the darkness of half-sleep, he felt something slapping his cheek. He opened his eyes.

"Wake up fuck-nuts," the voice continued as Al blinked the sleep out of his eyes.

As his vision became focused, Al recognized the voice of his roommate, Bub. He also realized what was causing the annoying slapping sensation on his face. He grabbed Bub's warty demon cock with lightning acuity and twisted.

Bub howled and grabbed Al's wrist in a futile attempt to escape. Al tightened his grip as he sat up. "How many times do we have to go over this? I don't like it when you touch me with your penis. Understand?"

Bub was panting from the pain. "I understand!" he screeched.

"The Big D has seen fit to bless us with genitalia for the explicit purpose of tormenting damned souls. Count yourself lucky. Angels don't have dicks, and they don't bust nuts. Having a dick in the afterlife is a privilege—not a right. Repeat after me: I WILL SAVE MY DICK FOR THE MEAT SACKS."

Bub moaned. "Ah—ah—ah—"

"Say it!" Al yelled, giving Bub's dick an extra squeeze.

"I—will—savemy—d—d—dickforthemeatsacks!" Bub screamed and fell to the floor when Al released his member.

"And don't ever forget it." Al adjusted himself on the couch. He licked his thumb and index finger before bringing his hand up to polish the horn protruding from the center of his forehead. He always engaged in this involuntary grooming habit when first waking up from a nap. "Now, what is so important that you felt the need to wake me up in such a manner?"

Al couldn't help but admire Bub's resilience as he hopped

off the floor like his dick hadn't almost been ripped off seconds earlier.

"Woo!" Bub cheered as if he'd just taken a shot of whisky. "That was quite a tug!" He shook his hips like he was dancing an accelerated version of the twist. His dick made thwapping sounds as it slapped against his pelvis on either side.

Al sighed at this display. "Well?"

"Well, what?" Bub asked as he came to a halt with a puzzled expression.

"Why'd you wake me up, dumbass?"

Bub rolled his eyes and chuckled. "Oh yeah. Duh. Some stupid delivery reaper dropped us off a free soul by mistake."

"So what? I'm sure whoever ordered it is going to want it back. It's not ethical to steal the souls that our fellow demons have ordered."

"But this one wasn't ordered by a demon," Bub said as a wicked smile bisected his face.

"What do you mean?" Al asked, his interest piqued.

Bub only giggled and stared at Al, his mischievous grin never faltering.

Understanding began to spark in Al's mind. "No way!"

"Uh-huh," Bub giggled.

"You're shitting me. They gave us a Heaven-bound soul?"

"Uh-huh," Bub giggled again.

"How do you know the soul's Heaven-bound?"

"The address on the box was 32 Charity House Way. That's a Heaven address. We live at 32 Charnel House Way here in Hell. They fucked up!" Bub giggled, his mischievous expression brimming with excitement.

Al rubbed his hands together in a pensive, sinister manner. "How fortuitous. The Demon Code only states that we can't steal from other demons. Dishonesty and malice are inherent in our demon nature, and if we all gave into these instincts regarding other demons, Hell would collapse on itself. But nowhere in the Demon Code does it say that we can't steal from angels."

"Uh-huh," Bub giggled a third time.

"And do you know what's amazing about this? Do you know why I've been hoping for this very thing to happen to us for so long?"

"No. Tell me," Bub said, still giggling as he sat beside Al on the couch.

Al shifted in his seat to face Bub. "We've been doing good work here. Our energy output is steady for a small operation such as ours. But lately, I've been feeling the urge to upgrade. We do a quality job of torturing and tormenting damned souls, but we are by no means being noticed by the Big D. I've been looking for a way to bolster our numbers in a way that will finally get us some attention. You may have just stumbled on our ticket, my friend."

"How so?" Bub asked.

"Hear me out. We acquire the souls of the damned. We put the screws to them in mostly physical ways to generate that energy that the Big G or D loves so much. After all, that's why we have dicks, right? And that's why Hell-model c-bodies are equipped with genitals and assholes—so we can mutilate and fuck the hell out of them. You with me so far?"

"Yes."

"Good. Now, pay attention. The butt stuff and genital mutilating are fun and all, but for the amount of work we put in, there's not a huge return on energy. Physical pain doesn't generate the same quantity as mental and emotional pain. But the unfortunate truth is that most of the souls we get are sociopaths who are virtually impervious to mental and emotional pain. This is Hell, after all."

"Damn right!"

"Here's an example. We had the Empathizor-3000 Chamber installed a while back. Remember all the commercials? It was supposedly designed to crank out huge energy numbers by making souls feel the world's woes. The only problem is that the machine draws on the soul's already existing sense of empathy. If a soul has no empathy to begin with, the machine doesn't really work. Remember that group of religious nuts who came to us a few months ago—the ones who were out picketing with hateful signs at that gay person's funeral when they got hit by that bus? We figured that since they proclaimed to be so deeply religious, maybe they possessed a more robust sense of empathy than most of the fuckers we get around here. So, we stuck them in the Empathizor-3000, expecting a decent energy return. And what did we get?"

"Bupkis" Bub snarled.

"That's right. We didn't get shit. The Empathizor-3000 has been used as a storage locker for spiked dildos and hydrochloric colonics ever since. But what *did* work on those assholes?"

"Butt stuff," Bub said as he nodded.

"Yep. Those bastards hate the butt stuff. The irony is hilarious when these bigoted morons arrive here to experience a smorgasbord of ass-play. The dopey looks on their faces when they realize that most gay people go to Heaven are absolutely priceless."

"Priceless," Bub mimicked as he emphatically nodded along.

"Nonetheless, the energy output of physical pain is pitiful. Like most demons, we are forced to intake large numbers of cheap souls and over-exert ourselves for mediocre numbers. Between the two of us, we don't have the workforce to do any better."

"We do our best," Bub replied.

"I know we do. But our best just hasn't been enough… Until now."

"What's gonna change things, Al?"

"This new Heaven-bound soul that's fallen into our laps, that's what."

A puzzled expression came over Bub's face. "How so?"

"Think about it. Theoretically, when a Heaven-bound soul is activated in a Hell-model c-body and finds themself in Hell, being subjected to all the tortures and torments that Hell has to offer, for no good reason, the energy they output is supposedly off the fucking chart. And on top of that—the real icing on the cake—Heaven-bound souls are, by nature, all empathic. Not only can we juice this fucker's ass, but we can finally get some good use out of the Empathizor-3000. Our numbers will be through the fucking roof! We are sure to be noticed by the Big D!"

"Holy shit! This is amazing!" Bub clapped his hands.

"What's the name of this soul, anyway?" Al asked.

"Hold on a sec." Bub got up and scurried off toward the front door.

Al watched as Bub returned to the room with an open SI package. Bub sat back down and rummaged through the packing paper.

"They always use so much packaging for one small order," Bub complained.

"I know, right? Save some for the trees, why don't you?" Al replied.

Bub pulled a single glowing orb from the packaging, squinting as he examined it. "It looks like its name is Mark Goodfellow."

Al's jaw dropped. "You're fucking with me."

"What?" Bub asked.

The idiotic look on Bub's face reassured Al that he was not being fucked with. "You're serious. Mark Goodfellow?" Al asked.

Bub shrugged. "Here, see for yourself." He handed the orb to Al.

Al squinted as he held the orb close and read the name inscribed in white letters just beneath the sheen of glowing purple. *Mark Goodfellow.*

Al turned back toward Bub, lowering the orb to his lap. "You don't know who this is, do you?"

Bub shook his head.

"You need to pull your head out of your ass, you dumb fuck," Al admonished.

"Why?" Bub asked.

"It's been in the news. This guy's a big deal. His obituary is all over the fucking place. I just read about him this morning in the Hades Pit Times."

"What's so special about him?" Bub Asked.

"Mark Goodfellow was this generation's golden boy on earth. His GA evaluation was off the chart. This mother fucker makes Jared from the Bible look like Jared from Subway."

Bub laughed.

"The energy we're going to generate with this guy isn't just going to get us noticed and promoted," Al continued. "We'll be on top of the fucking food chain around here. Get started on cleaning out the Empathizor-3000. I'll pick out a nice c-body for our honored meat sack."

———

"How could I have helped more?" Mark Goodfellow asked the two figures standing at the foot of his hospice bed.

The sound of the heart monitor and the quiet, angelic music faded as his vision went black.

Then there was nothing…

Darkness.

Muffled sounds.

Speaking.

Something lightly caressing his cheek.

A thought came to Mark. *Could it be the hand of my Lord and Savior — my Redeemer coaxing me awake into a new heavenly existence?*

The darkness receded into brilliant white light. Mark had to squint against the brightness as he struggled to gain focus. Two blurry figures stood before him. *God the Father and the Son?*

"Wakey, wakey," a shrill voice said.

Then everything came into focus…

Oh, God. Oh, Jesus Christ!

The two figures Mark saw before him were hideous, like something from one of his worst nightmares. They were humanoid in structure, each having all of a human's essential limbs and features. But the one on the right had green skin that appeared to be covered in warts and boils. He was tall and emaciated, with limbs that defied normal expectations of length. His fingers were bony and tipped with menacing claws. His face was devilish, with protruding cheeks and a sharp jaw. Set among his foul features were two red eyes that glowed like embers. And in the center of his forehead, a long, tapered horn jutted out and curved toward the sky.

Standing considerably closer, the figure on the left was similar in form. His skin, however, was red, and he had no horns.

Mark knew both figures were male because they were both naked. The green one's penis hung like a cured sausage in the window of an Italian deli. The red one was using his penis to slap Mark on the cheek. The pungent odors of sulfur and smegma invaded marks nostrils.

"Wakey, wakey. Suck my snakey!" the red one screeched.

"Give him some air. Let him wake up," the green one said.

The red one stepped back and stood beside the green one. They stared down at him.

Mark felt dumbfounded as he stared back from the chair where he sat, quickly scanning his surroundings. He appeared to be sitting in the center of a white room, with his chair being the only piece of furniture. The room was brightly lit despite no apparent light source. He looked back up at the strange, scary figures.

"I bet you have lots of questions," the green one said.

"Uh—wha—ye—," Mark stammered. His disorientation and fear made it hard for him to form a coherent thought, let alone speak properly.

"My name is Halphas, but you can call me Al—just like the Paul Simon song. This idiot standing beside me is Beelzebub. He goes by Bub. We are demons," the green one said.

Mark felt a new pang of terror. "I'm in Hell? You're Beelzebub? The Devil?" Mark pointed at Bub.

The two demons eyed each other and burst into laughter.

"Pull your head out of your ass," Al laughed. "This guy, the Devil? He's a fucking moron!" Al slapped Bub on the back. "No offense, buddy."

"None taken." Bub continued to laugh.

"Are you Mark, the apostle from the Bible?" Al asked.

"N—no," Mark replied.

"Right. You're just some schmuck who inherited your name from some famous schmuck in history. It works the same way here. We're just a couple of working-class demons with common demon names—his more so than mine."

"Oh. Sorry," Mark apologized. The gravity of his situation was beginning to sink in, and he felt a deep, sinking feeling of despair. Tears welled up in his eyes, and he began to weep. As he lowered his gaze to his lap, he noticed, for the first time, that his body was different. His thighs were lean and muscular. The skin on his forearms was taught and healthy, with no traces of melanoma or liver spots. He had the hands of a young man—not a hint of arthritis.

"Why are you crying? It's not that bad," Al said.

Mark shook his head. Thoughts of all the projects he and his organization never got around to accomplishing plagued his mind—all the potential aid he could have administered, all the lives he could have improved. "I should have done more."

"What are you blabbering about?" Bub asked.

Mark lifted his tearful gaze. "I could have helped so many more people in my life. But there was always an excuse for why I couldn't. The money wasn't there; the logistics weren't right. I'm selfish. If anyone deserves to be in Hell, it's me."

Bub snorted. "Pfft. No, y—"

Al interrupted, slapping Bub on the back again. "God-damn right, you deserve to be in Hell, you self-centered twat. You could have done so much more with your life. You could have helped many more people achieve the type of fulfill-ment and sense of accomplishment you enjoyed. You prob-ably got off on feeling superior."

"I never thought about it before, but you're probably right," Mark blubbered. "I probably did feel superior."

"Well, it's scum like you that truly makes me sick," Al continued. "But it's also scum like you who ensures that I have a job, a purpose in life, a reason to wake up in the morn-ing. Do you know what that reason is?"

"No," Mark replied, still crying.

"My whole purpose in life is to punish assholes like you. And let me tell you, I love my fucking job. First, we'll let you sit here a while and ponder all the mistakes you made—all the missed opportunities. Then, we're going to get into the butt stuff."

"Butt stuff?" Mark asked, sniffling through his tears.

"Your ass's pain will be legendary—even in Hell," Al said in a deep, ominous tone.

Mark watched as the two demons left the room. Though he didn't like the idea of this so-called "butt stuff," it wasn't foremost in his thoughts. All he could think of were the anonymous and numberless masses of people he could have helped. He'd been vain to indulge in any satisfaction over his life's accomplishments. His whole life had been a fable of self-servitude.

As he wallowed in self-loathing, the light in the room, which seemed to come from nowhere, went out. Before the darkness could set in, the light came back on. But now, instead of white light, the room glowed dark red. The redness swirled around Mark, seeming to take substance; the glow pulsated like a heartbeat. It fractured into snakelike tendrils as it circled, vectoring nearer and nearer to Mark like a whirlpool of water being sucked down a drain. Then, the ropey, transparent limbs of light shot into Mark's eyes, ears, nose, and mouth.

A scene—like a movie—immediately began playing in Mark's mind. It wasn't, however, a scene of people he *could have* helped. The people and place in this vision were familiar. It was the Central African village of Jou Ma Se Gat.

He watched as children he once knew, who were now adults, were herded, along with their own children, by pro-government militiamen into a school he had built. The male adult villagers were cut down with machetes. Little boys were separated from screaming mothers and loaded onto trucks. Mothers and daughters were shoved into the schoolhouse and gang-raped repeatedly. When the militia had finished its despoilment, the mothers and daughters who had not been murdered during the attack were locked inside the school-house. Their screams tore through the night as the building was set ablaze. Mark recognized several of the militiamen. They had also once been children he had known from the village—children who had once occupied desks at the school he had built.

This was the first vision Mark was treated to, courtesy of the Empathizor-3000 in which he sat. Over a period of celestial time incomprehensible to humans, he witnessed many more. He felt the physical, emotional, and psychological pain of every atrocity. And though the torment was immeasurably horrible, it paled in comparison to the sorrow he felt for not having done enough to help and the shame he felt for any sense of fulfillment he had ever enjoyed from his life's work.

In the brief juncture between visions, a simple thought came to Mark:

Hell is my reward. Hell is my home.

TAKE GOOD CARE OF MY BABIES

CHISTO HEALY

LIA SMILED AT HER FRIEND. "Thanks for inviting me. It feels good to get out."

Mandy put a hand on her shoulder and returned the smile. "Of course, honey. I'm just glad you came. You can't spend your life crying under your covers. Larry was a dick. The world is full of dudes. Who knows… maybe you'll meet one here tonight."

Lia laughed shyly. "I'm not looking for all that. I just want to have some fun, let loose."

Mandy nodded and smiled again. "And dicks are fun, girl. I'm saying. Put one in your vag. How long has it been?"

"You're gross. Where's the beer?"

"Kitchen. Have fun, baby. Live a little. Do something you've never done before. Put it in your butt or something."

Lia shook her head and made her way into the house. She b-lined straight for the kitchen. There was a square-jawed blonde man with a shirt that looked purposely a size too small so it would accentuate his muscles standing at the keg. He winked at her, and she groaned. "Just pour me a beer."

"I'd like to pour you something else," he said.

She glared at him. "Seriously? Awesome. Is there a punch-line? What would you like to pour me, good sir?"

"Huh? Oh, uh… how 'bout my jiz?"

"Like in a shot glass or what? Please enlighten me."

"Like in your mouth, babe."

"It literally took four seconds for me to hate you. Are you gonna pour my beer or move out of my way so I can pour it myself?"

"I got you, girl. I'm not just muscles, you know. I got a good heart."

Lia sighed, took the plastic cup of beer from him, and said, "Yes, the sweet, kind heart that offers girls a cup of jiz."

As she walked off, rolling her eyes, he said behind her, "Exactly!"

People were dancing to loud music in the other room. Lia decided to join them, sipping her beer and shaking her hips. She started to feel glad she came and was beginning to have fun when she felt a hand on her back.

She turned to look, and a smiling guy flipped his hair out of his eye. He must have known the music was too loud because he didn't even bother with talking. He just started grinding his crotch into her rear. Lia was about to hit him with her elbow when she saw Mandy dancing across the room. Mandy winked at her and gave a thumbs up. Lia decided to relax and let go.

She danced for a bit until the man had two hands on her ass and was practically fucking her. Then she'd had enough. She reached behind her, grabbed his balls, and squeezed. When the stranger broke away and fell to his knees, Lia stormed out of the room and the house.

She stood outside in the cool air, feeling like she'd made a mistake. Coming here was not the answer. She didn't need mindless man meat. They wouldn't mend her broken heart.

A minute later, Mandy came outside and stood beside her. "What happened, girl? That guy was hot."

"I don't even know him, and he just felt like he could help himself to me like I was an all-you-can-eat buffet."

Mandy sighed and raised her hands defensively. "Alright, okay. We're different people, and we want different things, but I'm still your friend, so what do you think will help you get over that cheating shitbag? You need to do what makes you feel better."

"Honestly, I think I need to get away for a bit, go to a cabin by the lake or something, but I don't want to leave my cats. I know cats don't need much care, but still."

Mandy laughed. "Girl, I will go feed your cats."

"You will?"

"Of course."

"Oh my God, thank you. Red Beard the purr-rate likes the salmon treats, but Marilyn Monrowr only eats the chicken. If the litterbox isn't kept clean twice a day, they will pee and poop on everything. But you can't put too much litter in, or they'll throw it all over the floor, and it's such a mess."

"How about this? I won't just swing by. I'll stay for a few days so you know they're good. I want you to be able to go heal, not worry about your cats the whole time."

"Oh, Mandy. That would be wonderful. They're not just cats. They're my babies. I know we weren't that close in college, but I wish we were closer. You're a good friend. I haven't had that many. It means a lot."

"And here I thought you didn't want to suck a dick tonight," Mandy said.

Lia shook her head and laughed. "If you had one, I'd suck it."

"Would you? Aww, that's so sweet. Who's the good friend now?"

Lia laughed and hugged her. "I love you."

"I love you too, honey. I'll come by on Friday."

"Perfect. I'll tape the key to the underside of the welcome mat. I'll see you on Sunday night."

————

Mandy showed up at Lia's place. She had gone out too many times this week, and the hangover had her head pounding. *I'm probably dehydrated. I hope she has bottled water. I don't do tap.*

Holding her head, she squatted down and lifted the doormat. She pulled the taped-on key off the bottom, groaned, and stood. Mandy realized it was strange she'd been friends with Lia for so long and had only been to her house a couple of times.

She put the key in the lock and turned it. Lia was always nice. They were just so different. They had different interests and different crowds. Strangely, it was Larry who made them friends. He was part of her crew. Of course, she stopped hanging with him when she found out he was a cheating asshole, but it was disappointing. Still, girls have to stick together. That's why she was here.

She pushed her way into the house and shut the door behind her. "Here, kitty, kitty," she called out, throwing her purse on the couch. She thought they would be hungry and come running, but maybe they were hiding because they didn't know her. Once she was here for a little while, they would probably get more comfortable and come out.

Mandy figured she should fill their food dishes anyway. They might sneak by when she wasn't looking and eat. Cats were private creatures. She went to the kitchen and scrunched her face. *There are no cat bowls. Maybe they're upstairs in the bedroom.* She looked around for the cans of food. They weren't out on the counter anywhere.

Mandy frowned and started opening cabinets. She still didn't see any cat food, but roaches scurried away from her in every direction with every door she opened. "Okay, I am *not* staying here," she said to the house. "I know why Larry left. Hell, I can't believe he stayed as long as he did if it was like this. Yuck."

A fly buzzed by her head. She swatted at it and felt something on her other hand that rated on the edge of the sink. A giant roach antenna twitched around as the insect stared up at her. Mandy screamed and yanked her hand away. The bug didn't let go. She smacked it against the counter, and it stepped off indignantly before scurrying away. "No!" she yelled. "No. This is not okay. I'm gonna call this bitch."

Mandy stormed to the couch but was afraid to sit on it. She snatched up her purse and dug out her phone. Immediately, she found Lia's number and placed the call. It went straight to voicemail. "Roaches?" Mandy retorted. "You didn't tell me there would be roaches. If I'm staying here, I'm gonna bomb this place, and you will absolutely be billed for it. What the fuck?"

Frustrated, she threw her phone down. She needed to find these cats, feed them, and clean their box. Then she would have done what she said she would, and she could get out of this disgusting house.

She checked the dining room. Still no cat food, bowls, or boxes, but something stunk to high heaven. It smelled so bad she could taste it. It was like she was eating someone's ass after they chugged a tray of bean burritos. It was like the one time she was drunk enough to let Tommy Bunson talk her into a Rusty Trombone. That was the most one-timey a one-time thing has ever been.

"Where the fuck are these cats?" she moaned as she made her way to the stairs. They had to be up there. There wasn't anywhere else they could be. She stopped and peeked into the half-bath just to be sure. No cats. No litterbox. Just more horrible odors. This was enough to ruin a friendship, she thought, and she'd been through some gross shit with friends before… literally.

Mandy wrinkled her nose as she climbed the steps. She was two seconds from saying fuck the cats and just bailing on this crap. She entered the first room and heard a loud bang downstairs, which made her pause. She stopped and listened but heard nothing else. *This is the last time I volunteer to house-sit for anyone, ever.*

Shaking off the willies, she stepped further into the room. A pet carrier sat at the back of the room with an open can of cat food in front of it. "Oh, thank God," she said, though she cringed at the flies buzzing around the cat food.

"Aww, she must have locked you guys up to keep you safe until I got here. How old is that food, though? Jesus. Why wouldn't she put it in there with you so you could get it?

Mean Mommy. Why don't I let you out so we can find something better? Maybe you can show me where she keeps it."

Mandy moved the can of food, and the flies scattered. She groaned and swatted at them before opening the gate on the pet carrier. Nothing ran out. She bent over and peered inside, but it was hard to see. Something was definitely in there.

Mandy reached in, and her eyes went wide. It didn't feel like a cat. It felt like a person. She pulled it free and saw she was holding a blood-stained baby, umbilical cord still attached and hanging like a rope. The child's eyes were gone, and the holes where they should be were charbroiled black and smelled like meat left on the grill for too long.

Mandy couldn't even scream. She was in shock, trembling and holding the dead child, staring at it with wide eyes. She dropped it, and it hit the hardwood floor with a smack. "What the fuck? What the fuck? What the fuck?" she mumbled as she backed away.

"Thanks for staying here for a few days," Lia said.

Mandy whirled around and saw no one.

She turned back and found herself face to face with Lia, who was twirling the dead infant over her head by the umbilical cord. Mandy found her scream, but it was short-lived as Lia swung the baby and hit her in the side of the face, knocking her to the ground.

"This belonged to that bitch Larry was fucking," Lia snapped as she brought the baby down on Mandy's head again and again.

Mandy raised her arms in front of her face to defend herself, but the assault was relentless. The baby was like a fleshy nine-pound hammer. She punched it away, her fist connecting with the tiny face, but Lia spun that cord and brought it back for another swing. The full weight of the dead child caught Mandy in the temple, and the world went black.

Mandy awoke in bed with a walloping headache. She looked around, took in the room with seemingly endless shelves covered in porcelain dolls, and quickly realized she must be in Lia's house. She didn't remember going to bed, but she'd been hungover and half-drunk when she arrived.

Maybe all that terrible stuff was just a nightmare. *It might be my sign to quit drinking.*

Holding her head and squinting against the headache, she sat up. "Fuck's with all the dolls. Creepy."

When she stood from the bed, Mandy swayed dizzily. She held her head and looked around at all the strange dolls. She felt like they were staring at her. "How does she sleep in here?" she groaned.

Then she saw that one doll was not a doll at all. The cord hanging from the shelve like a bloody fleshy string gave it away. Mandy stared in horror at the dead baby squeezed in among the dolls and staring at her from its burned-out cavernous eyes. She shook her head as tremors moved through her body. It was real. It was all real. "My head hurts because she beat it with a fucking baby. Oh God…"

Mandy realized Lia might still be somewhere in the house with her. The thought was terrifying. Where was she? Were there even any cats? What the hell was going on? Mandy wondered how long she was asleep. Was it the same day? The next day? She needed to find a window. It seemed odd that there were none in the bedroom. She thought that was standard.

She scanned the room for something she could use to defend herself if Lia should attack her again. Her eyes fell upon the infant. Mandy shook her head. *No. Absolutely not. I can't.*

She grabbed one of the porcelain dolls instead and held it by the arm as she walked from the room. "Lia?" she said quietly. "I came here to help you remember? We're friends."

"You are helping me," Lia said from behind before shoving her, sending her tumbling down the stairs.

Mandy screamed as she went down. The porcelain doll shattered beneath her as her face landed on top of it. The shattered doll sliced through the flesh of her face, shredding her cheeks, lips, nose, and forehead. Mandy whimpered in pain as she slowly lifted her head. Her lower lip hung from her face in a meaty chunk, blood running in streams. She cried at the white-hot pain as she prodded it with her fingers, and the chunk of lip meat fell off onto the floor. Mandy's cries became wails. Then she looked ahead through her tear-filled eyes and fell silent.

The front door was gone, as were the windows beside it. The area was now a solid wall covered in wallpaper. Two pictures hung from it filled with smiling stock photos of families. "What is this?" she cried quietly, blood flowing from her torn mouth.

"Assurance," Lia said as she strolled down the stairs. "I can't have you trying to go home when you promised to stay a few days and feed my cats. It's a hidden wall coming up from the floor. It cost a fortune. That's why I couldn't afford a real vacation. But it was worth it. How fun is this? I saw it on a survivalist show and just had to have it. Now, you should apologize for breaking my doll."

Mandy turned and found herself alone. *Where did she go?* "Broke your doll? You had a dead baby up there? Let me out! I want to go home!"

She got to her feet. Her mouth was still pouring blood. She had to find a way to stop it. She couldn't sew it up the way they did in action movies. There was no way Lia would let her. Even if she did, she didn't have a clue how to sew. It wasn't like an inherently female skill like people made it out to be. You had to be taught that shit, and she never was. *Fuck!*

She hurried to the kitchen and looked for something to fill the hole. She grabbed a bag of flour from the cabinet. It was open, and roaches poured over the sides. Mandy reached in, grabbed a handful of powder, and caked it into the open wound in her mouth. It turned red and crumbled free, but she replaced it and felt roaches scurrying over her hands and face. "How can you afford extra electronic walls but not get rid of the fucking bugs?" she whined.

"Those bugs aren't from filth," Lia's voice said. Mandy looked where it was coming from and saw a small speaker above the sink. "I brought them here. I just felt they added to the ambiance. Don't you?"

Lia was laughing when Mandy finally stopped caking her wound with roach-filled flour. "Who are you?" she cried. "Why are you doing this?"

She opened the fridge, looking for bottled water. The hard-shelled, antenna-wielding bugs were scurrying all over everything. There was no bottled water, but she saw a Tupperware container—the type her mom would fill with iced tea. *Please let this be something normal.* She took it out of the fridge, looking over her shoulder for the homeowner.

Mandy tipped up the container and poured its contents into her mouth. Brown sludge poured onto her wounded face. She immediately jerked the pitcher away and gagged. She tore the lid off the top and finally found one of the cats. It looked like it had been marinating in there for a while. The organs had broken down and leaked into the water, creating the brown sludge she had just poured into her mouth.

She moaned and ran into the half bath by the stairs.

Dropping to her knees by the toilet, Mandy threw the lid

up and leaned over to vomit. Larry's face stared up at her. His severed head floated in toilet water. The skin was severely rotted, and maggots poured from the wounds and flopped into the water. His mouth was open, displaying half a tongue. A spider walked over it. One of his ears was missing, and a broken piece of spine stuck out the bottom of his neck.

Mandy wanted to scream, but she couldn't hold it in anymore and vomited all over Larry's dead face. Her steaming, acidic puke washed the maggots from his face. Chunks of old food took their place and stuck to his rotting cheeks. "Larry?"

A hand came from behind and seized the back of Mandy's head, forcing her face into Larry's. His face caved under hers, and she kept going through his broken skull and the things squishing behind it into the puddle of vomit, water, maggots, and death. Mandy tried to scream and felt her mouth fill with the thick, syrupy contents of the toilet. She choked and gagged, swallowing the horrible stew. It burned her open eyes, and she could feel the sludge seeping into her ears.

Then, she was thrown back onto the bathroom floor. Mandy looked up and found herself alone. She started screaming and shaking, convulsing, crying and vomiting.

Mandy pulled herself up the sink on trembling limbs. She turned on the faucet and splashed water over herself, mumbling and rambling incoherently as she did. After struggling to wash the filth from her face and take a few painful sips of water, she stumbled from the bathroom to the living room, where she collapsed onto the floor.

She looked up at the ceiling. "There are no windows and no doors. I'm here, okay? I'm here. Why are you doing this?

Do you think I did something to you? I never slept with Larry or anything like that. I even stopped talking to him when I found out he was a creep."

"Oh, I know," Lia's voice came from a speaker somewhere. He slept with that girl, Chelsea, who worked at the diner down the road. He knocked her up, too. But you already met Larry Junior."

Mandy was exhausted, in pain, disgusted, and scared. She cried quietly and hugged herself. "Then what is this? Why are you doing this to me? Is it because I'm a slut, and you don't like that? What?"

Lia laughed. "Of course not. Women are allowed to enjoy sex, too."

"Then what the fuck is it? Tell me why!"

There was a pause... Then a creak... Then a pop.

The floor opened, and Lia emerged naked as the day she was born, smiling like a gleeful child. "It's quite simple," she said. "You told me I needed to do what made me feel better. This is what makes me feel better."

Mandy stared at her through wet, bloodshot, vomit-singed eyes. "That's it?"

"That's it. But if you want to fuck Larry, you can. We're not together anymore. I give you my blessing."

"What?" That's when Mandy noticed the testicles between Lia's thighs. Lia moved her hips, gyrated, and pushed the entirety of an erect penis out of her vagina onto the floor. She smiled at Mandy and pointed to the penis's glistening, creamy surface. "That was his. I freeze it so it stays hard. Go on. Have a turn. We're friends, right? Share, share, that's fair."

Mandy was staring at the severed hard-on on the ground. "I'm not putting that thing anywhere near me."

Lia looked suddenly angry. She bent and retrieved the

frozen discharge-coated member of her ex-boyfriend and stood to her full height.

"What are you doing?" Mandy asked, scurrying backward like a crab. "Stay away from me."

Lia's smile returned. She walked toward Mandy, who backed further away. "Larry was always good in the sack. You'll see. I mean, hey, you're the one who told me dicks are fun. Try something you've never done. That was your advice. How about trying one that's not attached to a man?"

"I've done that plenty. I have a drawer full of them at home. You can keep that one."

"No!" Lia lashed out and whipped her across the face with the frozen cock. "I want you to play with me. Undress."

"Or what?"

Lia lashed her with the frozen dick again. Blood flew from Mandy's swollen, broken nose. It came back again across her forehead and took her to the floor. She moaned shakily, looking up through blurry eyes. Lia beat her on the stomach with Larry's missing member as she gasped and groaned. "Please," she said quietly. "Just stop."

Lia squatted over her. Her naked asshole flexed above Mandy's face. "The cock wasn't my only surprise," she said, sounding exasperated.

"Wait, what are you doing?" Mandy cried from below her. She stared up at that brown eye as it expanded and shrunk repeatedly. There was something in it, something dark and wet. "What the fuck is that?"

The wet, fur-matted head of the other missing cat emerged from Lia's asshole like a giant anal bead.

Mandy screamed. In mid-scream, the shit-stinking severed cat head fell into her mouth, becoming lodged behind her jaws. It was too big to pass through her throat. She started choking and turning blue, grasping at her throat.

She saw Lia staring down at her, smiling and laughing—masturbating with Larry's severed dick as she choked to death. The last thing Mandy heard was Lia's orgasm.

———

Lia finished with a bang, squirting all over the woman beneath her. She was sad Mandy was too dead to taste it. She breathed heavily and wiped her forehead with her moist arm.

"Woo, you're right," she said. "Dicks are fun. I got rid of the rest of him—well, except the head. I saved that for you, haha. But his body went right down the gullet one bite at a time. The bastard deserved it. Now that you're dead, and I don't need it for effect, I'll probably eat his kid, too. Be right back."

Larry's member was defrosting and beginning to hang as opposed to the girthy, rigid stance she preferred, so Lia sauntered into the kitchen and shoved it back into the freezer. She felt so much lighter now that the cat head was out of her ass. She laughed at the thought as she walked back into the living room.

"What a way to go," she said. "I planned to play with you a bit more, but that was pretty fucking epic. Sometimes fate writes a better script than I ever could." She pantomimed choking and gagging, holding her throat and dying, and then burst out laughing. "Good times, am I right?"

She sat down beside Mandy and patted the dead woman's chest. "You were right about another thing, too," she told her. "I do feel much better now. You're a good friend, Mandy."

Lia patted the dead woman again. Then she noticed the lip that had fallen off of Mandy's face earlier, lying on the floor. "Ooo," she said excitedly.

She picked it up and tossed it into her mouth, sighing with

delight as she chewed through it and felt the blood squish out. "Suth a goo fwend," she said, with her mouth full. Delicious," she said as she finished and burped. Then she giggled at herself.

"I guess I ought to start cleaning up now, huh? Playtime is over."

Lia patted her dead friend one more time and worked to stand on trembling, sweaty limbs. As she stood, she farted. Only with the cat head expelled, her asshole was loose, and it turned out to be more than a fart. A spray of liquid shit sprayed out with a loud whistle and coated the dead woman, leaving her with a muddy exterior. Lia laughed again and slapped her thigh. "Oops," she said. "Gotcha again."

Six Months Later

Carey smiled at the girl when she came in. She was very pretty in an ordinary, girl-next-door kind of way. He knew her through some friends and made a point of inviting her because she'd been having a hard time lately. He figured she could blow off some steam, but he also understood that some people wanted nothing less than to be around people when they were grieving, so he wasn't sure she would show.

Now, here she was, walking into his house and looking like a deer in headlights. Carey tried to look welcoming as he walked over. "Hey, thanks for coming. I'm so glad you could make it. I know you've been through a lot lately. I wasn't sure what you needed because everyone is different, but I thought maybe this would help at least take your mind off things for a bit."

"You're not kidding. I think I need more than a party, though. I might take some time off and try to get away for a few days this weekend," Lia said to him.

"Who can blame you? First, your boyfriend cheats on you and bales, then your best friend turns up dead. That would be a lot for anybody. Please let me know if there's anything I can do to help. I mean it—in a real friend way—not in a guy-trying-to-get-something way. Okay?"

"Hmmm… Actually, there is something you can do," Lia said with a smile. "How do you feel about cats?"

Carey smiled. "They're great. I love all animals. I grew up with them. Let me guess, you need someone to cat-sit for you while you go away."

Lia's eyes lit up. "Oh my God, actually, yes, that's exactly what I need. I hate to ask when we don't know each other that well, but I don't know who else to ask. You know, it was Mandy who would cat-sit for me… and now…."

Carey looked at her with sympathy. He put a supportive hand on her shoulder. "Listen, it's okay. I'd be happy to cat-sit for you. I'll stop by and feed them, whatever you need me to do."

"Oh, would you? That would be wonderful. After everything else, if anything were to happen to little Tiger Woots and Purrtricia Arquette, I don't know what I would do. They're cuddle babies, and they're gonna miss their mama. Do you think you could stay at my place for a few days? I promise to fully stock the fridge for you. I'll leave some fun surprises for you as well."

Carey wondered if she was flirting with him. He certainly wouldn't mind it, but he also knew she was grieving, so he didn't want to overthink it. He did his best to give a supportive smile. "Yeah, of course. Definitely. Don't even sweat it. I've got you. Tiger and Purrtricia are in good hands."

"Oh wow. I'm so glad I came to this party. You're a life-saver. Can I hug you?"

Carey's smile widened. "Absolutely."

Lia embraced him. While she pulled him tightly into her, she thought, *I'm gonna have to get more cats.* "Well, come on," she said as she let go and grinned lovingly. "We're at a party. Show me where the beer is."

"Yes, ma'am," Carey said happily. Then, he led the way.

Backwoods Gothic

DAN SHRADER

CRINKLING the beer can in his hand, he watched it collapse into an uneven cylinder. The sound was so satisfying. James couldn't help but let out a massive belch, followed by a hearty laugh at his own antics. He was piss drunk, so much so that if he were to get out of the back seat of the car, he would surely fall. James loved getting smashed on a Friday night.

He'd woke up in the morning, getting ready for school,

filled with excitement for the night. He and his friends always went cruising, which was the best pastime in this small town. There wasn't much to do with cornfields and tractors in every direction. Only one small grocery store in the entire area, and nothing to do. It wasn't his fault that getting drunk would be the pinnacle of his high school memoirs.

It was his shithead parents' fault for moving him here.

James was going to graduate soon and didn't have a clue as to what he wanted to do. College was an option all his friends were opting out of. Some were actually staying in the sleepy town, but he wanted something more. James dreamed of bigger things, and tonight, as he gulped one beer after another, he decided why not try to start it now.

James always had his handheld camera with him and was notorious for making videos at parties and other fun events. He would upload them to his YouTube channel and get a lot of views. The last one was his biggest hit yet.

He and his friends captured a tornado on film. The footage was swiftly uploaded, and within hours, it went viral, captivating the hearts of countless viewers. Tonight, he pondered the possibility of something even more incredible, an epic undertaking. If only he could persuade his friends to join him.

The issue was that nobody was willing to visit *Hills Have Eyes* due to the rumors. Not being a born local to the area, to him, these were just that… rumors. He didn't believe in the bullshit that had almost every teenager scared to go out there. The moment he heard of this place, James knew he had to go, and now he had the right group to go with. He wanted to make tonight something epic. After all, they needed to find somewhere to dump the body in the trunk of Rex's car.

"Hey, hey. Listen, I know where we can dump this fucker off," James said from the backseat. "I got it."

Rex peered in the rearview mirror at him. He was calm as ever. It had been Rex who killed the guy, not James. But James immediately jumped into action and helped Rex move the man's body to the trunk and claimed they were in it together. James would be damned if Rex would go to prison for killing the creep. The guy deserved it for what he tried to do.

Tabitha sat in the passenger seat, trembling like a leaf. To calm her nerves, she slowly sipped on a beer at Rex's persistence, though she didn't want it. Although the murder had occurred hours ago, she was still a wreck.

In the backseat sat James, with Barbie by his side. She was his on-again, off-again fling, or whatever she wanted to call it. James liked her but knew she was too wild to be tamed. His grandfather once advised him that while the crazy ones may be exciting in bed, they weren't wife material. "The best sex a man will ever have," he'd said, "won't ever be with his wife. It's always the youthful flings… The ones you let get away… You don't marry the wild ones." And that's precisely what Barbie was.

"Talk to me, Jamie!" Rex screamed out, amped up. His adrenaline had been jacked up since the incident.

"It's simple. We've been cruising around looking for a spot no one would think of, and it's been right under our noses the whole time," James said, taking a beer from the cooler and popping the top. "Hills Have Eyes."

"Hills…" Tabitha said, trailing off. "No—no fucking way, James."

"What? It's brilliant! No one would think of it. Or even connect it to us," James exclaimed.

"Brilliant, bro. It's fucking brilliant!" Rex laughed. He banged his hand off the steering wheel a few times to release unwanted energy. Tabitha nearly jumped through the roof from her seat.

"I think it's hot," Barbie said, licking her lips.

"Of course you do, Barbs. You're a twisted bitch!" Rex added.

"Rex, please, I don't like this," Tabitha cried. We don't know what is out there."

"It's just people talking shit. Bunch of inbred river rats living like fucking shack house bums," James explained. He lit a cigarette and watched Barbie take it from his lips and inhale a large drag before giving it back. "Tab, you need to lighten up."

"Don't tell me to lighten up!"

"Babe, relax," Rex said gently. "Come on. You want me to go to prison? Is that what you want? You want to put money on my books and have to talk to me nightly on a phone?" He watched the tears swell in Tabitha's eyes. "I thought not."

"No, I don't want that," Tabitha lied. In reality, she wasn't okay with any of this. She was mainly there because she feared what Rex would do to her. After seeing what he did to Mr. Winters, she was even more scared of him. "I just believe we could go somewhere else. There's no need for us to venture out there. The place is…"

"…is what?" James interrupted. "No one knows because we've been conditioned to stay out of there by our parents and the local asshole sheriff," he explained, leaning forward from the backseat, breathing beer into her face. "You're being a fucking child, Tab, really. Please don't puss out on me."

"Well, we are going. I'm driving. End of it!" Rex declared, lifting his beer and pounding it back. He crushed the can and tossed it out the window.

"Yeah, we don't want him to go down for that fucking perv," James said, kicking the back of her seat. James lifted the handheld camera and started recording. "Let's go. Let's go. Meet the gang on another Friday night!"

Tabitha turned and immediately got angry at seeing the camera. "James! The fuck! Why are you recording?"

"I'm making another video, duh."

"No, dumbass. Not tonight. Not with the fucking body—"

"Seriously, discussing that on here is stupid. Like you, Tab. Just stop bringing it up. It'll save me the hassle of editing out unnecessary stuff while I'm recording," James condescendingly explained.

"Yeah, Tabitha. Shut up," Barbie laughed.

"It's cool, babe. This will be like proof we weren't even there, ya know?" Rex said.

"You guys are dumb," Tabitha mumbled.

Without giving her any chance to prepare, Rex backhanded her hard across the face. "Say something out the side of your face again, bitch!" he growled.

Tabitha leaned back, shifting her gaze to the window, hoping to conceal her tears from him. Meanwhile, Rex faced the camera and playfully gestured, forming devil horns with his hands.

Barbie reached over and placed her hand on James's lap. "You're such a badass, baby. I can't believe we're going to the Hills."

"I know. It's gonna be sick!" James replied as Barbie unzipped his pants. He leaned back and shut the camera off.

"No, leave it on. I like it when you record me." Barbie smiled up at him.

"You two are kinky as fuck, bro," Rex laughed and looked over at Tabitha, hitting her on the shoulder. "Why can't you be more adventurous like Barbs? Huh?"

Tabitha chose not to acknowledge him. She despised it when he behaved this way, and now, to make matters worse, Rex had taken someone's life. Her mother's words echoed in the depths of her mind as she questioned why she was even in the car. *"You find yourself a good, strong man, and you protect him. That's what a good woman does. Bury a body for him if you have to."* Her mother ended up in prison for doing just that, all for her worthless boyfriend.

Tabitha's actions, however, stemmed more from fear. Rex became violent when he drank, and he'd strangled her on multiple occasions. A feeling of helplessness consumed her. She found herself trapped in a constant struggle, torn between survival and breaking free from the cycle of abuse.

The sounds of Barbie slurping and gagging on James's member in the backseat broke her concentration. She hated Barbie and wondered why they'd picked her up. She hadn't been there earlier when everything happened. It was more than likely she would run around and tell everyone about it tomorrow. But Tabitha planned on being ten steps ahead of her. As soon as she could get away from Rex, she would go to the police.

Mr. Winters was a fantastic history teacher and an even better lover, far more exceptional than Rex would ever be. He taught Tabitha things about sex she never dreamed of. If only Rex had known the truth—she'd been in his car willingly. But he was too dumb to figure it out.

Tabitha had told Mr. Winters of Rex's violence, but he'd kindly pushed her warnings aside. He'd been too caught up in their carnal escapades. She could tell he was smitten by her. That was all sadly gone now.

Tabitha was in a position she desperately wanted out of, feeling trapped and obligated to help get rid of his body. To make matters worse, they were heading out of town to the Hills Have Eyes.

———

Hills Have Eyes was a little slice of hell on the outskirts of the county, snuggled deep in the marshy and swampy areas. The actual name of the lawless village had been forgotten. It picked up the moniker after Wes Craven's film was released, and the name had stuck. In the 60s, it became a rite of passage for young boys to venture down the town's filthy and rugged road, honking their horns to startle the river rats before speeding away like bats out of hell, never to return. Problems arose when kids started doing it too frequently. In 1968, a car filled with youngsters entered the village and vanished without a trace. Despite extensive searches, no evidence of their presence was ever found, except for a tree bearing an inscription.

During the 1980s, there were widespread rumors about toxic chemicals in the area due to drug manufacturing activities along the river. The whispers became so intense that most children from neighboring areas avoided it altogether. The local sheriff even held a meeting during PE class one day a year to discuss the dangers of fooling around. It was common knowledge that everyone should avoid the notorious Hills Have Eyes.

So this is where they were headed, highly intoxicated, with a body in the trunk of their car. Tabitha was a nervous wreck. Against her better judgment, she decided to crack open a pint of vodka from the cooler and gulp down two large helpings, convinced it would provide some form of relief.

James had the video camera and was hanging halfway out the car window. He recorded the surroundings as the vehicle crept slowly off the asphalt road and onto a dirty path. Compared to the main roads, it looked like an old wagon trail. Rex maneuvered the car slowly, trying to avoid massive potholes and craters.

Barbie was holding onto James's legs and peeking past him to look around. "Holy shit, do you see it?"

"Oh, yeah," James declared, tossing an empty beer can into the field.

As the car descended into a narrow space, an entirely new world came into view beyond the dense trees. A vast river appeared, lined with numerous huts and trailers of varying sizes and heights. Evidently, there was no electricity, as lanterns and dying campfires provided the only light sources. The entire area emitted a foul odor and exuded a sinister and intimidating aura.

As the car passed through a narrow space, the dense trees parted, revealing an entirely new world. A vast river stretched before them, its murky waters reflecting the dim light of lanterns and dying campfires. The riverbanks were dotted with huts and trailers of varying sizes and heights, giving the impression of a makeshift settlement. The absence of electricity was palpable, as the flickering lanterns and dying embers were the sole sources of light, casting eerie shadows that danced in the night. The air was heavy with a foul odor, assaulting their senses and adding to the sinister and intimidating aura that permeated the entire area.

A shiver ran down Tabitha's back as she surveyed the cluster of shacks. The whole scene appeared deserted and unsettling.

A sudden banging on the car jolted Rex into a panic. James also heard it and turned to look behind them. Nothing was there, but the banging grew louder and louder from the car's rear end. It almost sounded like the car was making the noise.

"Rex!" James spat.

"What the fuck is that?" Rex called back in a panic.

"It's… it's the car, man. I think it might be in the trunk," James said, second-guessing himself.

The car jerked to an abrupt halt.

"Rex, you can't just stop in the middle of this place," Tabitha screeched.

"Shut up, bitch! There's no one here. Look around, ya," Rex snapped. "If you don't like it, then start walkin'!" He forcefully swung the door open and carelessly tossed his beer, causing it to land in her lap.

The banging noise subsided as the car came to a stop. Everyone stepped out of the vehicle and gathered at the rear. Amidst the silence, they heard someone screaming, pleading to be set free.

"I'll be damned. I didn't kill him," Rex exclaimed with relief. "The bastard's still alive!"

"Wow, it's a miracle!" Barbie smirked.

James chuckled and turned off the camera. "Well, damn, what's our next move here?"

"Let me out! Help!" the voice screamed. "Rex! What the hell are you doing?"

"We'll get him out and have a conversation with him," Tabitha exclaimed. "We'll make him promise to keep quiet. In return, we'll let him live!"

Rex smacked himself on the head. "Damn, why didn't I think of that from the start?" A creepy smile slowly appeared on his lips. "Do you really think I'm going to let him get away with what he did to you? …trying to rape you? No way, that's not happening."

"Fuck no!" James egged on.

"I'm just happy he's alive so that I can beat the living shit out of him properly," Rex said, popping his knuckles. "All I did was punch his lights out once, and he hit his head. I wanted to do so much more, and now I can."

Tabitha felt a wave of fear wash over her as she heard those words. Rex was a monster, and she hated him for it. She knew she couldn't watch what was about to happen. Rex popped the trunk and leered at Mr. Winters' bleeding and frightened form.

James noticed Tabitha's tears and was taken aback. He pressed the record button on his camera and focused on the disappointment etched in her gaze. "Why on earth are you crying? You got feelings for this old fucker?" he asked behind the camera, loud enough for the others to hear.

Rex helped Mr. Winters out of the trunk, only to knock him down in the mud once he was planted on both feet. As his body hit the ground, Rex delivered a blunt kick to the man's ribs.

"Fucking bastard," Rex said and spit on him. "I need a beer. Someone beer me."

"Tab, get the man a beer!" James mocked with the camera still on her. "Your man needs a beer."

"Beer your hero!" Barbie yelled out theatrically.

Mr. Winters looked up from the ground, his head smeared with dried blood, and a hint of terror reflected in his eyes. He caught sight of Tabitha, illuminated by the small light of the camera.

"Ta-Tabitha … tell them…" Mr. Winters pleaded.

Rex clenched his fist and glared at her. "Tell me? Tell me what?"

Fear crawled from her belly up to her throat, choking her. Tabitha didn't know what to do. But she was certain if she came clean to Rex, she would die alongside Mr. Winters; she knew that for a fact. At first, she hesitated but then gathered her courage and forcefully kicked her lover in the face to convince her peers. The depth of her pain was unfathomable.

"You pig!" Tabitha screamed out, playing the part. She felt disgusted with herself as she felt the kick connect and heard the crunch of his nose against her foot. "Tell them what? How you forced me into your car and put your hands all over me?"

More tears cascaded down Tabitha's cheeks as James erupted into a boisterous fit of laughter that could have easily awakened the entire neighborhood.

Rex approached her and planted a passionate, albeit messy, kiss on Tabitha's face. He fervently clasped both sides of her face. "This is the depth of my love for you! This is how much I fucking adore you, baby! Just watch!"

Rex released her face and swiftly turned around, quickly retrieving a tire iron from the car's trunk. With tremendous rage, he swung the weapon with all his might, repeatedly striking Mr. Winters' back with powerful blows, one after another.

"You like that fucker!" Barbie screamed.

"Aww, I think he shit himself!" Rex chuckled, relentlessly landing blows without missing a beat.

James persisted in documenting the entire attack, meticulously capturing each strike on film. He laughed in the background and hurled insults at the old man.

Overwhelmed by her nerves, Tabitha couldn't hold herself together anymore. She collapsed against the side of the car and instantly vomited.

Then she saw it.

Right there, amidst the repulsive splatter of vomit, lay a solitary boot or shoe. But someone or something connected to it. A pungent stench intensified, assaulting her nostrils as she glanced upward and locked eyes with a thing... a man. She marveled at how he'd gone unnoticed for so long. His tall, menacing stature in the pale glow of the car's interior lights filled Tabitha with terror. She turned as fast as she could, looked at the others in pure desperation, and unleashed a resounding scream. Its brash volume overpowered the relentless pummeling of Mr. Winters as all eyes turned to her.

The others' faces turned white as ghosts.

At least ten peculiar faces littered the darkness, glaring menacingly. After a tense moment of appraisal, their stillness broke. They moved like arachnids, scuttling with eerie motions. In seconds, utter chaos ensued as the strangers stormed in from all around.

Rex turned and rushed for the car. He reached the driver's seat and put the car in drive. A sting prickled his neck as one of the strangers tried to grab him. But he pulled the car out in time and sped away like a speeding bullet.

Rex cheered victoriously as he passed multiple figures in the darkness. They must have been sneaking up on them the entire time they were out of the car. He hit one, watching them flip like a top off the hood, but he didn't stop.

As he yelled victoriously, blood burst from his neck like a crimson geyser, hitting the windshield. Panic overwhelmed him as he clutched his throat. It had been cut half an inch deep on the side. Blood gushed from his body with alarming speed, and despite his efforts, he couldn't stifle the flow. Shock spread through him as his consciousness quickly faded, and he passed out behind the wheel.

Tabitha fell to the ground as the strangers swarmed all around them. "Rex, you fucking bastard!" she screamed at the top of her lungs.

James was dragged into the mud by a powerful group of smelly locals. He didn't even have a chance to put up a fight against their brute force. His efforts amounted to a leaf being swept away by a raging river. They ripped the camera from his hand and thrashed it into his head over and over.

Barbie attempted to save her lover and jumped on the back of one of the men attacking James. She quickly realized her mistake as the man effortlessly tossed her through the air into a patch of brambles.

Chaos erupted in every direction as the unified force of these people mercilessly attacked the poor teens.

Tabitha watched as the car collided head-on with a massive oak tree. The force of the impact caused its front to cave in.

A booming explosion caught everyone's attention. It wasn't from the car hitting the tree but from a shotgun, bringing the assault to an abrupt halt. Illuminated by the moonlight, a towering figure with long hair and a hat emerged near one of the decrepit river houses. Situated proudly at the vicinity's zenith, this house teetered on the riverbank's edge. The shimmering glow from the water lent it an eerie and unsettling ambiance.

"What are all of ya doin'!?" the man bellowed in a thunderous voice. "Momma won't be happy! Bring our guests inside now!"

It appeared his words held the weight of scripture. The figures quickly scooped up the semi-conscious bodies of the teenagers. They moved like their lives depended on it and carried the kids away to a towering house.

———

Fear had never been more present than in the moments when Tabitha opened her eyes to the disgusting ramshackle of a living room. It was vile, as if the occupants hadn't thrown an item of trash away in decades. The kitchen was filled to the brim, with items spilling onto the seating arrangements. Amongst the chaos was a chair covered in countless moldy Playboy magazines. Surprisingly, someone was sitting on them, using them as a makeshift bed. This person was peculiar—a half-man with no legs, an oversized belly, and thin, stick-like arms. When he winked his only eye at Tabitha in a flirting manner, she felt like she was going to puke again.

She fought the rising acid in her throat. She looked at several members of the group who, without a doubt, had attacked them. All of them were bizarre in appearance, displaying a myriad of physical defects: Sunken noses. Over-sized heads. Sickening white faces. Cleft lips galore. Before her eyes, she beheld a nightmare in the flesh. These people … these creatures… were so terrifyingly hideous that they exceeded the expectations of any cinematic portrayal.

Tabitha attempted to move, but she found herself tightly bound with ropes knotted so securely that there was no possibility of escape. James and Barbie were also lying on the ground beside her, their bodies tightly bound like helpless lambs for the slaughter.

Tears welled in Tabitha's eyes, and she let out a weak, pathetic whimper.

"Shut up…" a woman's voice hissed from the back of the room.

Slowly, several lopsided figures moved to reveal the most grotesque spectacle in the house—their momma. Her immense size defied human possibility, her swollen belly a repulsive sight that no shirt could contain. It was as if her gelatinous flesh melded with the cluttered surroundings. Momma's enormous form blended seamlessly with the floor beneath her. The dim light glowed on her gut, revealing the intricate network of blue veins meandering across her skin. Open sores and liver spots marred her flesh. Tabitha detected a subtle shimmer on her belly with each breath, as if tiny waves of movement danced before her eyes.

"You ain't gonna saves yourself cryin' like dat." She struggled to muster with labored breaths. "You done come here and caused us a whole lotta trouble. You ain't supposed to be here. Not-at-all."

Barbie and James woke up, their eyes scanning the room frantically. Fear gripped them as they desperately tried to speak, their pleas stifled by the chaos surrounding them. One of the peculiar figures with an oversized head knelt beside Barbie, mischievously toying with the part of her breast that was exposed from her top. A few chuckles echoed in the room, but Momma swiftly cleared her throat, prompting the nosy man to move away from Barbie.

Some other men moved forward, lifted James and Barbie to sitting positions, and removed their gags.

"What in the trailer park fuck is going on here?" James yelled, only to receive a sharp slap from one of the men.

"James... stop," Tabitha pleaded, her voice tinged with urgency. The pungent smell of feces and death floated in the air more now, adding to the tension that hung thickly around them.

"You better watch yourself, boy!" the man warned.

"Fuck you!" James cursed. "Let us go! My dad is a fucking lawyer. You fucking inbred cupcakes!"

The man released a sinister and belittling giggle while glaring at James. "Out here, son, there's no law. We abide by our own set of rules." He snickered some more. "You better watch your mouth, too."

As James prepared to speak, a shiver ran down his spine. A chilling touch grazed the back of his neck, sending a wave of fear through his body. James sensed the weight of the double-barrel shotgun pressed firmly against his head. It was a stark reminder to remain silent. He could see out of the corner of his eyes it was the man they'd encountered earlier— a balding, long-haired figure resembling a skeletal apparition.

"You all are left with a choice—somethin' we never had.

None of ya can leave here, not without earning ya keep," Momma explained, yellow spittle dripping past her lip sores. "Da Boys, gots to make it with some of the girls here in the village. 'Fraid our closed community has brung a curse on us lately. Most men here can't fire full live loads no more. I can taste the death in their cock snot. You girls… well, you stay here, with us, and get filled with the men that is good and can breed ya up. Break the chain a little in the DNA. That's my say in this matter."

Barbie gazed around the room, her frustration written across her face. "Please, just release us," she pleaded. "We won't tell anyone. Hell, we were trying to kill someone tonight!"

"Fraid I can't do that. Them's the rules," Momma said, holding firm.

"Is this about Rex?" Tabitha stammered. "We're good. We won't…"

"Yeah, fuck him," James shot back.

"No. That has nothin' to do with it. He gots the quick way, I'm 'fraid. Very rare. But lucky," Momma smiled.

"Well, fuck all this. I was willing to give all you guys blowjobs!" Barbie screamed, pointing her finger around the room like it was a weapon. "But now you all aren't getting shit!"

"Hush… you don't wanna…" Momma whispered, her calm voice falling on deaf ears.

Barbie slowly rose from the floor. Her legs wobbled like a newborn fawn, yet she managed to stand. She looked around the room. "I'm leaving! And you can't stop me, you fat Jabba the Hut looking—"

Before she could finish, she was cut down by a blast from the shotgun. The shot was aimed directly into her hip, shoving her a few feet across the room and onto her side.

Tabitha and James flinched from the power of the gun. Blood and chunks of flesh scattered in their direction. James put his head down, and his complexion went as pale as a ghost.

"She made her decision," Mamma shook her head.

"Hey, her mouth should still be good," one of the men said.

"Hell, it was just her hip. Ol' Jesse just made another hole in her, that's all," another person laughed, swooped in, and grabbed Barbie by the arm. A few more of them quickly lifted her.

Barbie looked down at her leg and let out a surprised cry as the men carried her out of the living room and into a back bedroom, tossing her onto the bed and slamming the door shut. Her screams shook throughout the entire house.

Momma glared at Tabitha and James with a sweet but devious grin. "What say you two? Choose?"

James hung his head as far as it would go, tears streaming down his face. His face was pale, and he was shivering uncontrollably. In a desperate tone, he muttered, "Oh, fuck. Oh, God. Please."

Closing his eyes, James could hear the men in the room snickering at him. He knew deep down that he couldn't fuck any of these horrid creatures. Their very presence made his stomach churn. The way they looked at him, he wondered if his dick would ever get hard again.

The thought of death seemed more appealing. Despite the slim chances, James felt compelled to seize an opportunity the moment he could try to escape—maybe get to the brambles and hide in the dark. They surely didn't possess night vision as a special power of their inbred traits.

James heard the double-barrel shotgun crack open. That was it. He glanced at the face of the long-haired troll, who was absorbed in emptying the chambers. James decided it was now or never. Miraculously, he stood from the ground and spun for the screen door, moving as swiftly as lightning. It was the fastest he'd ever moved in his life. Despite feeling the urge to vomit, he knew he had to suppress it. He pushed through the discomfort and continued like a bat out of hell.

Bursting down the creaky steps of the house, James sprinted across the mud. The river flowed fiercely. The moon's reflection created a breathtaking scene, but James had no time to appreciate it. He needed to find a path to escape. Urgent screams and threatening footsteps echoed behind him, signaling they were closing in.

James raced forward, his feet pounding against the earth. A gunshot pierced the air, but he felt nothing. Perhaps they'd missed. Regardless, he didn't waste a second and continued running.

Arriving at the muddy road, he discovered the car had been completely wrecked in the crash. Not only was it unsalvageable, but a group of the river rats were carefully dismembering Rex in the driver's seat.

James kept running, occasionally glancing back to see his pursuers limping and contorting their bodies in unconventional ways in their attempt to chase him. It was terrifying but oddly fascinating. James had a feeling he would pull through.

The spot where Mr. Winters was beaten was empty. Those barbarians must have taken him. He didn't have time to think about it—just kept moving.

Suddenly, James felt a sharp pain, causing his strength to dwindle. His leg gave way, and he crashed face-first onto the road. The impact left him breathless. As he struggled to shake it off, he realized something was seriously wrong with his leg. Debilitating pain surged through his body, rendering him unable to move it, no matter how hard he tried.

"No! No!" James screamed.

Some of the freakish women had Tabitha on the porch and were peering out at James on the road. Tabitha could see the mayhem and also wondered where Mr. Winters had gone. None of it would have happened if she hadn't slept with him. Or she could have told Rex, and things wouldn't have happened like they had. It was all her fault, one way or another.

The mob reached James and picked him up like a rag doll. He did his best to fight back but felt sharp stabbing pains in his back and stomach. No major organs were hit as the men peppered him with their knives, playing with him.

"Put him over on the bench!" one ordered.

James was slammed front first over the bench. Everything was a blur and happened so fast. They stabbed him repeatedly until he could taste crimson in his teeth. Tears flooded his eyes as he tried to scream. The stabbing stopped as they ripped James's pants and underwear from his body. He looked in a frenzy and could see the mob with their trousers down and their deformed penises dangling around him.

"It's tradition to play pin the hog with one of the boys," giggled one of the uglier women in Tabitha's face. "Don't worry, though. They treat girls better. Especially one's like y'all."

"Why? Why do … you have to…. do this?" Tabitha cried.

Another girl, missing an eye, ran her hand through Tabitha's soft hair. "Why, after all the things you pretty-faced people did to us? We've been this way since I remember. You made us like this." She got close to Tabitha's face, her breath rotten, and growled with deep anger, "You don't think we want to be like you? You ungrateful bitch. You should appreciate what your kind did to us."

James could finally scream. It was a blood-curdling cry for help as one of the larger men shoved his erect member in dry.

As the smelly hillbilly snorted and grunted behind James, he felt his world fading.

"PIN! THE! PIG! PIN! THE! PIG!" the others cheered. They jerked each other off, wrapped around James in a circle-like fashion, and waved their bloody knives in the air.

———

Tabitha was brought back into the house. The bedroom door was open, and she glimpsed Barbie's lifeless body. A torturous expression was frozen on her face.

A small group of men piled out of the room, snickering. Tabitha could tell, just by looking at Barbie's corpse, that they'd used every hole and even fashioned more on her body. A line of makeshift fuck holes oozed their contents down the length of her torso. The sight was more than Tabitha could bear. She shook with fear as she stood before Momma, once more having to answer the question that would seal her fate.

She accepted full blame for the situation, and the thought kept circling in her mind.

In the moonlight, Tabitha spotted a man camouflaged in the river, gripping a twisted branch extending from the riverbank. It was him… Mr. Winters… He was alive.

"Well, child? What are ya goin' to do?" Mamma questioned sweetly.

Tabitha's lip trembled as she contemplated the words she was about to utter. "I… um…" Tabitha struggled to articulate her thoughts, feeling a sense of unease as the words lingered on her tongue like a poison. "Who should I… fuck first, Momma?"

YOU MESS IT UP
YOU CLEAN IT UP

J. ROCKY COLAVITO

"DO you think you could drive any slower?" Krissy grunted at her boyfriend as he piloted the conversion van along the desolate stretch of highway toward the setting sun to the west.

"Got something poking out?" Matt asked her, receiving a hard backhanded smack for his trouble. Krissy had been fidgeting in discomfort for the last few hours, and her child-like questions about their speed had become more persistent.

"Look, I can pull off the road, you can unload, and we can get back to the trip."

"Not on your life. I'm not an animal. Why didn't you have toilet capability put in when you designed this thing?"

"This thing, as you refer to it, has served us very well on this trip. We've eaten well and slept safely and comfortably. We've not gone wanting for wi-fi service, and we've had ample juice when we needed it. The space for the toilet and shower provided us more room for a bigger bed and the his and hers closets, which you appreciate."

Krissy was persistent, "I gotta go, Matt. Do you want me to shit my pants here on these newly upholstered seats? Did we pack a bucket? I don't want to go outside!" Her whining on the last part of her plea sounded like she probably did at seven years old.

"The only bucket we have is for toting water. I'm not gonna let you take a dump in that because we will be using it later on during the trip. Even with a liner, it could get contaminated." He looked at his squirming girlfriend. "What the hell is the problem with the side of the road; hell, the hardest part is burying it."

"Cause there's stuff out there that can bite me, Matt. Oh god, ugh!"

Matt pulled off the road and put the van in park. He took an exasperated tone.

"Krissy, you should have taken care of this when we stopped outside El Paso. Get out and take care of your business." He handed her the roll of toilet paper they used for nose-blowing and other needs.

Krissy looked at him pleadingly, but the rapidly diminishing power of her sphincter forced her out the passenger door and onto the shoulder. She looked carefully in both directions, undid her shorts, and squatted.

She released a loud fart that brought a chuckle out of Matt. She glared at him as she strained to evacuate. The constipation turds were slow in coming. It was taking her a lot longer than she'd hoped.

"Christ, Krissy, you passing a puppy?" Matt needled as she finally finished and wiped. She threw the used toilet paper on top of the pile that she'd left. She pulled her shorts back up, slid back into the passenger seat, closed the door, and sat with her arms crossed and her eyes straight ahead.

"You finished?" Matt asked.

"Just drive. I don't want to talk to you at the moment."

"By your command." Matt put the van in gear and merged back onto the highway. The trip started well; they'd grown a group of followers and established a brand. The Taboo Travelers were becoming a viral sensation; their full nude frolics in all kinds of places on the highways and byways of the United States had inspired copycats and, in their minds, had opened people's minds to the possibilities of sex in historic or naturally beautiful places. Matt was secretly angry with himself for not getting out the video camera while Krissy had shit on the roadside. He'd already performed that act on a Confederate monument in Louisiana, sneaking out in the early morning to drop a deuce at the ass of some Confederate general. The pile had been prodigious, and they'd sold the image online as a postcard with the title "Scared Shitless." Krissy captured the act on video and even complimented him on the quality and quantity of his output.

Matt settled into watching the road and the kept van at a clip just over the posted speed limit. Their exploits landed them followers, but also caught the attention of people who didn't appreciate their assignations at landmarks or their desecration—*defecation?* Matt thought and smiled—of those landmarks. Several of their followers warned them of places to avoid since eyes were everywhere. So, the deviant duo, as they referred to themselves, preferred to hide out in plain sight in larger cities. This paid off in several ways, not the least of which was access to chain gyms where they could shower. Laundromats and big box stores were plentiful, as were parking garages where the van was never questioned.

But they were several hours from such a place, and Matt was starting to flag. He caught himself nodding off several times and once was even woken up by the tires hitting the rumble cuts on the shoulder.

Krissy looked at him disdainfully. "Whatsa matter. You getting tired?"

"What tipped you off? Listen, I think we're gonna have to pit someplace. Check your phone and see if there's a truck stop or rest area anywhere near here."

"Your wish is my command," Krissy said sarcastically. She pulled out her phone and started looking.

"Listen, Krissy. You didn't give me much choice about the unscheduled pit stop. I didn't film it, although I'm pretty sure it would have been a hit with the fans. You unloaded a source of discomfort. Maybe something other than shooting me the death eye and radio silence is in order."

"I don't want to talk about that, Matthew."

"Well, maybe we should. Given some of the stuff you've done on this quest, it strikes me as funny that you have an issue with shitting on the roadside. Yeah, it's not pleasant, but it's a case of doing what you gotta do. Hell, if I remember right, you left a package inside a pillow at one of the hotels we stayed at because you thought it deserved less than one star."

"That's different. I showed the product, not the act. Do you understand I have limits?"

"I just find it funny that a public dump is one of them."

"I'm sure if you thought hard enough, you'd find you have limits as well." The conversation distracted her from looking for a place to pull off.

"Honey, I fingered you to orgasm in a revivalist church during a service. You blew me in the last row of a sold-out Broadway play. We did sixty-nine in an airplane lavatory; you did the equivalent of a keg stand on the damn toilet. I think my limits are limitless."

"I'm going to laugh my ass off when you find something that makes you cringe. Anyway, there's supposed to be a rest stop within ten miles. It's on the eastbound side, though. You'll have to find a way to cut across."

"That's weird. They normally put them on each side."

"The one on the westbound is listed as closed with access blocked. The next possibility is a truck stop fifty miles ahead. You think you can make it that far?"

"Why me all of a sudden? You can drive. Why don't you take the wheel?"

"Because I'm still mad at you for making me shit on the roadside."

"That's really short-sighted, Krissy. I'm falling asleep here."

"Suck it up, and be more respectful next time—you and your precious bucket."

"Our precious bucket. Hey, what the hell?!"

Something the size of a man but four-legged dashed in front of the van. Matt braked abruptly, tossing Krissy into the dashboard. He tried to steer around whatever it was but clipped it, knocking the creature through the air and onto the median, where it bounced and came to a stop.

"Goddamn, motherfucking, inattentive . . ." Krissy's lip was bleeding, animating her upbraiding of Matt.

"Did you see it?" Matt barked as he pulled the van to the

shoulder. He turned the van off and grabbed the keys and a flashlight.

"What are you doing?" Krissy yelped as Matt unbuckled and opened his door.

"Gonna check for damage first, then see what I clipped." He reached into one of the storage spaces on the door and pulled out his pistol, a Glock. They hadn't needed it yet, but Matt kept it handy for emergencies. "You wanna wait?"

"Like hell." Krissy slid out of her side of the van, silently cursing. It never crossed her mind that she should have been wearing a seatbelt.

"Ahh, fuck." Matt growled as he looked at the driver's side. Whatever they hit had taken out the light assembly and left a sizeable dent in the grille. Matt shined the light underneath the van to check for drips. He didn't see any, but that didn't mean there weren't any. He noticed some things that looked like porcupine quills sticking out of the area where the light used to be. Whatever he'd hit, he'd hit it hard.

Shaking his head, he turned to the median, where his light picked up the mound of flesh lying on its side. As they approached, they could hear raspy breath and muted moans. Matt cursed; it was still alive.

They got near enough to take a closer look. Matt shined the light on it, and they both gasped.

At first glance, it looked like a dog of some kind. But what kind of dog was covered in cactus spines? And what kind of dog had a humanlike face, with eyes that darted from side to side, looking for an escape? Matt and Krissy didn't know what to make of it.

Out of habit, Krissy pulled out her phone, snapped pictures, and started recording. "Look what we found. Thanks to Matt's inattentive driving, we picked off this whatsit at mile marker one-seventy-seven, somewhere in

Arizona. It smashed our driver's side headlight and dented our grille. Any of you know what this thing is?"

The thing vomited up something that might have been blood, but it was green with flecks of black. It growled and tried to fling itself toward Krissy, who gracefully retreated, still aiming her phone at the thing. It pulled itself forward a couple of feet, tried to rise, and collapsed. The lower half of its body was misshapen and twisted. It howled pitifully and flopped its head onto the gravel.

Krissy pointed the video camera at Matt, who had the gun by his side. "So what, Matt? It's suffering, we've got places to be, and it fucked up our transportation. Sounds like three strikes." Krissy giggled.

Matt drew the pistol and pointed it at the creature. "Sorry, buddy. But it looks like you need a way out." Matt shot the thing in the side. The bullet blew completely through its flank, leaving a softball-sized hole on the exit side.

The thing screeched, the cry transitioning into a howl. The two influencers laughed.

"I'll give you something to cry about. This is for the van. Krissy, get a closeup!" Matt walked to the thing's head, which rose from the gravel to look at him almost defiantly. It drew back lips full of small spines and snapped at him.

"Oh, wise guy, huh?" Matt shot it in the face at close range. The creature's head exploded like a rotten pumpkin.

Krissy cheered as the faceless thing thrashed and shook its damaged head. "Double tap this fucking mutant, and let's get gone," she said.

Matt did as requested. The third shot tore what was left of the thing's head apart. The stump of its neck sank to the ground, weeping the same black and green fluid.

"To Oz?" Matt asked, lowering the Glock.

"To Oz." Krissy held out her arm for him to take and

filmed as they jigged their way back to the van, whistling the tune from the movie.

The broken headlight made things difficult in the darkness. Matt was sure he'd missed the rest stop on the eastbound side. He hummed through his teeth to keep his mind off the funny sound he thought he heard the engine making.

Krissy broke the silence after they'd picked their way along for ten miles. "What do you think that thing was?"

Matt was grateful; the question distracted his mind from his worries. "Hell, if I know, it looked like something a stoned cartoonist would come up with if you asked them to create something that combined human, animal, and vegetable."

"An ugly thing it was," Krissy said, imitating Yoda. She pulled up one of the photos and inserted it into an image search engine. Their wi-fi held, and the results eventually popped up.

"I'd show you, but you're driving. I ran an image search. There's stuff like it—but mostly art." She scrolled and then halted. "Wait a second. Let me look at this." She paused, lips moving and head shaking as she read. She finished and laughed.

"I take it you found something humorous?" Matt queried.

"Yeah. I found a drawing of the thing on *Clues to the Weird.* It's just like what we saw—a four-legged cactus with a slightly human face."

"Does it have a name?"

"Yeah. It's called a Cactumalina. It's like a mash-up of a javelina, a cactus, and a human being."

"Gimme the highlights."

Krissy read from the article, "First reported in March of this year, the creature was sighted trying to get into a shed. It howled and ran off quickly when two sheriff's deputies tried to lasso it. Witnesses claim the thing stood on its hind legs and tried to turn the knob to get the door open."

"Interesting," Matt said.

"The strangest thing about the creature was its face appeared to have tracks of tears running down it, but that couldn't be verified. The creature disappeared in the darkness. Since then, the sightings have been more infrequent. However, there have been parallel reports of hikers and migrants disappearing in the general area where the things have been sighted."

"That's very interesting," Matt repeated. "Do we have numbers?"

"Six hikers. The number of migrants is open to question for obvious reasons. A group of them was apprehended recently, and before they were forcefully deported, they told their captors about a group of animals that looked like cacti but ran on four legs, abducting several women and children from their group. One young man was shot trying to escape. His last words to the posse were, `Please find my family. Don't let the desert get them.'"

"So how did that get attributed? *Clues to the Weird* is a tabloid, and you know how reliable they are as far as sourcing goes."

"I'm not reading from *Clues*, Matt. This is from a local news article. The reporter sourced the men in the posse."

"So, someone admitted to murder in a newspaper interview?"

"No, the guy who got shot had wrestled a shotgun away from one of the posse members, fracturing his skull in the process. They claimed self-defense and were not charged. The reporter also cites some of the migrants before they were deported. Their stories were similar. A pack of the things came out of the darkness, focusing on the children first and then dragging off women who tried to save the children. Several of the men showed signs of injury resembling cactus wounds. One was pierced so badly his face looked like a pin cushion."

"Are there pictures?" Matt asked. He spied a light off to the side of the westbound highway about two miles in the distance.

"Hey, I think that might be the truck stop. With luck, maybe they'll have a parts store, and I can find a headlight assembly," he said.

"And I can use a restroom privately," Krissy said. "And then I'll tell you the rest of this."

The truck stop wasn't what Matt had hoped for. It was more of a gas station/convenience store with a shady-looking take-out joint advertising Mexican food attached to one side. Matt topped off the van while Krissy went inside. When he finished, he noticed the card reader on the gas pump hadn't taken his credit card, so he went inside to check on things.

He walked in on a bloodbath. Three twitchy men in luchador masks were holding shotguns on the proprietor, a mother and her two children, and Krissy. Matt instinctively raised his hands.

"That's right, fuckbucket. Raise 'em high and clench 'em tight over your head. Disco Strangler here is gonna come and frisk you. Don't pay him any mind if he helps himself to a squeeze. He plays for lotsa teams," one of the men, wearing a red and black mask, said.

Disco Strangler, who wore a pink and black lucha mask with lightning bolts, put his gun down and stepped forward. He spun Matt against the counter and kicked his legs apart. His hands paused over Matt's groin as he frisked him. He grunted and turned Matt around, pushing his back against the counter. "Drop 'em. It feels big. I want to see it," Disco Strangler grunted.

Matt's eyes widened. "Excuse me?"

The third man, who wore a blue and gold mask with stars on the eyes and mouth hole, grabbed one of the shrieking children from her mother and dragged her to the floor in front of him. He stuck the barrel of the shotgun behind her head. "Say goodbye," he said flatly, then pulled the trigger.

The blast blew the little girl's face clean off; it flew through the air like a frisbee and splatted against Matt's chest, sliding down and leaving a wake of viscera. Her mother and brother screamed and burrowed into each other for comfort.

The man in the blue mask kicked the little girl's body out of the way and trained his gun on Krissy. "I figure this bitch belongs to you. She can be next if you don't play along. But I can tell you, it won't be as merciful."

Matt raised his shaking hands and undid his belt. He slid his cargo shorts and boxer briefs down.

"Would ya look at that," Disco Strangler said. "It's probably nine inches when it's ready for action. Think she deep throats him?" He jerked a thumb at Krissy. "How 'bout it, Juan Long? Can she take it all and swallow?"

Matt shook his head; Krissy looked stricken.

"Sorry to hear that, but I bet ol' momma here can do it. Whatchu say, momma? How about giving this guy a blow job?"

The woman took on a flabbergasted expression amid her tears. She pulled her son closer.

"Lady, you better start crawling and get his dick in your mouth, or I will shove this up your son's bunghole and turn him into a sock puppet." The man wearing the red and black mask shoved his shotgun between them and separated them. "You think I'm joking? Here's one for you." He turned the shotgun on the child and blew off one of his feet. The child screamed as the man dragged him out of his mother's reach.

"He'll bleed to death!" Matt yelled.

"Maybe. It depends on how deep his mother can take you and how quickly she can get you off. You need some inspiration, momma? How's this?" He stomped on the stump where her son's foot used to be. The kid screamed again, but the blood flow was curtailed.

The woman crawled to Matt and took his penis in her hand. She spat on it, bringing up a gob of saliva and blood, then massaged him to an erection. Looking up at him, she mouthed, "I'm sorry." Her unpracticed tongue started licking.

Matt closed his eyes and fantasized that it was someone with more experience and talent at work. This was probably one of the first blow jobs the woman had ever given, and she was already coughing when she tried to take Matt's length in her mouth. She withdrew, gagged, and gamely tried again.

"I said take it all!" Disco Strangler growled. He came up behind the woman and shoved her head forward, burying her face in Matt's pubic hair.

Matt screamed as her jagged teeth bit his cock and torqued it while she struggled with his length down her throat. Disco Strangler held her there, then moved her head back and forth, giving her brief moments to get air. During these pauses, Matt saw the damage to his penis; it looked like she had bitten a little chunk out of the side, and there were small gashes along the length.

"There. I done showed you how to do it. Now get on it. And you better swallow every drop." Disco Strangler stepped back.

The woman tried anew, but her performance was still wanting.

"Goddammit bitch, can't you do anything right? Your

husband died not having any pleasure." Disco Strangler shoved her head against Matt's pubic hair again and held her there until she choked and died. He yanked her off and threw her body to the floor. "Finish yourself off there, partner. Hit her in the face."

Matt did as he was told. He had enough blood to use as lubricant. His ejaculation didn't seem to impress the masked men, but it did slick her face.

"Get her duds off her, you sick pervert," the man wearing the red and black mask ordered.

Once again, Matt didn't argue. He pulled the woman's clothes off.

Blue Mask pulled off the moaning child's shorts and underwear and dragged him to the body. "That's your momma there, lookin' fine and wet for you. Lick her pussy! She wants you to."

The child blubbered, both in pain and nonunderstanding, as Blue Mask pushed his face down.

"Lick it, see how good she tastes."

The child struggled but finally gave in.

Blue Mask yanked him up. "Ok, you got her ready. Get your cock up! You're gonna fuck her." Blue Mask guided the child's hand to his penis and started him stroking. The child simply went along until he achieved a small erection.

"Now put it in her," Blue Mask commanded as he positioned the child so that his penis was rubbing against his dead mother's vulva.

Blue Mask shot him in the back of the head when he inserted it. The child's head exploded, showering his mother's corpse with brain matter and baby teeth. The headless body flopped forward, neck nestling under her sopping chin.

The three masked men guffawed as the proprietor, Matt, and Krissy watched in horror.

"At least he went out with a bang." Disco Strangler said.

Matt couldn't take it anymore. He bent over and vomited. His spew hit the dead woman and her son.

"Now, that was a money shot there, podnah, but you know what Mama always said, right?"

"Yeah, you mess it up, you clean it up." Blue Mask guffawed.

Matt looked for a mop.

Disco Strangler stepped forward and hit him on the side of the head with his gun barrel. "Get on your knees and lick it up. Get the other two to help you."

He kicked one of Matt's legs out from under him, and Matt fell face-first into the dead woman's crotch. "Start right there. It's as good a place as any. Get going, you two." He motioned with the gun barrel to the proprietor and Krissy, who slowly moved toward the befouled bodies. Krissy was already gagging from the smell.

Then she saw that the masked men were filming and went ballistic. "Uh, uh, no way! You can kill me. I'm not going to be part of your freak show."

"Sorry you feel that way." Disco Strangler grabbed her by the hair and threw her into a rack of chips. The bags crumpled and ruptured with the impact, covering Krissy in crumbs. He took her by the hair again and rubbed her face in the pile of crunchy cheese products. Krissy screamed as he raised her face; she pawed at her eyes.

"Damn, those extra hot ones must hurt, don't they?" Disco Strangler knelt to Krissy's level. "But it won't hurt as much as what I'm gonna do." He threw Krissy face-down in the crumbs and yanked her shorts and panties down.

Matt stopped his cleanup and stared, the blood and bodily fluids giving him a clown's face.

"Open wide, tight ass." Disco Strangler snarled as he

drove the barrel of his shotgun into Krissy's anus. Krissy's scream blew a mushroom cloud of disintegrated chips into the air as she struggled and bucked against the metal intruder.

"Hold still, I got a finger on the trigger. Go with it, and you might survive." He started moving the gun barrel in and out, and Krissy's screams went higher and higher.

Matt couldn't help himself. He felt the erection stirring.

Red Mask noticed. "Hey. Look! Dude's getting himself a stiffie! You like what you see? Old man, help him get off!"

The old man, probably resigned to his fate, reached an arthritis-corrupted hand to Matt's penis and started gently rubbing.

Blue Mask fired a shot into the cooler that ran the length of the back wall, destroying a rack of energy drinks. "Spit out your teeth and suck him off, Grandpa."

The now-shaking man did as he was told. He took the teeth from his mouth and put them in his pocket. His toothless orifice fastened onto Matt's engorged penis and commenced sucking.

Disco Strangler finally grew tired of sodomizing Krissy with the shotgun and withdrew it. The barrel was streaked with a gelatinous mixture of blood and diarrhetic shit. He yanked Krissy around and wiped some of it on her face.

"You mess it up, you clean it up." He wiped the barrel along Krissy's lips. She gagged in protest but then started licking. Disco Strangler slammed the barrel against her teeth, cracking her incisors. "It's a cock, bitchcakes, treat it like one."

Krissy started licking the barrel as if she was warming it up. A swallow and a gag followed each lick, but she kept the foul substances down and kept at the cleaning. She finished off by deep-throating the barrel. Her lower body was slick with blood from her torn rectum, but she seemed to be in no danger of bleeding out.

"See, now that's how you put your mind to something. How'd you like to do that for each of us?" Red Mask started to pull down his zipper.

Krissy held up her hand. "Begging your pardon, but do you think I can at least rinse my mouth out? Not sure you want to be in something that just sucked my shit off a gun barrel."

"Good thinking, cum-twat. What do you want?"

Matt saw Krissy pull a lighter from her shorts pocket and hide it in her palm. "Whiskey." She said in a deep, throaty voice.

Red Mask grabbed a bottle of the cheap stuff and handed it to Krissy. She untwisted the cap, took a mouthful, swished it, and spit into the pile of crumbs.

"You ready?" Red Mask asked. Slowly lowering his shorts with one hand, he kept the gun trained on Krissy.

"Gonna give you a special treat. I learned this from a friend who turned tricks. She said guys came back for more if she blew them with a mouthful of whiskey." She took a mouthful and grabbed the guy's penis, slowly stroking it to life. She slowly brought up her other hand as if to two-hand it.

"Yeah, that's right. Ahh, ahh, aiiiieeee!" His moans descended to screams when Krissy lit the lighter and blew whiskey through it. The improvised fireball landed in the guy's pubic hair and clung. Red Mask was so startled that he raised his shotgun by reflex and fired.

The buckshot caught Blue Mask in the belly and blew him back over the counter. His shotgun fell to the floor and skittered to a stop between Matt, the old man, and Disco Strangler.

Matt tried to grab it, but the old man was faster. With unbelievable agility, the man slid to the gun, swung it up, and fired it. He hit Disco Strangler in the knee.

Disco Strangler collapsed, his leg buckling at an obscene angle.

The old man chambered another round and fired the shotgun at Disco Strangler's hand, which somehow still held a shotgun. He missed the hand but got the forearm and severed it.

Disco Strangler screamed as he tried to fire. Then he noticed his hand, still holding the gun, was six inches from his forearm. The raggedy stump of his handless appendage pumped blood in thick, red spurts onto the floor.

Krissy used her diversion to get a larger mouthful of whiskey. She stood and spit another ball of fire into Red Mask's face. He dropped the shotgun and pawed at his eyes.

The old man motioned for Krissy to step out of the way. He chambered another round and fired at Red Mask, disintegrating his crotch. Red Mask mewled and fell in a fetal heap, grasping at equipment that no longer existed.

Their three tormenters were now in a position to be tormented. Matt collected the guns. Krissy, who'd been running on adrenaline, started hyperventilating over the pain in her ruined anus. The blood and shit had slowed to a trickle, but her face was contorted out of pain and shame.

The old man pulled his teeth from his pocket and put them back in his mouth. He looked at the two young people, who stared at him with awe.

"Sorry, kids. I tried to warn you when you pulled in, but it didn't work." His voice was firm, but Krissy and Matt could see the toll the experience had taken on him. His shaking was visible, and the pain etched on his face was unmistakable.

"Were they," Matt pointed to the bodies of the woman and children, "family of yours?"

The old man shook his head, "Not by blood, but by responsibility. Her husband served under me—caught a bullet from an enemy sniper. I promised him I'd take care of them as best I could before he died. I failed."

"Unarmed against three guys toting shotguns... Hard to tussle with those odds. You'd have probably ended up shot and forced to watch whatever they did. At least you're still alive." Matt said.

Krissy had fallen to her knees and was growing pale.

The old man looked at her. "Young fella, go tend to her. She needs a hospital to address the damage. I can't do the surgery. You'll have to jury-rig it. Get some tampons, feminine napkins, and antibiotic ointment. Everything should be in the same general area. I'll handle the trash." He trained the gun on the three masked men, who were in no condition to mount any resistance.

Matt collected the first aid materials and waited for instructions from the man.

"Ok, what's her name?" the man asked.

"Krissy, and I'm Matt."

"Okay, Krissy, I need you to listen and pay attention. You're bleeding internally from what he did with the gun barrel. There's no way to tell how deep the wounds are. Matt is going to plug the bleeding by putting tampons covered with antibiotic cream in your rectum. It won't solve the problem completely, but it will at least help stop the bleeding and slow infection. When he's got them inside you, he will use a sanitary pad to cover the insertion point and hold them in. I need you to relax. Take a slug of that whiskey if you need to. The tampons will hurt going in, but you must keep them inside. Matt will take you to a hospital as soon as he is done. Do you understand?"

Krissy took a deep swig of the whiskey and nodded. She grabbed a ball cap that had fallen off a display, clenched it between her teeth, and turned away so Matt could get to work.

Matt gagged when he saw the damage. He would need more than one tampon to close the hole the barrel had made. He bundled two tampons together and covered them with the opaque cream. Krissy jerked as he attempted the first insertion. She pulled the ballcap from her mouth.

"Just-huff-just-huff- shove it in!" She jammed the hat back in her mouth.

Matt did. Krissy stiffened as the package went in. Matt pushed until only the retrieval strings showed. He covered the makeshift packing with two sanitary napkins shaped into an X. Krissy spit the hat out and moaned.

"You okay?" Matt asked.

Krissy glared at him. "I just had a very invasive colonoscopy with a gun barrel that I had to lick clean. How the fuck do you think I feel."

"There's some high-power pain reliever where you found the other stuff. Give her some. It won't do much, but it might cut some of the pain." The old man motioned with his head.

Matt found the pain pills and grabbed a bottle of cold water from the undamaged coolers. He brought everything to Krissy, who eschewed the water for a slug of whiskey to wash down the pain reliever.

"I strongly urge you two to hit the road. You don't want to be around for what's about to happen." The old man was nervously looking out the windows of the storefront.

"Why? Are you gonna go full Inquisition on these mother fuckers? If that's it, count me in." Matt offered.

"I'm not, but something else is. And if you're here when they show up, you might get the same treatment."

"What are you talking about?" Matt asked.

"It's too long a story to tell, and you both need to git. Let's just say that there are things out here that come out every so often and need to feed."

"What kind of things?" Matt asked. He had temporarily forgotten about Krissy.

"Son, stop with the questions, help your girlfriend up, and get her to a hospital." The old man's voice became insistent. He looked out the window again, and his eyes stayed fixed. He looked sadly at Matt and Krissy.

"It's too late," He intoned with a hint of sadness.

A howl from outside the doors drew Matt's gaze. He stared and gulped.

A pack of mutants like the one they'd encountered earlier waddled forward on four legs. Their bodies were covered with spines, and some had manes of pointed quills. As they approached, Matt saw their humanoid faces framed by green plant skin. The creatures snorted like pigs as they moved toward the door.

"Jesus, there's more of them?" Matt said in awe.

"Seen one of them?" the old man asked.

"Yeah, we hit one with the van. That's the damage you see. It was suffering, so we put it out of its misery."

The old man shook his head. He went and kicked the door open. Two of the creatures moved in and sniffed the air. They surrounded Red Mask, who was barely conscious.

The first one to reach the man swatted his masked face, driving spines into it and leaving them like a porcupine's quills. The second creature wielded what might have been an arm and thrust the appendage into the man's ruined crotch. It thrust in and out, hollowing out the already destroyed area.

Red Mask's slowly tapered off. He died as the inserted appendage worked its way up through his body and burst from his mouth. The creature tensed and slowly ripped the lengthy stalk upward, splitting the man's body and splaying punctured internal organs.

Matt and Krissy watched in horror as three creatures converged on Disco Strangler, who had somehow clung to consciousness. He struggled as the creatures fell on him, throwing punches with his remaining hand. His fist slowly filled with quills and then started expanding like a balloon.

The creatures stopped their attack and watched as he raised the hand and looked at it incredulously. Swollen larger than an animated cartoon character's after a hammer hit, the appendage exploded, covering Disco Strangler's masked face with yellow-green pus. He screamed when it began sizzling, taking no time to dissolve his face.

The creatures resumed their attack and slowly ripped the man apart. They separated the legs first and tossed them to some of the smaller creatures, who immediately went to work devouring them. The largest of the three took both arms and gnawed them nude. The last tore the torso open and wallowed in the gore as if at a feeding trough.

"What are these things?" Matt screamed. Krissy had pulled herself to Matt and held his waist. She buried her face in his side.

"It never should have happened." The old man took off his glasses to polish them. He returned them to his face, where they sat cockeyed. "Stupid experiments to mesh animal and vegetable. I told them not to get ahead of themselves, but would they listen?" The old man was close to tears as he watched the massing creatures converge upon the bodies of the woman and her two children. Matt had never wished for earplugs more as the relentless slurping and crunching assaulted his ears. The creatures soon devoured all the bodies and lapped up the last of the viscera and fluids. Loud noises permeated the air.

"Not too couth, are they?" the old man commented. He glanced at the creatures. "What did I tell y'all about eating too fast?"

"You can communicate with these things?" Matt gasped.

"Son, in some ways, they're my children. I ran the project that created them."

"We have to do something, shoot them! Set them on fire!"

"I can't do that. First and foremost, I'm a doctor. I swore to do no harm. Oh, I've made a few concessions, but this isn't one of them. Here, help me get the last one out from behind the counter. There are some who haven't eaten yet."

Matt stood his ground.

The old man pointed the shotgun at him. "That wasn't a request, sonny."

Matt disengaged himself from Krissy and slowly moved behind the counter. Blue Mask had been shot clean through. His stomach was completely disintegrated, and a cantaloupe-sized hole gaped in his back, but somehow, he clung to life.

"Old man, I am gonna come back as a zombie and eat you, starting with your asshole and working my way around and up."

"Tough talk from someone who's about to become a four-course meal. Grab his legs, Matt."

Matt did and half-carried-half-dragged the man from behind the counter. The minute they pushed him into an open spot on the floor, he was swarmed by the creatures. They covered him like a tide of weasels, leaving his face untouched until one of the things distended its mouth obscenely and engulfed it. Matt gagged at the crunching sound as the thing chewed the man's face while it was still attached. It finished, leaving a hollowed-out space with a visible spinal column reaching into the top of the head.

Another creature grabbed the spinal column and yanked. It pulled the brain free and sucked it in like a strand of spaghetti wrapped around a meatball. The sounds of sloppy eating and the flying goo torqued Matt and Krissy's stomachs. The creatures gorged and lapped until there was no evidence of the last of their tormentors.

The old man smiled as the creatures slunk toward him and rubbed against him. He reached a hand down to stroke the tops of what Matt hoped were heads. The creatures had formed a mob, crowding into the store like lemmings.

"Can we leave now?" Matt asked with a tremor in his voice. He already knew the answer.

"Sorry, kids, you sealed your fate when you said you killed one of them. If you'd just left it alone, it would have regenerated after being hit by the car. I'm sure there's no trace of it, which adds to your crime. See, you made some of these things into cannibals. Hell, for all I know, that poor creature might have been eaten by its own children."

A sea of strange eyes stared at the two young people. Matt dragged Krissy to her feet and slowly backed up. The cold of the cooler struck their backs, and they knew they were trapped.

"Hey, Mister, how about you shoot both of us before they get us?" Krissy asked.

"Sorry, I can't do that. You each have another purpose before you're consumed."

"What's that?" Matt asked. He shuddered as one of the things drew close and reached out, dragging a spined tendril across his face and leaving a gash.

"Been a while since these poor souls had any action. You're dessert and then the after-dinner mints."

Matt and Krissy were yanked apart as a flurry of spines stripped them naked. Matt was thrown on his back. A creature stood on two legs and loomed over him. An orifice like a lamprey's mouth hovered over his crotch and then slammed down.

Matt screamed as his cock was shredded. His voice was silenced by a similar orifice clamping over his mouth. He felt the spines within grab his tongue like talons. He choked on his own blood, only vaguely aware that another creature was impaling itself on what was left of his penis.

Krissy was flipped on her stomach as one of the creatures went behind her. She didn't know how, but it slammed two penises into her, one in her vagina and the other in her damaged anus. The napkins and tampons were thrust deeper into her. She screamed as the spined pounding commenced in earnest but soon found another creature in front of her, growing another appendage that entered her mouth and silenced her. Her mouth slowly filled as the appendage expanded. Soon, the spines exploded through her cheeks, making her face look like a pufferfish. She and Matt died long before the creatures were done with them.

The old man looked at their bodies, little more than punctured sex dolls at this point. The mewling creatures nudged at them and snaked out barbed tongues to get a taste.

"You all know what to do," the old man said with a hint of pride. "You mess it up, you clean it up."

THE LOST SON OF KRYPTON

TOM FOLSKE

FREDERICK ALVEREZ WAS CONCEIVED via the one-time copulation of a cheap whore and a long-haul trucker who usually took his women forcefully. When the trucker met Fred's mother at the truck stop, he had just won big on a scratcher, and since she was so cheap a fuck anyway, he decided to be uncharacteristically generous and actually pay her. About halfway through their encounter, he changed his mind and raped the poor, wretched woman, beating her so severely that her face resembled that of a blue and purple catfish. He sodomized her with a tire iron so violently it caused prolapsing, then left her for dead in a ditch before pissing on her and riding off into the sunset. When she came to at the hospital almost two weeks later, it was too late for the morning after pill, and she couldn't afford an abortion.

Fred knew none of this, though.

Fred didn't have a single memory of his mother. The reason for this being when he was six months old, he cried so loud that even the cokehead neighbor got scared and called the police. When the cops found him, they also found his mother dead in the bathroom from an apparent heroin overdose.

He'd been left screaming in his crib for at least twenty-four hours, wearing a diaper that hadn't been changed since several hours before that. It was no wonder that in the rat-infested dwelling, the rodents sniffed out little Fred's shit and feasted in his crotch. His cries were what motivated the coke-head to call the police.

When the doctors were finished, they managed to salvage most of the young boy's genitals, but he lost one testicle. Thanks to the foreskin, although its remains had to be removed, only a tiny, rat-bite-sized chunk had been taken out of the head of his penis, near where the lip of the head over-hung the shaft.

After that, Frederick Alverez was sent from one foster home to another. The best of them all was an old lady who used to get drunk and slap him around, but she never molested him or used a closed fist. That was the shining star of his childhood—an old woman whose name he couldn't remember, who always called him "Charlie" instead of his real name, which he didn't think she knew.

There were many bad ones, though. Some were worse

than others. The first time Fred was molested, he was only four years old. An old man, Mr. Johnson, used to stick his finger up Fred's ass as he smoked cigars and jerked himself off. It only got worse from there.

When he was six, he lived with a lady who used to burn him in the armpits with cigarettes. When he was eight, he lived with a woman who used to wake him up in the middle of the night by biting him on the thighs or triceps, sometimes on the sides of the stomach. Luckily, though, that one didn't last long. There were a couple of dishonorable mentions along the way, such as a guy who locked him in his room for three days without food because he left and forgot about him, the woman who used to take shits and wipe her ass in his hair and on his face, and two guys who made him suck their dicks.

But somehow, he managed to avoid sodomy until his penultimate foster home. They were the worst. It was a sadist couple named Beth and Harmon. They locked Fred up in a cage, and when they took him out, they put a broom horizontally against his back, made him fold his arms over the broom handle, and handcuffed him in the front. They then beat and raped him, the woman using a strap-on, until he eventually passed out from the pain.

Fred escaped after the second night but was picked up by the police only a few weeks later for breaking into cars. He spent a year in juvenile detention, and when he got out, right after his thirteenth birthday, they put him right back in the foster system. That is when poor Fred found himself in the custody of Hubert Anderson.

———

Hubert Anderson, or Jolly Papa as he liked to be called, was wealthy, yes, but he was entirely fucked up. Hubert was almost sixty years old and in no way should have been a foster parent. He was fat, greasy, quick to anger, and he reeked like stale onion rings mixed with what ferrets smell like.

Fred recognized the smell from when a lady used to lock him in a room with her ferrets at bedtime. They weren't fed enough, so they were always mean and bit him constantly.

Hubert started off okay. He was even kind of nice at times. But one night, he freaked out.

"WHAT IN THE FUCK? WHAT IS THIS, FRED?" Hubert shouted from the kitchen.

"What?" Fred approached with reluctant curiosity.

"Fred! This is unacceptable," Hubert scolded, glowering at the young boy as he pointed to a small spot of spaghetti sauce on the carpet next to the trash can.

"What?" Fred asked, at first not seeing what he was talking about.

Hubert grabbed Fred by the ear and pulled him down toward the ground. The big man knelt alongside and rubbed Fred's face in the sauce spot as if he were a dog who had an accident.

"Oh, this won't do at all," Hubert said in a cold, foreboding tone.

"I'm sorry, Hubert. I'm so sorry. I'll clean it right away," Fred whimpered.

"You call me Jolly Papa, and you'll clean it alright. You'll clean it with your tongue," Hubert commanded, grimacing menacingly down at the small boy. "I have to go get changed."

Jolly Papa didn't leave until Fred began licking the spot with his tongue. He let out a long exhale of satisfaction before turning around and running up to his bedroom. "Don't you dare go anywhere, Fred, or I might have to kill ya."

Hubert spoke in a joking tone, but Fred wasn't certain either way. As soon as Hubert was gone, he spat on the floor until the spaghetti spot was completely gone. What he'd seen in Jolly Papa's eyes scared him, and he contemplated escape. As he weighed his options and was about to flee, he heard Jolly Papa's heavy footsteps thudding down the stairs.

His stomach jumped into his chest as he anticipated what would happen. A moment later, Jolly Papa appeared, tromping down the stairs wearing a too-tight mask that looked like a cross between a clown mask and something a luchador would wear. He held a baby rattle in one hand and wore nothing but an adult-sized diaper.

"Jolly Papa wants to play," the big man said, his erection poking up from the top of his Depends. Pre-cum dribbled down the tip. "You've been a bad boy, Freddy. Jolly Papa thinks you need a spanking."

Fred turned to run. Jolly Papa caught him instantly, squeezing him by both shoulders hard enough to leave bruises. He forced Fred down onto his knees.

"You've been bad," Jolly Papa said seductively.

Fred whimpered in fear and anticipation. He felt sick to his stomach.

"You need to be punished," Jolly Papa whispered coldly, forcing Fred down on all fours.

"Please. No. Please stop," Fred cried so intensely he gagged.

"Tell Jolly Papa you love him," the vile man said as he ripped Fred's pants down, exposing his bare buttocks.

"No," Fred said, barely able to choke out the words.

"Tell Jolly Papa you love him," Jolly Papa screamed angrily as he grabbed the back of Fred's hair, simultaneously springing more of his dick from his diaper. He rubbed it against Fred's bare ass cheeks.

"No," Fred screamed determinedly. At that moment, he felt the pain and hurt of all the anger, fear, loneliness, depression, shame, regret, mistrust, and downright depravity he'd experienced in his short existence flowing through him. He felt charged, exalted. Just as Hubert was starting to moan in pleasure, Fred willed him backward, thrusting the fat man against the kitchen counter hard enough to make his spine crack.

"What the fuck? You hurt Jolly Papa! You're fucking dead," Hubert shouted, fuming with rage.

Fred stood up, quickly pulling up his pants as Hubert rose and immediately rushed him. Somehow, he was again able to will the big man back, slamming him against the counter even harder this time.

"I'll fucking kill you," Hubert yelled.

"Stop all that anger. You'll lose your hard-on," Fred said coldly, the anger still surging through him as he experienced power and security he had never known before. He raised one hand into the air, lifting Hubert off the ground and holding him there like he was Darth Vader. "I hate you. I fucking hate you and fucking wish you would fucking die, you stupid fucking worthless, child-raping piece of shit!"

Hubert started to speak. Fred lifted his other hand and used it to focus on smashing the foul man's bottom jaw up into his top jaw hard enough to produce an audible cracking of teeth.

Fred didn't know how he was doing what he was doing, but it felt natural. As long as it was working for him, especially in the heat of the moment like this, with the ability to release years of pent-up aggression, he went with it.

"You wanted to put this in me, didn't you?" Fred asked,

bringing the focus of his left hand, fingers now splayed, to Jolly Papa's pelvic area. He slowly squeezed his digits together as he concentrated on the man's cock. Indents appeared as if invisible fingers clamped onto the Jolly Papa's still tumescent penis. Fred began to turn his hand counterclockwise like he was untightening a valve.

At first, Hubert Anderson's dick turned slowly, then the skin around the base began to twist, and he screamed in misery. Fred raised his right hand and moved his grip toward Hubert's throat, forcing his head back and his chin into the air vertically, visibly stretching the veins and tendons in the man's neck. Fred continued to twist Hubert's cock, which was now turning maroon. Instead of screaming, Jolly Papa could only gargle pitifully.

"You are a sick fuck. I want you to fucking die," Fred screamed, twisting multiple times in anger. After the first twist, one of the veins on the side of the man's dick burst. By the second twist, the penis had turned bulbous and deep purple. By the third turn, blood began to squirt in a corona from the base of the shaft. With the fourth twist, the sex organ was almost completely removed from the man's body, save for a few tendrils of vein and nerve connecting the severed appendage to Hubert's groin.

Hubert was so agonized that his gurgling became choking as he bled out through his crotch.

Fred, in his fury, pushed the fat man's head and chin back even further, violently popping something in the man's neck, causing all his limbs to go limp instantly.

Hubert began to spasm and gyrate, still helplessly suspended in mid-air. His bowels evacuated into his diaper a moment later. Fred finally released him, letting him collapse into a pile on the floor.

"You are a worthless piece of shit. I hope you suffer forever," Fred said, stepping over Hubert's violently twitching body as he went to the door.

Fred had never done anything like that before in his life. He felt like a violent Harry Potter, from the book with its cover ripped off he'd found in the garbage—one of the few treasures he'd been granted temporary custody of during his lifetime.

Fred wondered if he could do it again, looking at his hands uncertainly as he walked. He had killed Hubert in the heat of the moment and wondered if that was what it took to utilize his new gift. Was it a gift? Because if that was what it took to activate it, he didn't want it.

Fred left Hubert Anderson's residence in an absolute tempest of thoughts and emotions. The world had scarred and battered him, but it hadn't yet broken him. Yes, he had just killed a man, but Hubert was an evil man. Fred had always had a kind spirit, and no matter how awful the things that happened to him, he fought hard to remain himself and avoid becoming a creature of defenses and dissociation for as long as he could. He had killed a monster, and he didn't feel bad about it, and he didn't think he should feel bad about it. Fred was an empath. He felt pain, shame, and regret on a deeper level than most. Anyone who could do to a kid what had been done to him didn't deserve to be merely killed. They deserved to be dealt justice.

———

Fred was starting to feel pumped, a little invigorated. He approached a car parked nearby. With his emotions still going wild, Fred experimentally focused his anger on the vehicle. As he did, the car's windows blew out, and the tires popped.

Fred was scaring himself, but he was also the most excited

he had ever been in his entire life. He imagined this was how kids who got to go to amusement parks felt. He fled quickly from the car and headed for the nearby park, though that was hardly what it was. Sure, there was playground equipment there, but everything was broken, sabotaged, burnt, or pissed on. There were used needles and condoms coating nearly every inch of the floor. A pair of shit-filled panties lay at the bottom of what remained of the slide. Any parent who would let their kid attempt to go down that slide had to be absolutely fucking crazy. Someone had even twisted used syringes, with the needles still connected, into the chains of every remaining swing. Fred figured this was the perfect place to experiment.

He took a deep breath, wondering if he really would be able to do anything, as he stared at some of the detritus on the ground, raised his hand, palm down, and tried to push it lightly away. The debris on the ground moved effortlessly as if a strong gust of wind centralized solely in that area. Fred smiled, one of the only true smiles to ever cross his face. He spent the next three hours in a state of delirium as he practiced and began to learn how to control his newly realized ability.

After a few days, Fred was able to move both big and little things as he gradually learned how to apply force to his talent. Near the end of the first week of training, Fred started to refine his precision. He could use his gift like phantom fingers, applying specific pressure to specific places. He even managed to take a pencil and manipulate it into drawing a picture that would have been of the same quality had he used his physical hand and fingers.

It was summer, so Fred slept outside, not at that park, but under an overpass, a dozen feet away from an elderly Hispanic couple, whom he would have felt comfortable with even if he hadn't acquired extraordinary powers. The old woman even offered to share their blankets, but after taking one look at the stained, ratty pieces of cloth, Fred politely declined.

Fred spent that first week alternating between practicing at what he now called "Heroin Park," eating meals at a soup kitchen the Hispanic couple had shown him, and sleeping under the bridge. He was developing quite a friendly relationship with the couple, whom he came to know as Julio and Miranda. He vowed that if he ever found a way to use his new talents to help them, he would. At the rate his training was going, he thought he just might be able to do that.

Fred was almost happy. He felt safer than he ever had and had found the first permanent friends he'd ever known. Sure, he'd met plenty of nice kids in the foster system. But they were co-survivors, more like colleagues than friends, especially when all parties involved knew their time together was fleeting, as no one ever stayed anywhere for very long. This was the best life had ever been for him, so much so that he'd almost talked himself out of punishing his abusers and letting bygones be bygones… almost.

Maybe if it had just been him, and his abusers had been done after that, Fred would have considered sparing their lives, even though their fleeting moments of satisfaction through depravity had warped and forever tarnished his undeserving youth. If it had just been him, he might have moved on. He didn't want to think about his past, let alone revisit it. Unfortunately, Fred didn't feel this was the case. Most of his abusers had treated him with a certain nonchalant attitude—or in the case of the couple who raped him, a prominent passion for the unspeakable—indicating that they had and would continue to abuse.

They all had to be stopped.

———

It was still another two weeks before Fred found enough courage and had refined his skills enough to finally start paying visits to the worst of his past tormentors. Ironically, the lady who burned him under the armpits died in a house-fire, which was okay. Fred felt she had gotten what she deserved, and besides, although she deserved to be hurt, he didn't feel as if her crimes warranted a complete death sentence. For the rest, however, he held much more certainty.

The lady who used to bite him was named Phyllis Morse. Fred remembered the neighborhood, and after some days of wandering down countless streets, looking for anything familiar, constantly training whenever he thought no one was looking, he finally spotted her.

Fortunate smiled on Fred, for the woman was outside. If she hadn't been, he wouldn't have recognized the house, would likely have just kept walking, and probably never found her. He walked by her home, even going so far as to wave to her and smile, and although there was a slight pause as if she sensed something was amiss, there was seemingly no recognition of the boy she'd harbored for several weeks and bitten countless dozens of times.

"Hello, mam?" Fred called, approaching the woman from the sidewalk.

"Hello," Phyllis Morse answered suspiciously.

"Can I use your bathroom? I really have to go, and I get nervous peeing in public."

Phyllis contemplated his question for a long time before something in her demeanor noticeably changed, though no actual physical change occurred.

"Sure," Phyllis answered. "Please do come in."

Fred and Phyllis both entered the house. His heart was a

mix of trepidation and excitement. He wondered if she felt something similar but for a different reason.

Phyllis led Fred to the living room, where he sat on the couch. "Would you like any tea?" she asked him cordially.

"Sure. That would be great," Fred answered.

Phyllis went to the kitchen for a minute before returning with a glass of hot tea while Fred waited patiently. She set the teacup down on the table in front of Fred, then sat in the chair next to him. "So, you little fucker, you some kind of masochist? You didn't think I would recognize you, Freddy? Finger-licking good, Freddy. Wanna get bit some more, you little bastard?" Phyllis asked fiendishly, grabbing the steaming teacup and tossing it at the boy.

Fred was able to evade most of the scalding liquid, but it still burned part of his arm. He let out a shriek of pain as the old woman lunged at him, grabbing him tightly, sinking her nails into the tender spots of his arms hard enough to draw blood, and holding him tightly as she plunged her teeth deep into the flesh of his shoulder.

Fred writhed in agony, completely forgetting both his plan and his powers, reliving the torment and fear of his past. It only lasted a moment before Fred reclaimed the situation. He bent all ten of Phyllis Morse's nails backward at the nailbed, causing little spurts of blood to erupt from each one as the old woman released her grasp and screamed in pain. Fred proceeded to curl her fingers backward, breaking each bone multiple times like the rolled-up arms from *Beetlejuice* before telekinetically throwing her to the floor in front of him. There was a loud crack, and from the way she landed and the shriek she let out, it would be surprising if she hadn't broken her ankle.

"Please," Phyllis begged. "I will do anything you want. I

swear—please, Freddy, sweet Freddy. I'll call the cops and turn myself in. I'm a bad person."

These words had no effect on the boy, so she changed her tactic.

"Money! I have money. I have just under three grand in a jar in my closet. It's in an old hat box. You can get it right now and count it all out. It's money like you've never seen, boy."

Fred snapped her mouth shut. "You use your mouth too much," he said, slowly applying pressure to the older woman's jaws, squeezing her teeth together painfully. "And it's never in a good way." He applied increasing pressure to Phyllis' jaws while simultaneously sending her canines up, into, and through her gums and all the way into her sinuses.

The white-hot pain Phyllis displayed in her face seemed worse than fire. Her teeth were being squeezed together so tightly they were beginning to crack and crumble into a chunky powder-paste on her tongue. Phyllis' eyes, nose, and lips simultaneously leaked tears, drool, and blood as she gagged and coughed. When her canines reached the bridge of her nose, blood poured from her nostrils. She couldn't move or struggle, not one iota. Fred had immobilized her entirely.

He looked the old woman in the eyes. "Never again," he said, just as Phyllis' jaws connected through the remains of her teeth.

As mostly bare, swollen gums and exposed roots rubbed together, Phyllis' eyes turned bloodshot, and the pupils developed little white protrusions in their very centers. The minuscule beads of achromatic expectation soon blossomed into full-grown teeth, slowly piercing through the protective membrane surrounding Phyllis' eye. She was still alive as her pupils burst, excreting copious globs of viscous fluid. A moment later, Fred blasted the rest of her teeth bits through her face and skull in a macabre human pipe bomb of gore, and Phyllis Morse was finally allowed to meet her maker.

Fred felt a little bad about killing the old woman so violently. But then again, he didn't. Justice was justice. Sometimes, a person had to do bad things for a good cause. Wasn't that why people went to war?

Young Fred was about to run away when he suddenly remembered what the old lady had told him. He quickly ran upstairs to Phyllis' bedroom, scared shitless like the place was haunted. Even with psychic powers, he had been and always would be afraid of ghosts. After a quick search, he found the jar of money the late Phyllis Morse had told him about and immediately ran out of the house.

Fred had learned two things that evening, which he decided to improve upon immediately. First, he wanted to see if he could create some sort of shield around his body, like Sue Storm from the *Fantastic Four*, with whom he'd instantly fallen in love. Luckily, Phyllis' bite hadn't hurt him too badly. But he still didn't want to be hurt anymore, not even a little, not by anyone. Secondly, Fred had felt too vulnerable, strolling out of her house and running down the street with her jar of cash. He wanted to see if he could possibly lift himself. If he could make things and people move, why couldn't he also move himself?

After two more weeks, alternating between training and sleeping under the bridge by Julio and Miranda, Fred eventually learned how to create a force field around his body and how to turn certain areas off. At first, Fred was unable to stop hovering inches off the ground since his force field was protecting him from everything. But before long, he learned how to adjust the force field, and although he was by no means proficient in his skills, he felt like he had the basics down and could now refine as he went. Fred was also slowly learning to levitate but was not very good at it. The first time he tried, he dropped himself onto his back from about eight feet up. Later, when he attempted to move himself while aerially suspended, he spun so fast in a circle that he made himself puke. Ultimately, Fred decided the force field was more important anyway. The levitation could and would come later.

It was roughly one month after the death of Phyllis Morse when Fred decided it was finally time to go. It was starting to get a little chillier at night, and the bridge provided less and less comfort. Fred grabbed the jar he had taken from his tormentor, which he had successfully hidden and ignored up until this point, and did what he'd always intended to do with it. He took a couple hundred dollars out for himself, for food and maybe a place to stay, then, when Julio and Miranda fell asleep, he set the remainder of the jar next to them before disappearing into the night.

———

Over the next month, Fred slept in unlocked cars as he began his journey to find the two foster fathers who'd forced him to perform oral sex on them. He never stopped training during this time, even though the hunt was taking far longer than expected. Not only was he forcing himself to recall things he didn't want to remember, but he also hadn't stayed with either person for more than a couple of months. He did eventually find them, though.

When he found the first guy, a fat man named Arthur Landry, he was sitting on his couch, drinking beer and watching football. Fortunately, like Phyllis Morse, Arthur had no foster kids around at the time, or he would have been taken off the list. The latter would have been better, but Fred knew even so, they would still find other ways to acquire victims.

While Arthur was watching football, his wife Jeanette was in the kitchen stirring what looked like chili. Seeing her reminded Fred of the time Jeanette opened the door when Arthur had been molesting him. He'd heard her scoff before she closed the door without a word.

Fred watched the Landry family go about their daily business from his post, about ten feet above their lawn, peering down through their kitchen window. A few moments later, he was knocking on their front door.

Jeanette Landry opened the door and appeared to recognize Fred instantly. However, it took a long moment before she finally spoke. "Oh, Freddy. How good it is to see you," Jeanette proclaimed cheerfully, her eyes scanning the area. "How did you get here?"

"I walked," Fred answered as tonelessly as possible, trying not to play any cards yet.

"Alone?"

"Yeah. I needed to clear my head."

Jeanette Landry visibly relaxed, her expression changing from distress to extreme confusion. "Did you miss us?"

"Who the hell is there?" Arthur asked, making a scene of getting his bulk up off the couch and coming to the door.

Fred couldn't speak for a moment; his nerves suddenly got the best of him.

"What the hell are you doing here?" Arthur yelled. He quickly added, "I don't care what he told you, that boy is a fucking liar. Always has been, ever since he first arrived on our doorstep."

"There is no one with him," Jeanette told her husband.

"Go finish the chili. I will deal with this dipshit," Arthur commanded his wife before turning brusquely toward Fred. "What the fuck do you want? If this is blackmail, I will fucking kill you right now." Arthur Landry lurched forward, grabbed Fred by the shirt, pulled him inside, and slammed the door behind them.

Once inside the entrance hallway, Jeanette Landry could just be seen stirring and tasting the chili she was cooking. She completely ignored the situation, just like she had the last time.

"I asked you a mother fucking question," Arthur screamed, raising his arm as if to backhand Fred.

"Okay, my turn," Fred told the angry, red-faced, fat man, freezing him mid-blow.

Arthur's expression of anger suddenly melted away, only to be immediately replaced with one of fear. Fred was beginning to recognize bullies of Arthur's kind for the cowards they were. As Arthur tried to talk, it looked like he would start pleading for his life or crying crocodile tears, but Fred forced the man's mouth closed so he couldn't. They then began their sojourn into the kitchen, Fred floating Arthur along the way like a child holding a man-sized balloon by an invisible string.

Once in the kitchen, Jeanette Landry turned, and just as she opened her mouth to scream, Fred twisted her whole body sideways, clumsily plunging her head, face first, into the boiling chili. Once her face was inside the pot, Fred released her body below the shoulders so Arthur could watch his wife squirm and writhe as she died.

Arthur Landry didn't look hurt or sad in the slightest by his wife's death. He looked angry like Fred guessed he would, but it was more that Fred had killed something belonging to him than any sense of vengeance. The young boy imagined all the threats that would come from the fat man's mouth if he let him speak, so he decided not to let him speak.

Instead of any dialogue, Fred flipped the fat man upside down telekinetically and, with no concerns for comfort, ripped all the clothes off the man's body. Arthur's rage-stricken face softened again, and he truly began to weep this time.

"Not so fun being helpless while others do what they want to you, is it?" Fred asked as he spread each of the man's legs straight out to the sides of his body, audibly ripping muscles and flagrantly tearing flesh. There were loud POPs as the man's hip bones dislocated from their sockets, tearing on both sides where the fat man's genitals met his thighs and pushing bloody, purplish meat out through the fresh wounds like rising dough.

Although the agony was apparent on Arthur Landry's face, Fred kept him silent as blood ran down his groin and onto the bulge of his fat stomach.

"Now, how about you blow yourself, so no one else ever has to again."

Arthur's eyes went wide in terror as he felt his body bending in half midway down his lower back. He felt his vertebrae being stretched, then cracking, then breaking apart from each other as his body folded itself around his enormous stomach. His eyes rolled back as he nearly lost consciousness.

Fred had used his powers to pull and stretch the man's penis into a thin, pointy facsimile of an erection.

Before Arthur could fade away from the pain, his flaccid, elongated penis entered his throat and gagged him back into semi-consciousness. Understanding dawned in his eyes as he realized that even his balls were in his mouth, and he could see his own shit-encrusted asshole an inch away from his nose. Fred witnessed a new expression form over Arthur's cock-stuffed countenance—one of shame and wretchedness.

Fred could see Arthur was dying and knew he had to finish quickly. He made a note to himself to study how pain worked, to see if one day he could use his new powers to stop it. But that would be years from now, so he remained focused on the problem at hand.

Fred removed Arthur's manhood from his mouth and let him take one breath of air before ramming the pointy, teleki-netically tweezed penis back into Arthur's mouth and through the back of his throat. When it pierced through the flesh of the back of his head, Fred let the fat man fall to the ground and die.

————

Gordon Matthews was the other man who had committed such acts upon Fred. There were two key differences between Gordon and Arthur, however. One, Gordon was significantly thinner than Arthur, and two, his wife, Regina, probably never knew what Gordon had done to Fred. She was beaten so severely and so regularly that she never would have opened a door without knocking. Hell, she wouldn't have even knocked if he wasn't expecting her.

When Fred arrived at the Matthews' household, he could hear Regina upstairs vacuuming while Gordon came to the door. The young boy wasted no time inflicting the same tortures he'd visited upon Arthur onto Gordon. Let the punishment fit the crime, he thought, and since they both did the same thing, they could both die the same way.

When the screaming started, Fred heard the vacuum shut off upstairs, though the door didn't open.

Another big difference between Gordon and Arthur was that Gordon's spine didn't break when he was forced to perform self-fellatio on himself. This didn't bother or hinder Fred, though. When he pierced the back of Gordon's throat with his own cock, Fred smooshed his whole body together, like a PB&J. And like a smooshed PB&J, dark jelly leaked from the sides.

When Gordon finally lay dead on the ground, Fred walked over and put one foot on the bottom step of the staircase leading upstairs. "You're free," he called up to the second floor.

There was no answer, but he did hear light sobbing, which sounded very much like the sobbing of unexpected relief.

———

Fred only had one more justice to deal on his own personal list of abusers, and the last one scared him to death. Of course, being molested was horrible, but Beth and Harmon had made it into something much worse—like whoever the hell decided coke wasn't sufficient, so they needed to make crack. They held him prisoner, they hurt him, they tortured him, and they raped him. What happened in that house would haunt him for the rest of his life. As he stood before the door leading into that house of nightmares, all of Fred's strength faded, only to be replaced by fear. Even though he had powers now, he was scared. What if his powers didn't work? What if they caught him again and put him back in the cage? Fred began to tremble.

He would have turned around and high-tailed it right there, save for one thing—a pink shoe, much smaller than his foot, lay upside down on the step. It looked like it had fallen off, probably when a child was forcefully brought back inside the house. Given its location, Fred knew it had recently been left there. He knew there was a child inside.

Fred didn't think about the next part. He just acted. The front door burst into splinters as he stepped purposefully through the threshold.

"What in the fuck is going on?" Harmon yelled from the living room, emerging onto the scene a moment later, a beer can grasped tightly in his hand.

Beth was right behind him. She came out of the kitchen and looked like she'd been doing dishes. "Freddy? You came back. Did you fall in love with us or something? Your butt-hole need another pounding?"

Fred gagged and almost lost his nerve.

"Let's catch this little prick, Beth. I'll fuck him right here like he ain't never been fucked before. He'll definitely be a fairy after I'm through with him!" Harmon began his soliloquy as he rushed forward to grab Fred.

Beth came at him from the other side.

Neither Beth nor Harmon could reach Fred, and their looks as they found themselves frozen in mid-moment were ones of nervous confusion.

"What the fuck?" Harmon shouted.

"What are you, some kind of witch?" Beth asked.

"Shut up," Fred told them, violently snapping their mouths shut, more forcefully for Harmon, who'd bitten off a half inch of his own tongue. "You guys are bad people. You hurt children. You steal innocence. You feed on pain and vileness. You're sick, and the world will be better without you. Children will be safer with you dead. No child should ever have to go through the evil you put me through. I don't even think Hell is good enough. You might like it too much."

Harmon and Beth frantically struggled to speak, but nothing distinguishable was to be heard.

"Maybe that's what Hell is, though. Maybe Hell is taking something you love and contorting it into something awful, a warped and twisted version of what you loved, just close enough to the real thing to constantly remind you of it and tarnish it in a way that plants bad memories over the good ones, so the good memories will always remind you of the bad…" Fred tried to grasp the concepts behind the words he was speaking. "Either way, you deserve worse than Hell, and that's exactly what I'm going to show you."

Beth and Harmon's eyes went wide as they involuntarily floated toward one another. A moment later, Harmon was turned to stand vertically and face the kitchen, floating a foot off the floor. Fred maneuvered Beth directly behind him as he guided the pair into the kitchen.

When they reached the linoleum, Fred tilted Harmon and laid him prostrate on the table, on his stomach, with his legs spread apart. The look of fear in his eyes grew substantially, and he began to cry. Beth stared in wide wonder, not knowing what to expect next.

"Not so fun to be held down against your will, is it?" Fred asked, violently ripping Harmon's pants from his body in one quick, agonizing jerk. One side of his waist and both of his thighs instantly turned red from the ferocity of his disrobing.

"You guys like shoving things up people's asses who don't want things shoved up their asses," Fred said calmly. "I think you guys should die doing what you love."

Frederick Alvarez released his hold on Harmon and Beth's mouths, allowing them to scream. He was sure no one would hear them, as no one had ever heard him. Besides, even if the cops did come, which was seldom in neighborhoods like this, he would be gone long before they arrived. Even if he wasn't, he was sure he could escape anyway.

Harmon and Beth struggled and screamed. All their

efforts were futile as Fred telekinetically tilted Beth horizontally, at roughly the same level as Harmon, and started moving her closer to the naked, prostrate man.

They realized what was going to happen right before it did. Their struggles intensified tenfold as tears streamed more heavily from their puffy, red, swollen eyes. As their screams grew louder and more frantic, both of them began coughing sharply and occasionally gagging.

Fred felt no remorse for what he was about to do as he slowly brought Beth's face closer and closer to Harmon's now tightened butt cheeks. She tried to look down or away from her partner's posterior, but Fred made her gaze directly at it.

When Beth's face reached Harmon's ass cheeks, she could smell sweat and shit. She tried closing her eyes before her nose and mouth finally touched the foul orifice, but Fred forced her to keep them open. She screamed one final time as her face smashed into Harmon's asshole, but all she got for her troubles was a mouthful of flesh and ass juice.

Harmon's eyes nearly popped from his head when he felt the slight tickle of Beth's nose against his brown eye turn into an intense, ripping pain. The coppery smell of blood was now mixing with the noisome stench of shit already pervading the air as Harmon's lowest orifice began to expand in unnatural ways, stretching, ripping, then imploding in on itself from the force of Beth's face being pressed into it.

Fred watched, slightly appalled but knowing he had to finish. He had to end this forever and achieve justice. He watched as Beth struggled for air, as she slowly suffocated in Harmon's ass until her body began to convulse and spasm—until it finally stopped moving, and she was dead. He watched as Harmon bellowed boisterously from agonies unknown to the modern world, as his hips and ass cheeks spread past the point of breaking to accommodate Beth's head, as his pelvis collapsed forward and the vertebrae in his spine bulged up and over Beth's skull, like a snake swallowing a rat, before they too seemed to break inside Harmon's body.

Harmon was still alive when Fred was finally finished—when Beth's head had been forced into his anus, all the way to her neck, and it looked like his back was pregnant underneath his shattered spine.

Fred walked over until he was standing directly above the face of the sniveling, incoherent, dying mess of a man. "Death will take you soon, and the devil will take you after," he lowered his head and whispered just before the poor wretch's soul faded from his body.

Fred went to the basement door, unlocked all three locks, and then went down and freed the young girl from the cage they kept her in—the same one he'd been kept in.

"I'm here to help," Fred told the shaking girl as he assisted her to her feet. She didn't say anything, and that was okay. She was hurt and scared. Fred remembered the feeling. He took the girl's hand, squeezed it tenderly, and led her back up the stairs.

They paused at the top of the stairs before opening the door.

"When we get out there, don't look. I'll lead you."

The girl remained silent as Fred opened the door and led her through the threshold between the basement/dungeon and the main level. He planned to guide her across the room as swiftly as possible and get her out of the house. They only made it a few feet before the girl came to a dead stop and refused to be pulled any further.

When Fred turned to look at her, she was staring at Harmon and Beth's corpses.

"Did you do this?" the girl asked, her voice petite but cold.

Fred nodded, unsure whether he should be proud or ashamed. But he knew in his heart his acts were just.

"Can you do it again?"

Another nod.

"Are you going to?"

Fred considered this question for a long time, and just when it seemed like he wasn't going to answer, he gave an almost imperceptible nod.

"Can I help?"

Fred smiled.

Who Fights the DEVIL When Our Limbs Are Broke

JUDITH SONNET

CAN WE PRAY TOGETHER? *Do you mind?*

Thank you.

Our Father, Who comforts us when we are in need, Who pleads for us when we ought be damned, and Who fights the devil when our limbs are broke. Hallowed be Thy name. Thy Kingdom come, Thy will be done, on Earth as it is above, as it isn't below.

Amen.

He frowned. The message was strange, and the changes in the standard prayer were somewhat jarring. He read over it again, wondering who'd left it. It was scrawled in an untidy hand on a crinkled piece of torn brown paper, and it'd been slipped into his pile of essays, which he'd be grading all weekend.

Why, oh, why did I require a four-thousand-word minimum? I'll bet half of these pages are padded. And who knows how many were written by AI or just ripped out of Wikipedia?

Don't think that. They're smart kids. Don't underestimate them. They aren't like the goons in your regular courses who could give half a shit and could somehow get every answer wrong on a true or false quiz—

Grover Birch sighed and set the paper on his desk. He smoothed it with his chubby hands, then reread the prayer. It was strange, he observed, that the message had started in a conversational tone. It asked his permission to pray and thanked him, even though he'd had no chance to deny the writer their wants.

Who fights the devil when our limbs are broke.

What a strange way of putting it.

Grover was in his late fifties. He was round, cherubic, and red-cheeked. His white beard was thick, and his head was balding, save for a horseshoe of brown fur around the top. He often wore dress shirts, ironed trousers, and tweed jackets. He dressed to impress, even though he taught at Whitmore High, a public school—not a fancy institute.

He looked around his empty classroom. Grover taught AP Ancient Civ, and the assignment had been to write on The Peloponnesian War, the text they'd been working their way through for an entire semester. It was almost summer break, and this was their final essay. Next year, his juniors would be seniors, and they'd have plenty to read over break. He could tell they were itching to get this project over and done with, but they'd still been diligent, open-eared, and interactive. His AP class was his best class. His easy favorite—and yes, he knew every teacher at Whitmore had favorites, even the touchy-feely teachers who denied such elitism.

That's the word. Elitism. You're a classist, Grover. You judge your students based on their status. And yes, you look down on the religious types. Not outwardly, no. You don't discriminate publicly. But you roll your eyes when you shuffle past the kids who willingly stand in a circle and pray around the American flag every Wednesday morning. And you laughed behind the back of that kid who argued with his biology teacher for instructing them on the merits of reading Charles Darwin. Yes, you don't like religion. But if any of the students in AP Ancient Civ are religious, they've done a damn good job keeping it secret. It never shows in their work. They don't argue over it in class. They certainly haven't tried to preach to me!

Well, maybe my reputation has proceeded me, and they know I'm a lost cause.

Or this is their way of slipping religion into my life. Like those disgusting comics fanatics hand out, espousing the evils of sin and the cold-hearted judgment of God. What are those called? Chic Tracts?

Grover sighed. He was overthinking it. There was nothing insidious about this piece of paper. Someone had written a prayer down and slipped it in with their homework as they left the classroom. It either belonged to Wallace Orvill, whose paper had been above it, or Norton Dash, whose paper had been below it—one or the other.

Well, Grover wasn't going to make a fool of them for a simple mistake, and he wouldn't think less of either one, even if they *were* religious fruitcakes. He respected the students in this class, and they respected him.

He crumpled up the paper and tossed it into the wastepaper basket. Forgiven and forgotten! Now, onto grading!

Grover read a few more papers, slashing out poor thoughts and complimenting studious ones. He was happy to see his pupils had all done a good job. So far, the worst grade he'd given was a C, and that was because he suspected that the student had let the deadline slip up on him. His thoughts were present, but the execution was sloppy. It wouldn't doom his academic progress since this student was usually one of his brightest, but it was disappointing. That said, everyone had their off days, so he decided to nudge the grade up to a B minus to encourage him.

See? Grover thought, filing the paper away. *I'm not that hard on them. In fact, I'm a pretty laid-back dude. I'm more interested in them learning than . . . than fretting constantly. The way Mr. Buckley is in Math. He puts those poor kids through boot camp with little payoff despite their efforts! I think that bastard gets off on giving out bad grades. I bet he gets hard when he sees their faces drop with disappointment. Well! Not me!*

What a foul thought that was. Grover made sure it'd stay in the chambers of his mind. He didn't like to gossip about his peers, although it could be tempting. Sometimes, in the teacher's lounge, Ms. Keller and Mrs. Daughtry chatted like no one could hear them—about students *and* faculty. He was shocked they hadn't been reprimanded for some of the beans they'd spilled.

A knock on the door startled Grover out of his thoughts. "Cripes!" he declared, putting a hand against his barrel-shaped chest.

"Sorry, man!" Wilbur, the janitor, said. The skinny man stood at the door, leaning against a pushcart filled with cleaning supplies and a mop attached to its front like a crude masthead. He'd come into the room and knocked when he realized Grover hadn't noticed him. "Mind if I clean in here?"

"No! God! Sorry!" Grover laughed.

"Scared ya pretty good, huh?" Wilbur smiled cheekily.

"Yes. Jesus!" Grover leaned forward and sighed. "You like sneaking up on people like that?"

"Just you!"

The two men chortled.

Grover watched Wilbur start to pick through the desks, washing them with a rag and a spray bottle. He got down and looked underneath them. "Christ. They leave boogers under these things the same way kindergarteners do. I thought I'd escape boogers when I switched districts. Nope. In fact, I think it's worse over here!"

"Yes. I even see my AP kids picking their noses some-times. They all think they're invisible when they do it. Good kids, but everyone is a little gross, I guess," Grover said.

"Yeah, you may be forgiving, but I'm the one who's gotta pick 'em out! Yeech!" Wilbur said.

Grover smiled. "Need help?"

"Nah. I'm just gabbing."

Grover nodded. "You doing okay?"

"Yeah. I'm fine. You know, just working until I can't. My back's been aching, but so's life."

"I hear you. In this economy, I doubt I'll ever retire. Sure, I'll probably stop working here when I'm too old and cranky to teach. . . but then I'll be checkin' bags at Wal-Mart after a few years."

"Christ. You know I wanted to be an astronaut when I was

a kid?" Wilbur grunted. "Now look at me. Scraping proteins off of school desks."

"Never say never."

"Then I'll say 'unlikely!'" the man chuckled.

Grover pulled one of the last three papers from his stack. His red pin went to work while he listened to Wilbur clean.

Wilbur intruded on Grover's work for the second time that night as he emptied the trash can. "Hey, you got one too?"

"Huh?" Grover looked up. The wall told him it was almost nine. He needed to head home. He'd gotten more work done than he'd planned, which would give him a mostly free weekend! He wanted to pour himself a stiff drink before sleeping.

"This," Wilbur held up the crumbled, brown paper and unfolded it. "I've found a bunch throughout the school today."

"No shit?" Grover asked.

"Yeah. All of 'em say the same thing. 'Bout broken limbs and the Devil an' shit. I dunno what it means. I'm Buddhist."

Grover smirked.

"Just because I scrub toilets doesn't mean I don't deserve enlightenment, you prude!"

"Sorry!" Grover held up his hands.

Smiling, letting Grover know he was just ribbing him, Wilbur crunched up the paper and deposited it back into the trash.

"Yeah. Some kids do weird shit like that. You see the Wednesday morning prayer circle? Some of them start crying during that. I mean, really let loose. It's because they think they're being persecuted. Every kid thinks that. Religious or not. They don't realize . . . you know . . . just how free they are."

Grover nodded. He'd seen kids get worked up into a storm over simple slights, reading deep malice in actions as benign as a misspoken word or a bump in the hallway. Kids these days, he'd decided, were being trained to be on edge. To see themselves as victims and taught to seek victimhood out when it wasn't readily available. It was one of many reasons he refused to become friends with his students and only referred to them by their last names. The last thing he needed was someone to read insidious causes for familiarity.

"Anyways, everyone is getting these weird prayer papers. It's been in every class. Hell, someone wrote 'Praise God' on Mrs. Lewis's whiteboard. She came into her classroom and found it after lunch. She wiped it clean before anyone saw it, but she told me it gave her the creeps. It was written all . . . drippy. And in red. Like blood."

"Christians—or believers—always seem fascinated by the red stuff. It's one of the few things I have in common with them!" Grover laughed. "History is filled with it. With sacrifice, and agony, and blood. Christians think they invented suffering—"

"Hey, at least you don't write your study notes in dripping gore!" Wilbur said. "Imagine the cleanup!"

Grover laughed. 'Well, Wilbur, I'll let you get to it. I should be heading home. The rest of these can be graded tomorrow." He opened his attaché case and began to put the papers away. He froze before snapping it closed. "Say, what are you doing tomorrow?"

"Me? Cleaning. Same old, same old," Wilbur said.

"What time are you off? Wanna grab a beer?"

"It's been a while! Sure! I'm done around six. Maybe we could go to Tuckman's and catch the game?"

"Sounds fine. I could use some time away from my

house," Grover said. "Let's hope we don't run into any students this time!"

Wilbur howled. The last time the janitor and the teacher had gone out for drinks, they'd found a sophomore trying to nab drinks with a fake ID. It'd put a kink in their plans, confronting the boy and calling up his father. The scandal had come with some backlash, with students glaring at Grover Birch like he'd stabbed them all in the back for doing his civic duty. But, after a few months, the students glommed onto other controversies and had forgotten all about Brad Tanner's fake ID.

See? Grover thought as he finished packing, slipped his jacket on, and left the classroom with a happy "goodbye." *I'm not a classist. I spend my time with the common man!*

That's exactly the sort of thing a classist would think, you prick! Besides, Wilbur is a smart cookie. He's only a janitor because he fell on hard times. The man has a PhD in art history. He can talk about Picaso and Bosche from sunup to sundown! That's why you two have made such good friends —

Grover walked down the hallway, his shoes clicking loudly and echoing through the lockers. He realized that—aside from the janitorial staff—he was most likely the only person in the building. All the extracurricular clubs finished around six, and play practice ended at seven. What play were they going to end the year with? He struggled to remember. Then it came to him. *The Crucible*—a good piece of work, with a lot of themes that seemed applicable to modern day society. It also touched on the subject of fanaticism and religious hysteria. He wondered, then, if the prayer was some strange promotion tactic—something a drama student had drawn up based on a line from the play.

Grover decided to re-read Arthur Miller's classic when he got home. He was sure he had a copy on one of his many shelves. For as long as Grover Birch had been alive, he'd never thrown out a single book he'd read. His house was like a library, filled to the brim with massive tomes and slim volumes alike. He read contemporary fiction as well as the classics. Sometimes, he needed a break from the lofty reads, and legal thrillers by John Grisham often did the trick. Hell, he'd even read *The Twilight Saga* when it was all the rage, under the guise of trying to find common ground with his students and their taste in literature. He'd understood the hype, but that didn't mean he enjoyed it. Still, those books sat on his shelf amid the works of such masters as Aristotle and Epicurious. Oh, the irony!

He realized his mind was wandering purposefully. Because the school felt like a hollow husk, and he didn't like walking alone through its darkened halls. There was always something surreal about an empty school. He'd felt that way when he was a student, and he felt that way now. There was something unnatural about it, as if he'd left the real world and entered a mirror dimension, where everything was close to the same . . . but slightly *off*. The theme music to *The Outer Limits* began to spin through his cranium.

Now, Grover, you stop that this instant. You'll spook yourself into an early grave and have no one to blame but—

He heard a locker slam shut. The sound of metal slapping metal was like a ricochet. It made him flinch and duck. He spun around, looking down the barrel of the hallway.

No one was there. The school was hollow.

Maybe it was Wilbur. On his way into a classroom, he'd banged his cart against a locker. He probably put his headphones on and didn't notice. Yes, that's it. Just Wilbur. Maybe he did it intentionally because he knows you're jumpy and likes to kid you.

Shuddering, Grover walked out of the hallway and into the high-ceilinged cafeteria. The left wall was all glass, and he could see the night was cloudy. The moon was hidden except for a silver fingernail, which offered no illumination. The tables cast deep, inky shadows. He realized anything could be hiding in there, crouching in the dark, waiting for him to walk by and then lunging out to grab him with—

He pictured ghoulish hands—crusty with sores, rotten from the inside out, and squirming with fat, beady-faced maggots. Long yellow nails as well, which would dig into his flesh and draw blood!

He was no better than a child, believing a monster was hiding in his closet! Or under his bed! Grover felt ashamed of himself. He also realized he was desperate for the drink he'd promised himself.

That was a warmer thought—tipping his head back and allowing a slender tendril of whiskey to curl up in his belly like a purring cat. Yes, he needed a drink, all right. And soon, he'd be home, getting precisely what he deserved. So long as he made it through the cafeteria, through the doors, across the parking lot, and into his vehicle.

He heard something whisper across the room. It fluttered like a paper bag caught by a cold wind. A shiver leaked down his spine and cupped his balls.

Turning on his heels, he looked around the cafeteria, investigating. He saw nothing. Only darkness, shadows, and the monsters in his imagination. Thick, wormy, crawling things with jagged teeth and sneaky hands, waddling around on all fours, just out of sight.

"H-hello?" Grover asked, hoping he sounded more confident than he felt. "Who is that? Wilbur?"

There was no response. Of course, there wasn't! Because no one was there! Grover Birch, a man of reason and intellect, was jumping at shadows! Like a little fool!

Imagine if anyone saw you like this. I bet you look like an idiot, talking to an empty room, squirming in your shoes like a goose walked over your grave! God!

Grover rushed toward the double doors leading out of the school. He scanned his ID badge and then tried the door. It clicked and jolted but remained locked.

Hmmm.

He scanned his badge again and repeated the gesture with the same results. The door remained firm, only moving a centimeter before catching. He jostled the metal bar loudly, hoping it'd snap open and throw the door wide—no such luck.

He looked out the rectangular window and toward the parking lot. His car was just in sight. An Oldsmobile he had to grunt and heave himself into since he was no longer the slim teen who'd first purchased the vehicle. He'd refused to upgrade. That car held many sentiments for him. For one, it was where he'd lost his virginity. Now that he was past the age where sex was appealing, he still liked to remember that hot summer night with Maribeth Turner, who'd eventually left town and married an absolute dolt—a jock with big arms, tree-trunk legs, and the intellect of a squashed frog.

Hey, at least she got married! You spent your whole life looking for love, only to give up by the time you hit thirty! You said you were above the institution of marriage and preferred solitude. Well, how do you feel now?

He felt fine. He didn't mind his life. He was happy with his books, his pursuits, and his meaningful friendships. Yet, this persnickety voice persisted in moments of distress.

Am I in a distressed moment? I've left late before. It's never been like this—*never been…scary!*

He shook the door, muttering curses, hoping it would snap open with a flourish, that the night air would *whoosh* in and calm his jangled nerves. The door held firm, refusing to budge.

Damn thing. Probably has a loose wire. I miss when doors were simple, when all I needed was a key and a strong wrist. Nowadays, everything has to be electronic! Well, damn it to Hell!

He thought for a moment, recalling the nearest exit. It was in the rear of the gym, at the end of the damp hallway, where the girls' and boys' lockers were.

Bracing himself, he turned toward the cafeteria. He didn't like the idea of walking back through its slippery shadows. Grover pitched himself into a brisk jog, hoping not to look like a fool to the security cameras, but he also wanted to get this whole business over and done with. He thought miserably of an old horror movie he'd seen as a kid. It was called *The Cabinet of Dr. Caligari* and frightened him deeply, not because of the lumbering, monstrous ghoul, or the mad doctor . . . but because the shadows in the film had been painted on the sets. They looked spiky, thick, and fractured— as if the sun itself was breaking.

The darkness in the cafeteria was much the same. Each shadow felt like a swiping paw, and each strip of illumination was a flashing knife!

You're so dramatic, Grover. You'll be out of here in no time. Then you'll feel like an idiot for having been afraid! The persnickety voice had returned. He hoped it would prove prophetic.

With his heart in his throat, Grover rushed to the cafeteria, rounded a small corner, and pushed through the doorway into the gymnasium.

The gym smelled like sweat. Grover's shoes squeaked against the floor. He held his briefcase to his chest as he walked, taking furtive glances around the area. There were bleachers, stray balls, and a few abandoned duffle bags. If he'd thought the cafeteria was scary, it was nothing compared to the gym.

Why is the ceiling so damn high? It isn't like our players are that good.

He looked over toward the wall opposite the bleachers with a start. The school mascot—a roaring tiger—looked like a demon drifting out of the darkness, its sickle fangs drooling and its eyes burning with white-hot hunger.

I should've left earlier. Or never left at all. At least I felt comfy in my room.

Not that I could've been comfy sleeping in there.

Would I have been able to wait until morning?

He shook his head, feeling dafter than ever before. The school's creepy after-hours atmosphere was getting to him.

During the day, this gym was lively and bright. Grover tried to picture it: basketballs knocking through hoops, loafers sitting in the bleachers, joking around rapaciously, and the sound of a whistle rasping intermittently. He could hear it now, sliding eerily through the darkness, like a ghost's call—

Getting morbid again. Just move on.

Grover came up to the archway leading to the locker rooms. He froze at the precipice. This section was even darker than the gym itself. Ink-black. He wondered if he'd vanish entirely if he stepped under the archway and into the hall. He wondered if the locker rooms were even darker.

Shuddering, he remembered last year's trouble.

A vagrant had snuck into the school over the weekend and camped in the locker rooms. On Monday, the bastard had squeezed himself into one of the lockers and watched the girls change through the slits in the middle. He wouldn't have been caught if one of the girls hadn't thrown the locker open to toss in her clothes. The screams could be heard in every classroom. Grover had shut his classroom down, locking the door and drawing the blinds in case of an active shooter. From what he'd heard, the tramp went running. Everyone kept their distance from him, terrified to block his exit. He charged through the double doors leading out the school's side and vanished into the forest. Of course, the police were called, parents were angered, and the girls were traumatized. The counselor had a busy semester, and a couple of students even transferred.

Grover had heard a description of the man from one of the girls, who'd been a favorite pupil. "He was so thin and short, like my kid brother. I thought he *was* a child at first until I saw his beard and bald spot. And he was wearing this threadbare sweater and a pair of shorts. He went running the moment we saw him, but I swear to God, he was *smiling*—almost like getting caught was part of the fun for him."

The man had never been caught. Whoever he was, he'd come and gone like a ghost. By now, most of the affected students had graduated or moved on with their lives. Instead of being a serious issue, the sneaky vagrant was now nothing more than an urban legend—something the students talked about when they were bored. And how they'd exaggerate, too! He'd once overheard a boy claim the voyeur had been wielding a machete! Like the villain in a slasher flick from the eighties!

Either way, the end result of the incident was that their school had more security and cameras, and teachers and students were scolded for leaving doors open.

And there is fear.

Lingering fear.

Grover swallowed a lump.

He was afraid. As silly as it was, he wondered if walking through the dark hallway would put him face-to-face with the creep who had snuck into their school last year—the violator who'd watched those girls while they were unaware. Knowing that maniac was still out there…somewhere… holding onto the memories of what he saw, made Grover sick to his stomach. It worried him, now and then, that maybe the guy would come back for seconds.

And what if he's here? Now? What if he did something to the door so he could slither in? What if he heard my footsteps, and now he's waiting for me to take one more step before he strikes—

Grover wondered if he should turn around. Maybe he could spend some more time with Wilbur. He could convince the janitor that he'd simply decided he wasn't tired enough to go home.

No. I'll look like a little kid. Too scared to check under the bed myself, so I'm waiting for Daddy to look for me.

Deciding he'd never hear the end of it—from either Wilbur or his own psyche—Grover took a tentative step into the hallway. He felt as if the darkness was closing in on him, swallowing his trembling body up.

He took another step. The air was colder here than it had been in the gym. Mustier too. He knew that there was mold in the showers, in the lockers, and on the tile floor. Wilbur was a good janitor, but he was fighting a losing battle when it came to teenage hygiene.

Breathing in deeply—too deeply—he continued ahead. When he fumbled past the boy's lockers, he realized he should have brought his cell phone. Its flashlight app could have proved useful. Although now he imagined swinging the light around and catching sight of some pale, toothy *thing* scuttling after him.

Hugging his briefcase, he plunged on. The sounds of his footsteps were like thunderclaps.

Grover caught sight of the rectangular windows on the double doors. They were a lighter hue of darkness but dark all the same. He wondered why there weren't any lights on the side of the school building. It made the small lot between the school and the forest somewhat dangerous.

When the doors whisked open, Grover was ecstatic. He didn't know what he'd have done if he'd found them locked. Most likely, he'd have started blubbering like the scaredy cat he was.

He stepped out into the cold night. His eyes quickly adjusted, showing him the soggy side lawn and the asphalt drive that wrapped around the building. Jovially, he moved toward the front, swinging his briefcase as he went. He avoided looking toward the forest. The last thing he needed was to give his brain more ammunition and nightmare fuel.

Briskly, he came upon his old car. With a satisfied smile, he yanked at the door. His face fell.

Of course. You need to unlock the damn thing, you idiot!

Huffing, he set his briefcase on the car's top and began digging around in his pockets.

Where's my fob?

He became more frantic, rootling through his pants and jacket like a pig digging up truffles.

Where the fuck is it?

Of course, it couldn't be *that* easy, could it? No. Not only were the doors closed and the gym dark, but he'd left his key fob…

…on my desk!

He did feel like crying. Felt like punching something, too.

Damn it to hell! Damn it all! What a moron!

Swearing at himself, he looked down the lot and toward the school. There was no way he'd go back. No way in hell. He'd rather walk all the way home than trudge back through the darkness, worm his way into his classroom, and scurry out.

Thunder crackled like cellophane.

Great. Just great, Grover Birch thought. *Just fucking great!*

He didn't have his cell phone, so he couldn't call an Uber. He liked to leave the pesky device at home while he taught— besides, who'd be calling him aside from tax collectors and spam callers? Now, he understood the device's necessity.

Languidly, he took the briefcase in his hands and tested its weight. He could walk home. It wasn't all that far—probably about three miles. But it was dark out—dark and scary.

I can wait for Wilbur. He'd give me a ride home. I could wait by his truck and—

He spun around when he heard the whisper of bare feet against asphalt.

The encroaching figure froze.

Grover felt his blood grow thick, and his heart spiked with terror.

The man was standing a few yards away. He'd been approaching stealthily and quietly. If he hadn't dragged his foot, Grover would never have noticed him.

The man was naked. His white skin was so pale it was almost transparent. His eyes were small beads resting in deep bowls of sunken flesh. He'd shaved his head clumsily—hanks of blonde hair stuck out like tufts of hay from a weatherworn scarecrow.

He was skeletal—the thinnest, weakest-looking character Grover had ever laid eyes on. The naked man reminded him of a corpse brought inexplicably to life. Like Lazurus gone to seed.

The man smiled. His teeth were pearly and clean, like white blocks of ice.

Grover leaped back as if electrocuted. His rump slammed against the sealed door to his car.

"Stay back!" Grover shouted.

The man advanced, moving too quickly and comfortably. As if he wasn't at all bothered that he'd been caught.

"No!" Grover held up the briefcase like a shield.

The man froze, feet away from Grover. He could smell the stranger now. His aroma was spicy and perfumed. He saw that the man was coated in shimmering oils. It gave him a reptilian appearance.

His hands were painted black like they'd been dipped in tar.

"Stay back!' Grover reaffirmed.

The man cocked his head. His smile persisted.

"I mean it! I'll...I'll..."

"You must pray with me," the man's voice was alarmingly light and placid. As if he was worried they'd be overheard.

Grover gulped. "Please. Leave me alone—"

The man came jouncing forward, moving like a strange puppet. He breathed in heavily, releasing a huff with each footstep. Grover scootched around the car and backed away, knowing in his soul that it would be over the second this freak *touched* him.

The man froze again, mid-step, as if someone had hit "pause."

"Please," Grover repeated, "I didn't do anything to you."

The man continued to smile. Grover watched as his eyes began to leak. Slimy tears spilled down his cheeks like water from a broken bottle. His smile grew, stretching wide enough to split his face in half. Shakily, the man spoke.

"You are innocent. It's the devil we must punish. The devil lives in you. In all of you."

"I'm just a teacher! Please, leave me alone—" Grover called out.

The man suddenly landed on his knees and put his ink-black hands together. "Pray with me!" he screamed, his voice alarmed and desperate. "Please! Pray with me, before it's too late!"

Grover remembered the paper he'd found today. The strange prayer left amid the pile of homework—

He studied the man. There was no way this . . . creep . . . could have snuck into the school and laid it there himself— no way he could have gone undetected. He was in his forties, Grover saw, and he was just so disturbing to look upon.

There was no way this fiend was responsible for the prayer Grover had read.

—and Who fights the devil when our limbs are broke—

There was no way—

Grover heard another rustle of footsteps.

He spun around and caught sight of Wilbur.

The janitor had shed his clothes and painted his hands black. Naked, he stood by the school's doorway, posed mid-step, just as the creature had been—smiling just as ghoulishly.

"No," Grover mumbled.

He caught sight of another—a teenage boy, similar in appearance, crawling out from underneath Grover's car.

"NO!" Grover cried.

More came pouring out from the forest. Men, all nude, each with their hands painted black, each smiling at Grover as if they could somehow placate him with a grin. They all approached slowly, a diverse group of men, boys, and a few geriatrics. They said nothing, only came toward him.

Grover turned back toward the first. The skeletal man was still kneeling, hands clasped together, praying.

"I don't understand!" Grover cawed. "I don't—"

Wilbur's arm was suddenly around his throat. Grover knocked his head back, slamming his skull against Wilbur's. The janitor's nose crunched loudly, and there was a blast of hot blood. Wilbur stumbled back, holding his face and crying out.

Grover swung his briefcase. The corner caught against Wilbur's chin, spinning his pal around in a circle before he plopped onto the pavement.

The rest of the ghoulish figures rushed toward Grover, arms held out like zombies, faces contorted with macabre smiles.

Grover whirled on his feet and rushed away, heading back toward the school. The swarm was close behind him, and although he'd been lucky with Wilbur, he knew it'd be impossible to fight the crowd off.

There must be twenty or thirty of them. I recognize a few—students of mine. One of the older ones...he's a teacher! But I don't know all of them.

He especially didn't know the first one. The frightening specter remained kneeling on the asphalt, praying loudly. He was repeating the verses written on the paper Grover had received.

And Wilbur knew all along. He put up a front like he had no clue what that shit was about. For all I know, he's the one who put it there! He lied to my face!

Grover charged toward the doors. He slammed into them roughly, just as a teenager grabbed him by the back of his jacket and tried to jerk him off his feet. Grover stooped over, dodging the pull, then slammed his fist into the boy's stomach. The child released a *whoosh* of air before pitching sideways and landing on the ground.

He considered stomping the kid, then decided he didn't have time. He rushed the other way, heading toward the woods. The mass of white bodies piled after him, soundless except for the slapping of their bare feet.

This is a nightmare. A terrible, awful dream—one I need to run to escape from!

Hazarding a glance over his shoulder, he spotted the stranger. He was standing now, gazing toward Grover with rapturous delight. Wilbur was on his knees, kneeling before the skeletal creature, his hands held out in supplication.

Much to Grover's shock, the creature began urinating directly onto Wilbur. The janitor reacted as if he was being anointed with holy water. He lapped at the golden liquid, crying out with mirth as he was doused in the strange man's fluids.

Crazy! Grover thought as he raced toward the forest. *Crazy! They're all crazy! Each and every one of them!*

He ran down the ditch, up a slope, and into the tree line. The overgrowth pawed at him, tearing at his clothes and searing claw marks over his face. He ignored the spurts of pain, driven onward by fear.

His arm became tangled in a thornbush. He wrenched it free, not caring that the thorns had gouged in deep, leaving finger trails of blood down his arm.

Hoping the thorns and thickets had dissuaded the group, he looked once more behind him. He was alarmed to see their naked bodies diving through the forest after him. They didn't even flinch as they were shredded by the thorns, nettles, vines, and outstretched limbs of the overcrowded trees.

Their holy purpose gives them strength.

His briefcase slipped from his hand. Grover felt naked without it, but there was no way he would stop to pick it up. He barrelled through the trees, praying he'd break through to the other side and cops would be waiting for him!

For the first time since childhood, he began to pray. It made him feel dirty, knowing he was praying to the same god these freaks worshipped. But he wanted to survive—wanted to live. He was not a great man, and he knew it. Barely noble, even. But he was one of God's creatures, and he wished the Great Almighty would protect—

He came through the trees.

Skidding to a stop, Grover took in the sights surrounding him.

The field was filled with people—men, women, children, all looking exactly like the brutes who'd been chasing him. They all converged on him in a great swell, arms held out and faces twinkling with tears.

"Praise be!" he heard a few shouts.

"No!" Grover turned, seeing the horde coming from behind him.

Surrounded! I've got nowhere to go! Nowhere to—

He was ensnared. Oily hands gripped him by his limbs and took him into the air. Kicking and screaming, he was thrown over the crowd, dragging toward its swirling middle. They all handled him roughly, digging through fingers into his flesh, leaving scrapes and bruises. Grover whined pitifully, begging to be set down—hoping for mercy.

"Release him!" a firm voice bellowed.

The crowd fell still. A long hush descended over them. He hung in the air, held by their cruel hands.

"Now!"

Calmly, Grover was set on his rump. The white, naked legs surrounding him were like tree trunks. They swayed, then parted, allowing the skeletal stranger to walk in.

Grover gazed at him, slack-jawed and terrified.

Wilbur stood by the man, still doused in his fetid fluids.

Grover tried to stand, but a hard hand knocked his shoulder and put him back on his ass.

"Grover . . . Birch . . . why do you not pray?"

Grover was confused. He looked around at the sea of

faces, realizing that all of them were gazing down at him with abject sorrow and pity—as if he was in the casket at a funeral.

Swallowing, he responded. "What do you mean?"

"Many times...we asked you to pray." The old man coughed. "And yet...you chose not to."

"You hate us!" someone cried.

"You hate God!"

The crowd grew rowdy again, screaming at Grover and hurling insults at him.

"Blasphemer!"

"Unbeliever!"

Grover rotated in his spot. "No! No! I prayed! I just prayed!"

"You prayed when it was beneficial to you!"

"We all heard it! All heard your simpering prayers!"

"Pathetic!"

Grover began to plead his case when the crowd parted again. An eight-year-old charged out, holding a long, sharpened lance of wood. The spear slammed into Grover's side, nestling just beneath his ribcage. There was a squirt of blood followed by a long, screaming roar of pain. The child backed away, dragging his weapon with him. Its point was so blood-soaked it looked like it was coated in scarlet frosting.

Grover fell onto his hands and knees, wheezing with agony. He felt sheets of blood slip out of the wound and pool beneath him.

"All we wanted, Grover, was for you to accept Him!" Wilbur cried, standing by the ghostly man's side. "Yet, you ignored him! You ignored the signs and calls! We've been praying for you, Grover, but you didn't even *acknowledge* that!"

"How could I know?" Grover cried. "I... I didn't *know*."

"It's too late! Now that you know, you can't have faith!"

Wilbur brayed. "Now that you've seen Him, you can't be accepted! Oh, Grover, you ignorant fool! We tried! We tried!"

"No! Wait!" Grover started.

Another spear came out of the crowd. An elderly woman carried this one. She plunged its tip into Grover's lower back. He turned upright, crying as the spear dove in, then slipped out. Blood flew from his back, painting the chests of those who stood nearby.

"He's doing this because He loves you!" someone cried.

"He loves all of His creations!"

"It's up to you to love Him back!"

"No!" Grover cried. "No! Please! I'm sorry! I'm sor—"

A third spear slashed through the night. It drove deep into Grover's gut, doubling him up. He grabbed the shaft with his grimy, chubby hands. His teeth clacked closed over his tongue, severing the tip. When the spear left him, it drove splinters through his palms.

As soon as one spear was gone, another appeared. It slid into his calf, grinding against his bone. Blood poured out in waves. He was surrounded by crimson.

Four spears drove into him in one quick blow. One burst through the front of his chest and pinned him to the ground. Another went through his upraised hand and stapled it to his shoulder. The next went in between his buttocks, destroying his anus. The last went through his throat and out the back of his neck.

Held in place, Grover coughed and sputtered like a struggling engine. His left eye turned backward, and his right bugged out of his skull. His teeth were clenched so hard that the enamel began to splinter. From all of his wounds, blood dribbled and sprayed. He felt as if he'd become an open faucet.

The skeletal man stooped down toward him, smiling

peacefully. The strange man's eyes turned milky white, and his breath came out in foggy clouds.

"Grover Birch...*I forgive you.*"

Grover screamed directly into God's face as all the spears were ripped away from his body, leaving it a gory mess in the center of the field. By the time the crowd amassed over him and began to stomp Grover into the dirt... he was long dead.

ABOUT THE AUTHORS

K.L. ALLISTER is an avid fan of horror, metal music, and the macabre. He loves all things eerie. He hails from the Northeastern United States, where he spends his time as a father, husband, and author. He constantly forgets to take his meds so that the voices can help him come up with ideas for his next story. He's a pretty cool guy. You should read his books.

SHAUN AVERY has been published in many anthologies, comics, and magazines, normally with tales of a horrific or satirical nature, and often both at once. He has won competitions with both prose and comic scripting and was shortlisted in a screenwriting contest once upon a time. As this story shows, he has a fascination with furries . . . sorry, he means a fascination with *writing* about furries. That is what he means. Yes.

J. ROCKY COLAVITO (aka The XXX EX-Academic and Dr. Damned to those in pro wrestling circles) writes and publishes in a variety of genres because he's spicy and likes spicy. Select works include the Neo-Giallo series (*The Night Scavengers, Shards of Shattered Dolls, Classes After Dark, Snuff n Stuff, and Bathed in Crimson You Shall Suffer*) and *Tales from the Road, Whatever Happened to Helles Belles?*, and the forthcoming *Squared Circles of Hell* (for the professional wrestling horror fans out there). He is the creator of Buck Neighkyd, porn star turned occult detective whose cases are solved in *Caveman Magazine*, the origin novel *Creative Control*, and the forthcoming *Hawaiian Hardcore.*

ABOUT THE AUTHORS

R.J. DALY lives a somewhat quiet life with his family. Growing up in the '80s & '90s, he quickly developed a fascination with all things horror-related. Despite the sound and loving upbringing his parents provided, they eventually learned their son had different interests from his siblings. Realising they couldn't turn around this predestined collision with the macabre, they decided to allow it to run its course—hoping it was just a phase… Nowadays, R.J. prefers his horror to lean towards the darker edge of the genre, with themes and imagery that push boundaries in every way imaginable. What that says about him—who knows? When he's not annoying his wife and kids, you might find him reading, writing, listening to music, watching films, or, indeed, just staring out of the window, watching the world go by.

SARAH DEROSA can be found deep within the Michigan forests where she was raised. Her fascination with horror was ignited by the chilling tales of the Goosebumps series and the forbidden thrill of watching the Nightmare on Elm Street franchise at a very impressionable age. When she is not weaving dark tales or delving into the depraved worlds of other writers, she prefers to get lost wandering the haunting wooded trails with her husky, Big Pollo. She has an affinity for indulging in the sinister delight of poutine and loves playing in the rain.

TOM FOLSKE lives in Minnesota with his wife, soon-to-be five kids, and three black cats. He holds a BA in creative writing and has been creating stories for over two decades. He has had or is in the process of having over 20 short stories published. Tom loves horror in all forms, especially 80's and 90's horror, and is a comic nerd, a cinephile, an audiobook junkie, a horror buff, and above all things, a storyteller.

CHISTO HEALEY is extremely prolific. He's been actively writing for four years and has over 300 stories in anthologies, over 20 solo books out, and almost 40 stories on podcasts and YouTube channels, with a lot more on the way. He lives in North Carolina with his partner, their amazingly talented kids, an adorable dog, and an ungodly amount of cats. Follow him on Amazon, Facebook, and Instagram. He loves to connect with readers and other authors.

CHUCK NASTY resides in a small town in Kentucky. He mostly keeps to himself and works on multiple writing projects (as well as music and podcasts). R.L. Stine, Stephen King, Clive Barker, Hunter S. Thompson, and Edward Lee are a few of his biggest influences.

HARRISON PHILLIPS is an English author of extreme horror and splatterpunk fiction. His literary influences range from Clive Barker and Stephen King to Jack Ketchum and Edward Lee. He enjoys playing video games and watching 70s/80s exploitation movies. He was born and raised in Birmingham, England, where he still resides with his long-suffering wife, their two daughters, and a schnauzer named Minnie.

DAN SHRADER, hailing from Southern Indiana, is a mastermind of spine-chilling stories that will stay with you. His life took a turn the day he stumbled upon a large box of VHS tapes filled with titles: TEXAS CHAINSAW MASSACRE, BLACK CHRISTMAS, and NIGHT OF THE DEMONS. From that moment, an insatiable appetite for horror was awakened within his very soul. He cut his teeth on the Royal Road website in early 2023 under the pseudonym Sutter_Cain. Dan Shrader is the author of Those Who

Live in Darkness, VOL 1 (his debut book), which ranked #2 on "New Horror Releases" for over two weeks on Amazon. He draws inspiration from acclaimed authors like Clive Barker, Edward Lee, Kristopher Triana, David Sodergren, and Brian Keene.

SIDNEY SHIV is an American horror fiction author, editor, and illustrator. Several of his short stories have been published in various anthologies. In 2023, he published his first short story collection, Where Demons Dine. He edited, illustrated, and published his first anthology, Fall Equinox – An Anthology of Halloween Horror, under his Gaping Maw Anthologies imprint. Sidney lives in England with his wife and daughter.

JUDITH SONNET is a very sad girl. She writes gross and disturbing horror books and collects old paperbacks and '70s action movies. She grew up in Missouri, but now she lives in Utah. She's trans, asexual, and is an abuse and suicide survivor. If you want to know more about her, check her out on Facebook . . . or contact her through your nearest Ouija board. She is the author of No One Rides for Free, Beast of Burden, and Low Blasphemy. Scraps is her first curated anthology. She plans on doing a few more.

THOMAS STEWART is a young ghoul fascinated with the art of terror and the macabre. When he's not watching horror movies or reading horror books, he's crafting his own chilling gospels of horror to terrify and eternally rob you of a peaceful slumber. He publishes most of his work on Reddit under the pen name "Corpse Child." Many of his horror stories have been adapted for audio narrations by a wide variety of YouTube narrators and those commissioned on the Chilling-

App. He's released several horrifying titles on the Chilling Tales for Dark Nights podcast. You can follow him through his Facebook, SubReddit r/CorpseChildGospels, or Corpse Child's Sanctuary website. His books Damned Whispers, The Other Side, and his debut horror novella, Mortimer, are available on Amazon.

Printed in Great Britain
by Amazon